A TEXT BOOK OF

DATA STRUCTURES AND FILES

FOR
SEMESTER – II

SECOND YEAR DEGREE COURSE IN INFORMATION TECHNOLOGY

**Strictly According to New Revised Credit System Syllabus
of Savitribai Phule Pune University**
(w.e.f June 2016)

Dr. SACHIN R. SAKHARE
Ph. D. (Comp. Sci. & Engg.)
Professor & Head,
Computer Engineering Department,
Vishwakarma Institute of Inform. Technology
Kondhwa (Bk), Pune.

NITIN N. SAKHARE
M. E. (Comp. Networks)
Assistant Professor,
Computer Engineering Department,
Vishwakarma Institute of Inform. Technology
Kondhwa Bk., Pune

N 3585

DATA STRUCTURES AND FILES (SE IT)   **ISBN 978-93-86353-17-7**

First Edition : **January 2017**

© : **Authors**

Published By :   **Polyplate**

NIRALI PRAKASHAN

Abhyudaya Pragati, 1312, Shivaji Nagar,
Off J.M. Road, Pune – 411005
Tel - (020) 25512336/37/39, Fax - (020) 25511379
Email : niralipune@pragationline.com

☞ **DISTRIBUTION CENTRES**

PUNE

Nirali Prakashan	:	119, Budhwar Peth, Jogeshwari Mandir Lane, Pune 411002, Maharashtra Tel : (020) 2445 2044, 66022708, Fax : (020) 2445 1538 Email : bookorder@pragationline.com, niralilocal@pragationline.com
Nirali Prakashan	:	S. No. 28/27, Dhyari, Near Pari Company, Pune 411041 Tel : (020) 24690204 Fax : (020) 24690316 Email : dhyari@pragationline.com, bookorder@pragationline.com

MUMBAI

Nirali Prakashan	:	385, S.V.P. Road, Rasdhara Co-op. Hsg. Society Ltd., Girgaum, Mumbai 400004, Maharashtra Tel : (022) 2385 6339 / 2386 9976, Fax : (022) 2386 9976 Email : niralimumbai@pragationline.com

☞ **DISTRIBUTION BRANCHES**

JALGAON

Nirali Prakashan	:	34, V. V. Golani Market, Navi Peth, Jalgaon 425001, Maharashtra, Tel : (0257) 222 0395, Mob : 94234 91860

KOLHAPUR

Nirali Prakashan	:	New Mahadvar Road, Kedar Plaza, 1st Floor Opp. IDBI Bank Kolhapur 416 012, Maharashtra. Mob : 9850046155

NAGPUR

Pratibha Book Distributors	:	Above Maratha Mandir, Shop No. 3, First Floor, Rani Jhanshi Square, Sitabuldi, Nagpur 440012, Maharashtra Tel : (0712) 254 7129

DELHI

Nirali Prakashan	:	4593/21, Basement, Aggarwal Lane 15, Ansari Road, Daryaganj Near Times of India Building, New Delhi 110002 Mob : 08505972553

BENGALURU

Pragati Book House	:	House No. 1, Sanjeevappa Lane, Avenue Road Cross, Opp. Rice Church, Bengaluru – 560002. Tel : (080) 64513344, 64513355,Mob : 9880582331, 9845021552 Email:bharatsavla@yahoo.com

CHENNAI

Pragati Books	:	9/1, Montieth Road, Behind Taas Mahal, Egmore, Chennai 600008 Tamil Nadu, Tel : (044) 6518 3535, Mob : 94440 01782 / 98450 21552 / 98805 82331, Email : bharatsavla@yahoo.com

niralipune@pragationline.com | www.pragationline.com

Also find us on www.facebook.com/niralibooks

PREFACE

It gives us great pleasure in publishing this text book on **"Data Structure and Files"** for the students of Second Year Degree Course in Information Technology. This book is strictly written according to **New Revised Credit System Syllabus** of Savitribai Phule Pune University (2015 Pattern).

As per the policy of the University, Engineering Syllabi is revised every five years. Last revision was in the year 2012. New revision is coming little earlier, as university has introduced **Online System of Examination** from year 2012.

As per the **New Credit System**, the **Online Examinations** Phase-I will be conducted based on First & Second Units and Phase II on Third & Fourth Units. The **Online** examinations will have objective types of questions with multiple choices. End Sem. Theory Examination will be based on all the six units and that will be conducted in traditional way and the Theory Course will have 4 credits.

It is our objective to keep the presentation systematic, consistent, intensive and clear presentation of concept through explanatory notes and figures. So we are sure that this book will cater for all your needs for this subject.

Main feature of this book is, **Complete Coverage** of the New Credit System Syllabus with large number of **Worked (Solved) Programs Examples and Exercises.**

We have given Separate Book of Multiple Choice Questions (MCQ's) which will be very useful to the students especially for Online Examinations.

We take this opportunity to express our sincere thanks to Shri. Dineshbhai Furia, Shri. Jignesh Furia, Mrs. Nirali Verma and Shri. M. P. Munde and entire team of Nirali Prakashan namely Mrs. Deepali Lachake (Co-ordinator), who really have taken keen interest and untiring efforts in publishing this text.

The advice and suggestions of our esteemed readers to improve the text are most welcomed, and will be highly appreciated.

Pune   **Authors**

SYLLABUS

Unit I : Stacks and Queues   8 Hours

Concept of stack, stack as ADT, Implementation of stack using linked organization. Concept of implicit and explicit stack, Applications of stack.

Concept of queues as ADT, Implementation of queue using linked organization. Concept of circular queue, double ended queue and priority queue. Applications of queues.

Unit II : Trees   10 Hours

Difference in linear and non-linear data structure, Trees and binary trees-concept and terminology. Expression tree. Conversion of general tree to binary tree. Binary tree as an ADT. Recursive and non-recursive algorithms for binary tree traversals, Binary search trees, Binary search tree as ADT, Applications of trees

Unit III : Graphs   8 Hours

Graph as an ADT, Representation of graphs using adjacency matrix and adjacency list, Depth First Search and Breadth First Search traversal. Prim's and Kruskal's algorithms for minimum spanning tree, shortest path using Warshall's and Dijkstra's algorithm, topological sorting.

Unit IV : Tables   8 Hours

Symbol Table: Notion of Symbol Table, OBST, Huffman's algorithm, Heap data structure, Min and Max Heap, Heap sort implementation, applications of heap

Hash tables and scattered tables: Basic concepts, hash function, characteristics of good hash function, different key-to-address transformations techniques, synonyms or collisions, collision resolution techniques- linear probing, quadratic probing, rehashing, chaining without replacement and chaining with replacement

Unit V : Advance Trees   7 Hours

Concept of threaded binary tree. Preorder and In-order traversals of in-order threaded binary tree, Concept of red and black trees, AVL Trees, B trees, B+ trees, Splay trees

Unit VI : File Organization   7 Hours

External storage devices, File, File types and file organization (sequential, index sequential and Direct access), Primitive operations and implementations for each type and comparison

CONTENTS

Unit I : Stacks and Queues

Chapter 1 : Stacks — 1.1-1.48

1.1	Introduction	1.1
1.2	Stack Using Array	1.1
	1.2.1 Stack as an Abstract Data Type (ADT)	1.11
1.3	Stack Using Linked List	1.12
1.4	Concept of Implicit and Explicit Stack	1.16
1.5	Application of Stack	1.17
1.6	Arithmetic Expression : Polish Notation	1.18
	1.6.1 Evaluation of Postfix Expression	1.21
	1.6.2 Conversion of Infix Expression to Postfix	1.24
1.7	Recursion and Stack	1.30
	1.7.1 Removal of Recursion	1.33
•	Exercise	1.45

Chapter 2 : Queues — 2.1-2.34

2.1	Introduction	2.1
2.2	Queue Using Array	2.1
2.3	Queue Using Linked List	2.10
	2.3.1 Queue as an Abstract Data Type (ADT)	2.14
2.4	Circular Queue	2.14
2.5	Double Ended Queue (Deques)	2.19
2.6	Priority Queue	2.21
2.7	Applications Of Queue	2.22
	2.7.1 Categorizing Data	2.22
	2.7.2 Simulation of Queues	2.26
	2.7.3 Job Scheduling	2.27
•	Exercise	2.32

Unit II : Trees

Chapter 3 : Trees — 3.1-3.70

3.1	Introduction	3.1
3.2	Basic Terminology	3.2
	3.2.1 Difference between Linear and Non-Linear Data Structures	3.3
3.3	Binary Tree	3.4
	3.3.1 Representation of Binary Tree	3.6
	3.3.2 Binary Tree Traversal	3.8
3.4	Binary Search Tree (BST)	3.21
3.5	Operations On Binary Search Tree	3.21
	3.5.1 Creating BST	3.23
	3.5.2 Searching in BST	3.24
	3.5.3 Tree Traversal Operations	3.25
	3.5.4 Delete Operation	3.27
	3.5.5 Insert Operation	3.30

3.6		Operations On Binary Tree	3.38
	3.6.1	Creating a Binary Tree	3.39
	3.6.2	Traversal Operation	3.40
	3.6.3	Insert Operation	3.40
	3.6.4	Binary Tree as an ADT	3.45
	3.6.5	Recursive and Non Recursive Algorithms for Binary Tree Traversals	3.46
	3.6.6	Non-Recursive Traversal	3.52
3.7		Binary Search Tree as an ADT	3.55
3.8		Applications Of Trees	3.57
•		Exercise	3.67

Unit III : Graphs

Chapter 4 : Graphs — 4.1-4.56

4.1		Introduction	4.1
4.2		Graph Theory and Terminology	4.1
4.3		Representation of Graph using Adjacency Matrix	4.4
4.4		Representation of Graph Using Adjacency List	4.9
4.5		Traversals of Graph (DFS and BFS)	4.11
	4.5.1	Depth First Search (DFS) Traversal	4.11
	4.5.2	Breadth First Search (BFS) Traversal	4.16
4.6		Topological Sorting	4.26
4.7		Minimal Spanning Tree	4.29
	4.7.1	Prim's Algorithm	4.30
	4.7.2	Kruskal's Algorithm	4.35
•		Exercise	4.50

Unit IV : Tables

Chapter 5 : Tables — 5.1-5.68

5.1		Symbol Table	5.1
5.2		Optimal Binary Search Trees	5.3
5.3		Huffman's algorithm	5.12
	5.3.1	Huffman's Algorithm	5.14
5.4		Heap Data Structure	5.20
5.5		Min Max Heap	5.27
5.6		Applications of HEAP	5.30
5.7		Hash Tables	5.31
	5.7.1	Basic Hashing Techniques	5.34
	5.7.2	Forms of Hashing Data Structure	5.36
5.8		Collision Resolution Methods	5.38
•		Exercise	5.67

Unit V : Advance Trees

Chapter 6 : Advance Trees — 6.1-6.48

6.1		Threaded Binary Tree	6.1
	6.1.1	Create/Insert Operation	6.4
	6.1.2	Non-Recursive Traversals	6.5

6.2	Height Balance Tree (AVL Tree)	6.11
	6.2.1 Binary Tree	6.25
	6.2.2 Representation using Sequential and Linked Organization	6.28
	6.2.2 Height of the Tree	6.31
6.3	Types of Binary Tree	6.31
	6.3.1 Full Binary Tree	6.31
	6.3.2 Complete Binary Tree	6.32
	6.3.3 Skewed Binary Tree	6.32
	6.3.4 Strictly Binary Tree	6.33
	6.3.5 Extended Binary Tree	6.33
	6.3.6 Splay Trees	6.34
•	Exercise	6.47

Unit VI : File Organization

Chapter 7 : File Organization		**7.1-7.86**
7.1	Introduction to Files	7.1
7.2	External Storage Devices	7.2
	7.2.1 Magnetic Tape	7.2
	7.2.2 Magnetic Drums	7.3
	7.2.3 Magnetic Disks	7.4
7.3	File Handling in C	7.5
	7.3.1 File Opening Modes	7.20
	7.3.2 Storing File on External Storage Device	7.21
7.4	Primitive File Stream Operations and implementations in C++	7.21
7.5	Primitive Functions in C++ for Files	7.22
7.6	Comparison Between Text file and Binary File	7.30
7.7	Sequential File Organization	7.31
7.8	Direct Access File Organization	7.47
7.9	Index Sequential File Organization	7.59
	7.9.1 Primary Indexes (Indexed Sequential File)	7.59
	7.9.2 Secondary Indexes (Simple Index File)	7.60
	7.9.3 Clustering Indexes	7.67
	7.9.4 Indexed Sequential Characteristics	7.68
7.10	Difference Between Sequential File organization and Direct Access File	7.81
7.11	Difference Between Sequential File and Index Sequential File	7.82
7.12	Indexing and Hashing Comparison	7.82
7.13	Linked Organization of a File	7.83
7.14	Inverted File Organization	7.83
7.15	Cellular Partitions	7.83
•	Exercise	7.84
•	**Sample Question Paper for End. Sem. Theory Exam.**	**P.1-P.2**
•	**University Question Papers (May 2016 to Nov. 2016)**	**P.1-P.8**

Unit I

CHAPTER 1
STACKS

1.1 INTRODUCTION

Stack is a linear data structure where the element which is inserted last can only be taken out first. Thus, it is called LIFO (Last In First Out) type of data structure.

Stack is also defined as a data structure where all addition and deletion are made only at one end called top. It is similar to a real life situation of stack of things. If we keep things stacked one on to the another, we can take out the thing at the top. Similarly, we can keep a new thing on the top.

Stack can be implemented using :

1. Arrays

2. Linked lists

Following four operations can be done on a stack :

1. **Push Operation :** In this, an element is stored at a location indicated by top.

2. **Pop Operation :** In this operation, the element at the top is removed.

3. **Stack Full :** When all the locations reserved for stack are occupied, we can't insert any more elements. This condition is called as stack full condition.

4. **Stack Empty :** When there is no element left on a stack, we can't pop any element. This condition is called as stack empty condition.

1.2 STACK USING ARRAY

To represent a stack using array, we require an array of some size to be declared say int a[4]. This will create a space for storing elements on stack. The size of the stack is 4. We will require one more variable say top which will be an index to the top element of the stack. Initially, the stack is empty. The variable top will be initialized to −1.

Push Operation :

Now, if we want to store a number 10 on the stack, we can increment top and the element 10 will be stored at location a[0].

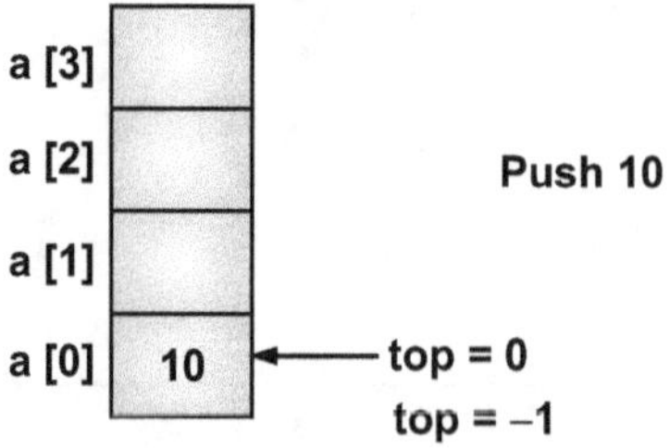

Fig. 1.1 (a) : Push (10)

Next, we store a number 20 on the stack, top will be incremented to 1 and element 20 will be stored at location a[1].

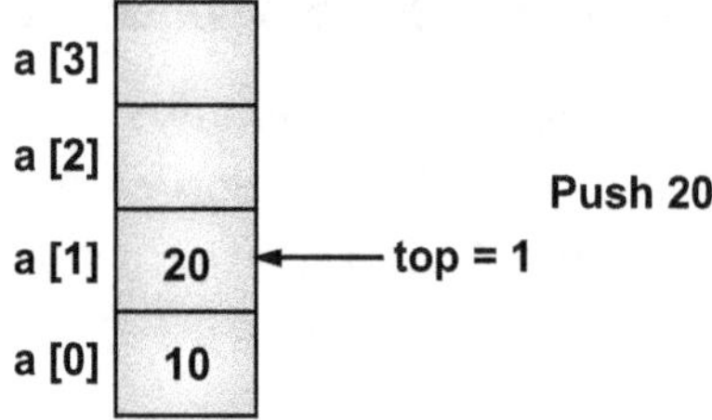

Fig. 1.1 (b) : Push (20)

Next, we store a number 30 on the stack, top will be incremented to 2 and element 30 will be stored at location a[2].

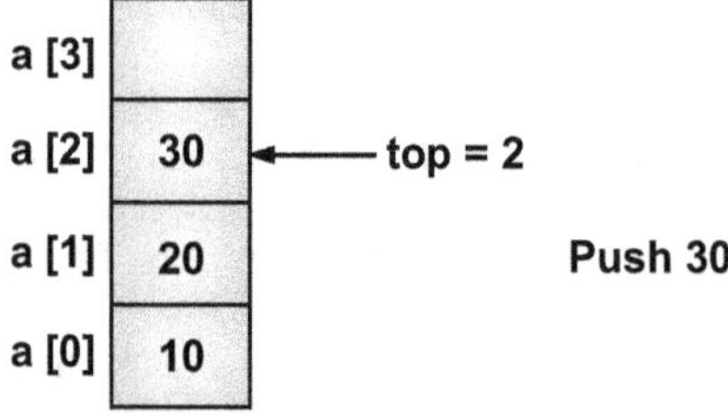

Fig. 1.1 (c) : Push (30)

Next, we store a number 40 on the stack, top will be incremented to 3 and element 40 will be stored at location a[3].

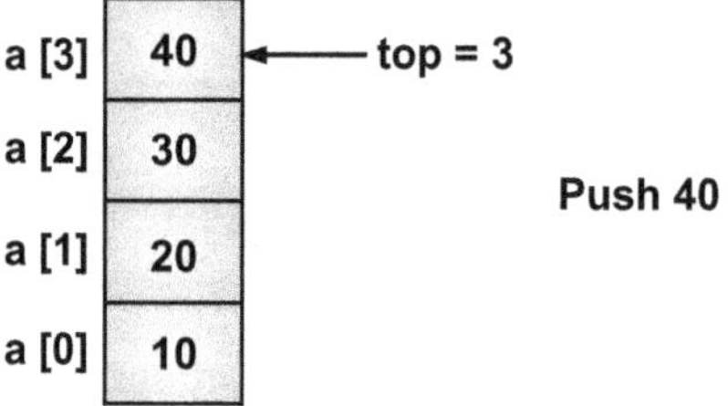

Fig. 1.1 (d) : Push (40)

Now there is no space left on the stack, hence, the stack is full. The condition for stack full is top becomes equal to maximum size of array −1.

Pop Operation :

Now, suppose we want to remove an element from the stack, we can access element at the top which is given by the index value in top. Consider the stack where we have already pushed four elements. If we carry out pop operation, the element at the top i.e. 40 will be accessed and top is decremented to 2.

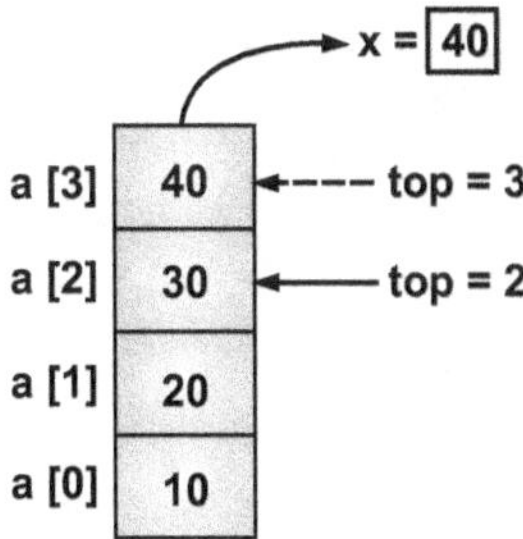

Fig. 1.2 (a) : x = pop( )

The next pop operation will remove 30 from the stack and top will be decremented to 1.

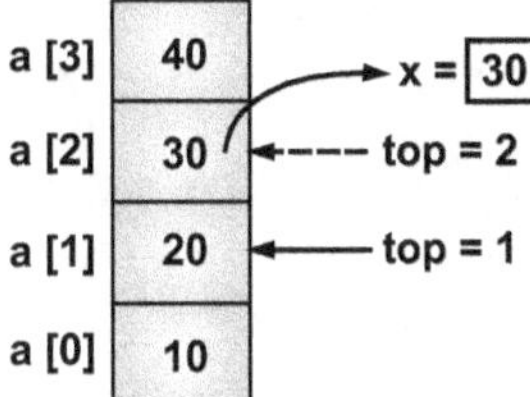

Fig. 1.2 (b) : x = pop( )

Another pop operation will remove 20 from the stack and top will be decremented to 0.

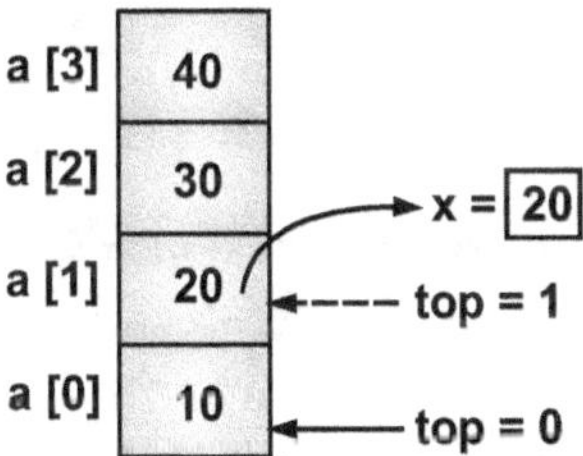

Fig. 1.2 (c) : x = pop( )

If the operation is carried out again, element 10 will be removed and top becomes −1.

Fig. 1.2 (d) : x = pop( )

Then we can't remove any more elements because stack is empty. The condition for stack empty is top = −1. The program for implementation of stack will require two functions push and pop whose algorithms areas follows :

1. Push (x) :

> (i)   If top == MAX −1
>
> > print "stack full";
>
> (ii) else
>
> > top ++;
> >
> > a [top] = x;
>
> (iii) Return.

Every time we do a push operation, we need to increment top and store the data at the location given by top in the array. But before we do this operation, we must check whether the stack is full or not. Hence, the condition top == MAX −1.

2. x = pop( ) :

> (i)   If top==−1
>
> > print "stack empty";
> >
> > return −9999;
>
> (ii) else
>
> > x = a [top]
> >
> > top −−;
> >
> > return x;

Every time we do a pop operation, we remove an element and then decrement top. But before we do this, we must check whether the stack is empty or not. Hence, the condition top == −1. Note that we are returning −9999 when stack is empty. This is an indication for the calling function, so that it takes appropriate action when the stack is empty. The complete program for stack implementation is as follows :

Program 1.1 : To implement stack using array (Version 1)

```
#define MAX 5
int a [MAX];
int top = -1;
void push (int x)
{
    if (top == MAX - 1)
```

```c
        printf("Stack is full");
    else
    {
    top ++;
    a[top]=x;
    }
}
int pop( )
{
    int x;
    if (top == -1)
    {
        print("Stack is empty \n");
        return (-9999);
    }
    else
    {
        x = a[top];
        top --;
        return (x);
    }
}
main( )
{
    int ch, x;
    do
    {
        clrscr( );
        printf(" 1. Push \n. 2. Pop \n. 3. Exit \n");
        printf("Enter your choice \n");
```

```c
            scanf("%d", &ch);
            switch (ch)
            {
                    case 1 : printf("Enter a number \n");
                            scanf("% d", &x);
                            push (x);
                            break;
                    case 2 :    x = pop( );
                            if (x!= -9999)
                                    printf("% d", x);
            }
            getch( );
        } while (ch!=3);
    }
```

We can implement separate functions for stack full and stack empty conditions as follows :

```c
    int stk_full( )
    {
        if (top == MAX -1)
        {
            printf("Stack full");
            return (1);
        }
        else
            return (0);
    }
```

The function returns 1 when stack is full otherwise 0.

```c
    int stk_empty( )
    {
        if (top == -1)
        {
```

```
        printf ("Stack is empty");
        return (1);
    }
    else
        return (0);
}
```

The function returns 1 when stack is empty otherwise 0.

These functions can be used in functions 'push' and 'pop' as follows :

```
void push (int x)
{
    if (!stk_full( ))
    {
        top ++;
        a[top] = x;
    }
}
int pop( )
{
    if (!stk_empty( ))
    {
        int x;
        x = a[top];
        top --;
        return x;
    }
    else
        return (-9999);
}
```

The stack consists of an array and top. If multiple stacks are to be implemented in single program, we need to define separate arrays and tops for each stack. Instead, we can define a stack variable for a stack which combines array and top together.

```
typedef struct stack
{
    int a[4];
    int top;
} STK;
```

Now if we declare a variable STK s1; it consists of an array and top as shown in Fig. 1.3.

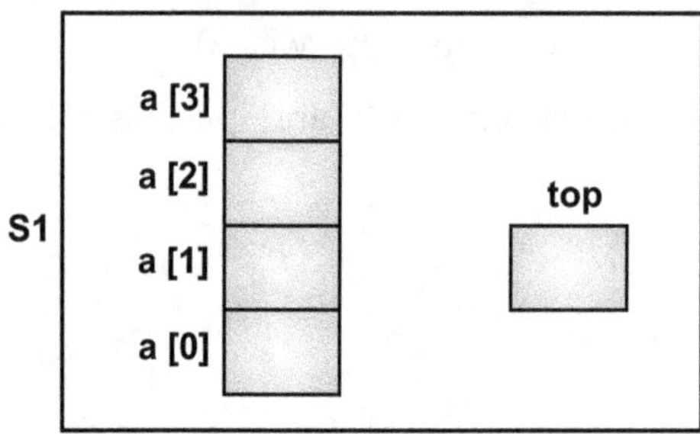

Fig. 1.3 : Stack using structure

The elements in the stack can be accessed using dot operate, For Example, if top of the stack is to be initialized, we can write s1.top = −1 or if 10 is to be stored at the top of the stack; we can write s1.a [s1.top] = 10. But the major advantage of this struct type stack will be when more than one stack is to be implemented. The push and pop functions require the stack variable to be passed to them. Since these functions are going to modify the contents of the stack variable, we must pass it by address. Hence, the function parameter will be pointer to a structure.

The push function will have prototype as,

```
void push (STK*, int)
```

The first argument is the pointer to the stack in which we are going to store the element and second argument is the integer number to be stored on the stack.

The pop function will have prototype as,

```
int pop (STK *)
```

The argument is the pointer to the stack from which number returns will be popped. A complete program using this is given as follows :

Program 1.2 : Implementation of stack

```
#define MAX 5
typedef struct stack
{
    int a[MAX];
```

```c
        int top;
} STK;
void push (STK*, int);
int pop (STK *);
main( )
{
        STK s1, s2;
        s1.top = -1;
        s2.top = -1;
        push (&s1, 10);
        push (&s1, 20);
        push (&s2, 100);
        push (&s2, 200);
        x = pop (&s1);
        printf("%d", x);
        x = pop (&s1);
        printf("%d", x);
        x = pop (&s2);
        printf("%d", x);
        x = pop (&s2);
        printf("%d", x);
}
void push (STK *s, int x)
{
        if (s->top == MAX -1)
            printf("Stack is full");
        else
        {
            (s->top) ++;
            s->a [s->top] = x;
```

```c
        }
}
int pop (STK *s)
{
    int x;
    if (s->top == -1)
    {
        printf("Stack is empty");
        return (-9999);
    }
    else
    {
        x=s->a [s->top];
        (s->top) --;
        return (x);
    }
}
```

Explanation :

- The main function has two variables s1 and s2 which are stacks.

- The functions push and pop are passed addresses of stack. It is because the functions are going to change the contents of stack. Since we are passing the structure variable by address, the structure members are accessed using –> operator, For Example, top of stack is accessed through s as s –> top.

- Note that though we are using two stacks, we have only one structure declaration and same functions push and pop for both the stacks.

- We can modify the menu driven program we had written earlier for implementation of stack.

Program 1.3 : To implement stack using array (version 2).

```c
    void push (STK *, int);
    int pop (STK*);
    void main( )
    {
```

```c
        STK s1;
        int ch, x;
        s1.top = -1;
        do
        {
            clrscr( );
            printf(" \n 1. Push \n 2. Pop \n 3. Exit \n");
            printf("Enter your choice");
            scanf("%d", &ch);
            switch (ch)
            {
                case 1 :  printf("Enter data \n");
                          scanf("%d", &x);
                          push (&s1, x);
                          break;
                case 2 : x = pop (&s1);
                         if (x! = -9999)
                             printf ("%d \n", x);
                         break;
            }
            getch( );
        } while (ch!=3);
}
```

1.2.1 Stack as an Abstract Data Type (ADT)

The ADT for stack can be given as follows :

Definition : A stack is a restricted list in which entries are added and removed from the same end, called the top. This strategy is known as last-in-first-out (LIFO) strategy.

Operations (Methods) on Stacks :

push(item)	Inserts item on the top of the stack
pop( )	Removes the top item
size( )	Returns the number of items in the stack

empty( )   Returns true if the stack is empty

full( )   Returns true if the stack is full

ontop( )   Returns the top element without removing it from the stack

Multiple Stacks using Single Array :

We have seen that multiple stacks can be implemented using multiple arrays. We can use single array also to implement multiple stack. For this we can divide the array into number of parts. Each part will be used as one stack. The top of each stack will be initialized to the starting index of each part in the array. For implementing stack full or stack empty condition, we can use a counter for each stack. The counter will be incremented when push operation is done and decremented when pop operation is done. Stack full condition occurs when the counter reaches maximum value (size of each stack). Stack empty condition occurs when counter becomes starting index of each stack.

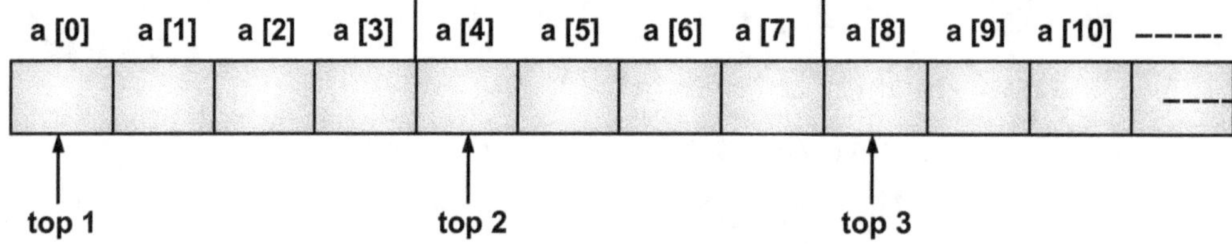

Fig. 1.4 : Multiple stacks using single array

Two stacks can be efficiently implemented using single array by using the upper part of the array for first stack and lower part for second array, The top of first stack will be initialized to −1, it will be incremented when push operation is done and decremented in pop operation. The top of the second stack is initialized to MAX (size of the array). It is decremented in push operation and incremented in pop operation.

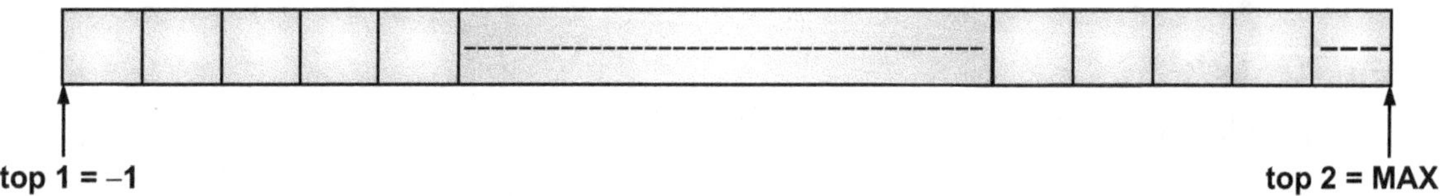

Fig. 1.5 : Two stacks using single array

1.3 STACK USING LINKED LIST   [May 05, 06, 07, 08, DEC. 06, 10]

The array implementation of stack is not efficient from the point of view of memory utilization. The fixed size of array is required and it remains allocated for the entire duration of the program. Linked list implementation will have advantage over the array implementation because we can allocate memory as and when it is required.

The stack using linked list consist of nodes having data and address of next node. The node definition will be,

```
    typedef struct node
    {
        int data;
        struct node *next;
    } NODE;
```

A pointer called top can be declared (NODE *top) which will always point to the top of the stack. The operations push and pop will be implemented as follows :

Push Operation :

Step 1 : Create a node.

Step 2 : Store the data in the node.

Step 3 : Link the next field of the node to the node where top is pointing.

Step 4 : Point top to the recently created node.

Following figures show this operation.

Push (10) :

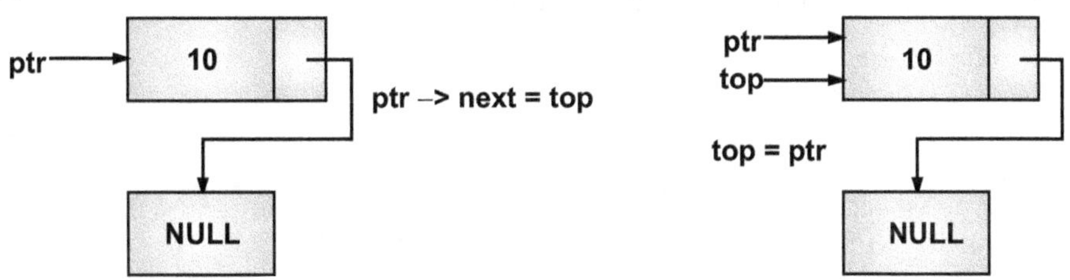

Fig. 1.6 (a) : Stack using linked list push (10)

Push (20) :

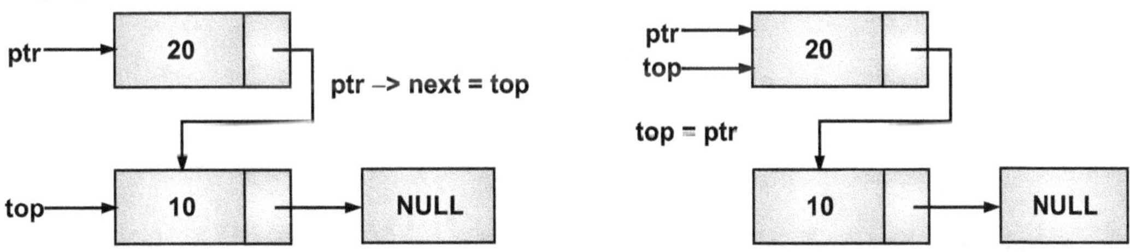

Fig. 1.6 (b) : Stack using linked list push (20)

Pop Operation :

Step 1 : Make a pointer temp point to the top of the stack.

Step 2 : If it is NULL, then stack is empty.

Step 3 : If not, remove the data from this node then advance top.

Step 4 : De–allocate memory pointed by temp.

Following figures show this operation.

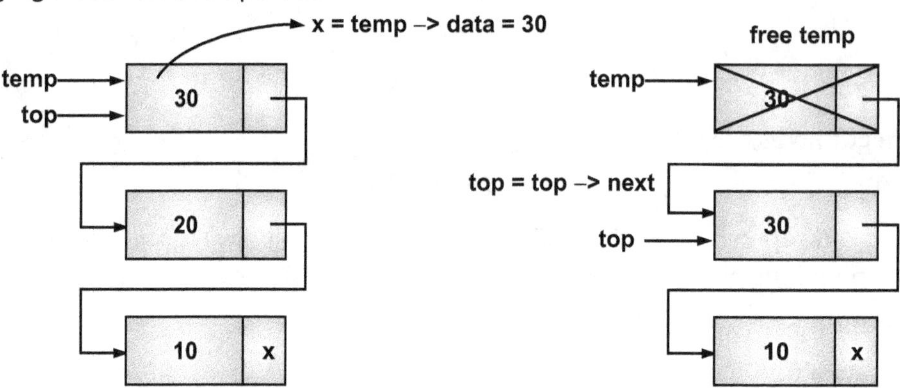

Fig. 1.7 : Pop operation in stack using linked list

Following program implements stack using linked list. It has the function push and pop which has the same prototype as that used in case of array. The function push accepts data, creates a node and puts it into a linked list. The function pop removes an element from the linked list and returns it.

Program 1.4 : To implement stack using linked list.

```c
typedef struct node
{
    int data;
    struct node * next;
} NODE;
NODE *top = NULL;
void push (int);
int pop( );
void main( )
{
    int ch, x;
    do
    {
        clrscr( );
        printf(" 1. Push \n 2. Pop \n 3. Exit \n");
        printf("Enter your choice");
        scanf("%d", &ch);
```

```c
            switch (ch)
            {
                case 1 : printf("Enter a number \n");
                         scanf("%d", &x);
                         push (x);
                         break;
                case 2 :      x = pop( );
                         if (x != -9999)
                              printf ("%d \n", x);
            }
          getch( );
      } while (ch!=3);
}
void push (int x)
{
    NODE *ptr;
    ptr = (NODE *) malloc (size of (NODE));
    if (ptr == NULL)
        printf("Insufficient memory");
    else
    {
        ptr->data = x;
        ptr->next = top;
        top = ptr;
    }
}
int pop( )
{
    NODE *temp;
    int x;
```

```
        temp = top;

        if (temp == NULL)

        {

            printf ("Stack empty");

            return (-9999);

        }

        else

        {

            x = temp->data;

            top = top->next;

            free (temp);

            return (x);

        }

    }
```

1.4 CONCEPT OF IMPLICIT AND EXPLICIT STACK

A stack is an ordered list in which all insertions and deletions are made at one end, called the top. A queue is an ordered list in which all insertions take place at one end, the rear, while all deletions take place at the other end, the front. Given a stack S=(a[1],a[2],........a[n]) then we say that a1 is the bottommost element and element a[i]) is on top of element a[i-1], 1<i<=n. When viewed as a queue with a[n] as the rear element one says that a[i+1] is behind a[i], 1<i<=n.

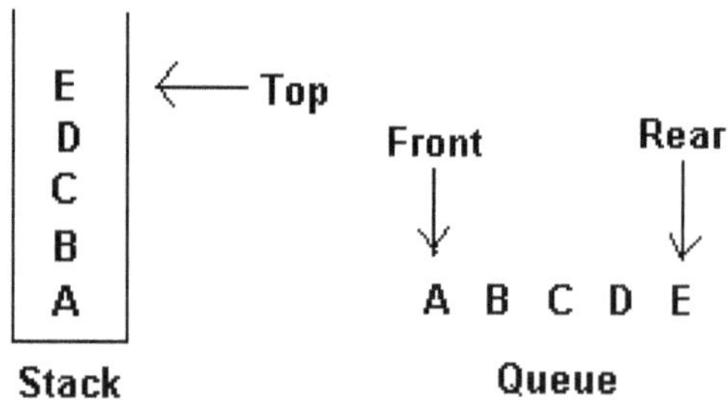

Fig. 1.8

The restrictions on a stack imply that if the elements A, B, C, D, E are added to the stack, n that order, then the first element to be removed/deleted must be E. Equivalently we say that the last element to be inserted into the stack will be the first to be removed. For this reason stacks are sometimes referred to as Last In First Out (LIFO) lists. The restrictions on queue imply that the first element which is inserted into the queue will be the first one to be removed. Thus A is the first letter to be removed, and queues are known as First In First Out (FIFO) lists. Note that the data object queue as defined here need not necessarily correspond to the mathematical concept of queue in which the insert/delete rules may be different.

You can see the algorithms you want by clicking on the items below:

- Adding an element into a stack.
- Deleting an element from a stack.
- Adding an element into a queue.
- Deleting an element from a queue.

One natural example of stacks which arises in computer programming is the processing of procedure calls and their terminations. Suppose we have four procedures as below:

The MAIN procedure invokes procedure A1. On completion of A1 execution of MAIN will resume at location r. The address r is passed to A1 which saves it in some location for later processing. A1 then invokes A2 which in turn invokes A3. In each case the invoking procedure passes the return address to the invoked procedure. If we examine the memory while A3 is computing there will be an implicit stack which looks like (q,r,s,t).

The first entry q is the address to which MAIN returns control. This list operates as a stack since the returns will be made in the reverse order of the invocations. Thus t is removed before s, s before r and r before q. Equivalently this means that A3 must finish processing before A2, A2 before A1, and A1 before MAIN. This list of return addresses need not be maintained in consecutive locations. For each procedure there is usually a single location associated with the machine code which is used to retain the return address. This can be severely limiting in the case of recursive and re-entrant procedures, since every time we invoke a procedure the new return address wipes out the old one. For example, if we inserted a call to A1 within procedure A3 expecting the return to be at location u, then at execution time the stack would become (q, u, s, t) and the return address r would be lost. When recursion is allowed, it is no longer adequate to reserve one location for the return address of each procedure. Since returns are made in the reverse order of calls, an elegant and natural solution to this procedure return problem is afforded through the explicit use of a stack of return addresses. Whenever a return is made, it is to the top address in the stack.

1.5 APPLICATION OF STACK

Stack can be used in number of applications such as :

- Conversion of expression.
- Evaluation of expression.
- Processing function calls.

- Handling recursive function or removal of recursion.
- Reversing a string.
- Syntax checking for Example, parenthesis check.

1.6 ARITHMETIC EXPRESSION : POLISH NOTATION

This is the most important application of stack. When we write a program, we write number of expressions (arithmetic, logical, etc.) in it. The compiler must interpret and convert these expressions into machine language.

An expression consists of operands and operators, For Example, the expression a + b has two operands a and b and one operator +. This is a very simple expression. Expression can be very complex consisting of number of operands and operators. While converting an expression into correct machine language format, compiler must take care of the priority of the operators. It is very difficult to directly produce a code for evaluation of expression. The solution to this is, convert the expression into a form which will not require priority of operators and the expression can be directly evaluated.

An expression can be written in three different forms :

- **Infix Expression :** Operator is in between the two operands, For Example, a + b.
- **Postfix Expression :** Operator is after the two operands, For Example, ab+. It is called Reverse polish notation.
- **Prefix Expression :** Operator is before the two operands, For Example, +ab. It is called Polish notation.

Suppose we have an expression in infix format a + b * c.

Its postfix is abc * +

and prefix is + a * bc

If you observe postfix and prefix expression, we find that these expressions can be evaluated directly without knowing the priority of operators. Whereas for infix expression we must find out priority and then evaluate.

Before we learn how to evaluate the postfix expression let us see how to convert an infix expression to postfix or prefix.

If we are given an infix expression a + b * c steps for conversion will be as follows :

1. Write the expression with full parenthesized as per the priority of operators.

   For Example, (a + (b * c))

2. Replace the innermost parenthesized expression with e_1

   exp = (a + e_1) where e_1 = b * c

- Replace the next innermost parenthesized expression with e_2 as :

  i.e. $exp = e_2$ where $e_2 = a + e_1$

  Continue till you get a single expression.

- Now go in reverse direction replacing each expression with postfix or prefix

  For Example, $exp = ae_1 +$ or $exp = + ae_1$

  $exp = abc* +$		$exp = + a * bc$

  Hence the postfix expression is abc * +

  and the prefix expression is + a * bc.

SOLVED EXAMPLES

Example 1.1 : Convert following expressions into postfix and prefix expressions.

1. a * b + c

2. a * b + c * d

3. a + b + c + d

4. a * b/c* d – e/f

5. a ** b * c ** d

Solution :

1.	$exp = ((a * b) + c)$

	$= (e_1 + c)$			$e_1 = a * b$

	$= e_2$				$e_2 = e_1 + c$

	Postfix			**Prefix**

	$exp = e_2$			$exp = e_2$

	$= e_1 c +$				$= +e_1 c$

	$= ab * c+$				$= +* abc$

2.	$exp = ((a *b) + (c * d))$

	$= (e_1 + e_2)$			$e_1 = a * b$			$e_2 = c * d$

	$= e_2$				$e_2 = e_1 + e_2$

	Postfix			**Prefix**

	$exp = e_2$			$exp = e_2$

	$= e_1 e_2 +$				$= +e_1 e_2$

	$= ab * cd * +$				$= + * ab * cd$

3. $\exp = (((a + b) + c) + d)$

$\qquad = ((e_1 + c) + d)$ 						$e_1 = a + b$

$\qquad = (e_1 + d)$ 						$e_2 = e_1 + c$

$\qquad = e_3$ 						$e_3 = e_2 + d$

Postfix						**Prefix**

$\exp = e_3$						$\exp = e_3$

$\qquad = e_2 d +$						$\qquad = + e_2 d$

$\qquad = e_1 c + d +$						$\qquad = + + e_1 cd$

$\qquad = ab + c + d +$						$\qquad = + + + \; abcd$

4. $\exp = a * b / c * d - e/f$

$\qquad = (((a * b)/c) * d) - (e/f)$

$\qquad = (((e_1/c) * d) - e_2)$ 				$e_1 = a * b$			$e_2 = e/f$

$\qquad = ((e_3 * d) - e_2)$ 				$e_3 = e_1/c$

$\qquad = (e_4 - e_2)$ 				$e_4 = e_3 * d$

$\qquad = e_5$ 				$e_5 = e_4 - e_2$

Postfix						**Prefix**

$\exp = e_5$						$\exp = e_5$

$\qquad = e_4 e_2 -$						$\qquad = - e_4\, e_2$

$\qquad = e_3 d * e_2 -$						$\qquad = - * \; e_3 d e_2$

$\qquad = e_1 c/d * e_2 -$						$\qquad = - * \; /e_1 cd \; e_2$

$\qquad = ab * c/d * ef/ -$						$\qquad = - * / * \; abcd / ef$

5. $\exp = a**b*c**d - e$

where ** is raised to operator

$\qquad = (((a**b)*(c**d)) - e)$

$\qquad = ((e_1 * e_2) - e)$ 				$e_1 = a ** b$			$e_2 = c ** d$

$\qquad = (e_3 - e)$ 				$e_3 = e_1 * e_2$

$\qquad = e_4$ 				$e_4 = e_3 - e$

Postfix						**Prefix**

$\exp = e_4$						$\exp = e_4$

$\qquad = e_3 e -$						$\qquad = - e_3 \; e$

$\qquad = e_1 e_2 * e -$						$\qquad = - e * e_1 \; e_2$

$\qquad = ab**cd***e-$						$\qquad = -e***ab**cd$

1.6.1 Evaluation of Postfix Expression

Now, let us see how we can evaluate a postfix expression. If we are given a postfix expression the expression is scanned from left till we come across an operator. The operator corresponds to previous two operands hence operate on the operand and result is an operand for next operator. Like this go on scanning till the end of the expression.

For Example, suppose we have the expression 456 * +

- The first operator is *. It will operate on 5 and 6 to give 30. The resultant expression is 430 +.

- Next operator is +. It will operate on 4 and 30 to give the result is 34.

  When we scan the expression and come across an operator we take latest two operands hence, we can use a stack to store the operands, so that latest two operands can be accessed. Hence, the procedure for evaluation of postfix expression will be as follows :

- Scan the expression.
- In case of operand.

  push the operand on stack.

- In case of operator

  Pop two operands from stack

  Do the operation

  Push the result on stack.

- Repeat 2 and 3 till the end of expression.

The expression can be stored in a string and can be scanned character by character. The procedure is illustrated with example below :

Suppose we have the expression 456 * +.

Expression Character	Action	Stack Content
4	push	4 ...
5	push	4 5 ...
6	push	4 5 6 ...
*	pop 6	
	pop 5	
	push (5 * 6)	4 30 ...
+	pop 30	
	pop 4	
	push (30 + 4)	34 ...

Fig. 1.9 : Evaluation of postfix expression 456*+

The detailed algorithm and program is :

Algorithm 1.1 :

1. Read expression in string expr[ ]

2. i=0

3. while (expr [i] !='\0')   // while it is not end of string

    {

        if(expr[i] is operand)

            push (expr[i]);

        else

        {

            op1 = pop( );

            op2 = pop( );

            v = op1 (operator in expr[i]) op2;

            push (v);

        }

        i++;

    }

4. result = pop( );

5. print result

Program 1.5 : To evaluate postfix expression.

```
#define MAX 10
int stk [MAX];
int top = -1;
void push (int);
int pop( );
void main
{
    char expr[40];
    int i, op1, op2;
    clrscr( );
```

```c
    printf("Enter expression \n");
    gets (expr);
    i=0;
    while (expr[i] != '\0')
    {
        if (isdigit(expr[i]))
            push (expr[i] -'0');
        else
        {
            op2 = pop( );
            op1 = pop( );
            switch (expr[i])
            {
                case '+' : push (op1 + op2);
                           break;
                case '-' : push (op1 - op2);
                           break;
                case '*' : push (op1 * op2);
                           break;
                case '/' : push (op1 / op2);
                           break;
            }
        }
        i++;
    }
    result=pop( );
    printf("The result is %d", result);
    getch( );
}
void push (int x)
```

```
{
    if (top == MAX -1)
        printf("Stack is full");
    else
    {
        top ++;
        stk [top] = x;
    }
}
int pop( )
{
    int x;
    if (top == -1)
    {
        printf ("Stack is empty \n");
        return (-9999);
    }
    else
    {
        x = stk [top];
        top --;
        return (x);
    }
}
```

1.6.2 Conversion of Infix Expression to Postfix

The evaluation of postfix expression requires stack and the priority of operators need not be considered for evaluating the expression. Normally, we write the expression in infix format. It needs to be converted into postfix format. The procedure for conversion is as follows.

A stack is used this time to store operators. The infix expression is scanned from left to right. Incase of operands, the operands are directly copied to postfix expression. In case of operators, either of two decisions is taken.

- If priority of operator is greater than operator on top of stack, the operator is pushed on stack.

- If priority of operator is less than operators on stack, the operators on stack are popped and copied into the output expression and the operator is pushed on to the stack.

Following examples illustrate the process of conversion of infix to postfix.

Example 1 : a+b*c

Incoming Character	Action	Postfix	Stack Contents
a	Copy to output	a	
+	Push	a	`+` ...
b	Copy to output	ab	
*	Priority more than +, Push *	ab	`+` `*` ...
c	Copy to output	abc	
c	Pop all operators copy to output	abc* +	

Fig. 1.10 : Conversion of infix to postfix

Example 2 : a*b+c

Incoming Character	Action	Postfix	Stack Contents
a	Copy to output	a	
*	Push	a	`*` ...
b	Copy to output	ab	
+	Priority less than *, pop *, copy to output, push +	ab*	`+` ...
c	Copy to output	ab*c	
End of expression	Pop all operators copy to output	ab*c+	

Fig. 1.11 : Conversion of infix to postfix

Example 3 : a + b * c / d − e

Incoming Character	Action	Postfix	Stack Contents
a	Copy to output	a	
+	Push	a	+ | | | ...
b	Copy to output	ab	
*	Priority more than +, push	ab	+ | * | | ...
c	Copy to output	abc	
/	Priority equal to *, pop*, copy to output, push /	abc*	+ | | | ...
d	Copy to output	abc*d	
−	Priority less than /, pop /, copy to output	abc*d/	
	priority equal to +, pop +, copy to output, push −	abd*d/+	− | | | ...
e	Copy to output	abc*d/+e	
End of expression	Pop all operations copy to output	abc*d/+e−	

Fig. 1.12 : Conversion of infix to postfix

The algorithm for conversion of infix to postfix is :

Algorithm 1.2 : To convert infix expression to postfix.

```
1.  Read infix expression

2.  i=0, j=0;

3.  while (infix[i] != '\0')
    {
        if (infix[i] is operand)
        {
            postfix[j] = infix[i];
            j++;
        }
        else
```

```
        {
            if (stack empty)
                push (infix[i]);
            else
            {   if (priority (infix [i])>priority (stack[top]))
                    push (infix[i]);
                else
                {
                    do
                    {
                        postfix[j] = pop( );
                        j++;
                    } while (priority (infix[i]))<=priority(stk[top])&& (!stack_empty);
                    push (infix[i]);
                }
            }
        }
        i++;
    }
4.  while (!stack_empty)
    {
        postfix[j] = pop( );
        j++;
    }
5.  postfix[j] = '\0';
6.  print postfix
7.  stop.
```

For Implementation of above Algorithm following considerations are required :

- A stack of characters need to be defined along with the operations push and pop.
- A function called priority needs to be defined which will return address of operator passed to it.

- Two string variables will be required one for storing infix expression and other for postfix expression.

- To make the program simple, the stack is implemented using array and it is declared globally along with the top of stack, so that we can directly access it in main function.

- Only four operators +, −, *, / are taken for the conversion. Otherwise the program will be bit complex since apart from priority; associativity of operators also plays an important role in the conversion.

- The expression is assumed to have variable with single character or digit for example, a + b * c and not like sum = n1 + n2.

Program 1.6 : To convert infix expression to postfix

```c
#define MAX 50
char stk[MAX];
int top = -1;
void push (char);
char pop( );
int priority (char);
void main( )
{
    char infix[MAX], postfix[MAX];
    int i, j;
    clrscr( );
    printf("Enter infix expression \n");
    gets (infix);
    i=0; j=0;
    while (infix [i]!='\0')
    {
        if (isalpha(infix[i]) || isdigit(infix [i]))
        {
            postfix [j] = infix [i];
            j++;
        }
        else
```

```c
        {
                if(top == -1 || priority(infix[i])>priority(stk[top]))
                    push (infix[i]);
                else
                {
                    do
                    {
                        postfix[j] = pop( );
                        j++;
                    } while (priority (infix [i])<=priority(stk[top]) && top!=-1);
                    push (infix[i]);
                }
            }
            i++;
        }
        while (top!=-1)
        {
            postfix[j] = pop( );
            j++;
        }
        postfix[j] = '\0';
        printf("%s", postfix);
}
void push (char x)
{
        if(top!=MAX-1)
        {
            top ++;
            stk [top] = x;
        }
```

```
}
char pop( )
{
    char x;
    if (top!=-1)
    {
        x = stk[top];
        top --;
    }
    return(x);
}
int priority (char ch)
{
    switch (ch)
    {
        case '*' :
        case '/':   return (2);
                    break;
        case '-':
        case '+':
        return (1);
    }
}
```

Note : If at all you want to include the raised to operator ($ or ^) you can assign priority 3 (highest) to it.

1.7 RECURSION AND STACK

A function that calls itself is called recursive function. When a recursive function is called, following actions are performed :

- Allocation of space for parameters.
- Saving of local variables.
- Saving return address.

When the function returns back to a point in previous call, following actions are performed :

- Retrieval of return address.

- Retrieval of local variables.

Now in case of recursive calls, where the function is called repetitively, number of copies of local variables and return addresses are to be saved and when return takes place, the most recent copy of local variables and addresses are required i.e. last in will be first out. This calls for use of stack for handling recursion. The C compiler does exactly this for handling recursion. Let us consider the recursive function to find n!.

```
int fact (int n)
{
    int x, y;
    if(n == 0 || n==1)
        return (1);
    else
    {
        x = n - 1;
        y = fact (x);
        return (n*y);
    }
}
```

- Let the function be called with n = 4 i.e. fact (4). Three stacks of integer will be required for 3 variables involved in function n, x and y. Initially, the stacks will be empty, when fact (4) is called value 4 and is stored in stack of variable n as,

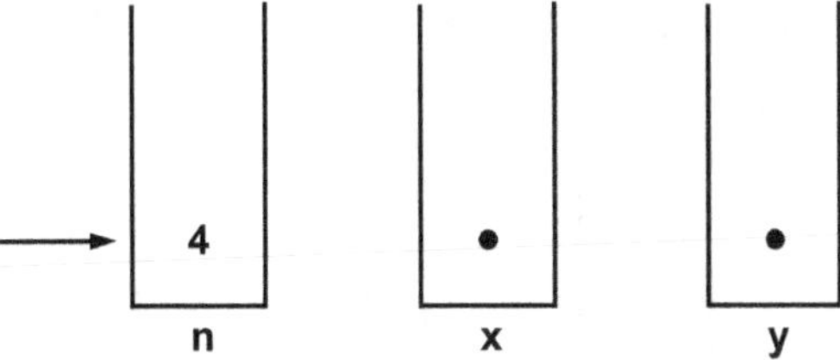

Fig. 1.13 (a) : Recursion stack n = 4

During this call, x = n − 1 = 3 and function call y = fact (3) takes place.

- The function call fact (3) will put the most recent values of n = 3, x = 3 on stacks as,

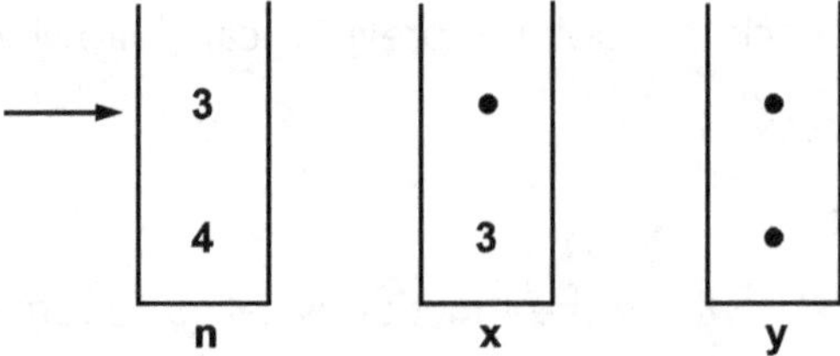

Fig. 1.13 (b) : Recursion stack n = 3

During this call, x = n – 1 = 2 and function call y = fact (2) takes place.

- The function call fact (2) will put the most recent value of n = 2, x = 2 or stacks as,

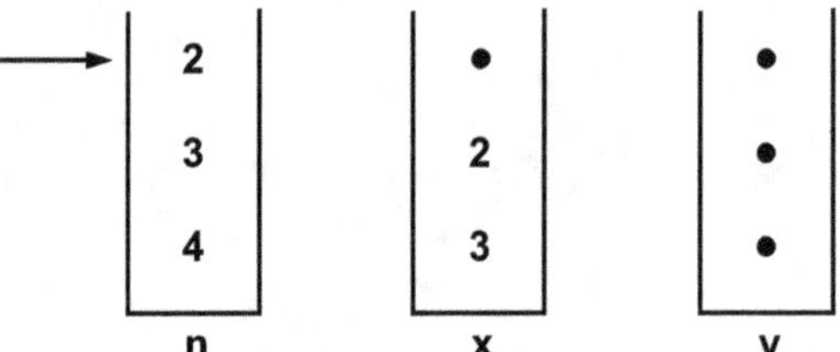

Fig. 1.13 (c) : Recursion stack n = 2

During this call, x = n – 1 = 1 and function call y = fact (1) takes place.

- The function call fact (1) will put values of n = 1 and x = 1 on stacks as,

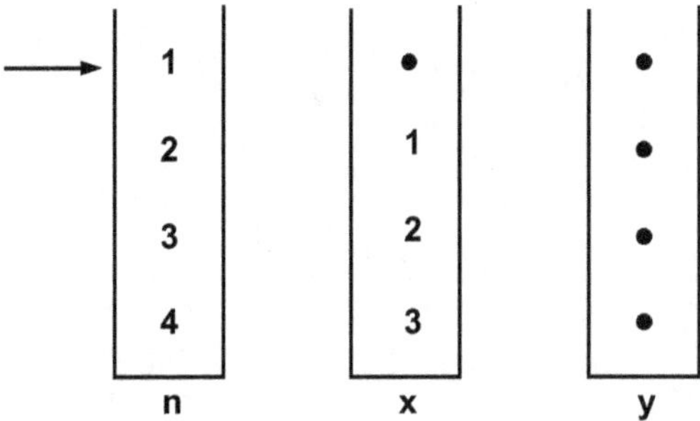

Fig. 1.13 (d) : Recursion stack n = 1

During this call, x is garbage and return(1) will be executed which will return value 1.

- The return statement will assign returned value y = 1. It will free the values allocated during fact (1) to n, x and y.

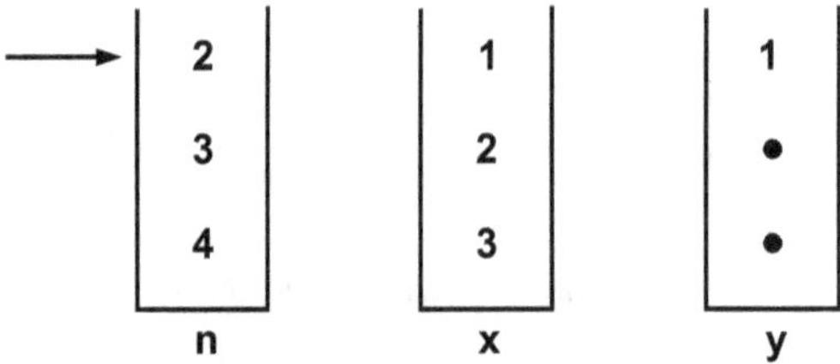

Fig. 1.13 (e) : Recursion stack n = 2

- The return statement return (n * y) is executed which will return the value 2 to fact (3). It will be assigned to y and free the locations allocated to n, x and y.

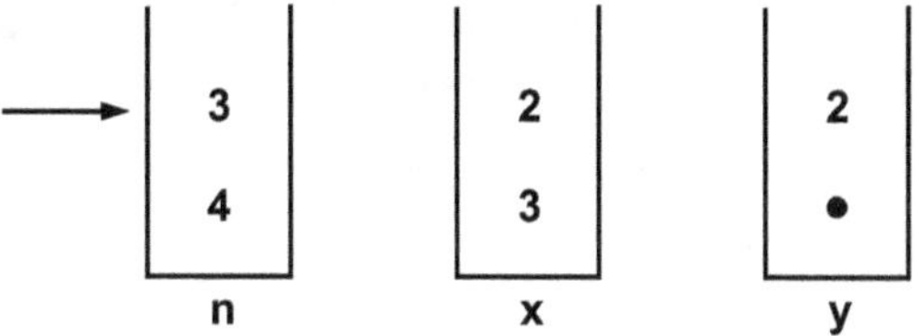

Fig. 1.13 (f) : Recursion stack n = 3

- The return statement in fact (3) will return 3 x 2 = 6 to fact (4) and free the location n, x, and y.

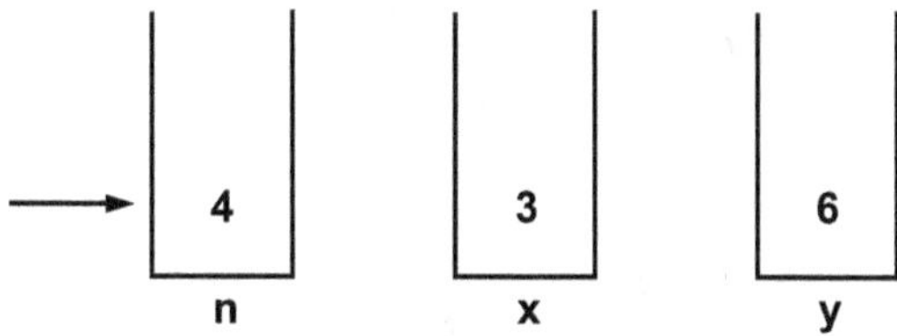

Fig. 1.13 (g) : Recursion stack n = 4

- Finally fact (4) will return 6 x 4 = 24 to the main function and free n, x and y.

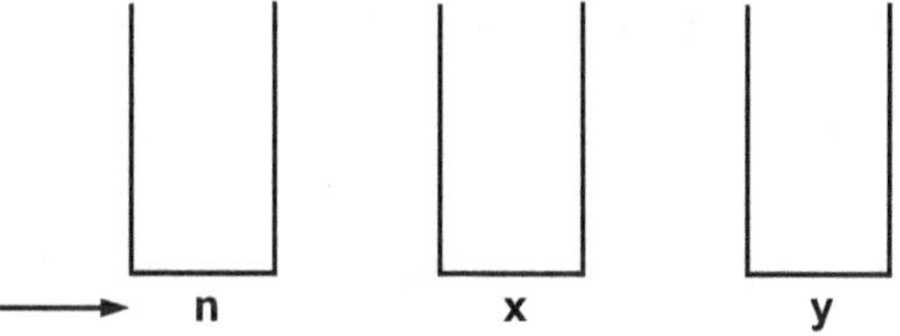

Fig. 1.13 (h) : Recursion stack empty

1.7.1 Removal of Recursion

A recursive function uses internal stack. It can be converted into non-recursive function using stack. Whenever a function is called; its local variables, actual parameters and return address are stored in memory and retrieved back whenever the control returns.

Hence, if we want to remove recursion, we can use a stack which can store the local variables, actual parameters and return address.

Let us consider the example of recursive function to find n!. The function can be converted into non-recursive using stack as follows. It is assumed that the stack is existing.

```
int fact(int n)
{    int p;
     if(n == 0 || n == 1)
         return (1);
```

```
    else
    {
        do
        {
            push(n);
            n=n-1;
        } while (n!=0)
        p = pop( );
        while (!stack_empty)
        p = p*pop( );
        return (p);
    }
}
```

In the above function, we have used stack to hold the value of n, i.e., actual parameter. Hence, the steps for removal of recursion are as follows :

- Implement a stack to store suitable values like local variables, parameters, return address, etc.
- Whenever there is a call, push all local variables, parameters, return address on stack.
- Execute the function call after assigning actual parameters to formal parameters.
- After the function call is over, retrieve the return address from stack and go back to that location.
- Retrieve (pop) the local variables and actual parameters and continue.
- Above steps will be repeated for every call that we make in case of recursion.

SUMMARY

- Stack is a linear data structure where all additions and deletions are made only at one end called top.
- The operations performed on stacks are :

  (i) Push, (ii) Pop, (iii) Stack-empty, (iv) Stack full.
- Stack can be implemented using array or linked list.
- Stack can be used for expression conversion and evaluation, handling recursion, reversing a string, language processing applications, etc.
- An expression can be written in infix, postfix and prefix format.

- Postfix and prefix expressions are easier to evaluate than infix since priority of operators need not be considered.

SOLVED PROBLEMS

1. Write a program to reverse string using stack.

Solution :

```c
#define MAX 80
int top=-1;
char stk[MAX];
void main( )
{
    char s [MAX];   // String variable
    int i;
    printf("Enter a string \n");
    gets(s);                 // Accept a string
    i=0;
    while(s[i] !='\0')         // while it is not end of string
    {
        push(s[i]);            // Push character on stack
        i++;
    }
    i=0;
    while(top!=-1)            // while stack is not empty
    {
        s[i]=pop( );            // Pop a character from stack
        i++;
    }
    printf("Reversed string is %s", s);
}
void push (char x)
{
```

```
        if(top!=MAX-1)
        {
                top ++;
                stk [top] = x;
        }
}
char pop( )
{
    char = x;
    if(top!=-1)
    {
            x = stk [top];
            top --;
    }
}
```

2. Write necessary 'C' functions to implement stack of characters using array.

Solution :

```
    #define MAX 10
    char s[MAX];
    int top=-1;
    void push (char x)
    {
        if(top == MAX-1)
            printf("Stack full");
        else
        {
            top ++;
            s[top] = x;
        }
    }
```

```
char pop( )
{
    char x;
    if(top == -1)
        printf("Stack full");
    else
    {
        x = s[top];
        top --;
    }
    return (x);
}
```

3. Modify program 1.6 to incorporate bracketed expression for example (a*(b+c)).

Hint : Assign lowest priority (say 0) to opening bracket '('. Whenever there is opening bracket push it on the stack. Whenever there is closing bracket pop all the operators and copy them in output, till you get an opening bracket in the stack. The procedure for expression (a + (b * c / d) − e) is as follows :

Incoming Character	Action	Postfix	Stack
(	Push		(
a	Copy to output	a	
+	Priority more than (, push)		(+
(	Push		(+(
b	Copy to output	ab	
*	Priority more than (, push	ab	(+(*
c	Copy to output	abc	
/	Priority equal to *, pop*, copy to output, push/		
d	Copy to output	abc*d	
)	Pop /, copy to output, Pop (	abc*d/	(+
−	Priority equal to +, pop +, copy to output push -	abc*d/+	(−
e	Copy to output	abc*d/+e	
)	Pop-, Copy to output	abc*d\+e−	
End of expression		abc*d\+e−	

4. Evaluate the following postfix expression using stack.

623 +− 382/+*2$3+

Incoming Character	Action	Stack
6	Push	6
2	Push	6, 2
3	Push	6, 2, 3
+	Pop 3, 2 Push 2 + 3 = 5	6, 5
−	Pop 5, 6 Push 6 − 5 = 1	1
3	Push	1, 3
8	Push	1, 3, 8
2	Push	1, 3, 8, 2
/	Pop 2, 8 Push 8/2 = 4	1, 3, 4
+	Pop 4, 3 Push 3 + 4 = 7	1, 7
*	Pop 7, 1 Push 1 * 7 = 7	7

| 2 | Push | 7, 2 |

| $ | Pop 2, 7 | |
| | Push 7^2 = 49 | 49 |

| 3 | Push | 49, 3 |

| + | Pop 3, 49 | |
| | Push 49 + 3 = 52 | 52 |

$\therefore$ result = 52

5. Convert following expression into prefix and infix.

(a + b * c) / (x + y / z)

Solution :

$$\begin{aligned}
\text{Postfix} &= (a + b * c)\ (x + y/z)\ / \\
&= (a + (bc\ *))\ (x + (yz/))/ \\
&= abc*+xyz/+/ \\
\text{Infix} &= /\ (a + b * c)\ (x + y/z) \\
&= /\ (a + (*\ bc)\ (x + (/\ yz)) \\
&= /\ + a * bc + x / yz
\end{aligned}$$

6. What is stack? Explain how stack is used to check validity of parenthesis with suitable example.

Solution : (Refer Section 1.1 for definition of stack)

Validity of parenthesis using stack :

- Stack can be used to check validity of parenthesis.

- For example, if you are given an expression ((a + (b + c / d)) − e), we can scan the expression from left to right.

- We can create a stack of characters and when we came across a (opening parenthesis) we push it on stack and whenever we get (closing parenthesis)) an opening parenthesis will be popped.

- At the end of the expression, if the stack is empty it means we have equal number of opening and closing parenthesis, otherwise the expression is invalid.

The algorithm for the same is given as follows :

1. Input exp
2. i=0;
3. while (exp[i]!='\0')
    {   if(exp[i] == '(')
            push('(')
        if(exp[i] == (')')
            pop( );
    }
4. if(stack_empty( ))
        printf ("Valid expression");
    else
        printf ("Invalid expression");

7. Consider infix expression.

a + (c / d) * (e * f)

Convert it into postfix and prefix. Evaluate postfix expression for a = 2, c = 4, d = 2, e = 3, f = 5.

Solution :

Given : a + (c / d) * (e * f)

$$expr = (a+ ((c/d) \quad * \quad (e * f)))$$
$$\downarrow \quad \downarrow$$
$$= a \quad cd\backslash \quad ef ** +$$

Hence, postfix is acd \ef ** +

$$expr = (a + ((c/d) * (e * f)))$$
$$= +a * / cd * ef$$

Prefix is a * / cd * ef

Evaluation : acd \ ef ** +

Incoming Character	Action	Stack
a	Push a = 2	2
c	Push c = 4	2, 4

d	Push d = 2	2, 4, 2
/	Pop 2, 4	
	Push 4/2 = 2	2, 2
e	Push e = 3	2, 2, 3
f	Push f = 5	2, 2, 3, 5
*	Pop 5, 3	
	Push 3 * 5 = 15	2, 2, 15
*	Pop 15, 2	2, 2, 15
	Push 15 * 2 = 30	2, 30
+	Pop 30, 2	
	Push 2 + 30 = 32	32

$\therefore$ result = 32

8. Convert the following expression in other two forms where $ stands for unary minus.

(i) **ab + cd – ***　　　　　　　　　　　(ii) **$a + (b – c) ↑ d**

(iii) **/– * abc + ef**　　　　　　　　　　(iv) **$a + p ↑ q ↑ r**

Solution :

(i) ab + cd – *

The expression is postfix.

$$exp \rightarrow ((ab +) (cd -) *)$$
$$\rightarrow (((a + b) * (c - d)) \qquad \text{Infix}$$
$$\rightarrow * + ab - cd \qquad \text{Prefix}$$

(ii) $a + (b – c) ↑ d

The expression is infix.

$$exp \rightarrow \$a + (b - c) \uparrow d$$
$$\rightarrow (\$a) + ((b - c) \uparrow d)$$
$$\rightarrow + \$a \uparrow - bc\ d \qquad\qquad \text{Prefix}$$
$$\rightarrow a\$\ bc - d \uparrow + \qquad\qquad \text{Postfix}$$

(iii) /– * abc + ef

The expression is prefix.

$$exp \rightarrow (/ (- (* a\ b)\ c) + (ef))$$
$$\rightarrow ((a * b) - c) / (e + f) \qquad\qquad \text{Infix}$$
$$\rightarrow ab * c - ef +/ \qquad\qquad \text{Postfix}$$

(iv) $a + p \uparrow q \uparrow r

The expression is infix.

$$exp \rightarrow \$a + p \uparrow q \uparrow r$$
$$\rightarrow (\$a) + ((p \uparrow q) \uparrow r)$$
$$\rightarrow a\$\ pq \uparrow r \uparrow + \qquad\qquad \text{Postfix}$$
$$\rightarrow + \$a \uparrow\uparrow pqr \qquad\qquad \text{Prefix}$$

9. **Explain the necessity of representing expression in prefix and postfix. Evaluate the following expression. Show stepwise stack contents.**

$$\textbf{ABC * DEF ^ \backslash G * – H +}$$

A= 6, B = 1 C = 4, D = 16, E = 2, F = 3, G = 2, H = 5.

Solution :

Incoming Character	Action	Stack
A	Push A = 6	6
B	Push B = 1	6, 1
C	Push C = 4	6, 1, 4
*	Pop 4, 1 Push 4	6, 4

D	Push D = 16	6, 4, 16
E	Push E = 2	6, 4, 16, 2
F	Push F = 3	6, 4, 16, 2, 3
^	Pop 3, 2 Push 2 ^ 3 = 8	6, 4, 16, 8
/	Pop 8, 16 Push 16/8 = 2	6, 4, 2
G	Push 4 = 2	6, 4, 2, 2
*	Pop 2, 2 Push 2 * 2 = 4	6, 4, 4
−	Pop 4, 4 Push 4 − 4 = 0	6, 0
H	Push 5	6, 0, 5
*	Pop 5, 0 Push 5 * 0 = 0	6, 0
+	Pop 0, 6 Push 6 + 0 = 6	6

Result = 6

10. Convert the following expression into postfix. Show all steps.

Solution :

a + b * c / d – e

Incoming Character	Action	Stack	Output
a	Print		a
+	Push	+	
b	Print	+	ab
*	Push	+ *	a
c	Print	+ *	abc
/	Pop Push /	+ /	abc*
d	Print	+ /	abc*d
–	Pop / Pop + Push	–	abc*d/+
e	Print		abc*d/+e
\0	Pop –		abc*d/+e–

Postfix is abc*d/+e–

11. Explain the application of stack to check the validity of parentheses in the expression. Also, write the pseudo code for the same.

Solution :

- We can use stack to check validity of parentheses.

- The opening parentheses can be pushed into stack and as soon as a closing parenthesis comes, one parenthesis is popped. In the end, if the stack is empty there will be equal number of opening and closing parentheses.

- Pseudo-code will be as below :

```
1.  Read expr

2.  i=0;

3.  while expr[i] != '\0'
    {
        if(expr [i] == '(')
            push('(');
        if(expr [i] == ')')
            pop( );
    }
4.  if(stack_empty( ))
      print "Valid";
    else
        print "Invalid";
```

EXERCISE

1. Write 'push' and 'pop' functions in C to implement stack in an array.   **(4m)**

    Solution : (Refer Program 1.1)

2. Explain the stack with the help of suitable example. Also, write the pseudo-code for the operations performed in stack.   **(8m)**

    Solution : (Refer Sections 1.1 and 1.2)

3. Write necessary 'C' functions to implement stack using array.

    Solution : (Refer Section 1.2)

4. Write functions in 'C' for push, pop is empty for stack using linked list. Give declaration in 'C' for implementing above functions for stack.   **(8m)**

    Solution : (Refer Section 1.2)

5. Write a program to perform following operations :

   (i)   Push 10 and 20 on first stack.

   (ii) Push 100 and 200 on second stack.

   (iii) Pop all elements from both stacks one by one and display.

   Solution : (Refer Section 1.2 and Program 1.2)

6. Write an ADT for stack. .   **(6m)**

   Solution : (Refer Section 1.2.1)

7. What do you mean by ADT? Write an ADT for stack.   **(8m)**

   Solution : (Refer Section 1.2.1)

8. Define ADT. Write down ADT of stack.

   Solution : (Refer Section 1.2.1)

9. Write necessary 'C' functions to implement stack using linked list.

   Solution : (Refer Section 1.3)

10. Write all the necessary functions to represent stack using linked list. Write a C function using stack to determine whether the given string is palindrome or not.   **(8m)**

    Solution : (Refer Section 1.3)

11. Give a 'C' declaration to define a node structure for a stack using linked list.   **(2m)**

    Solution : (Refer Section 1.3)

12. Write function in 'C' to 'push' and 'pop' an item from a stack using linked list.   **(6m)**

    Solution : (Refer Section 1.3)

13. Explain how stack is implemented using linked list.

    Solution : (Refer Section 1.3)

14. Write a 'C' function for push, pop, is stack empty using linked list.

    Solution : (Refer Section 1.3)

15. Explain the necessity of representing expression in prefix and postfix notation. For the given postfix expressions, evaluate it for the values given. Show stepwise stack contents.   **(8m)**

    $$A\ B\ C * D\ E\ F \wedge / G * - H +$$

    A = 6 B = 1, C = 4, D = 16, E = 2, F = 3, G = 2, H = 5

    where $\wedge$ = exponential operator

    Solution : (Refer Section 1.5 and Solved Problem 9)

16. Write pseudo C algorithm for postfix evaluation.   **(4m)**

    Solution : (Refer Section 1.5.1)

17. Give an algorithm for evaluation of a postfix expression.   **(8m)**

    Solution : (Refer Section 1.5.1)

18. Write a function in 'C' to evaluate postfix expression and explain with suitable example.

    (8m)

    Solution : (Refer Section 1.5.1 and Program 1.5)

19. Write pseudo C algorithm for infix to postfix conversion.   **(8m)**

    Solution : (Refer Section 1.5.2)

20. Write an algorithm to convert infix expression to postfix. Convert the following infix
    expression to postfix using stack.   **(8m)**

    A / B $ C + D * E − A * C where $ is an exponentiation. Show stepwise conversion.

    Solution : (Refer Section 1.5.2 and similar to Example 2, 3)

21. Write pseudo-C algorithm to convert infix expression to postfix using stack.   **(10m)**

    Section : (Refer Section 1.5.2)

22. Write an algorithm to convert infix expression to postfix.

    Solution : (Refer Section 1.5.2)

23. Give the postfix and prefix forms of the infix expression given below. Also write an
    algorithm or pseudo 'C' code to evaluate a postfix expression.   **(8m)**

    infix expression − (a + b * c) / (x + y/z).

    Solution : (Refer Solved Problem 5)

24. Convert the following expressions into other two forms :   **(8m)**

    (i)   ((A − (B + C)) * D) $ (E + F) where $ = exponentiation

    (ii) /m n $ q p $ y $ / − r s * +

    Solution : (Similar to Solved Problem 8)

25. Convert following infix expression into postfix using stack. Show all steps.   **(6m)**

    A/B**C+D*E−A*C where ** is exponentiation.

    Solution : (Similar to solved problem 10)

DRILL PROBLEMS

1. Write a function using stack to determine whether the given string is palindrome or not.

2. Modify Program 1.5 to include variables in postfix expression instead of digits, i.e. input will be of the form abc*+ or 4a*c+.

   Hint : When the operand is pushed on the suck and if it is alphabet accept its value from user and push the value on the stack.

CHAPTER 2
QUEUES

2.1 INTRODUCTION

Queue is a linear data structure in which the first element inserted is taken out first. Thus, Queue is a first in first out (FIFO) type of a list where all insertions are made at one end called rear end and all deletions are made at the other end called front end. It is just like queue for railway reservation or buses. The first person in the queue will be first to go out.

Queue can be implemented using :

1. Arrays
2. Linked lists

Following four operations can be done on a queue :

- **Insert Operation :** In this, an element is stored at a location indicated by rear.
- **Delete Operation :** In this operation, the element at the front is removed.
- **Queue Full :** When all the locations reserved for queue are occupied, we can't insert any more elements. This condition is queue_full condition.
- **Queue Empty :** When there is no element stored in a queue, we can't delete any more elements. This condition is called as queue_empty.

2.2 QUEUE USING ARRAY

To represent a queue using array we require an array of some size to be declared say int a[4]. This will create a space for storing elements of queue. The size of the queue is 4. We will require two more variables say front and rear which will be indices to the front and rear element of the queue. Initially, the queue is empty. The variables front and rear will be initialized to −1.

Insert Operation :

Now if we want to store a number 10 on the queue, we can increment rear and the element 10 will be stored at location a[0].

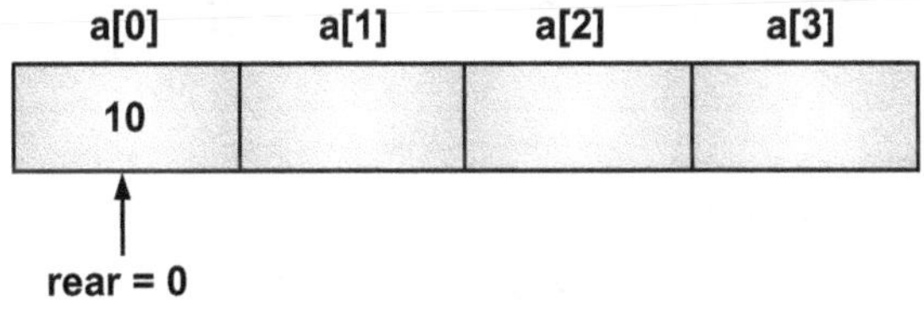

Fig. 2.1 (a) : Insertq (10)

Next we store a number 20 on the queue, rear will be incremented to 1 and element 20 will be stored at location a[1].

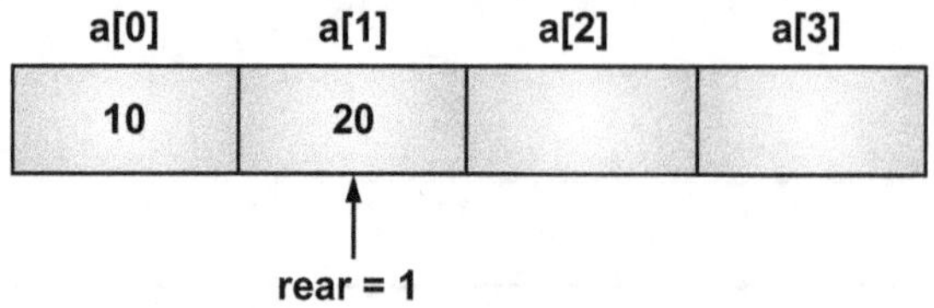

Fig. 2.1 (b) : Insertq (20)

Next we store a number 30 on the queue, rear will be incremented to 2 and element 30 will be stored at location a[2].

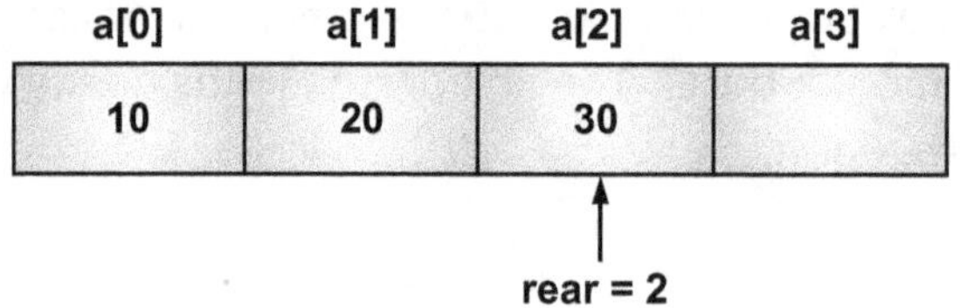

Fig. 2.1 (c) : Insertq (30)

Next we store a number 40 on the queue, rear will be incremented to 3 and element 40 will be stored at location a[3].

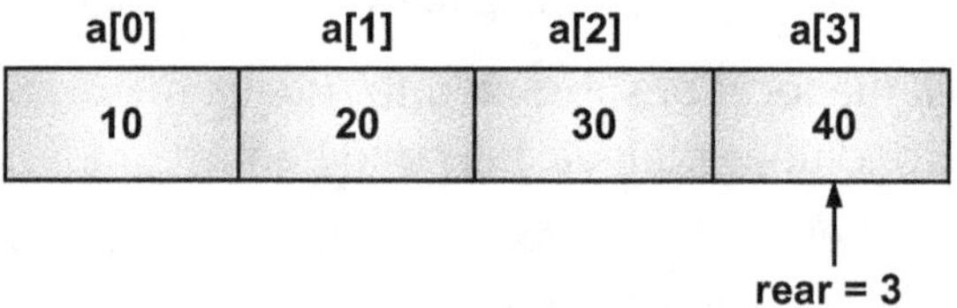

Fig. 2.1 (d) : Insertq (40)

Now there is no space left on the queue hence, the queue is full. The condition for queue_full is rear becomes equal to maximum size of array −1.

Delete Operation :

Now suppose we want to remove an element from the queue. We can access element at the front which is given by the index value in front. Consider the queue where we have already inserted four elements. If we want to carry out delete operation, front is incremented to 0 and element at the front 10 will be accessed.

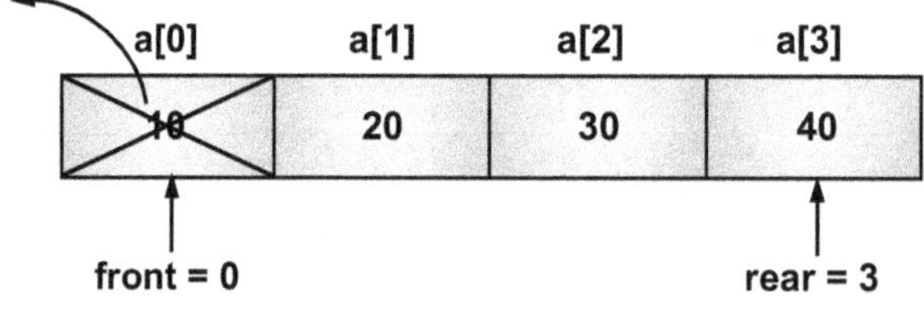

Fig. 2.2 (a) : x = delq( )

The next delete operation will increment front to 1 and remove 20 from the queue.

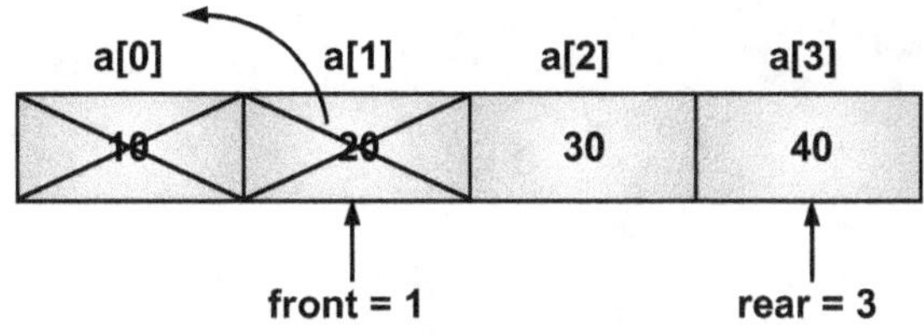

Fig. 2.2 (b) : x = delq

Another delete operation will increment front to 2 and remove 30 from the queue.

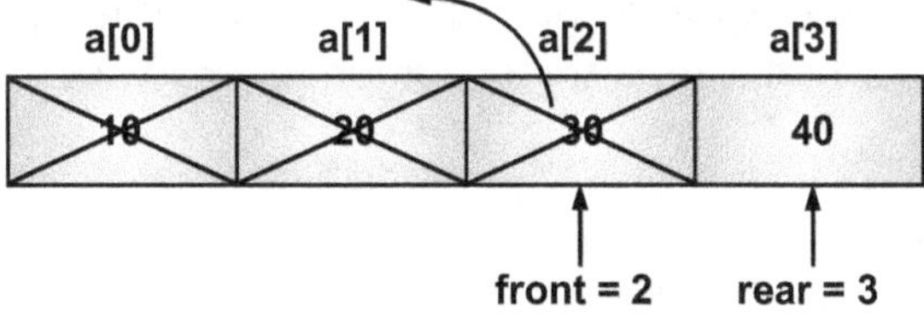

Fig. 2.2 (c) : x = delq ( )

If the operation is carried out again, element 40 will be removed and front becomes 3 equal to rear.

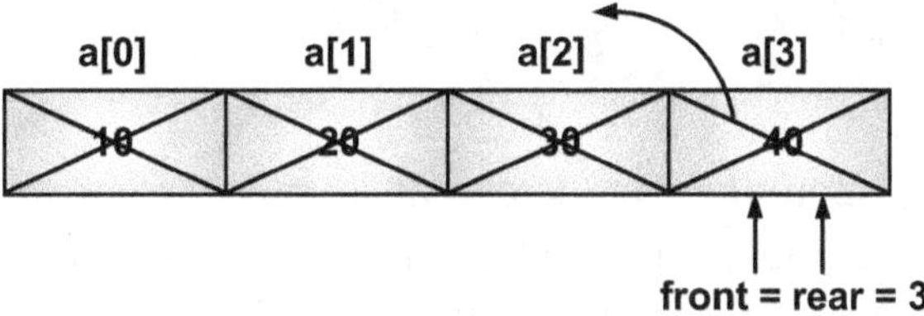

Fig. 2.2 (d) : x = delq( )

Then we can't remove any more elements because queue is empty. The condition for queue_empty is front == rear.

The disadvantage of linear queue is when rear reaches the value MAX-1, queue full condition occurs. Now if we remove some elements from front end of the queue, we will not be able to store or insert element in these locations as rear remains MAX-1.

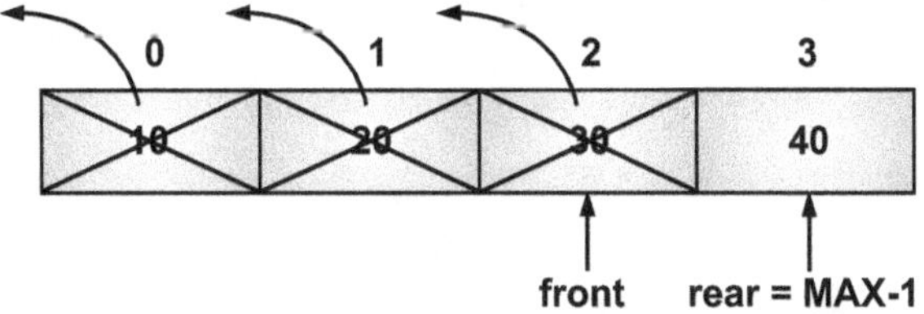

Fig. 2.3 : Problem with insert operation even if queue is not full

The program for implementation of queue will require the two functions insertq and delq whose algorithms are as follows :

1. Insertq (x)

1. If rear == MAX −1

```
            print "queue full"
2.   else

            rear ++;

            a [rear] = x;

3.   stop.
```

Every time we do insertq operation, we need to increment rear and store the data at the location given by rear in the array a. But before we do this operation, we must check whether the queue is full or not. Hence, the condition rear==MAX-1.

2. x = delq( )

```
1.   If front == rear

            return –9999

2.   else

            front++;

            x = a [front];

            return x;
```

Every time we do a delq operation, we increment front and remove an element. But before we do this operation, we must check whether the queue is empty or not. Hence the condition front == rear. Note that we are returning –9999 when queue is empty. This is an indication for the calling function so that it takes appropriate action when the queue is empty. The complete program for queue implementation is as follows :

Program 2.1 : To implement queue using array.

```c
#define MAX 4

int a[MAX];

int front = -1, rear = -1;

void insertq(int);

int delq( );

void main( )

{

    int ch;

    do

    {

        clrscr( );
```

```c
                printf ("1. Insert \n 2. Delete \n 3. Exit \n");
                printf ("Enter your choice");
                scanf ("%d", &ch);
                switch (ch)
                {
                    case 1 :  printf ("Enter data \n");
                              scanf ("%d", &x);
                              insertq (x);
                              break;
                    case 2 : x = delq( );
                             if (x!=-9999)
                                 printf ("%d \n", x);
                             break;
                }
            getch( );
        } while (ch!=3);
}
void insertq (int x)
{
    if (front == MAX -1)
        front = rear = (-1);
    if (rear == MAX -1)
        printf ("Queue full");
    else
    {
        rear ++;
        a[rear] = x;
    }
}
int delq( )
```

```
{
    int x;
    if (front ==rear)
    {
        printf ("Q is empty");
        return (-9999);
    }
    else
    {
        front ++;
        x=a[front];
        return (x);
    }
}
```

We can implement separate functions for queue_full and queue_empty conditions as :

```
int q_full( )
{
    if (rear==MAX -1)
    {
        printf("Queue full");
        return (1);
    }
    else
        return (0);
}
```

The function returns1, when queue is full; otherwise 0.

```
int q_empty( )
{
    if (front == rear)
    {
```

```
        printf("Queue is empty");
        return (1);
    }
    else
        return (0);
}
```

The function returns 1, when queue is empty, otherwise 0.

These functions can be used in functions 'insertq' and 'delq' as :

```
void insertq (int x)
{
    if (front == MAX -1)
    front = rear = -1
    if(!q-full( ))
    {
        rear ++;
        a[rear] = x;
    }
}
int delq( )
{
    int x;
    if (!q-empty( ))
    {
        front ++;
        x = a[front];
        return (x);
    }
}
```

The queue consists of an array, front and rear. If multiple queues are to be implemented in single program, we need to define separate arrays, font and rear for each queue. Instead, we can define a structure variable for a queue which combines array, front and rear together.

The structure definition for queue is

```
typedef struct queue
{
    int a[MAX];
    int front, rear;
} Q;
```

Now if we declare a variable Q q1; it consists of an array, front and rear as :

q1

a[0]	a[1]	a[2]	a[3]	front
				rear

Fig. 2.4 : Queue using structure

The elements in the queue can be accessed using dot operator, For Example, if front of the queue is to be initialized we can write q1. front = −1 or if 10 is to be stored at the rear end of the queue we can write q1.a [q1.rear] = 10. But the major advantage of this struct type queue will be, when more than one queue is to be implemented. The insertq and delq functions require the queue variable to be passed to them. Since, these functions are going to modify the contents of the queue variable; we must pass it by address. Hence, the function parameter will be pointer to a structure.

The insertq function will have prototype as,

```
void insertq (Q*, int)
```

The first argument is pointer to the queue in which we are going to store the element and second argument is the integer number to be stored on the queue.

The delq function will have prototype as,

```
int delq (Q *)
```

The argument is pointer to the queue from which number returned will be popped. A complete program using this is given as follows :

Program 2.2 : Implementation of queue using structure

```
#define MAX 5
typedef struct queue
```

```c
{
    int a[MAX];
    int front, queue;
} Q;
void insertq (Q*, int);
int delq (Q*)
main( )
{
    Q q1, q2;
    q1.front = q1.rear = q2.front = q2.rear=(-1);
    insertq(&q1, 10);
    insertq(&q1, 20);
    insertq(&q2, 100);
    insertq(&q2, 200);
    x = delq(&q1);
    printf("%d \n", x);
    x = delq(&q1);
    printf ("%d \n", x);
    x = delq (&q2);
    printf ("%d \n", x);
    x = delq (&q2);
    printf ("%d \n", x);
}
void insertq (Q *q, int x)
{
    if (q->front == MAX-1)
        q->front = q->rear=-1;
    if (q->rear == MAX-1)
        printf("Queue is full");
    else
```

```c
    {
        (q->rear) ++;
        q->a[q->rear]=x;
    }
}
int delq (Q *q)
{
    int x;
    if (q->front == q->rear)
    {
        printf("Queue empty");
        return (-9999);
    }
    else
    {
        (q->front) ++;
        x = q->a [q->front];
        return (x);
    }
}
```

2.3 QUEUE USING LINKED LIST

The array implementation of queue is not efficient from the view point of memory utilization. The fixed size of array is required and it remains allocated for the entire duration of the program. Linked list implementation will have advantage over the array implementation because we can allocate memory as and when it is required and memory can be deallocated (free) when not in use.

The queue using linked list consist of nodes having data and address of next node.

The node definition will be

```c
    typedef struct node
    {
        int data;
```

```
    struct node *next;

} NODE;
```

Two pointers called front and rear can be declared (NODE *front, *rear) which will point to the front and rear end of the queue. The operations insert and delete will be implemented as follows :

Steps for Insert Operation :

1. Create a node and store data in the node.

2. Link rear node to new node, if it is not first node.

3. Point rear to the recently created node.

    Following figures show this operation.

    Initially, front = rear = NULL

1. Insertq (10)

Fig. 2.5 (a) : Insertq (10) in queue using linked list

2. Insertq (20)

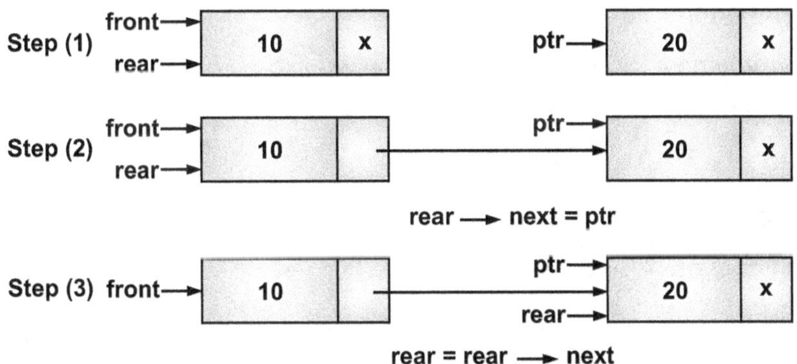

Fig. 2.5 (b) : Insertq (20) in queue using linked list

Steps for Delete Operation :

1. Make a pointer temp point to the front end of the queue.

2. If it is NULL, then queue is empty.

3. If not, remove the data from this node and advance front.

4. De-allocate memory pointed by temp.

Following figures show this operation.

1. x = delq

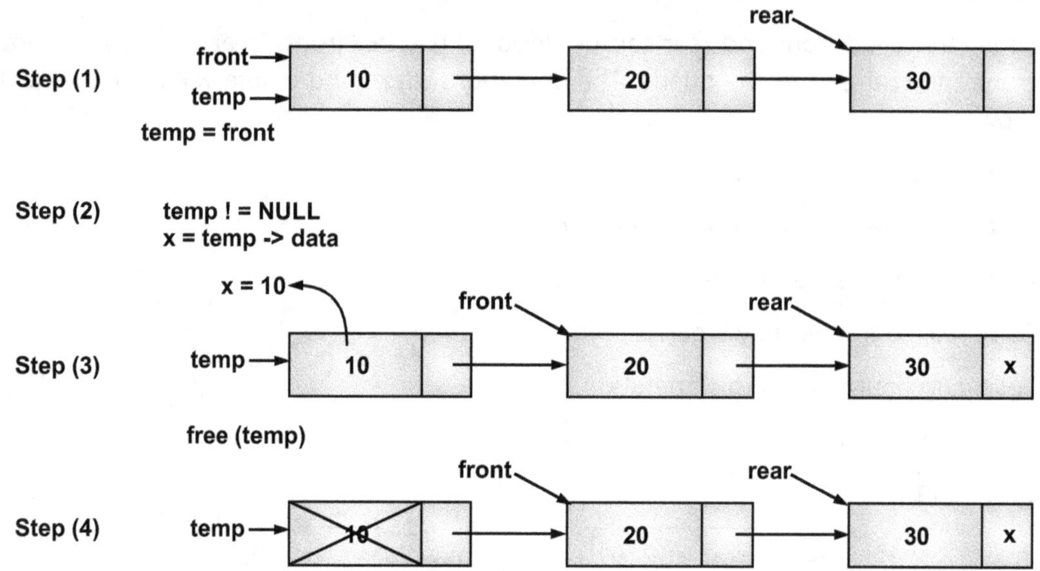

Fig. 2.6 : Delete operation in queue using linked list

Following program, implements queue using linked list. It has the function push and pop which have the same prototype as that used in case of array. The function push accepts data, creates a node and puts it into linked list. The function pop removes an element from the linked list and returns it.

Program 2.3 : Implementation of queue using linked list.

```
typedef struct node
{
    int data;
    struct node*next;
} NODE;
NODE*front=NULL, rear=NULL;
void insertq (int x)
{
    NODE*ptr;
    ptr = (NODE*)malloc(sizeof(NODE));
    if (ptr == NULL)
        printf("Insufficient memory");
```

```c
        else
        {
            ptr->data = x;,
            ptr->next = NULL;
            if (rear == NULL)
                front = rear = ptr;
            else
            {
                rear->next = ptr;
                rear ptr;
            }
        }
}
int delq
{
    NODE = temp, int x;
    temp = front;
    if (temp == NULL)
    {
        printf("Queue empty");
        return(-9999);
    }
    else
    {
        x = temp->data;
        front = front->next;
        free (temp);
        return (x);
    }
}
```

To implement queue using linked list you can use two pointers, front and rear. Front will point to first node and rear to the last node. Whenever insert operation is done, a new node is created, it is attached to the last node in the list and the pointer rear points to this new node. Whenever delete operation is done, an element from front end is accessed, front is advanced to next node and the node is deleted.

2.3.1 Queue as an Abstract Data Type (ADT)

//Queue data definition

```
typedef struct queue
{
    <datatype> data;
    struct queue*front, *rear;
}Q;
```

//Operation definition

```
initializeq(Q);           // Initialize front and rear
insertq(Q, x);            // Insert into Q
x = delq(Q);             // Remove x from Q
int qempty(Q)            // If Q is empty return 1 else return 0
int qfull(Q)             // If Q is full return 1 else return 0
```

The above data definition can be written as :

```
typedef struct queue
{
    <data type> data [size];
    int front, rear;
} Q;
```

2.4 CIRCULAR QUEUE

The disadvantage of linear queue is that, even if some locations are available for storage, we will not be able to use them when rear becomes MAX −1. Hence, when rear reaches MAX −1, we should be able to come back to location 0 in case it is empty. Hence, rear ++ can be replaced by rear = (rear + 1) % MAX.

Similarly, when front reaches MAX-1 we should be able to come back to location 0 which is done using front = (front + 1) % MAX. This implementation is called circular queue. In order to handle queue full and queue empty conditions, one more variable called counter will be required. The counter c is incremented whenever insert operation is performed and decremented when delete operation is performed. The program for circular queue is as follows :

Program 2.4 : To implement circular queue.

```c
#define MAX 5
int a[MAX];
int front = 0, rear -1, c = 0;
void insertq (int);
int delq( );
void main( )
{
    int ch;
    do
    {
        clrscr( );
        printf ("1. Insert \n 2. Delete \n 3. Exit \n");
        printf ("Enter your choice");
        scanf("%d", &ch);
        switch (ch)
        {
            case 1 :printf ("Enter data \n");
                    scanf ("% d". &x);
                    insertq (x);
                    break;
            case 2 : x = delq( );
                    if (x!=-9999)
                        printf ("%d \n", x);
                    break;
        }
        getch( );
    }while (ch!=3);
}
```

```
    void insertq (int x)
    {
        if (c==MAX)
            printf("Q is full");
        else
        {
            rear = (rear + 1) % MAX;
            q[rear] = x;
            c++;
        }
    }
    int delq( )
    {
        int x;
        if (c == 0)
        {
            printf("Q is empty");
            return(-9999);
        }
        else
        {
            x = q[front];
            front = (front + 1) % MAX;
            c --;
            return (x);
        }
    }
```

Explanation :

- Let us assume queue size 5. Initially when queue is empty.

    front = 0   rear = -1   c = 0

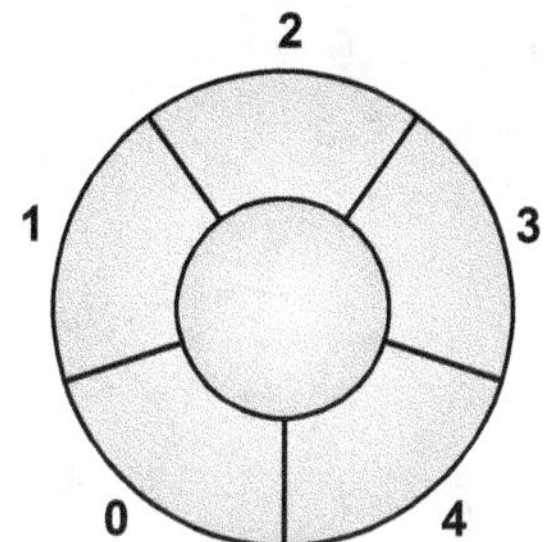

Fig. 2.7 (a) : Circular queue

- Insert(10) operation
  front 0
  rear = 0   c = 1

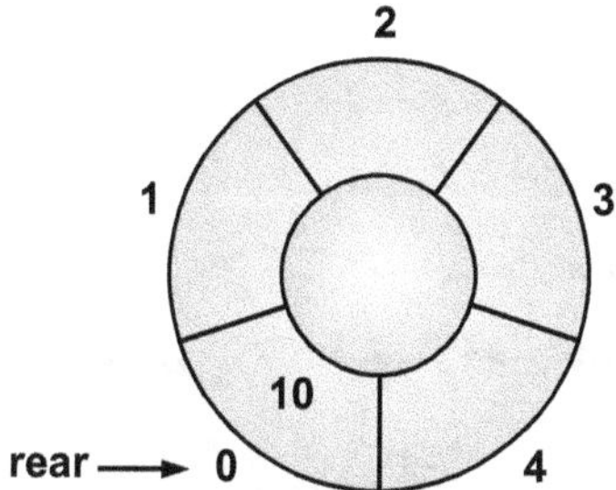

Fig. 2.7 (b) : Insert (10)

- Insert(20) operation
  front = 0   rear = 1   c = 2

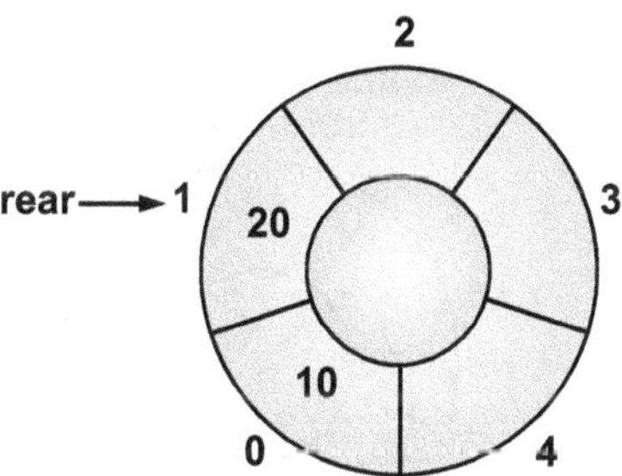

Fig. 2.7 (c) : Insert (20)

- Like this if we insert 30, 40, 50
  front = 0   rear = 4   c = 5
  The queue is full i.e., c=MAX=5

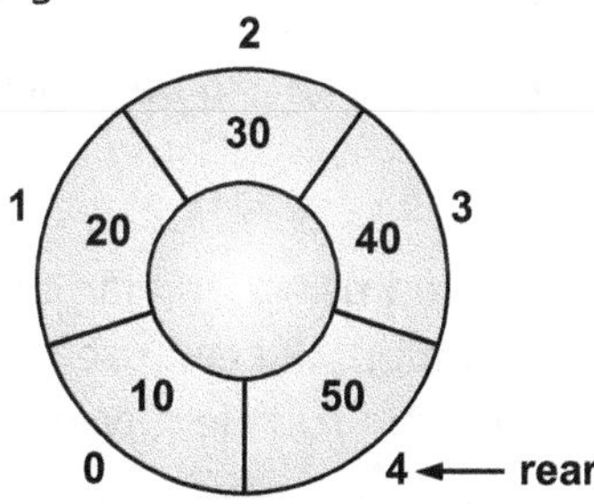

Fig. 2.7 (d) : Insert (30), Insert (40), Insert (50)

- Now if delete operation is performed, 10 will be removed,
  Before delete, front = 0   rear = 4   c = 5
  After delete,   front = 1   rear = 4   c = 4

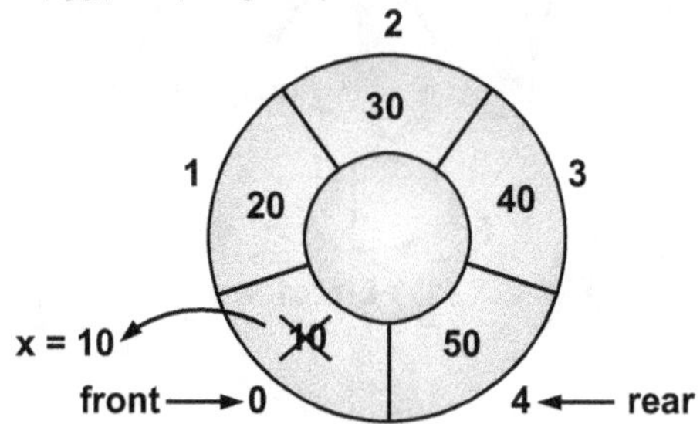

Fig. 2.7 (e) : Delete operation in circular queue

- One more delete operation will remove 20
  Before delete; front = 1   rear = 4   c = 4
  After delete,   front = 2   rear = 4   c = 3

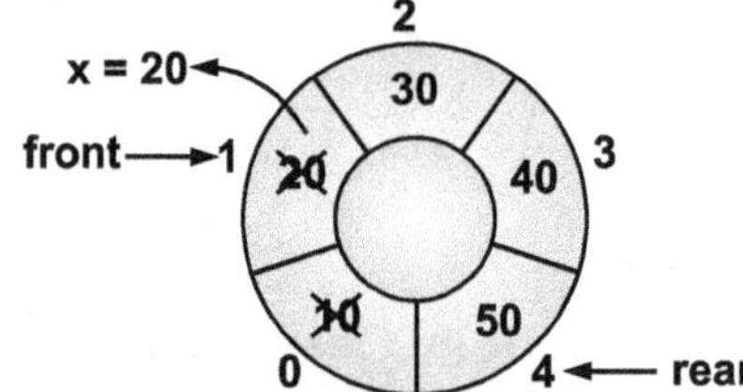

Fig. 2.7 (f) : Delete operation in circular queue

Now, if we want to insert say 60,

rear = (rear + 1)% MAX.= (4 + 1)% 5 = 0 and we can store/insert the element at location 0.

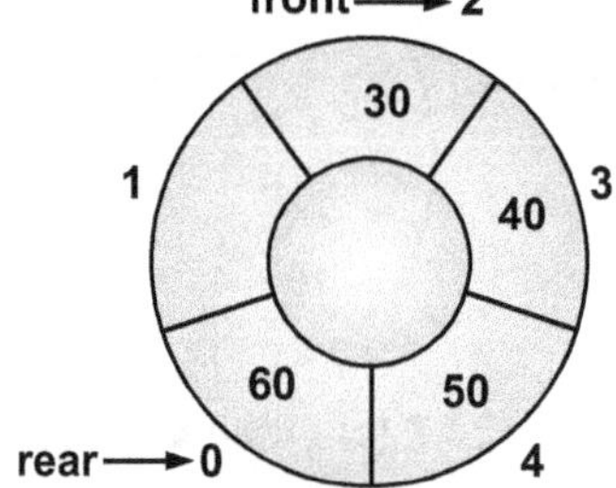

Fig. 2.7 (g) : Insert operation

Thus, we can insert the element in the queue at location 0 even if rear has reached value MAX−1.

Note : If we don't use counter, the implementation becomes slightly complex, we must keep one location empty in the queue.

Circular Queue using Linked List :

A circular queue can also be implemented using circular linked list. This implementation will be most efficient than array implementation. We can use two pointers front and rear. In fact, a single pointer to last element will also be sufficient. We can access the front element with this pointer as list is circular.

2.5 DOUBLE ENDED QUEUE (DEQUES)

It is a linear list in which data can be inserted or deleted at both ends. It is a double-ended queue.

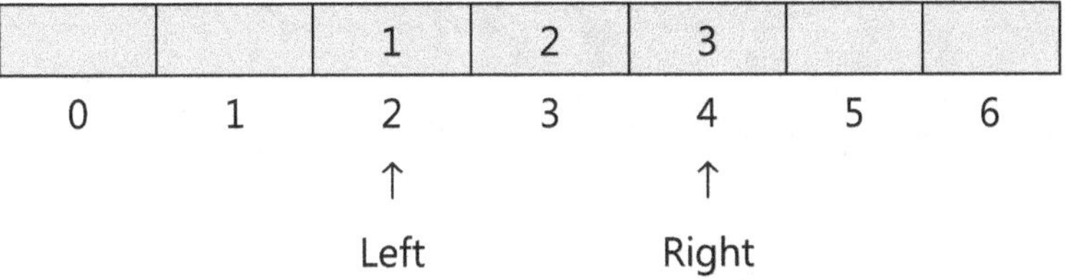

Fig. 2.8 : Double Ended Queue

The dequeue is shown in Fig. 2.8. It consists of two pointers left and right. They point to the two ends of queue. There will be four operations that can be performed on the dequeue. There will be four operations that can be performed on the dequeue.

- Insert left : Insert into left end of queue.
- Insert right : Insert into right end of queue.
- delright : Delete from right end of queue.
- delleft : Delete from left end of queue.

The implementation can also be done using circular queues.

There are two variations of deque.

(i) Input-restricted Dequeue : In this the insert right operation is invalid. Other three right operation is invalid. Other three operations are used.

(ii) Output_restricted Dequeue : In this delright operation is invalid. Other three operations are used.

Priority Queue :

The priority queue is a data structure in which each element is assigned a priority. Based on this priority the insert and delete operation is performed. The rules for insert and delete are :

- An element with higher priority will be removed for processing before the elements with lower priority.
- If two elements have same priority they will be removed from queue for processing in the order in which they were inserted.

The priority queue can be implemented in number of different ways. Some of these are :

- One way list representation of priority queue.
- Array representation of priority queue.
- Ascending order priority queue.
- Descending order priority queue.

One-Way List :

We can maintain a linked list of nodes in memory containing the job to be performed and its priority number as shown below. The higher priority jobs will be stored before the lower priority jobs in the list. The priority number 1 indicates highest priority.

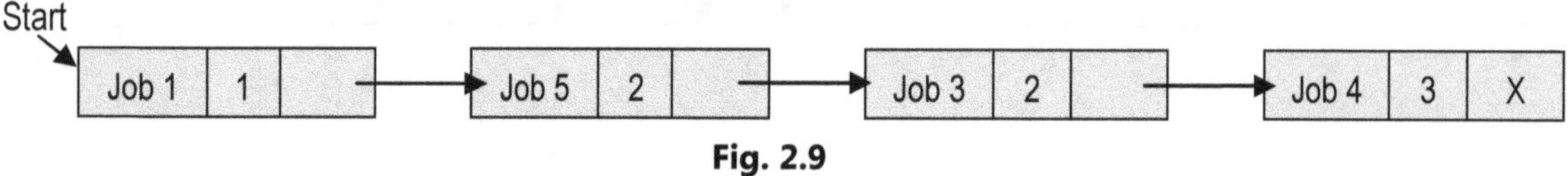

Fig. 2.9

Note that job 5 and job 3 have same priority (Priority No. 2).

The algorithm for delete operation will be

1   temp=start

2   Access into at first node (item=temp→data)

3   Delete the node

4   Process the item (job)

5   temp=temp→next

6   stop

To insert an element into priority queue, we need to find the correct place according to its priority. The algorithm for the same will be as below.

Step 1 : temp=start

Step 2 : p = temp → priority

Step 3 : if priority of current item is less than p

      temp = temp → next

      else break

Step 4 : go to step 3

Step 5 : insert new item before the current node

Step 6 : stop

Array Representation of Priority Queue :

We can use multiple queues having their own front and rear. Each queue will store elements as per their priority i.e. for each level of priority there will be separate queue. Each queue is allocated same amount of space by using a two-dimensional array as shown in Fig. 2.10. below.

The algorithm to delete an element will be as shown below.

Step 1 : i = 1

Step 2 : if q[i] is not empty delete element from q[i] goto to step 2

Step 3 : i=i+1

Step 4 : if i is less than number of queues/rows go to step 2

Step 5 : stop

The algorithm to insert an item into the queue will be as below.

Step 1 : read item

Step 2 : read priority say P

Step 3 : insert item in rear end of q[p]

Step 4 : stop.

2.6 PRIORITY QUEUE

The priority queue is a data structure in which the ordering of elements decides the two operations insert and delete. The elements from the priority queue are removed as per their priority. There are two types of priority queues :

1. Ascending order Priority Queue,

2. Descending order Priority Queue.

1. **Ascending Order Priority Queue :** It is collection of elements into which the elements are stored or inserted in any order but the smallest element can be removed.

2. **Descending Order Priority Queue :** It is collection of elements into which elements are inserted at any order but only larger element can be removed. The other operations on priority queue will be queue empty and queue full. There are several implementations of priority queues.

The priority queue can be implemented in number of ways. One method can be :

*   When insert operation is done, the element is stored in an array in the continuous locations.

*   But when the element is removed, we must search for maximum in case of descending priority queue or minimum in case of ascending priority queue.

*   In place of deleted element an invalid element (say −1) is stored.

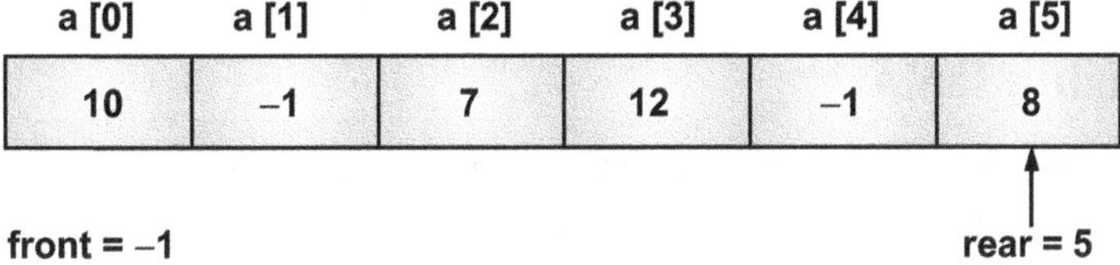

Fig. 2.10 : Priority queue

*   When an element is inserted, we can increment rear but if rear reaches maximum size, we can do compaction i.e. rearrange the array to remove invalid elements as shown in Fig. 2.11.

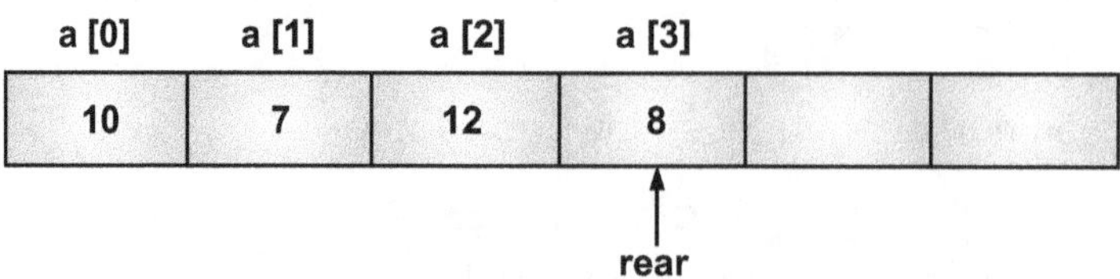

Fig. 2.11 : Priority queue after compaction

Second method can be

- Instead of maintaining the priority queue as an unordered list of elements, we can maintain it as an ordered (sorted) list of elements but then this will require more work while inserting the element in the queue.

- The delete operation will be simple as the minimum or maximum element is available as front end of queue.

The priority queue is used for scheduling of jobs by operating system programs. The priority queue can be used in job scheduling where the execution of job is required to be done based on the priorities. The jobs will be kept in a queue along with their priority numbers. Whenever a new job is to be executed, the job with highest priority will be taken up from the queue.

2.7 APPLICATIONS OF QUEUE

There are several applications of queues in real world. Some of these applications are :

- Railway/Bus/Airplane Reservations.
- Processing of customer requests.
- Processing of online applications.
- In a computer system processing of jobs such as print spool (printing of multiple files/pages).
- In a operating system scheduling of jobs as per their priority in multitasking operating system.
- Categorizing of data can be useful in many problems.
- Queue simulation can be used to study performance of any application involving queue like situation.

2.7.1 Categorizing Data

We need to organize the data into groups. For example, if we have a list records having empno, name and age and we may want to group them as per their age as 21-30, 31-40, 41-50, 51-60 etc. While rearranging these records into groups, the original order is to be maintained.

The following algorithm implements categorizing of data into four groups of 1-10, 11-20, 21-30 and 31-40.

Algorithm 2.1 : The algorithm reads integers between 1-40 and inserts them into four queues.

```
Step 1 :Read n          // Number of data items
Step 2 :    i=1
Step 3 :    while(i<n)
        {
            Read x          // Enter data
            if(x<=10)
                insertq (&q1, x);
            if(x>10 && x<=20);
                insertq(&q2, <=30);
            if(x>21, &&xx<=30);
                insert(&q3, x);
            if(x>31 && x<=40);
                insert(&q4, x);
            j=x+1;
        }
Step 4 : Stop
```

The complete program is given below.

/*Program for Categorizing Data :

Input is a list of integers between 0-39

Output is four groups (queues)*/

```
#include <stdio.h>
#include <conio.h>
#include <stdlib.h>
#define MAX 5
typedef struct queue
{
    int ar   [MAX];
    int front, rear;
}Q;
```

```c
void insertq (Q*, int);
int deleteq (Q*);
void main( )
{
    Q q[4];
    int x, i, n;
    clrscr( );
    for(i=0;i<4;i++)
        q[i].front=q[i].rear=-1;
    printf("How many numbers\n");
    scanf("%d",&n);
    i=0;
    randomize( );
    while(i<n)
    {
        printf("Enter number between 1-40\n");
        scanf("%d",&x);
        x=rand( )%100;
        if (x>=0 && x<40)
        {
            insertq(&q[x/10],x);
            i++;
        }
        else
            printf("Invalid number\n");
    }
    printf("\nThe categorised data is\n");
    i=0;
    while(i<4)
    {
```

```c
            printf("\nData between %d to %d is \n", 10*i, 10*i+9);
            while (1)
            {
                x=deleteq(&q[i]);
                if(x!=-9999)
                    printf("%d\t",x);
                else
                    break;
            }
            printf("\n");
            i++;
        }
}
void insertq (Q *q, int x)
{
    if(q->front == MAX-1)
        q->front = q->rear = -1;
    if (q->rear == MAX-1)
        printf("queue is full");
    else
    {
        (q->rear) ++;
        q->ar[q->rear] = x;
    }
}
int deleteq (Q *q)
{
    int x;
if (q->front == q->rear)
{
```

```
        printf("queue empty");

        return (-9999);

    }

    else

    {

        (q->front) ++;

        x = q->ar [q->front];

        return (x);

    }

}
```

2.7.2 Simulation of Queues

Any real life application involving queue like activity can be simulated and the performance of the system can be analysed under different conditions. Thus, we can create a model of the real life application.

Suppose a shop is open for 8 hours a day for 6 days in a week. The shop activity can be studied in different situations i.e. busy day, average day, busy hours etc. We need to simulate the activities of the shop as queue. The events that can take place are as below :

- A customer arrives

- The counter is free

- The customer is served

When the customer arrives and counter is not free he waits in a queue. Hence, we need to create a queue of customers.

When the counter becomes free to serve next customer, we need to start a timer to find out how much time is taken by each customer. When a customer is served, we should count time taken by the server, waiting time for the customer in queue etc. This can be used to find average taken to serve each customer, average waiting time for each customer etc.

We can use random numbers to generate the inputs such waiting time for a customer, time taken to serve a customer etc.

2.7.3 Job Scheduling

The operating system programs like Window, Unix etc, which are multitasking operating systems, execute number of programs simultaneously. It is required to do scheduling of executions of these programs. There are number of techniques for scheduling some of them are :

- First Come First Serve (FCFS)
- Round - Robin Technique

Both these technique uses queues for the implementation of scheduling program execution.

First Come First Serve (FCFS) : The FCFS technique stores the programs in the queue on first come first serve basis. The program which comes first will be executed first. This technique is useful for scheduling of print jobs in a print server.

The disadvantages is that if one of the jobs in queue takes more time the other jobs have to wait for a long time.

Round Robin Technique : In this technique, the programs to be executed are stored in a queue. But each program is given a fix time slot for execution. If execution is over in time slot allotted, the program is removed otherwise the program is kept in the rear end of queue so that it gets another turn. The next program in the queue will be given its turn of execution for the next time slot as shown in Fig. 2.12 (a) and (b).

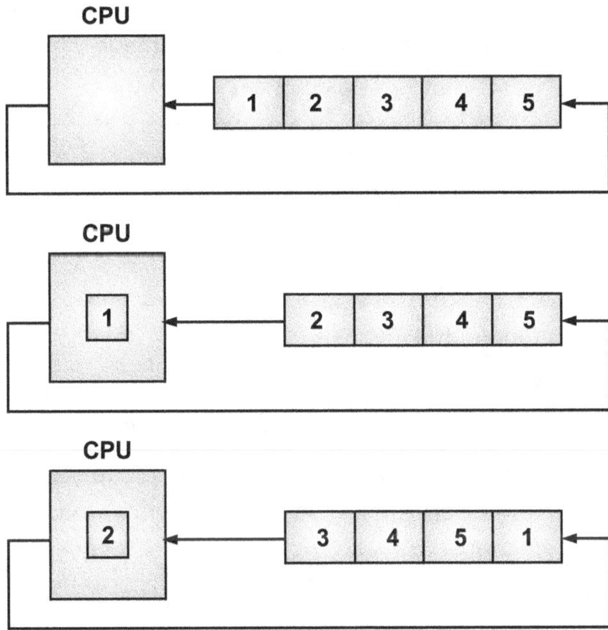

Fig. 2.12 (a) : Round Robin technique

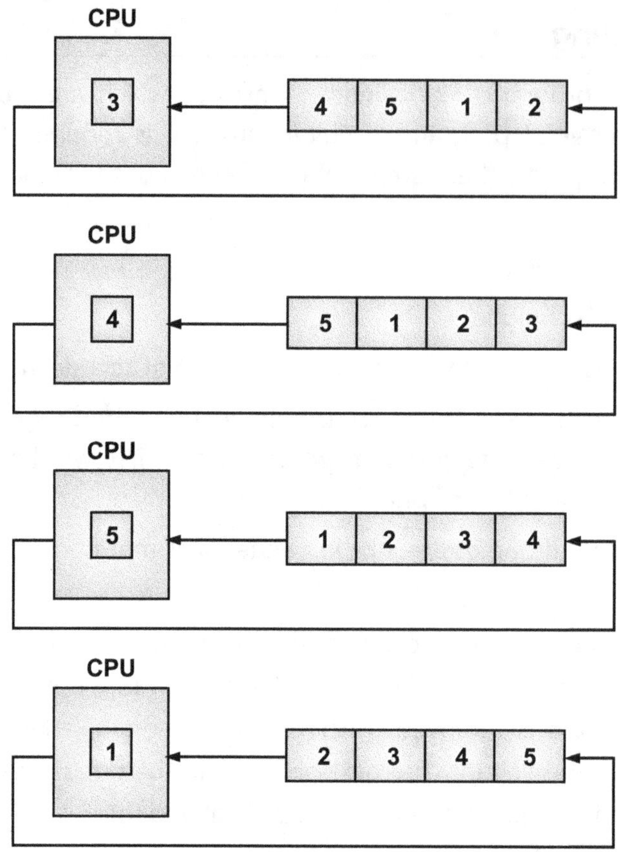

Fig. 2.12 (b) : Round Robin technique

SUMMARY

- Queue is a linear data structure in which all insertions are made at rear end and all deletions are made at the other end called front end.

- Queue can be implemented using array or linked list.

- The four operations done on queue are :

  (i) Insert, (ii) Delete, (iii) Queue full, (iv) Queue empty.

- Linear queue has the advantage that when queue becomes full, rear reaches to end of queue and even if we remove some elements we cannot insert elements in it.

- Circular queue is used to avoid disadvantage of linear queue stated above. We can go to the front end of queue and insert the elements if it is empty in circular queue.

- In priority queue, the elements are stored as per the priority. The priority queue can be ascending or descending.

- Queue can be used in scheduling techniques like First Come First Serve or Round Robin Technique.

SOLVED PROBLEMS

1. Write a program to reverse a queue using stack.

Solution :

```c
#define MAX 5
int q[MAX];
int front = 1, rear = -1;
void insertq (int);
int delq( );
int front -1, rear -1;
int stk[MAX]
int top =-1;
void main( )
{
    int i, x, n;
    printf ("Enter n \n");
    scanf("%d", &n);
    for(i=0; i<n; i++)
    {
        scanf("%d", &x);
        insertq(x);
    }
    while(front!=rear)
    {
        x=delq( );
        push(x);
    }
    while(top!=-1)
```

```c
        {
            x=pop( );
            insertq(x);
        }
}
void insert q (int x)
{
    if (front == MAX -1)
    front = rear = -1;
    if (rear = MAX -1)
        printf ("Queue full");
    else
    {
        rear ++;
        q[rear] = x;
    }
}
int delq( )
{
    int x;
    if (front == rear)
    {
        printf ("Q is empty");
        return (-9999);
    }
    else
    {
        front ++;
```

```c
            x = q [front];
            return (x);
        }
    }
    void push (int x)
    {
        if(top == MAX-1)
            printf("Stack is full");
        else
        {
            top ++;
            stk [top] = x;
        }
    }
    int pop( )
    {
        int x;
        if  (top == -1)
        {
            print ("Stack is empty \n");
            return (-9999);
        }
        else
        {
            x = stk [top];
            top- -;
            return (x);
        }
    }
```

2. Differentiate between circular and linear queue.

Solution : (Also refer Section 2.4).

No.	Linear Queue	Circular Queue
1.	When rear becomes MAX −1, we cannot insert elements at front end even if space is available.	When rear becomes MAX −1, we can continue adding elements at front end if space is available.
2.	Counter is not required to check Q full or Q empty.	Counter is required to check Q full or Q empty.
3.	Easy implementation.	Difficult implementation.

EXERCISE

1. Explain the concept of queue with suitable example. Also, explain any one application of queue with Pseudo-Code. **(8m)**

   Solution : (Refer Sections 2.1 and 2.7)

2. What is queue? Explain circular queue and priority queue with suitable example. **(8m)**

   Solution : (Refer Sections 2.1, 2.4 and 2.5)

3. Write a menu driven program for implementation of queue using structure.

   Solution : (Refer Program 2.2)

4. Write necessary 'C' functions to implement Queue using array.

   Solution : (Refer Section 2.2)

5. How can queue be implemented using array and linked list? Explain. **(8m)**

   Solution : (Refer Sections 2.2 and 2.3)

6. Explain array and linked list implementation of queue. **(8m)**

   Solution : (Refer Sections 2.2 and 2.3)

7. Write necessary 'C' functions to implement Queue using linked list.

   Solution : (Refer Section 2.3)

8. Write 'insert' and 'delete' operations to implement a linked queue. **(6m)**

   Solution : (Refer Section 2.3)

9. Compare linear and circular queue representations using arrays. Give a node structure in 'C' to define a queue using linked list. Also, write a function to add an item into a queue using linked list. **(8m)**

   Solution : (Refer Sections 2.3 and 2.4)

10. Write necessary 'C' functions to implement Circular Queue using array.

    Solution : (Refer Section 2.4)

11. Write necessary functions in C to implement circular queue in all array. Assume rear=front=0 initially.   **(6m)**

    Solution : (Refer Section 2.4)

12. How circular queue is advantageous over sequential queue? Explain with an example.

                                                                                        (4m)

    Solution : (Refer Section 2.4)

13. Differentiate between linear and circular queue when represented using array.   **(8m)**

    Solution : (Refer Section 2.4)

14. Implement the following functions in 'C' to implement circular queue using array. **(8m)**

    (i)   Insert an element,

    (ii) Delete an element,

    (iii) Queue full,

    (iv) Queue empty.

    Assume data elements to be integer.

    Solution : (Refer Section 2.4)

15. Explain advantages of circular queue over linear queue.

    Solution : (Refer Section 2.4)

16. What is circular queue? Explain insert and delete operations in circular queue.

    Solution : (Refer Section 2.4)

17. Explain the concept of priority queue with suitable example. Explain one application of Priority queue.

    Solution : (Refer Section 2.6)

18. Explain the concept of priority queue with suitable example.   **(6m)**

    Solution : (Refer Section 2.6)

19. What is Priority Queue? Write Pseudo 'C' function to insert and delete item from Priority Queue.   **(8m)**

    Solution : (Refer Section 2.6)

20. Why do we need priority Queue? Explain with appropriate data structure, the implementation of priority queue.   **(8m)**

    Solution : (Refer Section 2.6)

21. What do you mean by priority queue? Explain any one application of priority queue with suitable example.   **(8m)**

    Solution : (Refer Section 2.6)

22. What do you mean by priority queue? Explain any one application in detail.   **(8m)**

    Solution : (Refer Section 2.6)

23. Explain the term priority queue and give the application for the same.   **(4m)**

    Solution : (Refer Section 2.6)

24. What is priority queue? What are the applications of priority queue? Write a 'C' function to perform insertion and deletion on priority queue.   **(8m)**

    Solution : (Refer Section 2.6)

25. Compare circular and linear queue.

    Solution : (Refer solved problem 2)

26. Write applications of queue.

    Solution : (Refer Section 2.7)

◈ ◈ ◈

CHAPTER 3
TREES

3.1 INTRODUCTION

Till now, we have seen data structures such as arrays, linked lists, stacks, queues, etc. All these are linear data structures. The data is stored in sequential locations. In order to retrieve data, we have to traverse in sequence. For large amounts of data, this kind of access is not efficient because, time complexity of retrieval in such data structures will be poor, i.e. O(n).

If we arrange the data in hierarchical manner, we can have more than one successor of a data element as shown in Fig. 3.1. Such a structure is called tree.

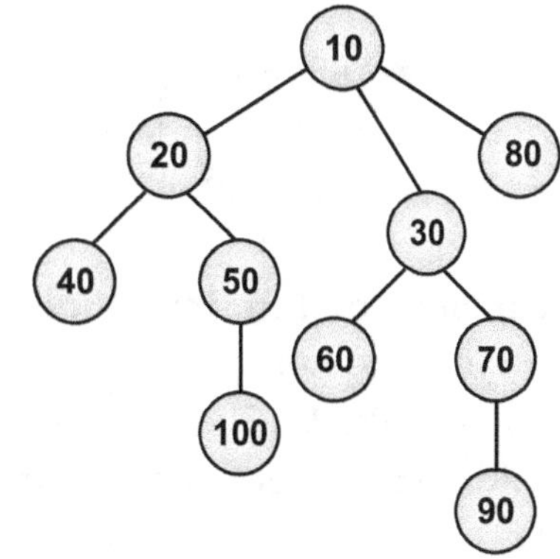

Fig. 3.1 : Tree

There are number of applications in computer science where we can use this data structure. A tree can be defined in several ways.

Definition 1 :

A tree (T) is a set of nodes. The set can be empty. If it is non-empty set it consists of a specially designated node called root node and zero or more (sub) trees $T_1, T_2, T_3, \ldots, T_n$, each of whose roots are connected by a directed edge from the root of T.

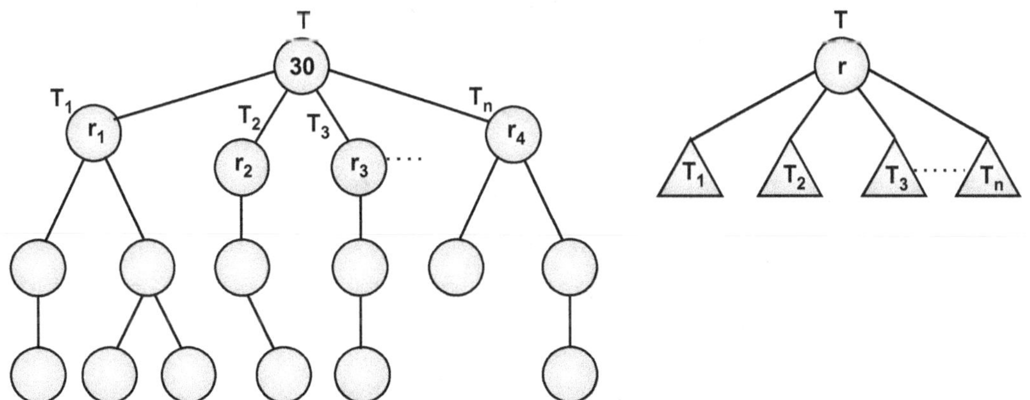

Fig. 3.2 : Tree definition

Definition 2 :

A tree consists of finite set of elements called nodes and a finite set of directed lines called branch edges that connect the nodes.

3.2 BASIC TERMINOLOGY

There are number of terms used with tree. Let us see the definition of each of them.

- **Node :** It stands for item of information plus the branches to other items.
- **Degree :** The total number of edges associated with a node is called degree of that node.
- **Indegree :** The total number of edges converging a node is called indegree of the node. Root node will have indegree 0.
- **Outdegree :** The total number of edges diverging from a node is called outdegree of the node.
- **Leaf Node or Terminal Node :** The nodes that have outdegree zero are called leaf node or terminal node.
- **Non-Terminals :** The nodes which have nonzero outdegree are called non-terminals.
- **Children :** The root nodes of the sub-tree of a node are called children of that node, i.e., they are immediate successors of node.
- **Parent Node :** If A is child of B then B is the parent node of A, i.e., it is immediate predecessor of a node.
- **Siblings :** Children of the same parent are called siblings.
- **Degree of a Tree :** It is maximum degree of a node in the tree.
- **Ancestor Nodes :** Ancestors of a node are all the nodes along the path from the root to that node.
- **Level of a Node :** Root node of a tree is said to be at level 1. Its children will be at level 2. In general, the node at level l will have its children at level $l + 1$.
- **Height or Depth of Tree :** It is the maximum level of any node in the tree.
- **Forest :** It is a set of disjoint trees, i.e., these trees will not have common node amongst them. Let us draw a tree and represent these terms.

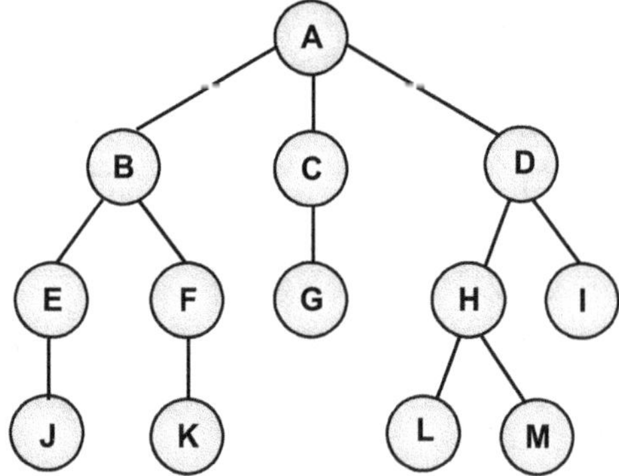

Fig. 3.3 : Tree

Observation :

- Total degree of A $\Rightarrow$ 3
- Indegree of H $\Rightarrow$ 1
- Out-degree of H $\Rightarrow$ 2
- Leaf nodes $\Rightarrow$ J, K, G, L, M, I
- Non-terminal $\Rightarrow$ A, B, C, D, E, F, H
- Children of B $\Rightarrow$ E, F
- Parent node of J $\Rightarrow$ E
- Siblings $\Rightarrow$ {B, C, D}, {E, F}, {H, I}, {L, M}
- Ancestors of J $\Rightarrow$ E, B, A
- Degree of Tree $\Rightarrow$ 3
- Level of H $\Rightarrow$ 3
- Height of Tree $\Rightarrow$ 4
- Forest : If we remove root A of the tree we get set of three trees which is a forest.

The tree can be represented in a linked list format, where each node in the tree will be as :

Data	Link 1	Link 2	......	Link 4

For a general tree there are no restrictions on the number of sub-trees. The data field will store the information. The link fields will store the addresses of children of the node. Now the question is how many link fields should be defined? It is going to depend on maximum number of branches a node can have. Hence, it is very difficult to create a general tree. Binary trees are used in most of the applications where the number of branches will be fixed to 2. Hence, we will restrict our study to binary trees.

3.2.1 Difference between Linear and Non-Linear Data Structures

Linear Data Structure :

- Those data structures where the data elements are organised in some sequence is called linear data structure.
- Here the various operations on a data structure are possible only in a sequence i.e. we cannot insert the element into any location of our choice. E.g. A new element in a queue can come only at the end, not anywhere else.
- Examples of linear data structures are array, stacks, queue, and linked list.
- They can be implemented in memory using two ways.
- The first method is by having a linear relationship between elements by means of sequential memory locations.
- The second method is by having a linear relationship by using links.

Non-Linear Data Structure :

- When the data elements are organised in some arbitrary function without any sequence, such data structures are called non-linear data structures.

- Examples of such type are trees, graphs.

- The relationship of adjacency is not maintained between elements of a non-linear data structure.

3.3 BINARY TREE

A binary tree is a tree in which no node has more than two sub-trees. It means any node can have at most two branches. i.e., there is no node with degree greater than two.

Definition :

A binary tree is a finite set of nodes which is either empty or consists of root and two disjoint binary trees called left sub-tree and right sub-tree.

Following are examples of binary trees.

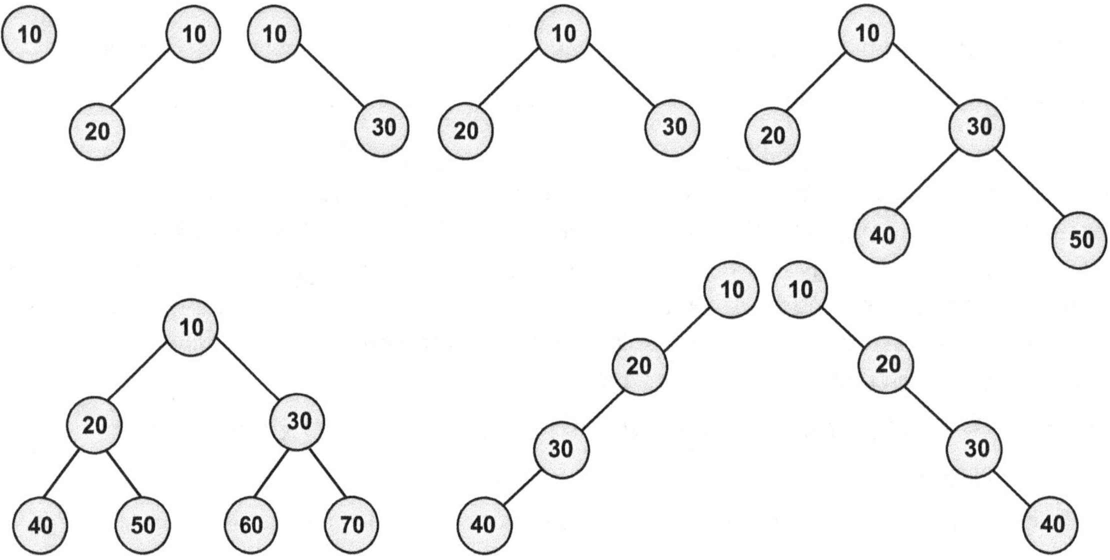

Fig. 3.4 : Binary trees

The maximum number of nodes in a binary tree will be $2^h - 1$ where h is height of the tree. The number of leaf nodes in the binary tree will be 2^{h-1}.

Depending on how the nodes are placed in the binary tree, we can have following types of binary tree.

1. Complete Binary Tree :

If the height of binary tree is h and there are 2^{h-1} nodes at least level, then it is a complete binary tree. Following are examples of complete binary tree. It is also called full binary tree.

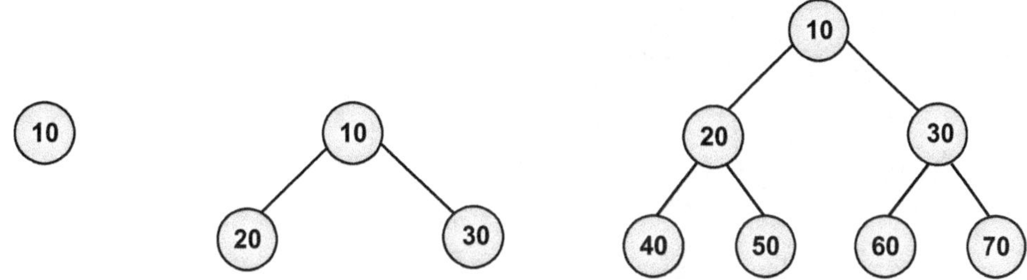

Fig. 3.5 : Complete binary tree

2. Almost Complete Binary Tree :

If the height of binary tree is h, then the binary tree is said to be almost complete if,

- The leaf nodes are at level h or h − 1.
- There is no leaf node at level h − 2 i.e., at h − 2 level every node has two children.
- At level h, the leaf nodes are as far to the left as possible.

Following are examples of almost complete binary tree.

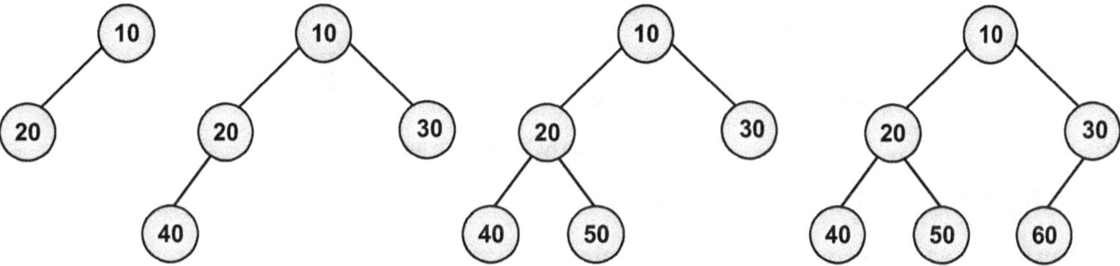

Fig. 3.6 : Almost complete binary tree

3. Left Skewed Binary Tree :

If the nodes in a binary tree have only left child, it is called left skewed binary tree.

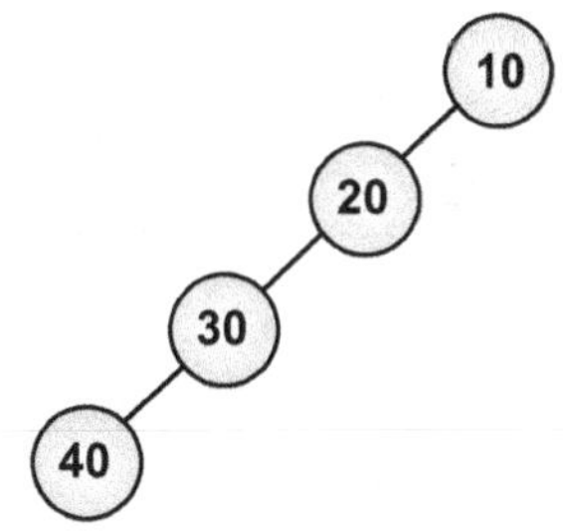

Fig. 3.7 : Left skewed binary tree

4. Right Skewed Binary Tree :

If the nodes in a binary tree have only right child, it is called right skewed binary tree.

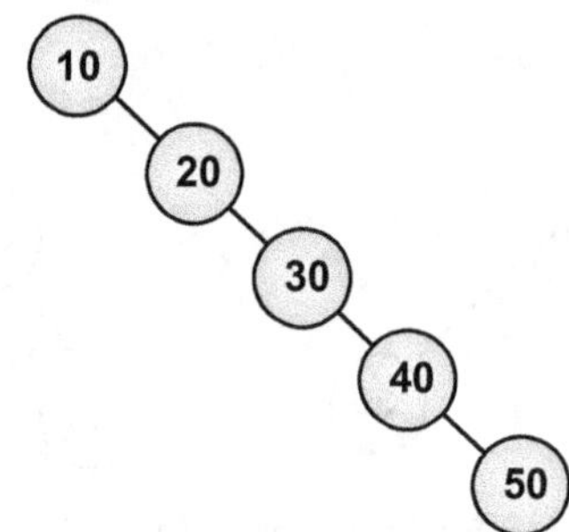

Fig. 3.8 : Right skewed binary tree

5. Strictly Binary Tree :

It is a binary tree in which each node will have either two children or no child. Examples of strictly binary tree are shown in Fig. 3.9.

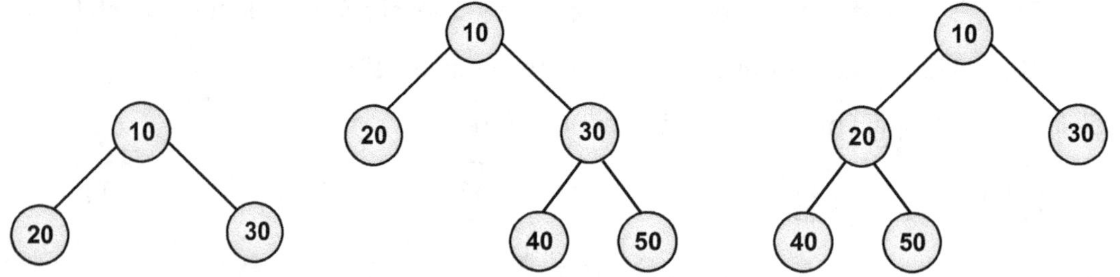

Fig. 3.9 : Strictly binary tree

3.3.1 Representation of Binary Tree

A binary tree can be represented using arrays or linked lists.

The array representation of binary tree is very simple for implementations where each node in binary tree will be stored in the array sequentially. Consider a complete binary tree as shown in Fig. 3.10.

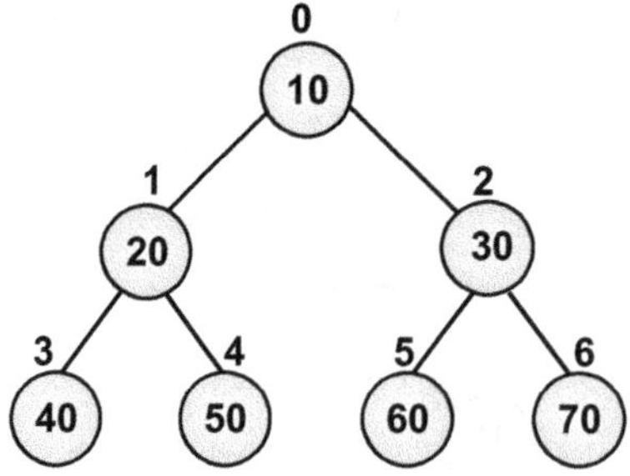

Fig. 3.10 : Binary tree

The nodes are designated by numbers which can be used as location number of the element in the array for example, the element 30 will be stored at a[2]. The array representation of above binary tree is shown in Fig. 3.11.

a[0]	a[1]	a[2]	a[3]	a[4]	a[5]	a[6]
10	20	30	40	50	60	70

Fig. 3.11 : Array representation of binary tree in Fig. 3.10

Observe that if an element is at i^{th} location, its left child will be at $(2i+1)^{th}$ location and right child will be at $(2i+2)^{th}$ location.

But, if we have binary tree which is not complete binary tree or almost complete binary tree most of the space in the array will be unutilized. For example, if we have a binary tree as shown in Fig. 3.12.

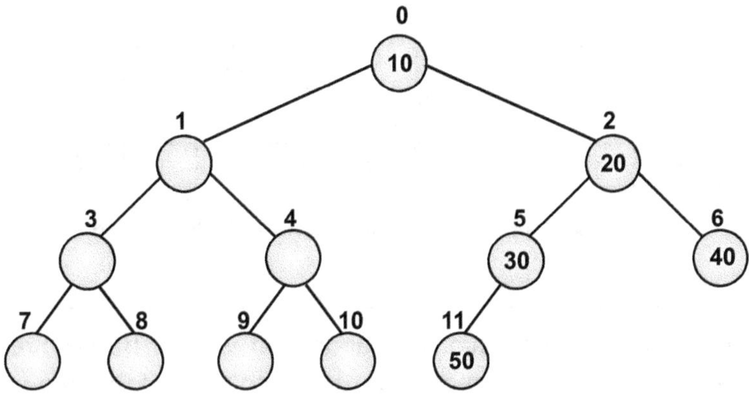

Fig. 3.12 : Binary tree

Its array representation will be,

a[0]	a[1]	a[2]	a[3]	a[4]	a[5]	a[6]	a[7]	a[8]	a[9]	a[10]	a[11]	a[12]
10	–	20	–	–	30	40	–	–	–	–	50	–

Fig. 3.13 : Array representation of binary tree in Fig. 3.12

It is not only wastage of space, the insertion or deletion of node is also going to cause lot of movements. These problems can be eliminated using linked representation.

In linked representation, each node will be having three fields viz., data, *l*child and rchild. The data field is information to be stored. It can be int, float, char, array or records. The two field's *l*child and rchild will be pointers storing the addresses of left sub-tree and right sub-tree.

The node structure can be defined as :

```
typedef struct node
{
    int data;
    struct node *lchild, *rchild;
} NODE;
```

The node will be as shown in Fig. 3.14.

lchild	data	rchild

Fig. 3.14 : Node in a binary tree

The binary tree in node structure will be as shown in Fig. 3.15.

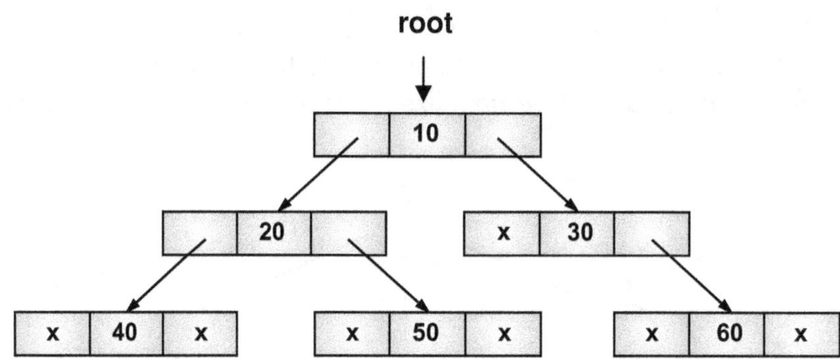

Fig. 3.15 : Linked list representation of binary tree

3.3.2 Binary Tree Traversal

Once a binary tree is created the major operation that we will be required to do will be traversal of the tree. Traversing a tree means, visiting each node in the tree exactly once.

While traversing a binary tree, if we are at-a particular node there are six different ways in which we can move. They are **LVR, VLR, LRV, RVL, VRL** and **RLV**. Where **V** is visit the node or access data, **L** move to left and **R**-move to right. There is a standard conversation that we should move to left first before right. Hence, there are only three standard traversals **LVR, VLR** and **LRV**.

LVR is called in order traversal where left sub-tree is processed first then root and finally right sub-tree. **VLR** is called preorder traversal where root is processed first followed by left sub-tree the right sub-tree.

LRV is called post order traversal where left sub-tree is processed first then right and finally root node.

Let us consider a binary tree.

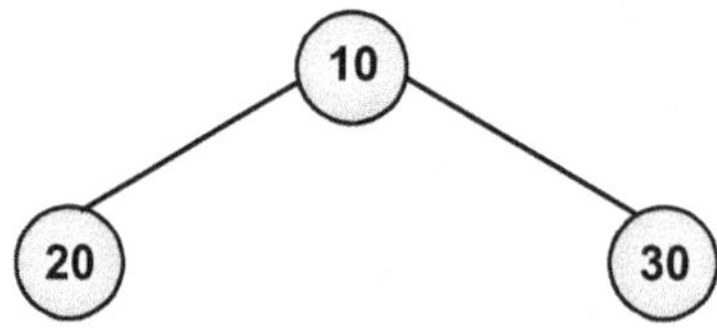

Fig. 3.16 : Binary tree

Inorder traversal for Fig. 3.16, is shown in Fig. 3.17.

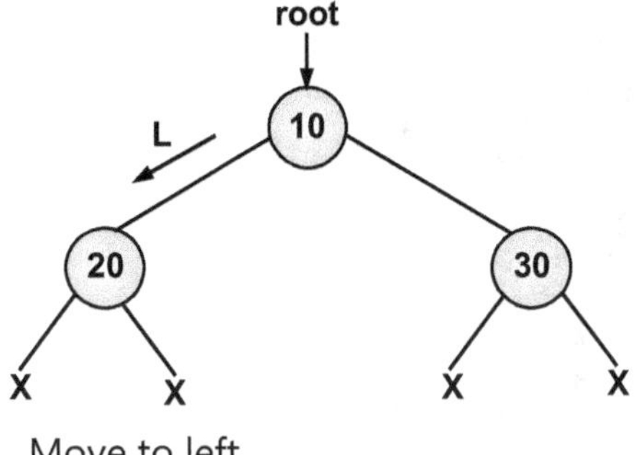

Move to left

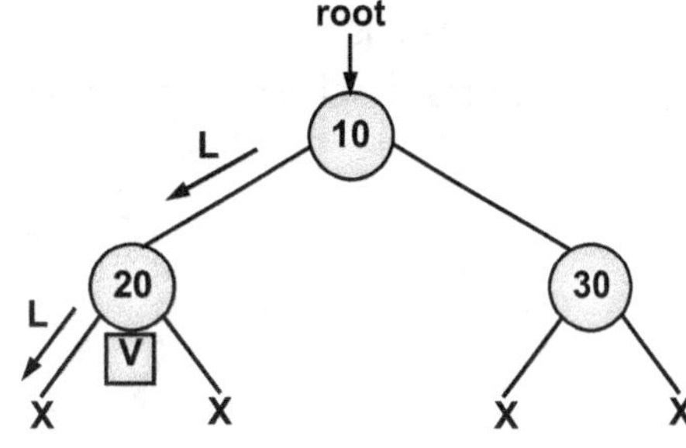

Move to left

left sub-tree of 20 is Null

Hence, visit node 20

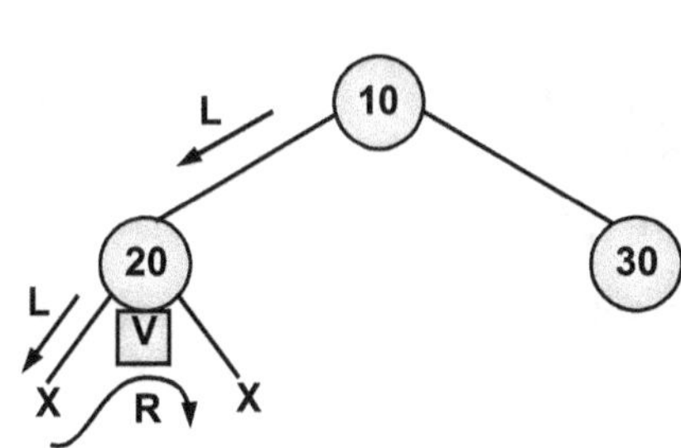

Move to right

Right sub-tree of 20 is Null

LVR for 20 is order

Go back to previous node

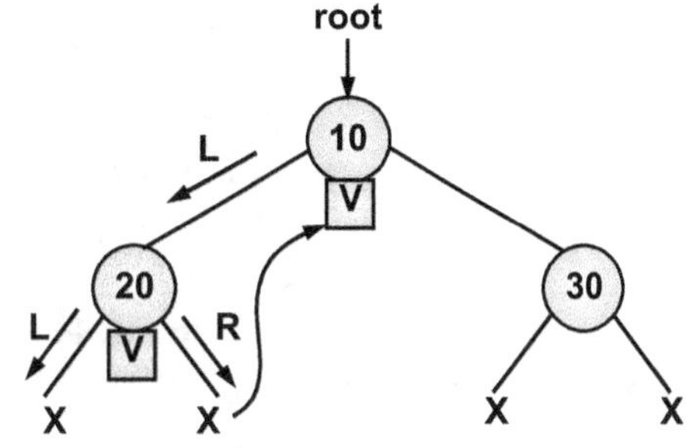

Left sub-tree of 10 is over

Visit the node 10

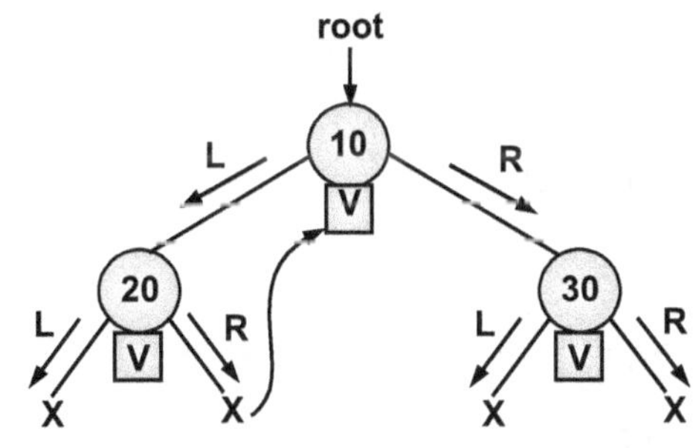

Move to right

Move to left, it is NULL

Visit 30

Move to right, it is Null

LVR for 30 is over, Go back to 30

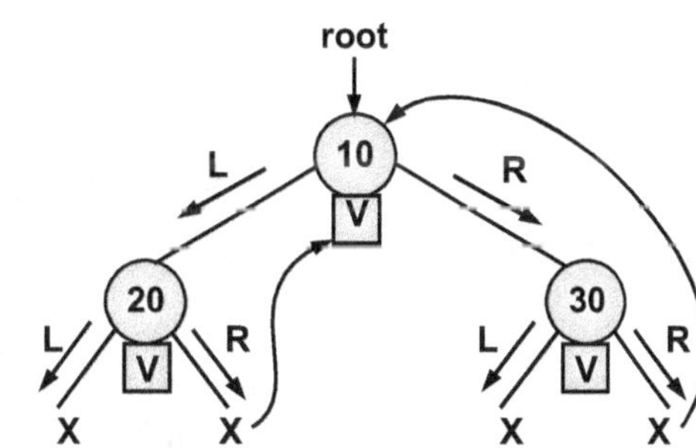

Go back to root

LVR for 10 is over

Fig. 3.17 : Inorder traversal of binary tree

Hence, inorder traversal is 20 10 30.

Similarly, preorder traversal will be as shown in Fig. 3.18.

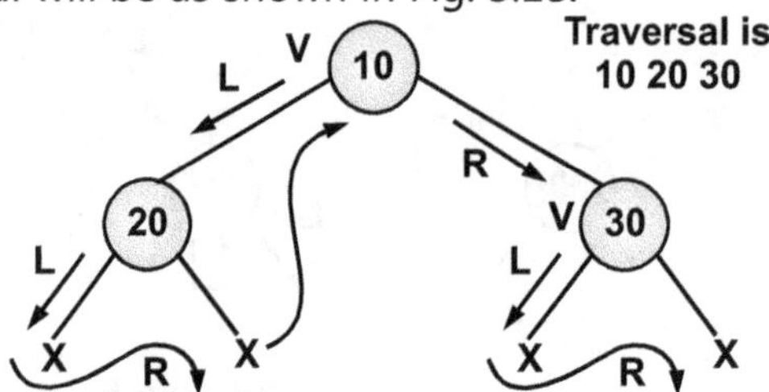

Fig. 3.18 : Preorder traversal

Postorder traversal will be as shown in Fig. 3.19.

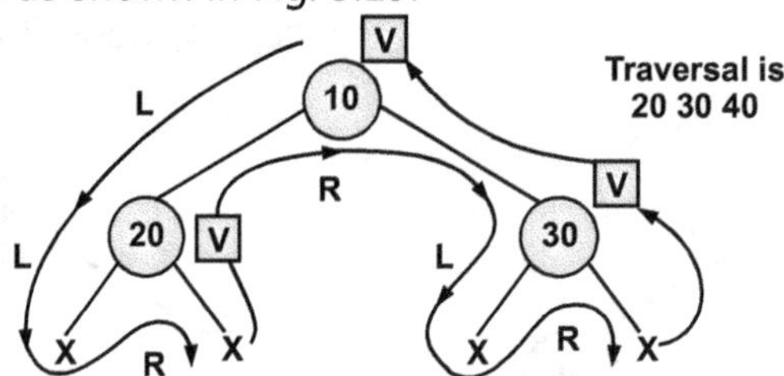

Fig. 3.19 : Postorder traversal

Let us consider another example.

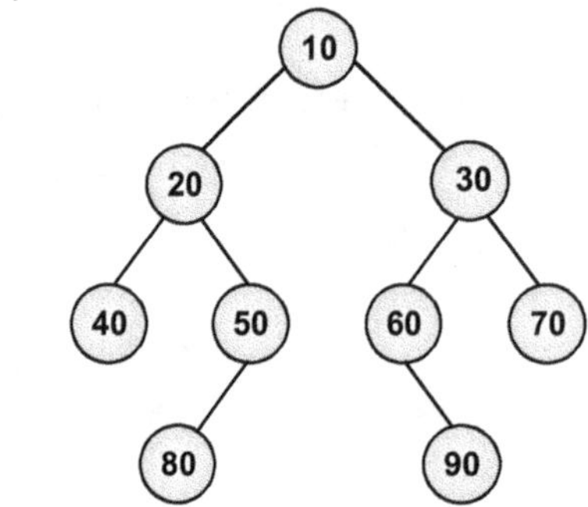

Fig. 3.20 : Inorder traversal

Inorder Traversal :

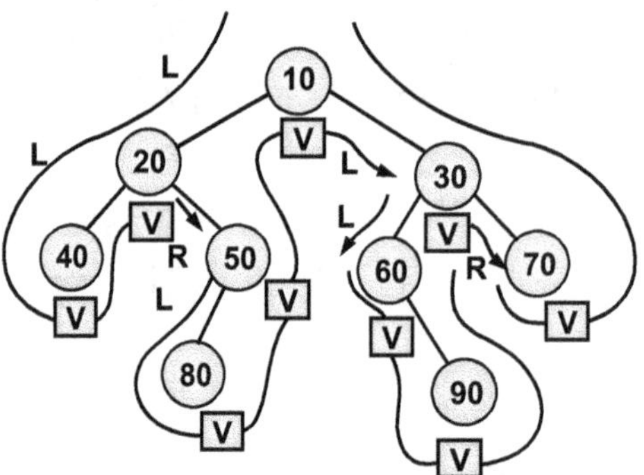

Fig. 3.21 : Inorder traversal

Traversal is 40 20 80 50 10 60 90 30 70.

Preorder Traversal :

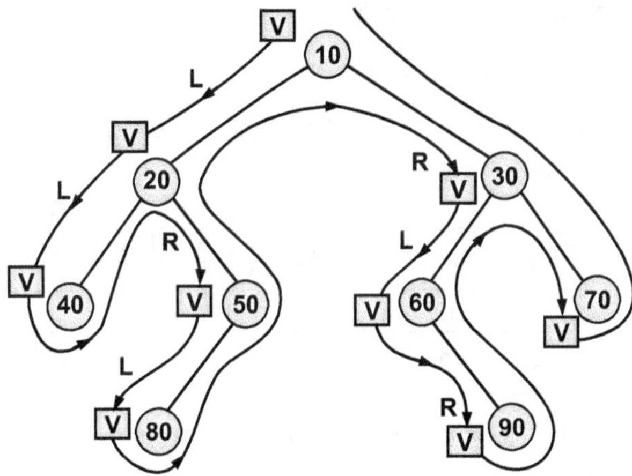

Fig. 3.22 : Preorder traversal

Traversal is 10 20 40 50 80 30 60 90 70

Postorder Traversal :

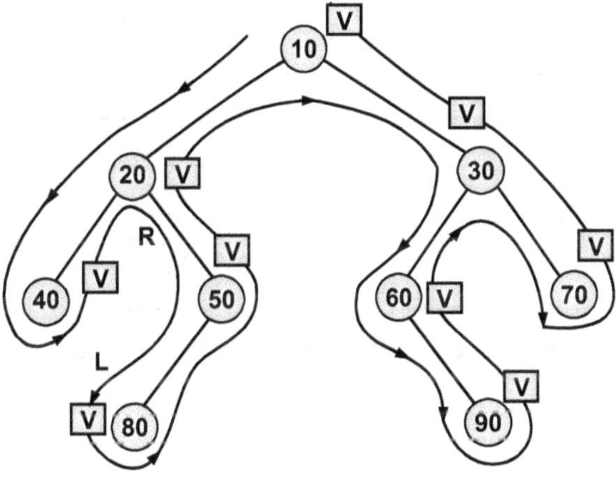

Fig. 3.23 : Postorder traversal

Traversal is 40 80 50 20 90 60 70 30 10

Observation :

- In inorder traversal, the root element is in between the left sub-tree and right sub-tree.

- In preorder traversal, root element is at the beginning.

- In postorder traversal, root element will be at the end.

- If we are given any two traversals of a tree we can draw the tree diagram.

Example : Let us take up the same traversals of Figs. 3.21 and 3.22.

Inorder :   40 20 80 50 10 60 90 30 70

Preorder :   10 20 40 50 80 30 60 90 70

Step 1 : From preorder, we find that root is 10. Hence, the right and left sub-tree elements will be as shown in Fig. 3.24 (a).

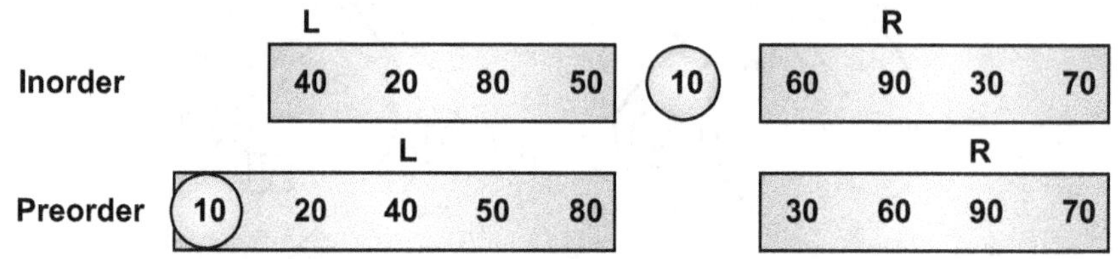

Fig. 3.24 (a) : Binary tree from traversal

Step 2 :   Left sub-tree has root 20 (first element of pre-order).

Right sub-tree has root 30 (first element of pre-order).

Hence, the division will be as shown in Fig. 3.24 (b).

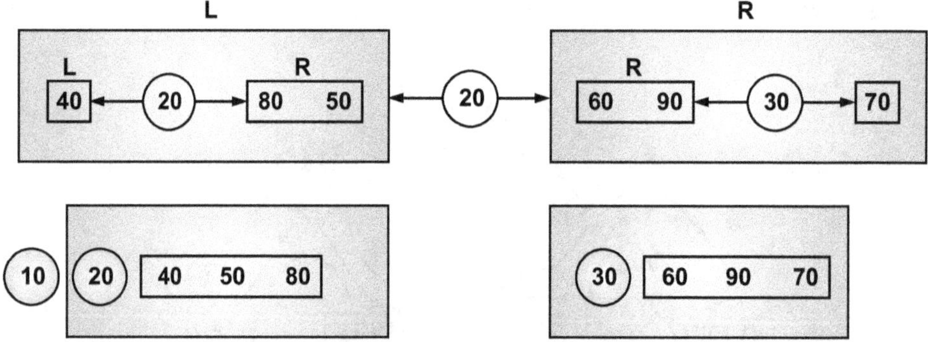

Fig. 3.24 (b) : Binary tree from traversal

Step 3 : Continuing on the same lines.

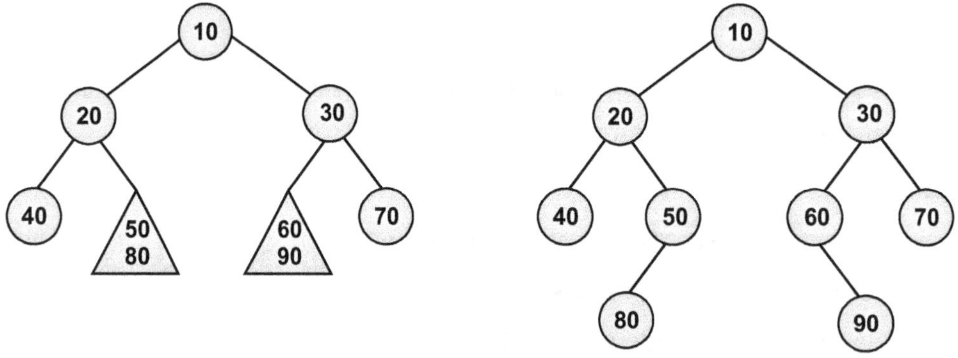

Fig. 3.24 (c) : Binary tree from traversal

Expression Tree :

Expression tree is a binary tree in which each internal node corresponds to operator and each leaf node corresponds to operand, so for example expression tree for 3 + ((5+9)*2) would be :

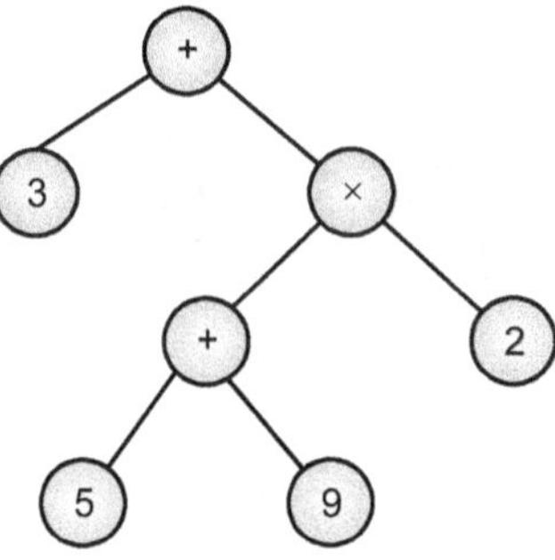

Fig. 3.25

Inorder traversal of expression tree produces infix version of given postfix expression (same with preorder traversal it gives prefix expression).

Construction of an Expression Tree :

The evaluation of the tree takes place by reading the postfix expression one symbol at a time. If the symbol is an operand, one-node tree is created and a pointer is pushed onto a stack. If the symbol is an operator, the pointers are popped to two trees T1 and T2 from the stack and a new tree whose root is the operator and whose left and right children point to T2 and T1 respectively is formed. A pointer to this new tree is then pushed to the stack.

Example :

The input is : a b + c d e + * * since the first two symbols are operands, one-node trees are created and pointers are pushed to them onto a stack. For convenience, the stack will grow from left to right.

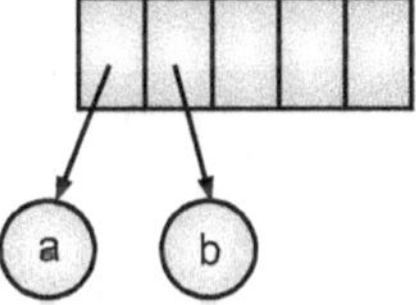

Fig. 3.26

Stack Growing from Left to Right :

The next symbol is a '+'. It pops the two pointers to the trees, a new tree is formed, and a pointer to it is pushed onto the stack.

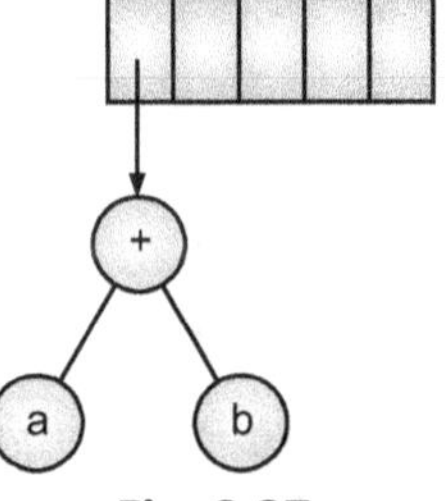

Fig. 3.27

Formation of a New Tree :

Next, c, d and e are read. A one-node tree is created for each and a pointer to the corresponding tree is pushed onto the stack.

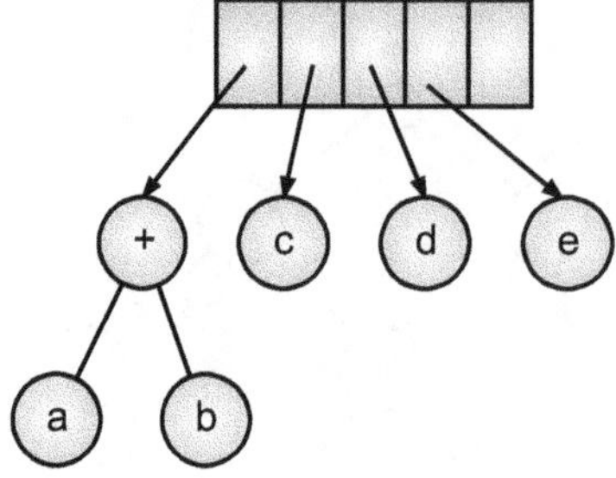

Fig. 3.28

Creating a One-Node Tree :

Continuing, a '+' is read, and it merges the last two trees.

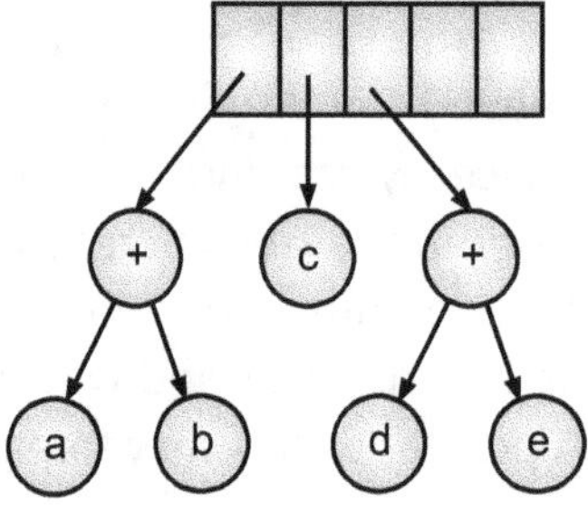

Fig. 3.29

Merging Two Trees :

Now, a '*' is read. The last two tree pointers are popped and a new tree is formed with a '*' as the root.

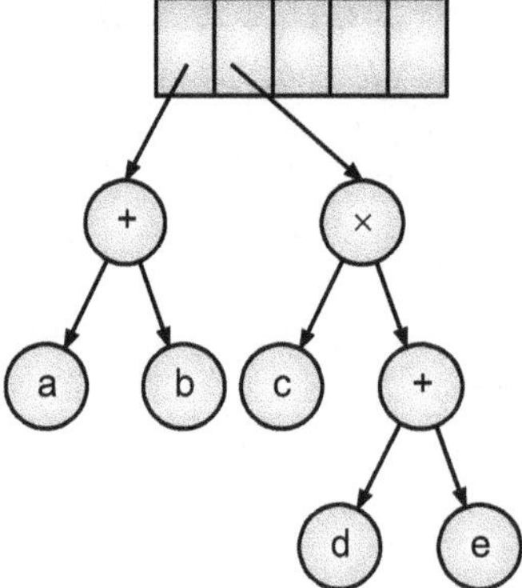

Fig. 3.30

Forming a New Tree with a Root :

Finally, the last symbol is read. The two trees are merged and a pointer to the final tree remains on the stack.

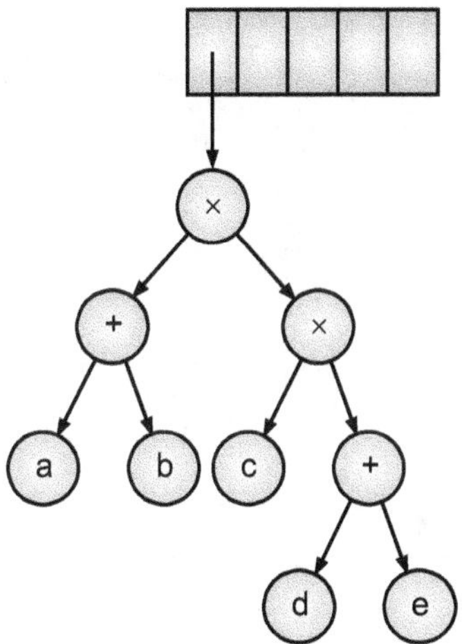

Fig. 3.31

Steps to construct an expression tree a b + c d e + * *

Evaluating the expression represented by expression tree :

Let t be the expression tree

If t is not null, then

    If t.value is operand, then

        Return t.value

    A = solve(t.left)

    B = solve(t.right)

    // calculate applies operator 't.value'

    // on A and B, and returns value

    Return calculate (A, B, t.value)

Construction of Expression Tree :

Now for constructing expression tree we use a stack. We loop through input expression and do following for every character.

- If character is operand, push that into stack.
- If character is operator, pop two values from stack, make them its child and push current node again.

At the end, only element of stack will be root of expression tree.

Below is the implementation :

```
// C++ program for expression tree
#include<bits/stdc++.h>
```

```cpp
using namespace std;
// An expression tree node
struct et
{
    char value;
    et* left, *right;
};
// A utility function to check if 'c'
// is an operator
bool isOperator(char c)
{
    if (c == '+' || c == '-' ||
        c == '*' || c == '/' ||
        c == '^')
        return true;
    return false;
}
// Utility function to do inorder traversal
void inorder(et *t)
{
    if(t)
    {
        inorder(t->left);
        printf("%c ", t->value);
        inorder(t->right);
    }
}
// A utility function to create a new node
et* newNode(int v)
{
```

```cpp
    et *temp = new et;
    temp->left = temp->right = NULL;
    temp->value = v;
    return temp;
};
// Returns root of constructed tree for given
// postfix expression
et* constructTree(char postfix[])
{
    stack<et *> st;
    et *t, *t1, *t2;
    // Traverse through every character of
    // input expression
    for (int i=0; i<strlen(postfix); i++)
    {
        // If operand, simply push into stack
        if (!isOperator(postfix[i]))
        {
            t = newNode(postfix[i]);
            st.push(t);
        }
        else // operator
        {
            t = newNode(postfix[i]);
            // Pop two top nodes
            t1 = st.top(); // Store top
            st.pop();      // Remove top
            t2 = st.top();
            st.pop();              //  make them children
            t->right = t1;
            t->left = t2;          // Add this subexpression to stack
            st.push(t);
        }
```

```
   }
   //  only element will be root of expression tree
   t = st.top();
   st.pop();
   return t;
}
// Driver program to test above
int main()
{
   char postfix[] = "ab+ef*g*-";
   et* r = constructTree(postfix);
   printf("infix expression is \n");
   inorder(r);
   return 0;
}
```

Output :

infix expression is

a + b - e * f * g

General Tree :

A Tree in which each node having either 0 or more child nodes is called general tree. So, we can say that a Binary Tree is a specialized case of General tree. General Tree is used to implement File System.

Consider Following Figure :

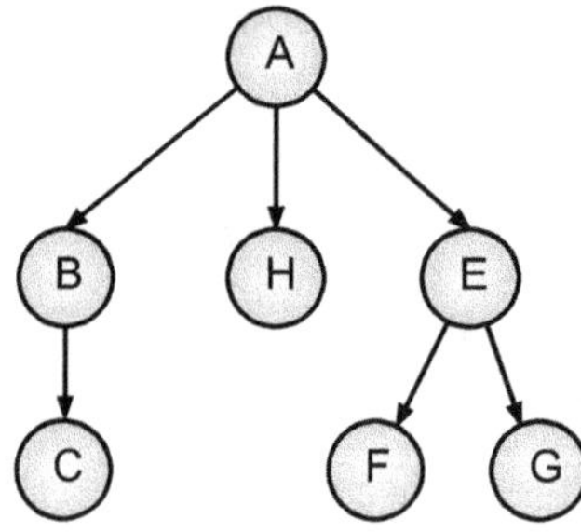

Fig. 3.32

Conversion of General Tree in to Binary Tree :

The process of converting general tree in to binary tree is given below :

- Root node of general tree becomes root node of Binary Tree.
- Now consider T1, T2, T3 ... Tn are child nodes of the root node in general tree. The left most child (T1) of the root node in general tree becomes left most child of root node in

the binary tree. Now Node T2 becomes right child of Node T1, Node T3 becomes right child of Node T2 and so on in binary tree.

- The same procedure of step 2 is repeated for each leftmost node in the general tree. Consider Following General Tree :

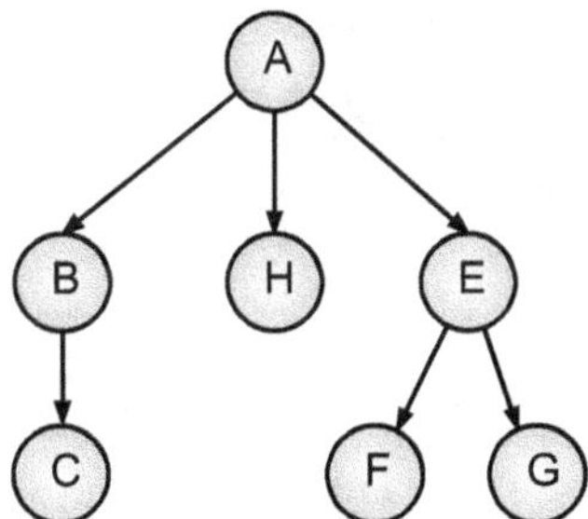

Fig. 3.33

Now step by step we convert general tree into binary tree.

Step 1 : Root Node of general tree becomes the root node of binary tree.

Fig. 3.34

Step 2 : Now **Root Node (A)** has three **child Nodes (B, H, E)** in general tree. The **leftmost node (B)** of the **root node (A)** in the general tree becomes the left most node of the **root node (A)** in binary tree.

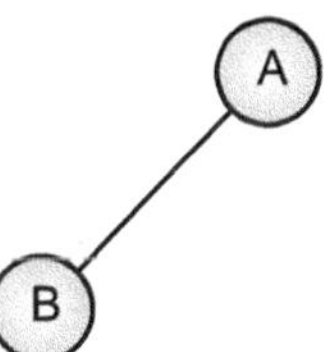

Fig. 3.35

Step 3 : Now **Node H** becomes the right **node of B** and **Node E** becomes the right **node of H**.

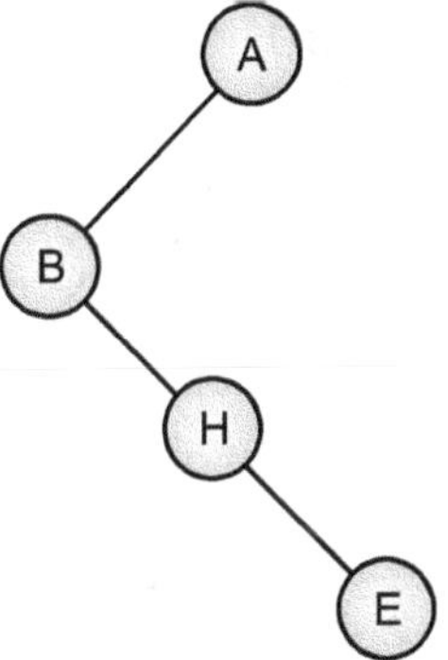

Fig. 3.36

Step 4 : Now **Node B** has only one left child node, which is C in general tree. So, **Node C** becomes left child of **Node B** in binary tree.

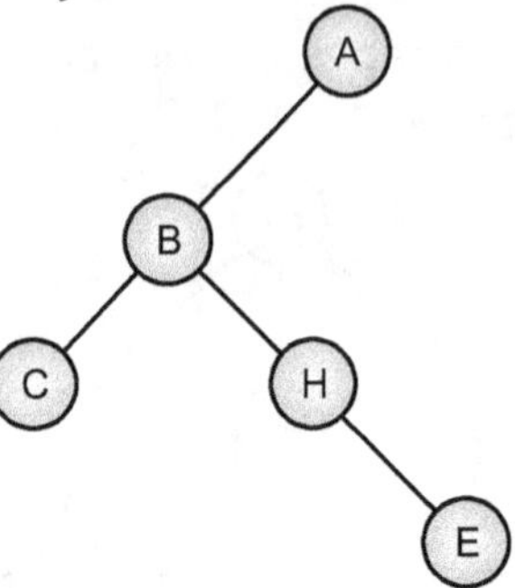

Fig. 3.37

Step 5 : Now **Node E** has two **child nodes (F, G)**. The leftmost **node (F)** of the **node (E)** in the general tree becomes the left most node of the **node E** in the binary tree.

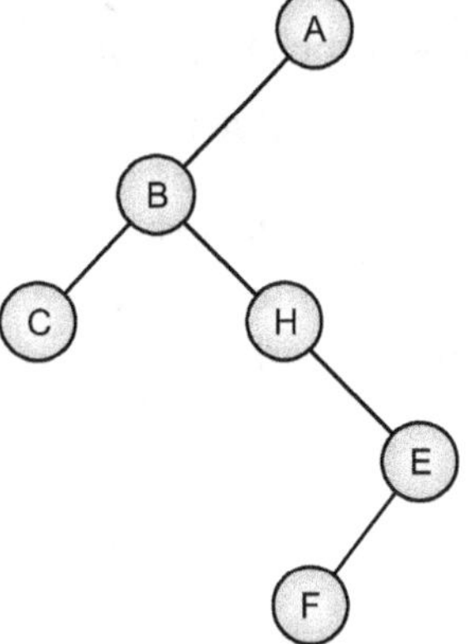

Fig. 3.38

Step 6 : Now **Node G** becomes right node of **Node F** in binary tree.

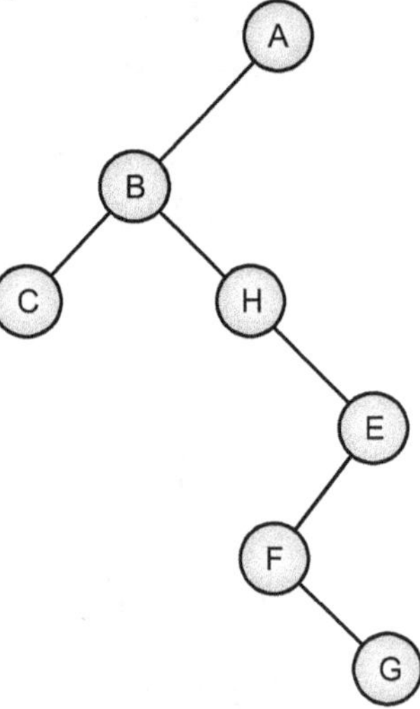

Fig. 3.39

3.4 BINARY SEARCH TREE (BST)

Binary search tree as the name suggests, is used for storing the data mainly for searching applications. We have seen that nonlinear data structures are used for speeding up the process of searching. If we store the data in binary tree in a particular way, we will be able to improve the efficiency of searching to the order of $\log_2 n$ similar to binary search. In fact, **BST** implements the same principle as that of binary search :

Definition 1 :

A binary search tree is a binary tree that is either empty or has each node that can satisfy following conditions.

- All the elements in left sub-tree of the root precede the element in the root.
- All the elements in the right sub-tree of the root succeed the element in the root.
- Left and right sub-trees are again binary search tree.

Definition 2 :

A binary search tree is a binary tree in which for each node the left sub-tree elements are less than the node element and right sub-tree elements are greater than the node element or vice versa.

The example of BST is shown in Fig. 3.40.

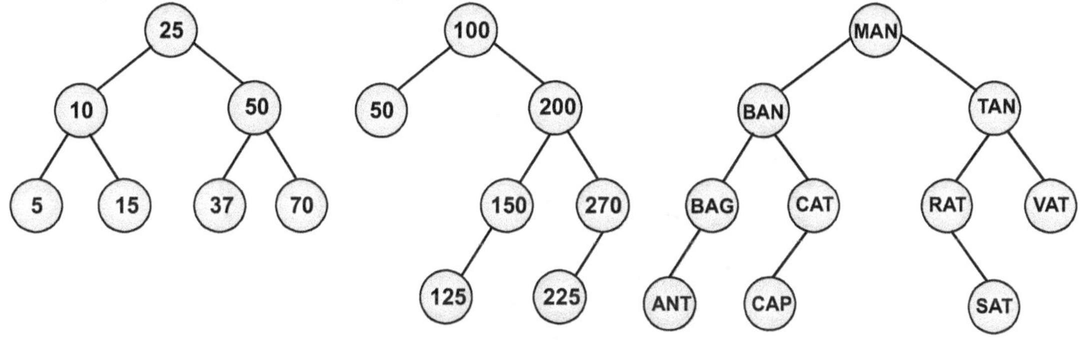

Fig. 3.40 : Binary search tree

3.5 OPERATIONS ON BINARY SEARCH TREE

We can use the traversals discussed earlier for the binary search trees. For example, for first tree the traversals will be as :

Inorder	:	5	10	15	25	37	50	75
Preorder	:	25	10	5	15	50	37	75
Postorder	:	5	15	10	37	75	50	25

Note that inorder traversal of BST will result into ascending order.

We can store the elements in BST in reverse order also. i.e., smaller element on right side and larger element on left side of root. In that case, the inorder traversal will result into descending order of the elements in the tree.

The main operation that we need to do on binary search tree is searching an element. Consider tree as shown in Fig. 3.41.

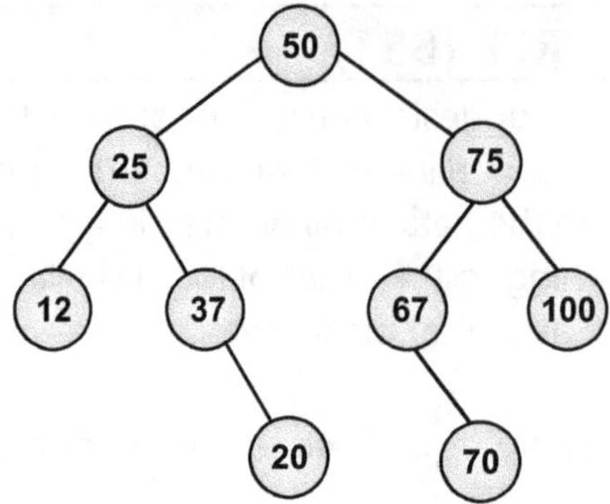

Fig. 3.41 : Binary search tree

Suppose we want to search 37 in the tree. We start from the root node and move to left or right side depending on whether the number is smaller or greater.

Step 1 : Compare whether element at current node is 37. The answer is no. Now since 37 < 50 we move to the left side.

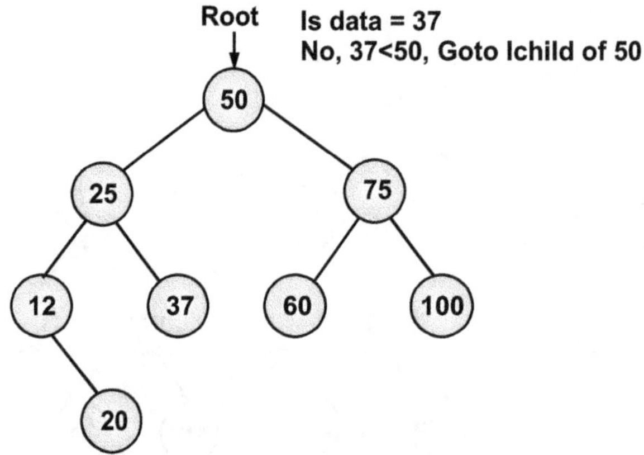

Fig. 3.42 (a) : Search operation

Step 2 :

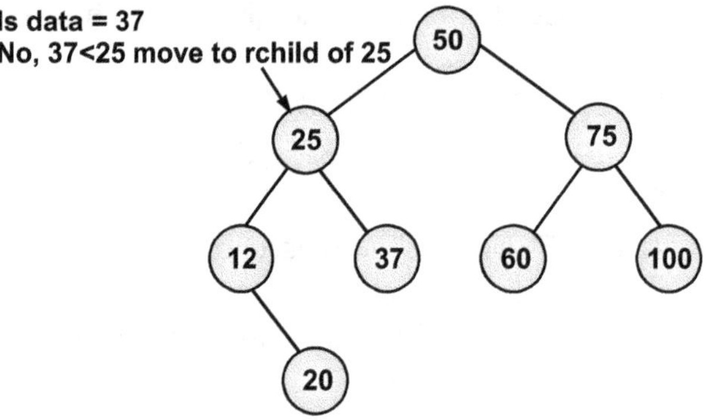

Fig. 3.42 (b) : Search operation

Step 3 :

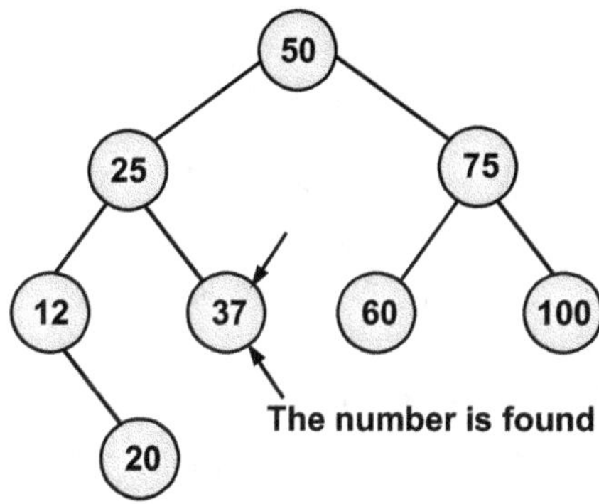

Fig. 3.42 (c) : Search operation

If the number to be searched is not there in the BST, we will reach the end of BST (i.e. Leaf node).

There are various operations that can be performed on BST viz., create, search and traverse.

Let us write the algorithms for various operations on BST.

3.5.1 Creating BST

1.   Read n {Number of elements}

2.   root=Null

3.   Repeat Steps 4 to 2 n times.

4.   Read x

5.   Create a node ptr

6.   ptr->data=x

7.   ptr->lchild=ptr->rchild=Null

8.   temp = root

9.   if (temp==NULL) root=ptr

10. while (temp!=NULL)

      {

         prev=temp;

         if (temp->data>x)

            temp=temp->lchild; flag=1;

         else

            temp= temp->rchild; flag=0;

```
        }
    if (flag==1)
        prev->lchild = ptr;
    else
        prev->rchild=ptr;
```

Explanation :

- n is number of elements to be stored in BST.

- The root pointer points to root node which is initially null.

- Every time we accept the data, we create a new node ptr, store the data in it and this node is to be placed in the BST.

- When first node is created, it will be pointed by root.

- Whenever a new node is created we start from root node and find a position for this node in BST. For this we compare the element in the tree with current element and move to right or left side. Before we move, pointer prev is kept behind so that we can connect new node to the current node, in case its lchild or rchild becomes null.

- The movement of pointer temp before it becomes null gives location where new node is to be inserted. It is tracked with the help of flag.

3.5.2 Searching in BST

```
1.  Read s
2.  temp=root
3.  while (temp!=NULL)
    {
        if (temp->data ==s)
        {
            printf("Found");
            break;
        }
        if (temp->data>s)
            temp=temp->lchild
        if (temp->data <s)
            temp=temp->rchild
    }
```

```
4.  if (temp==NULL)
        printf("Not found");
```

Explanation :

- The element to be searched is s.

- We start from the root and move into the tree either on left or right side depending on data at current node.

- If we find the data at a particular node, we exit.

- If we don't find the data, temp will finally become null.

3.5.3 Tree Traversal Operations

We can use recursive functions as :

```
Inorder (temp)
1.  {
2.      if(temp!=NULL)
        {
3.          inorder (temp- >lchild)
4.          print temp->data
5.          inorder (temp->rchild).
        }
    }
```

Explanation :

Let us take a BST as shown in Fig. 3.43 for this.

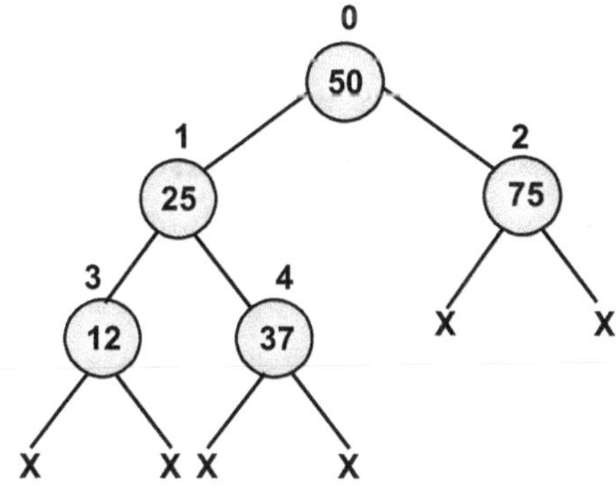

Fig. 3.43 : Binary search tree

Let 0, 1, 2, 3, 4 be the addresses of there nodes.

The function will be called as inorder (root)

The function gets address of root which is assumed to be 0. Temp is assigned this address. The following table shows how the function gets called recursively. Follow the numbered lines in that sequence.

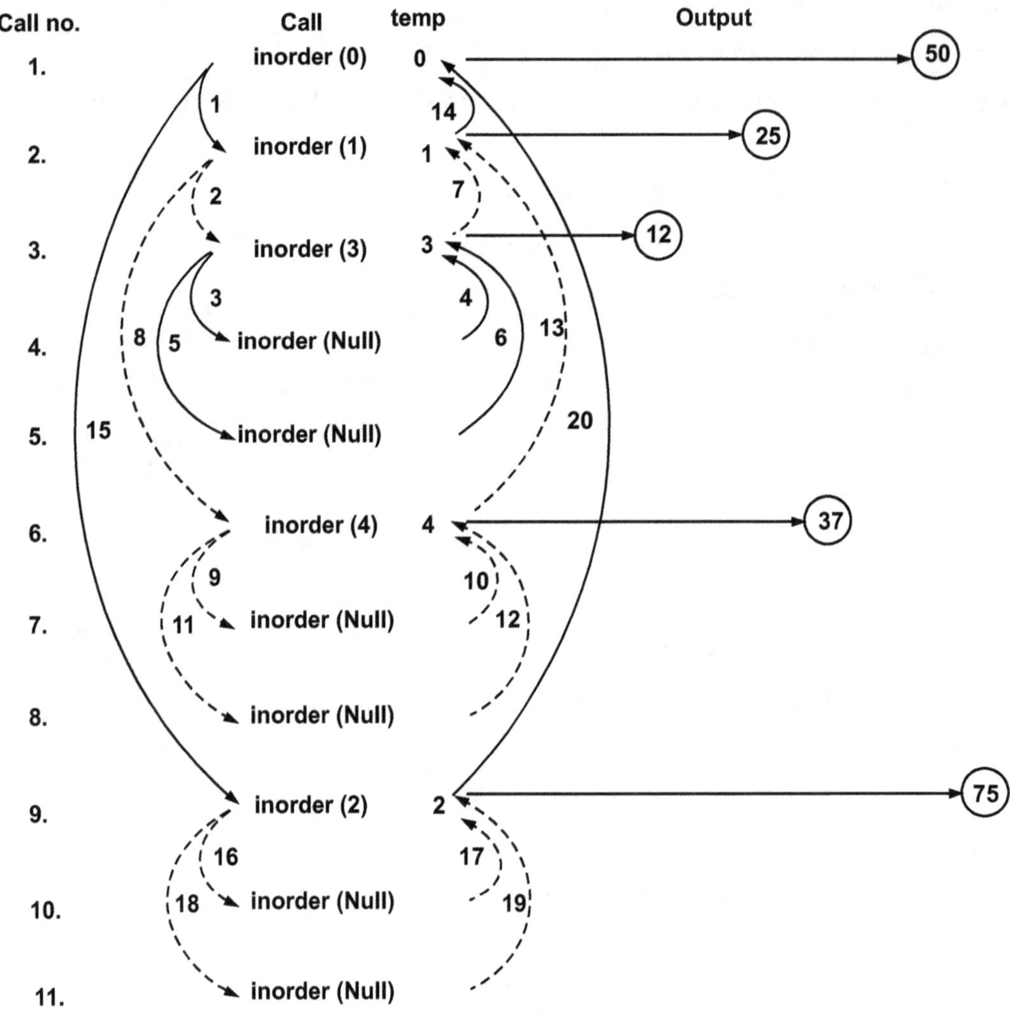

Fig. 3.44 : Recursive inorder traversal function trace

The other two traversal functions are as follows :

```
preorder (temp)
{
    if (temp!=Null)
    {
        print temp->data
        preorder(temp->lchild);
```

```
            preorder(temp->rchild);
        }
    }
    postorder (temp)
    {
        if(temp!=Null)
        {
            postorder(temp->lchild);
            postorder(temp->rchild);
            print temp->data;
        }
    }
```

3.5.4 Delete Operation

Deleting a node in BST is a complex operation because we need to readjust the nodes in the tree. There are four different situations in the BST for deleting a node. They are,

- The node to be deleted is leaf node.

- The node has right child only.

- The node has left child only.

- The node has both children.

Let us find out how to deal with these four cases with example

Case 1 :

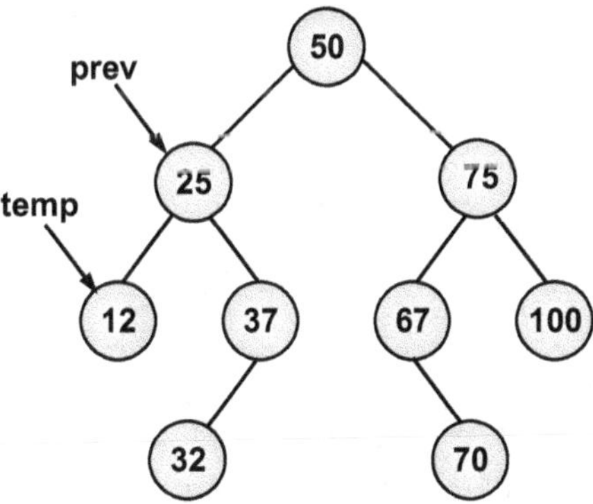

Fig. 3.45 (a) : Delete operation leaf node

Suppose, the node to be deleted is 12, we need two pointers one at 12 (temp) other at its parent node i.e. 25 (prev). We need to check whether the node to be deleted (temp) is connected to *l*child or rchild of prev.

if   prev->*l*child=temp make prev-*l*child=Null

if   prev->rchild=temp make prev->rchild=Null

and then free (temp)

Case 2 :

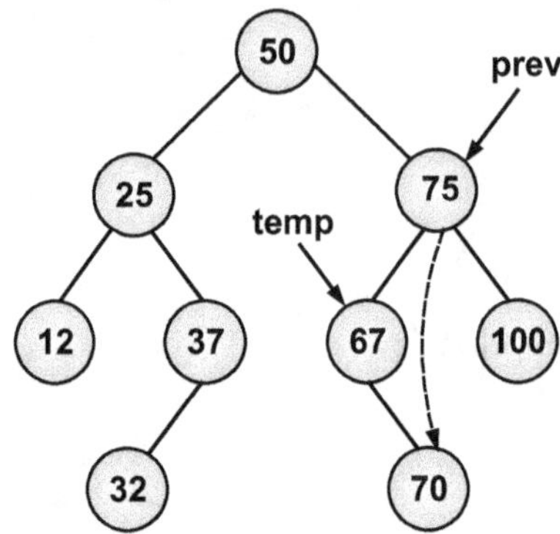

Fig. 3.45 (b) : Delete operation node with rchild

Suppose, the node to be deleted has right child as shown in Fig. 3.45 (b). In this case, since 67 is to be deleted, its successor 70 is to be made *l*child of its parent i.e. 75. The node to be deleted might be right child of its parent or left child. Hence, we must determine this first. The code will be :

```
if (temp->rchild != NULL &&temp->lchild == NULL)
{
    if(prev-lchild==temp)
        prev-lchild=temp->rchild
    else
        prev->rchild=temp->rchild;
}
```

Case 3 :

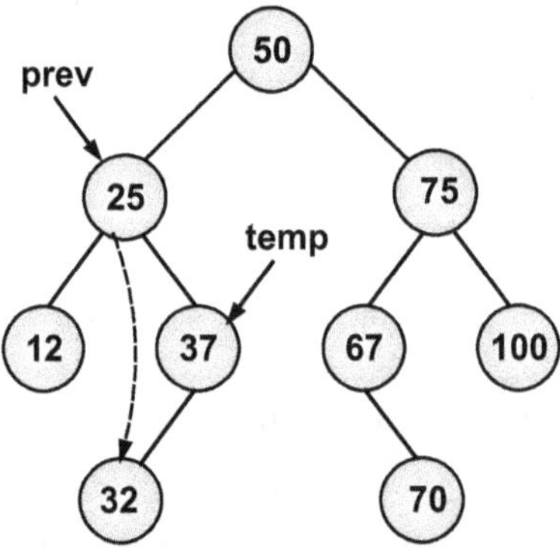

Fig. 3.45 (c) : Delete operation node with *l*child

If the node to be deleted has left child as shown in Fig. 3.45 (c). If 37 is deleted, its successor should be made right child of 25. We can have the node to be deleted as right or left child of its parent node. Hence, we will have two options :

```
if (temp->rchild==NULL &&temp->lchild!=NULL)
{
    if (prev->lchild==temp)
        prev->lchild=temp->lchild;
    else
        prev->rchild=temp->lchild;
}
```

Case 4 : The node to be deleted has both children as shown in Fig. 3.45(d).

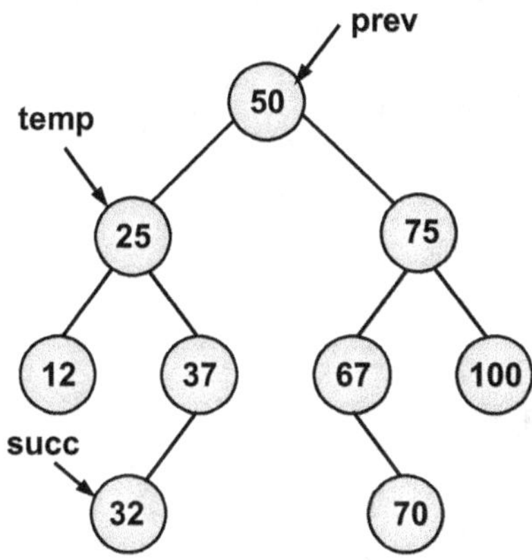

Fig. 3.45 (d) : Delete operation node with *lchild* and *rchild*

Let us say we want to delete 25. The inorder successor of 25 is 32. We can copy 32 in place of 25 and delete 32. Hence, the process is to find inorder successor of the node. Copy the successor in its place and delete the inorder successor node.

```
if (temp->lchild!=NULL, &&temp->rchild!=NULL)
{
    succ= temp;
    x=temp->rchild;
    while(x!=NULL)
    {
        prev=succ;
        succ=x;
```

```
        x=x->lchild;
    }
    temp->data=succ->data;
    temp=succ;
}
```

This will copy the value of inorder, successor into the node to be deleted. Now, that we have a pointer temp to the inorder successor node and prev to its parent node, this node will fall into one of the 3 cases considered earlier. If we write the cases after this case, automatically one of them will get executed and the node will be deleted.

3.5.5 Insert Operation

If new data is to be inserted in already existing BST, the position for this new data must be located. It will be inserted as a leaf node in the BST. The algorithm will be as follows :

1. Read x (Data to be added)
2. Create a new node ptr and store the data in it
3. temp=root
4. while(temp!=NULL)
   ```
   {   prev=temp;
       if(temp->data>x)
           temp=temp->lchild; flag=1;
       else
           temp=temp->rchild; flag=0;
   }
   ```
5. if (flag==1)
   ```
       prev->lchild=ptr;
   else
       prev->rchild=ptr;
   ```

Explanation :
- The new data to be inserted is accepted and stored into a new node ptr.
- Start from root node till you go bottom of tree. Compare at each node and move to left or right. Before you move to left or right keep a pointer prev to previous node so that if you fall into null, you have a pointer to the node on whose left or right side new node is to be attached. The decision of whether the new node will be attached to right or left will be made from the value of flag.

Now let us write a menu driven program to implement all these operations.

The functions that we are going to write are,

(i)	Create	: Creates a binary search tree and returns address of root node,
(ii)	Search	: Searches an element in BST.
(iii)	Inorder	: Display inorder traversal.
(iv)	Preorder	: Display preorder traversal.
(v)	Postorder	: Display postorder traversal.
(vi)	Delete	: Deletes a node.
(vii)	insert	: Inserts a new node.

Program 3.1 : To create and implement binary search tree.

```c
#include <stdio.h>
#include <conio.h>
typedef struct node
{
    int data;
    struct node *lchild,*rchild;
}NODE;
NODE*create( );
int search (NODE*, int);
void inorder (NODE*);
void preorder (NODE*);
void postorder (NODE*);
NODE*del(NODE*);
NODE* insert (NODE*);
void main( )
{
    int ch, s;
    NODE*root=NULL;
    do
    {
        clrscr( );
        printf("1.Create \n 2.Search \n 3.Inorder \n 4.Preorder \n 5.Postorder \n
        6.Delete \n 7.Insert \n8.Exit \n");
```

```c
        printf("Enter your choice \n");
        scanf("%d", &ch);
        switch(ch)
        {
            case 1  :  root=create( );
                       break;
            case 2  :  printf("Enter number to be searched \n");
                       scanf("%d", &s);
                       search(root, s)
                       break;
            case 3  :  inorder(root);
                       break;
            case 4  :  preorder(root);
                       break;
            case 5  :  postorder(root);
                       break;
            case 6  :  root=del(root);
                       break;
            case 7  :  root=insert(root);
                       break;
        }
        getch();
    }while(ch!=8);
}
NODE *create( )
{
    int x, i, n, flag;
    NODE *root, *ptr, *temp, *prev;
    root=NULL;
    printf("How many elements? \n");
    scanf("%d", &n);
```

```c
for(i=1;i<=n;i++)
{
    printf("Enter the number");
    scanf("%d", &x);
    ptr=(NODE*)malloc(sizeof(NODE));
    ptr->data=x;
    ptr->rchild=ptr->lchild=NULL;
    if (root==NULL)
        root=ptr;
    else
    {
        temp=root;
        while (temp!=NULL)
        {
            prev=temp;
            if (temp->data>x)
            {
                temp=temp->lchild;
                flag=1;
            }
            else
            {
                temp=temp->rchild;
                flag=0;
            }
        }
        if (flag==1)
            prev->lchild=ptr;
        else
            prev->rchild=ptr;
```

```c
        }
    }
    return (root);
}
int search (NODE *root, int x)
{
    NODE *temp;
    temp=root;
    while (temp!=NULL && temp->data!=x)
    {
        if(temp->data>x)
            temp=temp->lchild;
        else
            temp=temp->rchild;
    }
    if (temp!= NULL)
        return (1);
    else
        return (0);
}
void inorder (NODE *temp)
{
    if (temp!= NULL)
    {
        inorder (temp->lchild);
        printf("%d \n", temp->data);
        inorder(temp->rchild);
    }
}
void preorder (NODE *temp)
```

```c
{
    if (temp!=NULL)
    {
        printf("%d \n", temp->data);
        preorder(temp->lchild);
        preorder(temp->rchild);
    }
}
void postorder (NODE *temp)
{
    if (temp!=NULL)
    {
        postorder(temp->lchild);
        postorder(temp->rchild);
        printf("%d \n", temp->data);
    }
}
NODE *del(NODE*root)
{
    NODE *temp, *prev, *x, *succ;
    int s;
    printf("Enter data to be deleted \n");
    scanf("%d", &s);
    temp=root;
    prev=temp;
    while(temp!=NULL)
    {
        if (temp->data==s)
            break;
        prev=temp;
```

```
        if(temp->data>s)
            temp=temp->lchild;
        else
            temp=temp->rchild;
}
if(temp==NULL)
{
    printf("Not in the BST \n");
    exit(0);
}
if(temp->lchild!=NULL &&temp->rchild!=NULL)
{
    succ=temp;
    x=temp->rchild;
    while(x!=NULL)
    {
        prev=succ;
        succ=x;
        x=x-Achild;
    }
    temp->data=succ->data;
    temp=succ;
}
if(temp->rchild== NULL & temp->lchild!=NULL)
{
    if(prev->lchild == temp)
        prev->rchild=temp->lchild;
    else
        prev->rchild=temp->lchild;
}
```

```c
        if(temp->rchild!=NULL &&temp->lchild==NULL)
        {
            if(prev->lchild==temp)
                prev->lchild=temp->rchild;
            else
                prev->rchild=temp->rchild;
        }
        if(temp->lchild == NULL &&temp->rchild == NULL)
        {
            if(prev->lchild==temp)
                prev->lchild=NULL;
            else
                prev->rchild=NULL;
        }
        free(temp);
        return(root);
}
NODE *insert(NODE *root)
{
    NODE *temp, *prev, *ptr;
    int x, flag;
    printf("Enter data to be inserted \n");
    scanf("%d", &x);
    ptr =(NODE*)malloc(sizeof(NODE));
    ptr->data=x;
    ptr->lchild=ptr->rchild=NULL;
    temp=root;
    while (temp!=NULL)
    {
        prev=temp;
```

```
            if(temp->data>x)
            {
                    temp=temp->lchild;
                    flag=1;
            }
            else
            {
                    temp=temp->rchild;
                    flag=0;
            }
    }
    if(root==NULL)
        root=ptr;
    else
    {
    if(flag==1)
        prev->lchild=ptr;
    else
        prev->rchild=ptr;
    }
    return (root);
}
```

3.6 OPERATIONS ON BINARY TREE

We have seen Binary search tree and operations on it. The BST was relatively easy to implement along with the operations such as create, insert, delete traversals, etc. It was because of the relation that exists among the elements in BST. Now, if you are given a binary tree and asked to create it as it is, you have to ask the user to manually enter the data and their positions in the tree. The operators that we can have on this tree are insert, traversals (all three). The algorithms of these operations are as follows.

3.6.1 Creating a Binary Tree

```
1.  Read n
2.  root=Null
3.  for (i=1;i<=n;i++)
    {
4.      Read x
        //Create a new node ptr
        //store x in ptr->data
5.      if(root==NULL)
            root=ptr;
        else
        {
6.          temp=root;
7.          while(temp!=NULL)
            {
                prev=temp;
                //read side
                if(side=='l')
                    temp=temp->lchild;
                else
                    temp=temp->rchild;
            }
8.          if(side=='l')
                prev->child=ptr;
            else
            prev->rchild=ptr;
        }
    }
9.  Stop
```

Explanation :

- Read number of nodes (n) in the tree.

- root=NULL.

- Repeat for each element the following process.

- Read data and store it in a node ptr.

- If it is first node let it be pointed by root.

- If it is not first node, start from root node and traverse in the tree every time asking the user about which side of current node the new node is to be added.

- When temp becomes NULL, prev will be at a node in the tree on whose left or right side new node is to be inserted. Insert the node accordingly.

3.6.2 Traversal Operation

The inorder, preorder and postorder traversals can be implemented in the same way as discussed in BST.

3.6.3 Insert Operation

It will be similar to create operation except that the process is to be carried out only once.

Program 3.2 : To implement a binary tree.

```c
typedef struct node
{
    int data;
    struct node *lchild, *rchild;
} NODE;
NODE *create( );
void     inorder(NODE*);
void     preorder (NODE*);
void     postorder(NODE*);
NODE *insert(NODE*);
void main( )
{
    int ch;
    NODE *root;
    root=NULL;
```

```c
    do
    {
        printf("1.Create \n2. Inorder W. preorder \n4. Postorder \n5. Insert \n6.
        Exit \n");
        printf("Enter your choice \n");
        scanf("%d", &ch);
        switch(ch)
        {
            case 1  : root=create( );
                        break;
            case 2  : inorder(root);
                        break
            case 3  : preorder(root);
                        break;
            case 4  : postorder(root);
                        break;
            case 5  : root=insert(root);
        }
        getch( );
    } while(ch!=6);
}
NODE *create( )
{
    NODE *ptr, *temp, *prev;
    int x; n, i;
    char ch;
    printf("Enter number of nodes \n");
    scanf("%d",&n);
    root=NULL;
    for(i=1;i<=n;i++)
    {
```

```c
            printf("Enter data \n");
            scanf("%d", &x);
            ptr=(NODE*) malloc(sizeof (NODE));
            ptr->lchild=ptr->rchild=NULL;
            if(root == NULL)
                root=ptr;
            else
            {
                temp=root;
                while(temp!=NULL)
                {   prev=temp;
                    printf("which side of %d? (l/r) \n", temp->data);
                    ch=getch( );
                    if(ch=='l' || ch=='L')
                        temp=temp->lchild;
                    else
                        temp=temp->rchild;
                }
                if(ch=='l' || ch=='L')
                    prev->lchild=ptr;
                else
                    prev->rchild=ptr;
            }
        }
    return (root);
}
void inorder(NODE*root)
{   NODE *temp;
    temp=root;
    if (temp!=NULL)
```

```c
    {
        inorder(temp->lchild);
        printf("%d \n", temp->data);
        inorder(temp->rchild);
    }
}
void preorder(NODE*root)
{   NODE *temp;
    temp=root;
    if (temp!=NULL)
    {
        printf("%d \n", temp->data);
        preorder(temp->lchild);
        preorder(temp->rchild);
    }
}
void postorder(NODE*root)
{
    NODE*temp;
    temp=root;
        if(temp!=NULL)
        {
            postorder(temp->lchild);
            postorder(temp->rchild);
            printf("%d \n", temp->data);
        }
}
NODE *insert(NODE*root)
{
```

```c
    NODE *temp,*ptr, *prev;
    int x;
    char ch;
    printf("Enter data \n");
    scanf("%d", &x);
    ptr=(NODE*)malloc(sizeof(NODE));
    ptr->data=x;
    ptr->child=ptr->rchild=NULL;
    if (root==NULL)
        root=ptr;
    else
    {
        temp=root;
        while(temp!=NULL)
        {
            printf("which side of %d (l/r) \n", temp->data);
            ch=getch( );
            if(ch=='l' || ch=='L')
                temp=temp->lchild;
            else
                temp=temp->rchild;
        }
        if(ch=='l' || ch=='L')
            prev->lchild=ptr;
        else
            prev->rchild=ptr;
    }
    return(root);
}
```

3.6.4 Binary Tree as an ADT

The Binary Tree is a more general ADT than the linear list: it allows one item to have two immediate successors

ADT Binary Tree is a finite set of nodes which is either empty or consists of a data item (called the root) and two disjoint binary trees (called the left and right subtrees of the root), together with a number of access procedures.

Nodes with no successors are called leaves. The roots of the left and right subtrees of a node "i" are called the "children of i"; the node i is their parent; they are siblings. A child has one parent. A parent has at most two children.

The data organizations presented so far are linear in that items are one after another. The Binary Tree is a more general form of ADT, in which data are organized in a non linear, hierarchical form whereby one item can have more than one immediate successor.

A Binary Tree is a "position-oriented" ADT, as lists, stacks, queues. However, since it is not linear as the ADT lists we have seen so far, we will not reference items in a binary tree by using a position number. The Binary Search Tree is a value-oriented ADT whose elements are organized on the basis of their values.

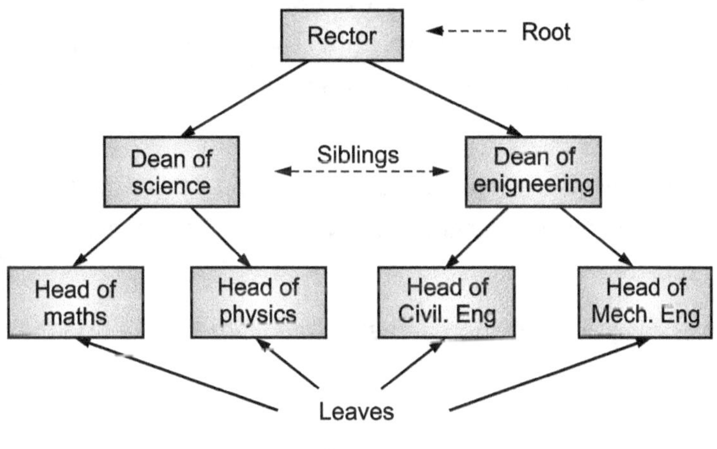

Fig. 3.46

All trees are hierarchical in nature. Intuitively, hierarchical means that a "parent-child" relationship exists between the nodes in the tree. If there is a link between a node "n" and a node "m", and "n" is above node "m" in the tree, then "n" is the parent of "m", and node "m" is a child of "n". Children of the same parent are called siblings. Each node in a tree has at most one parent, and exactly one node, called the root of the tree, has no parent. A node that has no children is called a leaf of the tree.

The parent-child relationship between the nodes can be generalised to the relationships "ancestor" and "descendant". The root of a tree is an ancestor of every node in the tree. A subtree in a tree is any node in the tree together with all its descendants. A subtree of a node r is a subtree rooted at a child of the node r. To give a formal definition of what a tree is, we say that a binary tree is a set of node which is either empty, or is partitioned into three disjoint subsets: (i) a single node "r", the root; and (ii) two (possibly empty) sets that are binary trees, called the left and the right subtrees of r. Each node in a binary tree has therefore no more than two children.

3.6.5 Recursive and Non Recursive Algorithms for Binary Tree Traversals

Once a binary tree is created the major operation that we will be required to do will be traversal of the tree. Traversing a tree means, visiting each node in the tree exactly once.

Traversal is a process to visit all the nodes of a tree and may print their values too. Because, all nodes are connected via edges (links) we always start from the root (head) node. That is, we cannot randomly access a node in a tree.

While traversing a binary tree, if we are at-a particular node there are six different ways in which we can move. They **LVR**, **VLR**, **LRV**, **RVL**, **VRL** and **RLV**. Where **V** is visit the node or access data, **L** move to left and **R**-move to right. There is a standard conversation that we should move to left first before right. Hence, there are only three standard traversals **LVR**, **VLR** and **LRV**.

LVR is called in order traversal where left sub-tree is processed first then root and finally right sub-tree. **VLR** is called preorder traversal where root is processed first followed by left sub-tree the right sub-tree.

LRV is called post order traversal where left sub-tree is processed first then right and finally root node.

Let us consider a binary tree.

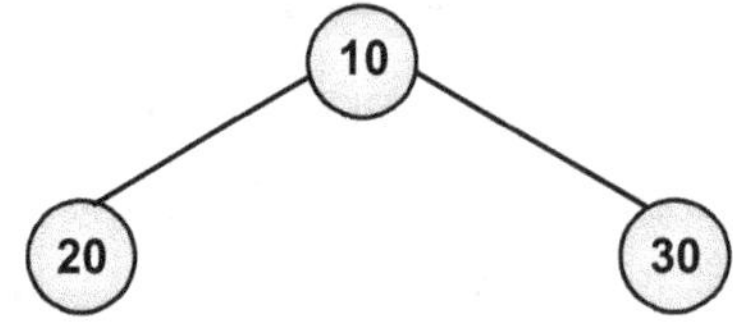

Fig. 3.47: Binary tree

Inorder traversal for Fig. 3.47, is shown in Fig. 3.48.

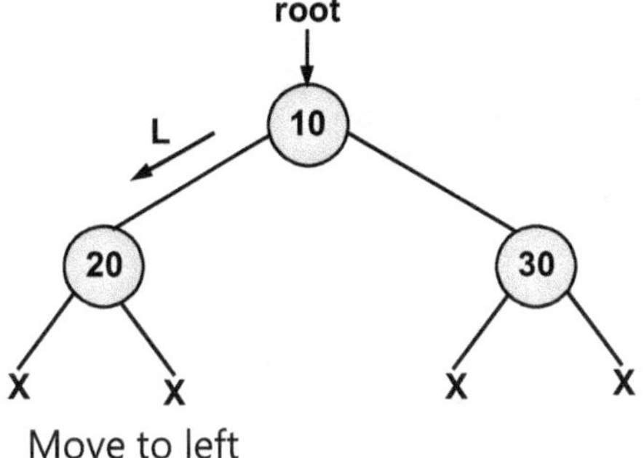

Move to left

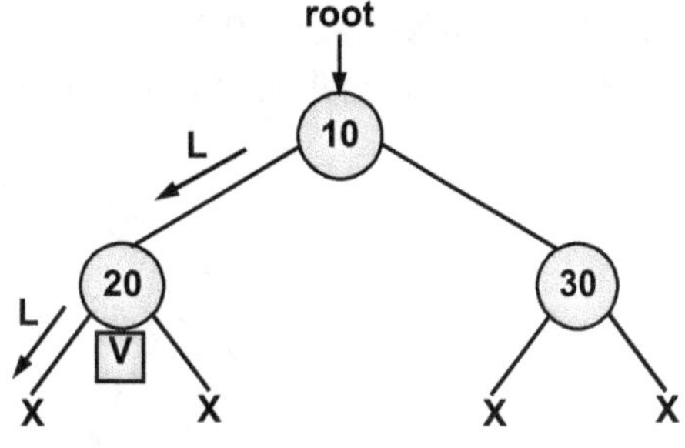

Move to left

left sub-tree of 20 is Null

Hence, visit node 20

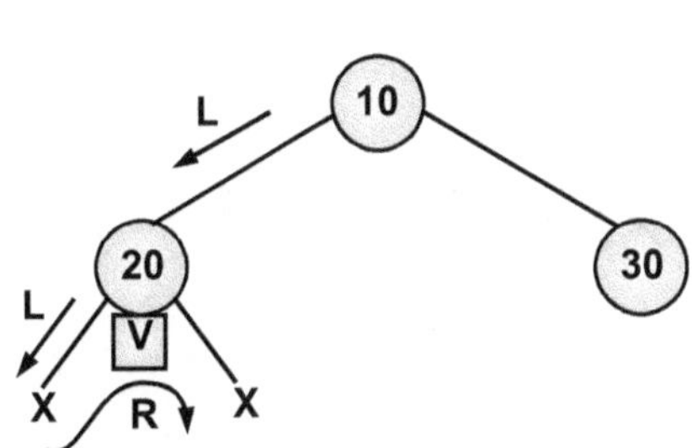

Move to right

Right sub-tree of 20 is Null

LVR for 20 is order

Go back to previous node

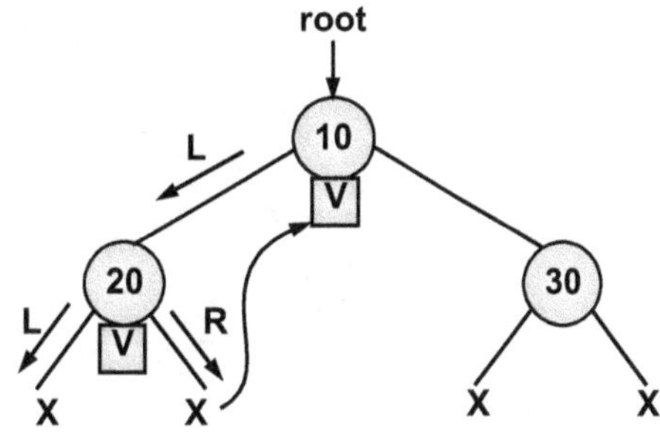

Left sub-tree of 10 is over

Visit the node 10

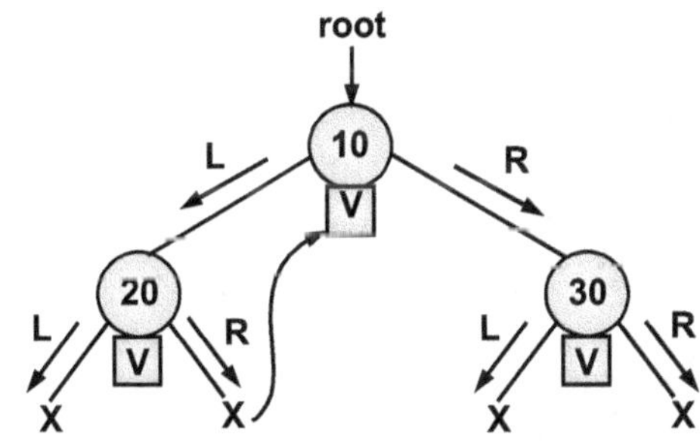

Move to right

Move to left, it is NULL

Visit 30

Move to right, it is Null

LVR for 30 is over, Go back to 30

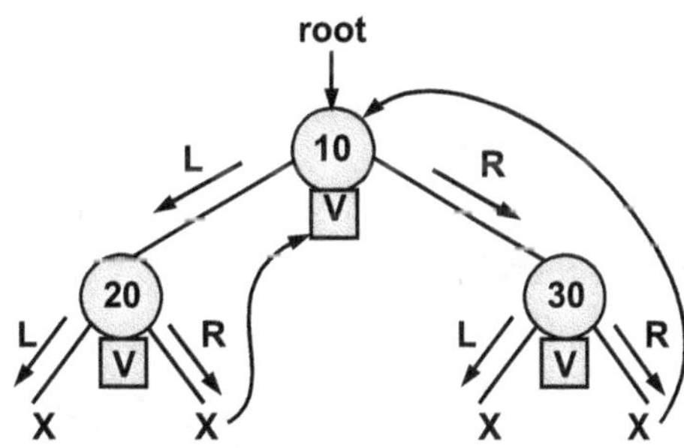

Go back to root

LVR for 10 is over

Fig. 3.48: Inorder traversal of binary tree

Hence, inorder traversal is 20 10 30.

Similarly, preorder traversal will be as shown in Fig. 3.49.

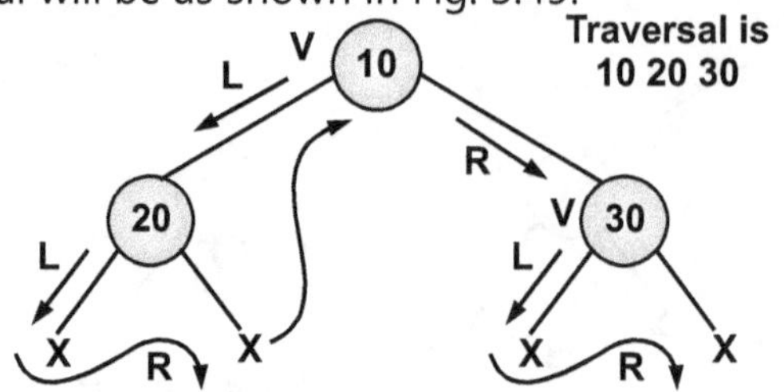

Fig. 3.49: Preorder traversal

Postorder traversal will be as shown in Fig. 3.50.

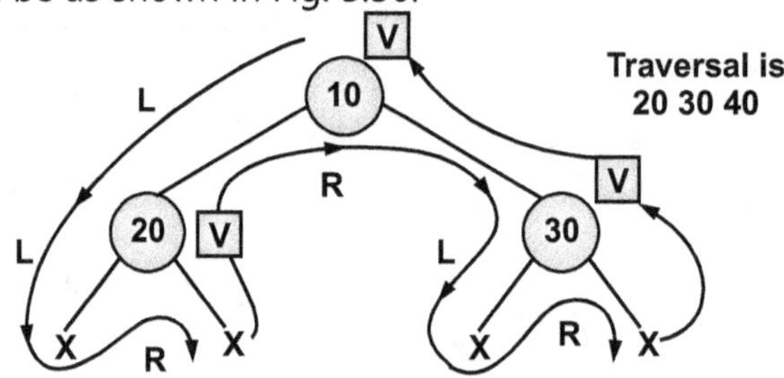

Fig. 3.50: Postorder traversal

Let us consider another example.

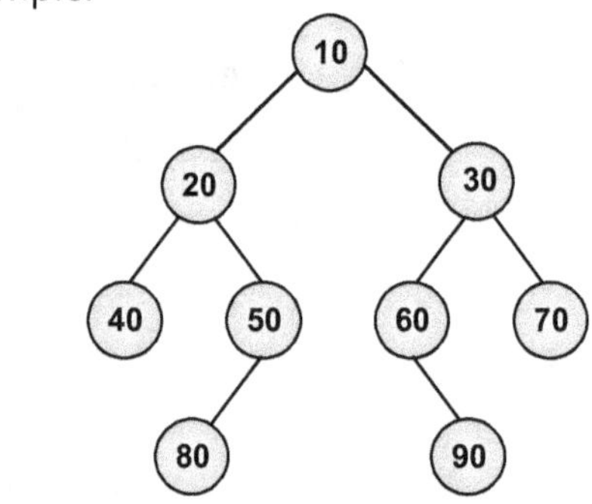

Fig. 3.51: Inorder traversal

Inorder Traversal :

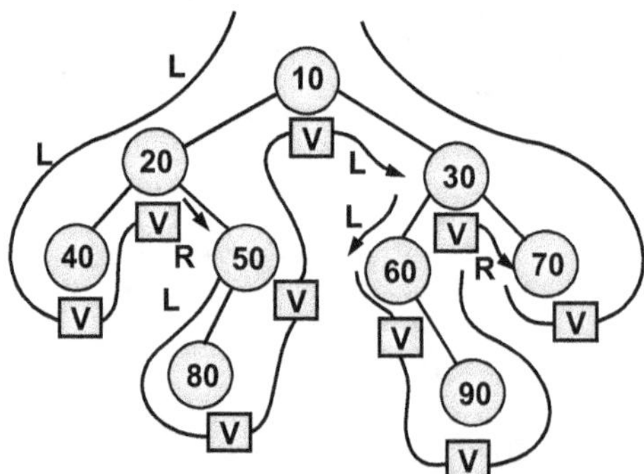

Fig. 3.52: Inorder traversal

Traversal is 40 20 80 50 10 60 90 30 70.

Preorder Traversal:

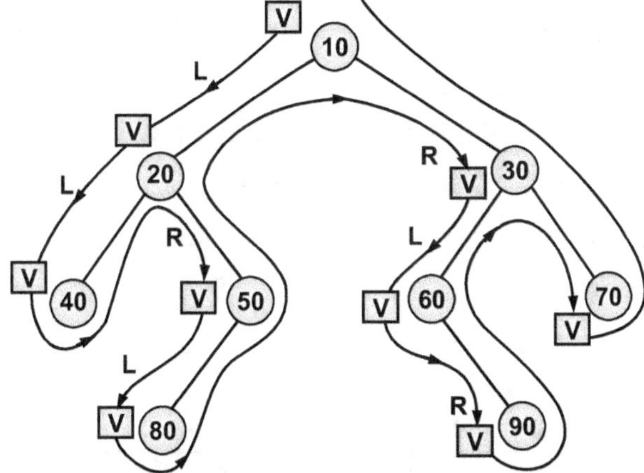

Fig. 3.53: Preorder traversal

Traversal is 10 20 40 50 80 30 60 90 70

Postorder Traversal:

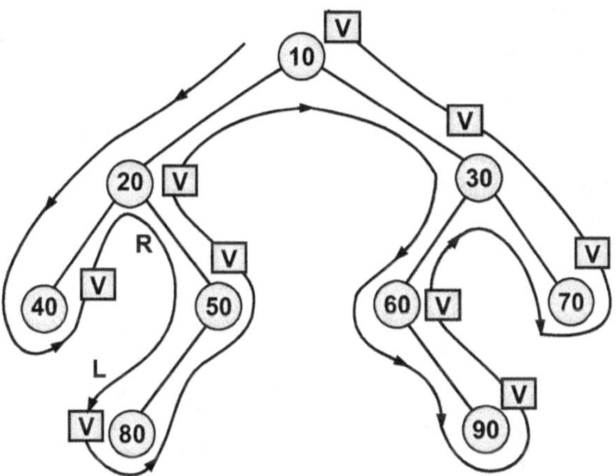

Fig. 3.54: Postorder traversal

Traversal is 40 80 50 20 90 60 70 30 10

Observation:

- In inorder traversal, the root element is in between the left sub-tree and right sub-tree.
- In preorder traversal, root element is at the beginning.
- In postorder traversal, root element will be at the end.
- If we are given any two traversals of a tree we can draw the tree diagram.

Example: Let us take up the same traversals of Figs. 3.21 and 3.22.

    Inorder: 40 20 80 50 10 60 90 30 70

    Preorder: 10 20 40 50 80 30 60 90 70

Step 1: From preorder, we find that root is 10. Hence the right and left sub-tree elements will be as shown in Fig. 3.55 (a).

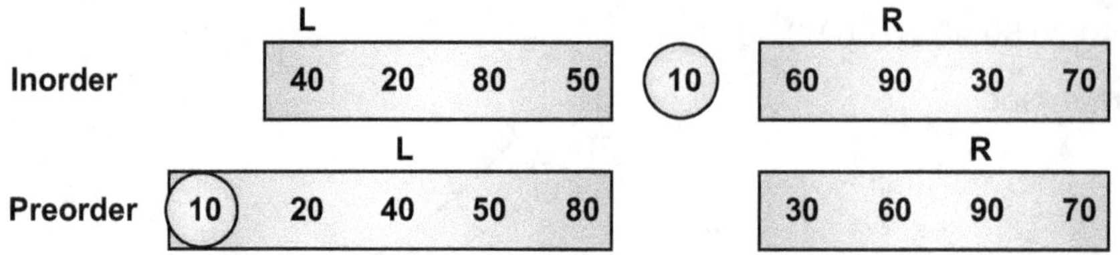

Fig. 3.55 (a): Binary tree from traversal

Step 2: Left sub-tree has root 20 (first element of pre-order).

Right sub-tree has root 30 (first element of pre-order).

Hence, the division will be as shown in Fig. 3.55 (b).

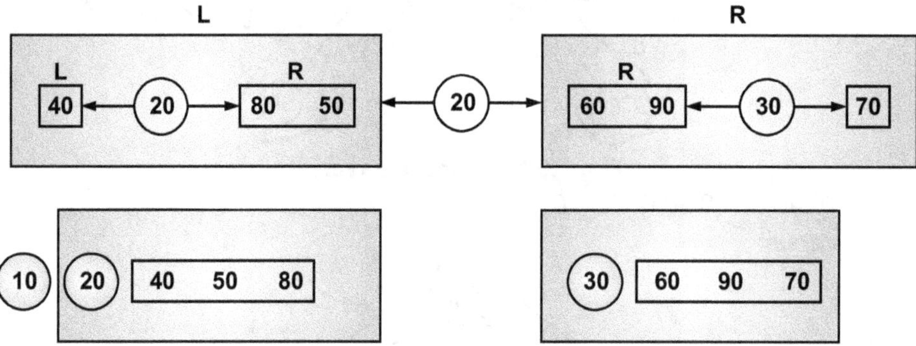

Fig. 3.55 (b): Binary tree from traversal

Step 3: Continuing on the same lines.

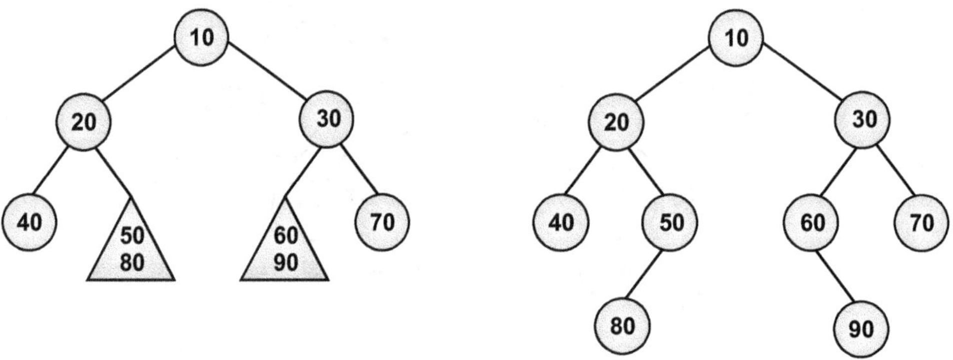

Fig. 3.55 (c): Binary tree from traversal

There are three ways which we use to traverse a tree –

In-order Traversal

Pre-order Traversal

Post-order Traversal

Generally, we traverse a tree to search or locate a given item or key in the tree or to print all the values it contains.

In-order Traversal

In this traversal method, the left subtree is visited first, then the root and later the right sub-tree. We should always remember that every node may represent a subtree itself.

If a binary tree is traversed in-order, the output will produce sorted key values in an ascending order.

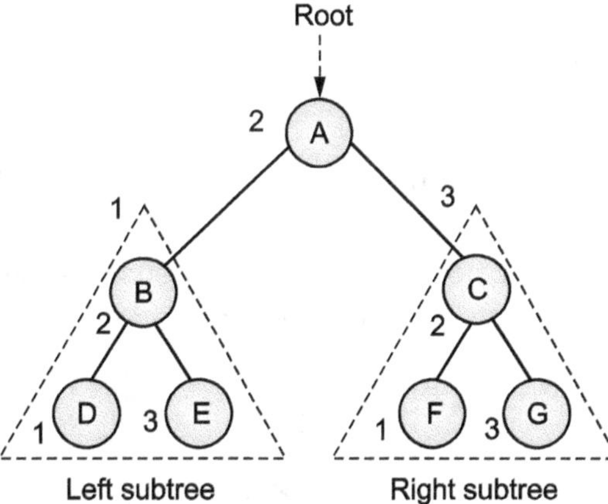

Fig. 3.56

We start from A, and following in-order traversal, we move to its left subtree B. B is also traversed in-order. The process goes on until all the nodes are visited. The output of inorder traversal of this tree will be –

$$D \rightarrow B \rightarrow E \rightarrow A \rightarrow F \rightarrow C \rightarrow G$$

Algorithm :

Until all nodes are traversed :

Step 1 – Recursively traverse left subtree.

Step 2 – Visit root node.

Step 3 – Recursively traverse right subtree.

Pre-order Traversal

In this traversal method, the root node is visited first, then the left subtree and finally the right subtree.

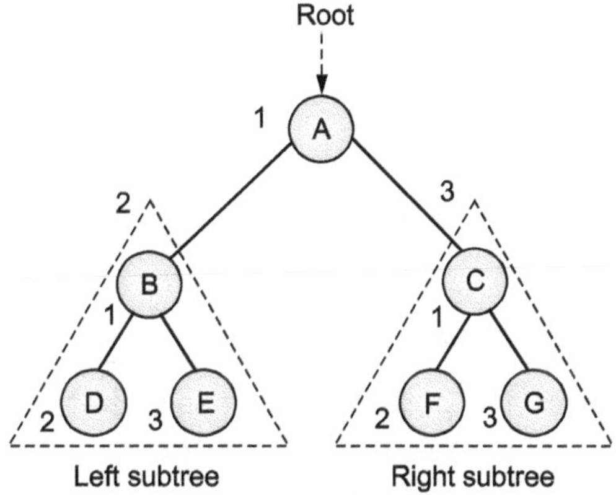

Fig. 3.57

We start from A, and following pre-order traversal, we first visit A itself and then move to its left subtree B. B is also traversed pre-order. The process goes on until all the nodes are visited. The output of pre-order traversal of this tree will be –

$$A \rightarrow B \rightarrow D \rightarrow E \rightarrow C \rightarrow F \rightarrow G$$

Algorithm :

Until all nodes are traversed :

Step 1 – Visit root node.

Step 2 – Recursively traverse left subtree.

Step 3 – Recursively traverse right subtree.

Post-order Traversal :

In this traversal method, the root node is visited last, hence the name. First we traverse the left subtree, then the right subtree and finally the root node.

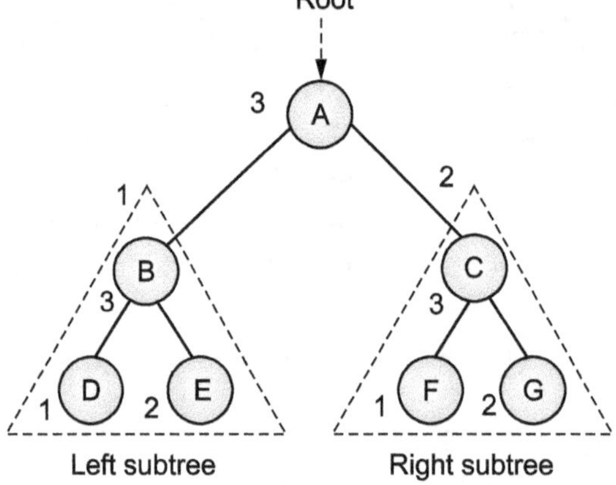

Fig. 3.58

We start from A, and following pre-order traversal, we first visit the left subtree B. B is also traversed post-order. The process goes on until all the nodes are visited. The output of post-order traversal of this tree will be –

$$D \rightarrow E \rightarrow B \rightarrow F \rightarrow G \rightarrow C \rightarrow A$$

Algorithm :

Until all nodes are traversed –

Step 1 – Recursively traverse left subtree.

Step 2 – Recursively traverse right subtree.

Step 3 – Visit root node.

3.6.6 Non-Recursive Traversal

The recursive inorder, preorder and postorder traversals use the program's recursion stack. The recursion can be removed by implementing user defined stack. Let us see, how we can write inorder and preorder traversals using stack.

1. Inorder Traversal

Algorithm 3.1 : Inorder traversal

```
1.  temp=root;
2.  do
    {
        while(temp!=NULL)
        {
            push(temp);
            temp=temp->lchild;
        }
            temp=pop( );
            print temp->data;
            temp=temp->rchild;
    }while(stack is not empty OR temp!=NULL);
3.  Stop.
```

Explanation :

- Start with root node.
- Traverse on left side while storing the address of each node on stack.
- Pop the address of a node from stack (it will be left most node). Display the data.
- Move to right side.
- Repeat above steps till all nodes are traversed.
- The stack will be stack of pointers as it has to store addresses of nodes.

Consider a binary tree as :

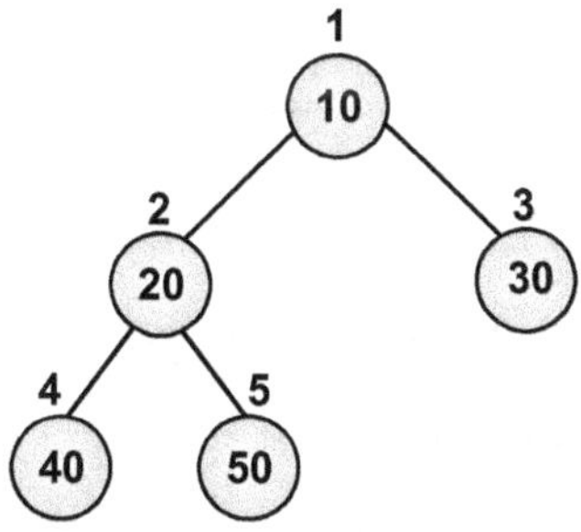

Fig. 3.59 (a) : Binary tree

Let 1, 2, 3, 4, 5, be the addresses of the nodes.

- We start with root node and move to left pushing every time address of node on the stack. At the end of inner while, the stack will be,

Fig. 3.59 (b) : Stack contents for non-recursive inorder traversal

- temp=pop( ) will pop node 4.

    data at node 4 i.e. 40 will be displayed.

- temp will be Null as rchild of 4 is Null.

    Since temp is NULL, 2 is poped.

    Data at 2 i.e. 20 is displayed.

    temp will move to rchild of 2.

    Hence, 5 will be pushed and stack will be

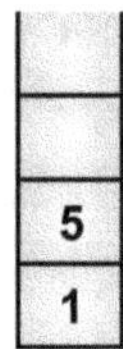

Fig. 3.59 (c) : Stack contents for non-recursive inorder traversal

- 5 is popped and data at 5 is displayed i.e. 50.

    Since temp is NULL,

    1 is popped and data 1 is displayed i.e. 2.

    temp will move to rchild 3.

    3 is pushed and stack will be,

Fig. 3.59 (d) : Stack contents for non-recursive inorder traversal

3 is popped. Data at 3. i.e. 30 displayed.

stack becomes empty and temp is null hence the function gets over.

2. Preorder Traversal : For preorder traversal (VLR) we used to make only one change the print statement will be written before left move as follows :

```
1.  temp=root;
2.  do
    {   while(temp!=NULL)
        {
            print temp->data;
            push(temp);
            temp=temp->lchild;
        }
        temp=pop( );
        temp=temp->rchild;
    }   while (stack is not empty OR temp!=NULL)
3.  Stop.
```

3.7 BINARY SEARCH TREE AS AN ADT

The Binary Search Tree is a particular type of binary tree that enables easy searching for specific items.

Definition :

The ADT Binary Search Tree is a binary tree which has an ordering imposed on the nodes, such that for each node:

- All values in the left sub-tree are less than the value in the node;
- All values in the right sub-tree are greater than the value in the node.

Searching for a particular item is an operation for which the ADT binary trees are not well suited. Binary search trees are particular type of binary trees that correct this deficiency by organising its data by value. Each node in a binary search tree satisfies the two properties that

(a) all the nodes in its left sub-tree are less than the value in the node, and (b) all the nodes in the right sub-tree are greater than the value in the node.

Items in a Binary Search Tree often have a special attribute used as search key.

The search key's value uniquely identifies a node in the tree.

For each node n of a binary search tree,

- n's search key is greater than all the search keys in n's left subtree;
- n's search key is less than all the search keys in n's right subtree,
- both the left and right subtrees of n are binary search trees.

Additional operations are insertion, deletion and retrieval of items by the search key's value, and not by position in the tree.

Traversal operations for binary trees are also applicable to binary search trees.

Additional operations are insertion, deletion and retrieval of items by the search key's value, and not by position in the tree.

A binary search tree is often used in situations where the data stored in the tree contain more than one field (attribute). For example, each item in the tree might contain the name of a person, his/her ID number, his/her address, etc. Often one of these fields is used as the sort key among the items in the tree. For instance, the person's ID, which is unique for each person, can be used as the information by which the nodes in the tree are sorted. This information is often called the "search key".

The search task would be, for instance, the operation of searching for a person whose ID number is equal to a given value. Searching is then the operation of finding the particular item in the tree whose key value is equal to the value given as input.

Given this concept of search key, we can say that a binary search tree can be recursively defined as follows. For each node n, n's search key is greater than all the search keys in the n's left subtree; n's search key is less than all the search leys in the n's right subtree,

Both the left and right subtrees of n are binary search trees.

As with all the other ADTs seen so far, a Binary Search Tree has operations that involve inserting, deleting, and retrieving data from a given binary search tree. The main difference compared with what we have seen so far is that in the case of a binary search tree, these operations are done by searching on the key value rather than by its position in the data structure, as we have seen for instance in the case of linked lists.

The operations of insertion, deletion and retrieval of items by their search key values are what extend a basic binary tree into a Binary Search Tree.

Access Procedures for Binary Search Trees :

The Access procedures createEmptyTree( ), isEmpty( ), getRootItem( ), getLeftTree( ), getRightTree( ) for binary trees are unchanged.

Additional access procedures are needed to add items to and delete items from a binary search tree according to their search key's value:

i.   **insert(newItem)**

    // post: insert newItem in a binary search tree, whose nodes have search keys

    // that differ from the newItem's search key.

ii. **delete(searchKey)**

    // post: delete from a binary search tree, the item whose search key equals

    // searchKey. If no such item exists, the operation fails and throws exception.

iii. retrieve(searchKey)

> // post: returns the item in a binary search tree whose search key equal
>
> // searchKey. Returns null if no such item exists.

As it is a binary tree, the binary search tree includes the basic operations for the ADT's binary tree seen in the previous lecture. In particular, the default constructor createEmptyTree( ), the operations isEmpty( ), getRootItem( ), getLeftTree( ), and getRightTree( ) defined for a binary tree are also applicable to binary search trees.

Note that the constructor createTree(root, leftTree, rightTree) cannot be used in the case of binary search trees. We'll say why later on. Similarly the operation of adding a left sub-tree, or adding a right sub-tree cannot be directly used for binary search trees.

But the ADT binary search tree includes additional access procedures, which allow insertion, deletion, retrieval of items from/to a binary search tree by their (search key) values and not by their position (as we have seen so far with ADT likes lists, stacks, queues).

In the remainder of this lecture we will see the implementation of these three new access procedures: insertion, deletion and retrieval. They all make use of an auxiliary method which is search(searchKey) that searches for an item whose search key is equal to searchKey.

Because a binary search tree is a recursive structure, it is natural to formulate the algorithms for these additional operations in a recursive way.

3.8 APPLICATIONS OF TREES

In computer science, trees have number of applications because they are most efficient for searching the data. Hence, they are used to store large databases. Some of the applications are as below.

1. Expression Tree :

The compilers and interpreters evaluate the expression based on the precedence of operators. Any arithmetic expression can be represented using binary tree. The evaluation of the expression becomes convenient with such representation. For example, the expression a + b * c/d can be represented as below :

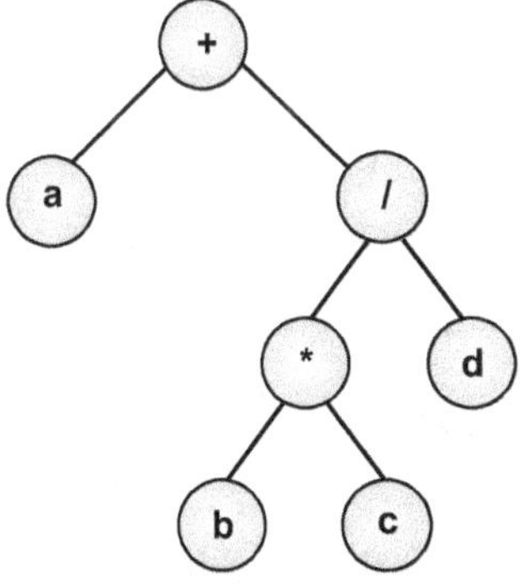

Fig. 3.60 : Expression tree for a + b * c/d

The expression 3 * 4 + (8 + 7) can be represented as

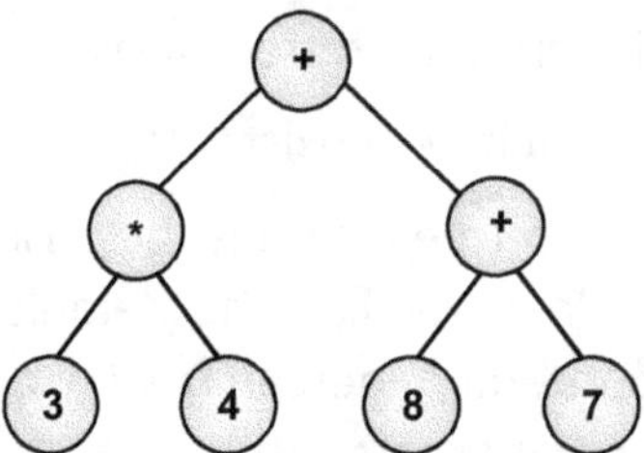

Fig. 3.61 : Expression for tree 3*4+(8+7)

Inorder traversal of tree will result into evaluation of the expression. Some more examples are as below.

d=a * b/d – 4.

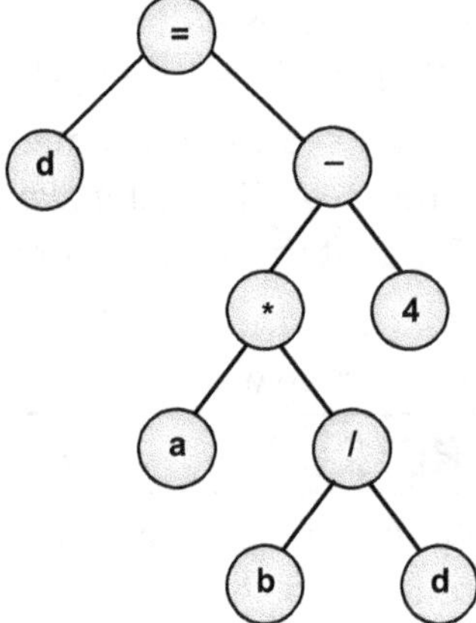

Fig. 3.62 : Expression tree for d = a*b/d–4

x=4 * 5 + 6 * 7 – 3/2

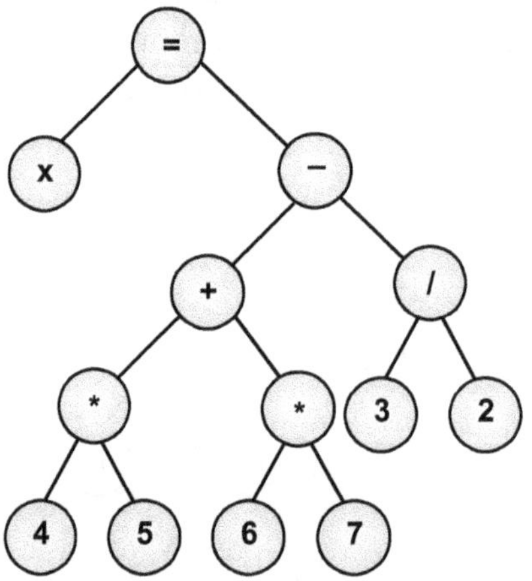

Fig. 3.63 : Expression tree for x = 4*5+6*7–3/2

2. Game Trees :

The trees can be used in many gaming applications. The different moves in the game can be represented using trees. From a given board position, we can represent all possible moves so that we can select best possible move.

Consider the problem of implementing a computer program to play a game. To simplify things a bit, we will only consider games with the following two properties :

- Two player - we do not deal with coalitions etc.

- Zero sum - one player's win is the other's loss; there are no co-operative victories.

Examples of these kinds of games include many classic board games, such as tic-tac-toe, chess, checkers, and go. For these types of games, we can model the game using what is called a game tree.

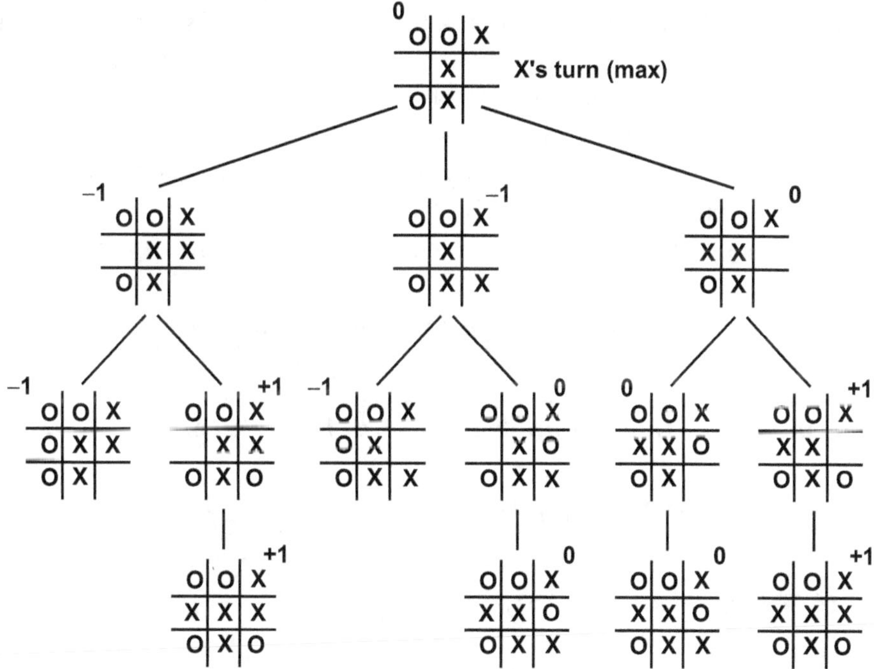

Fig. 3.64 : Game tree

Fig. 3.64 shows a section of a game tree for tic-tac-toe. Each node represents a board position, and the children of each node are the legal moves from that position. To score each position, we will give each position which is favorable for player 1 a positive number (the more positive, the more favorable). Similarly, we will give each position which is favorable for player 2 a negative number (the more negative, the more favorable). In our tic-tac-toe example, player 1 is 'X', player 2 is 'O', and the only three scores we will have are +1 for a win by 'X', −1 for a win by 'O', and 0 for a draw. Note that scores of current positions can only be calculated. To calculate the scores for the other positions, we must look ahead a few moves, by using tree traversal algorithms.

SUMMARY

- Tree is a nonlinear data structure used for efficient access or retrieval of elements.
- A tree (T) is a set of nodes. The set can be empty. If it is non-empty set, it consists of a specially designated node called root node and zero or more sub-trees (T_1, T_2, ..., T_n) each whose roots are connected by a directed edge from the root of T.
- Binary tree is a tree in which no node has more than two sub-trees.
- A binary tree can be represented using array or linked representation.
- A binary tree can be traversed in three different ways inorder (LVR), preorder (VLR) and postorder (LRV).
- A Binary Search Tree (BST) is used to store data for searching applications. A binary search tree is a binary tree in which for each node, the left sub-tree elements are less than the node elements and right sub-tree elements are greater than the node element.
- If binary search tree is height balanced, the time complexity of search is $0(\log_2 n)$.
- The traversals of binary tree can be implemented using recursive or non-recursive ways.
- A threaded binary tree makes use of NULL fields in the nodes of binary tree for spreading up the operations on binary tree.
- A height balanced or AVL tree is a binary tree with T_l and T_r as left and right sub-trees having heights h_l and h_r such that $|h_l - h_r| \leq 1$.
- In order to make a binary tree height balanced, we can use one of the four rotations LL, RR, LR or RL.
- Trees can be used for expression storage and evaluation and gaming applications.

SOLVED PROBLEMS

1. Write a recursive function to print leaf nodes of binary tree.

Solution :

```
void leaf node_check(NODE *temp)
{
    printf("The leaf nodes are \n");
    if (temp!=NULL)
    {
        leaf-node-check (temp->lchild);
        if(temp->lchild==NULL && temp->rchild=NULL)
        {
            printf("%d \n", temp->data);
        }
        leaf_node_check(temp->rchild);
    }
}
```

2. Write Inorder, Preoder and Postorder traversals for following tree.

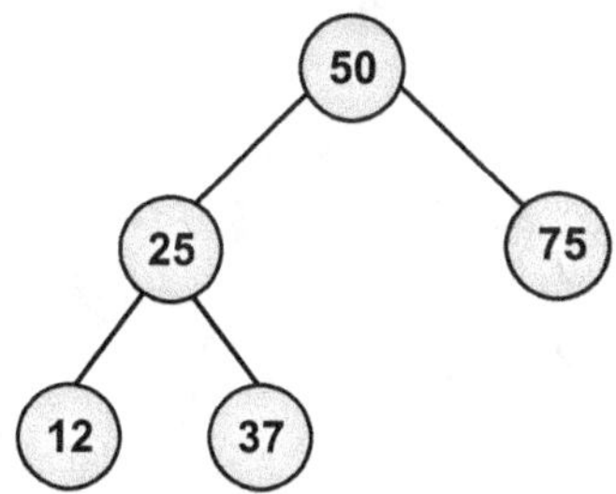

Fig. 3.65 : Binary tree

Solution :

Inorder	12 25 37 50 75
Preoder	50 25 12 37 75
Postorder	12 37 25 75 50

3. For the following data draw a binary search tree. Show all steps.

50 80 30 20 100 75 25 15 68

Solution : A binary search tree is shown in Fig. 3.66.

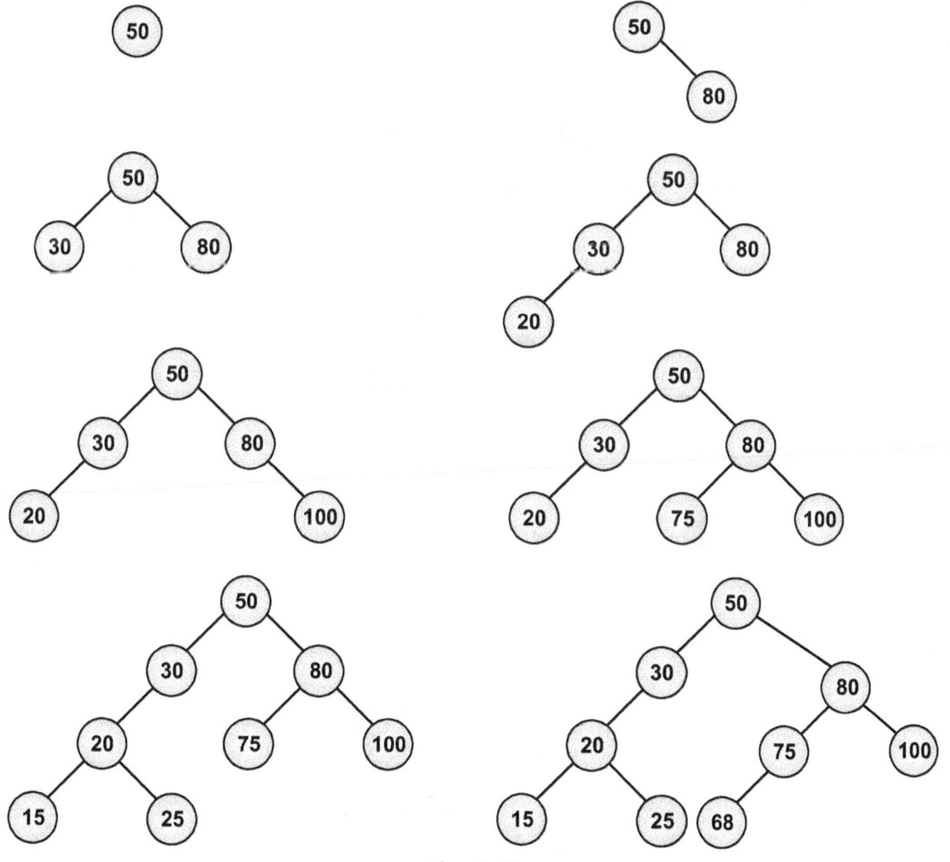

Fig. 3.66

4. Write Inorder, Preoder and Postorder traversals for the following. **[May 10]**

Solution :

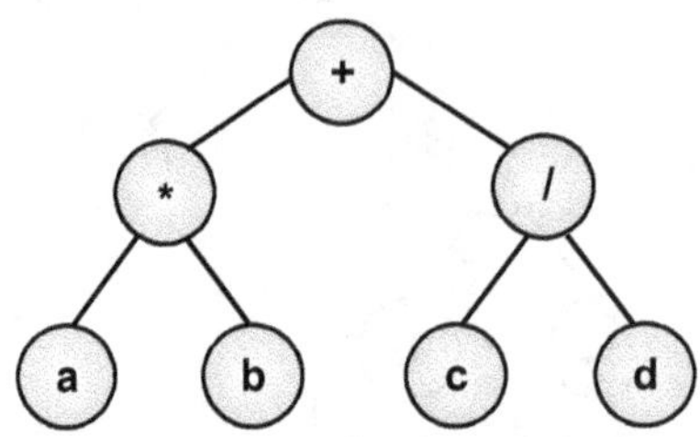

Fig. 3.67

Solution :

    Inorder   :   + *ab/cd

    Preoder   :   a * b + c/d

    Postorder   :   ab * cd \+

5. From given traversal, construct the binary tree.(May 05, May 08, May 09)

    Inorder   : DBFEAGCLJHK

    Preorder   : DFEBGLJKHCA

Solution :

Step I : From postorder we can see last element is root.

    Hence, the left sub-tree and right sub-tree from inorder traversal is

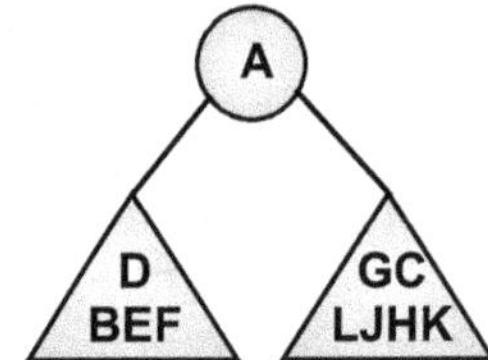

Step II :

    D (B) F E (A) G (C) L J H K

    D F E (B)   G L J K H (C) (A)

Step III :

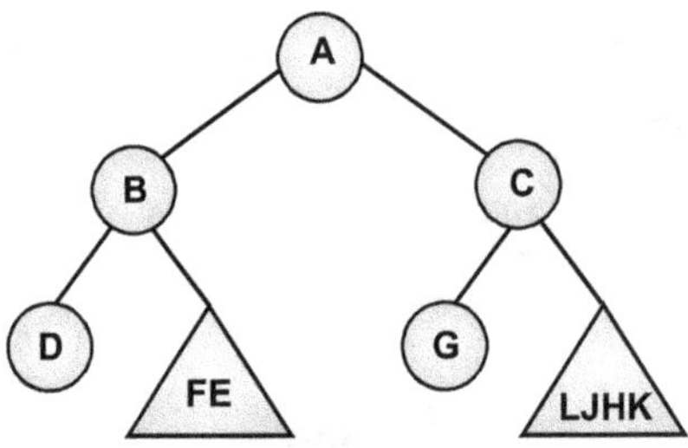

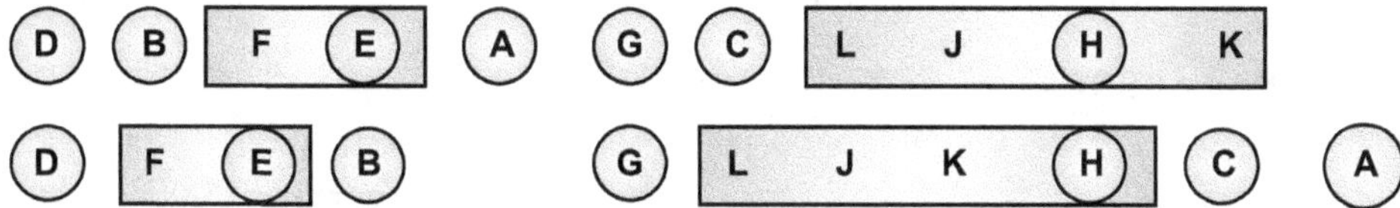

Step IV :

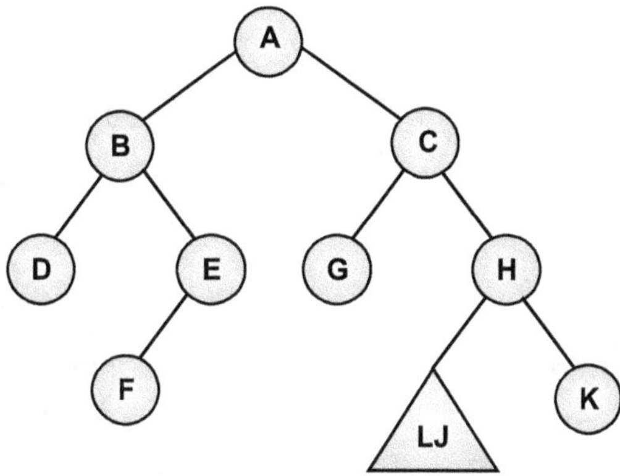

Step V :

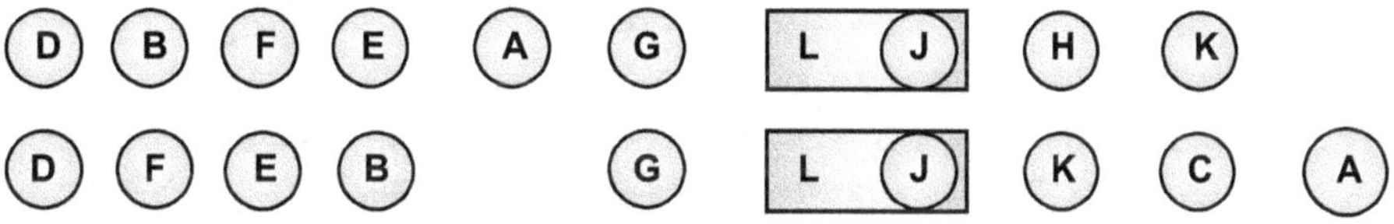

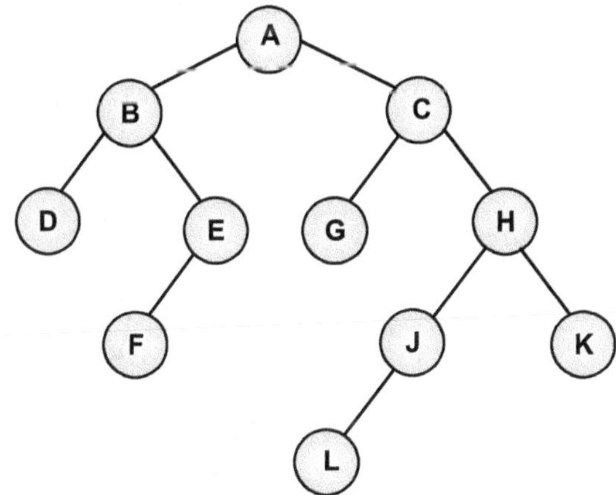

Fig. 3.68

6. **Define binary search tree. Construct binary search tree from following set of strings. Show all steps. Also write height of final tree.**   **[May 05, 06, 08, 09]**

JAN FEB MAR APR MAY JUN JUL AUG SEP OCT NOV DEC

Solution : (Refer section 3.4 for definition)

Steps for Creation of BST.

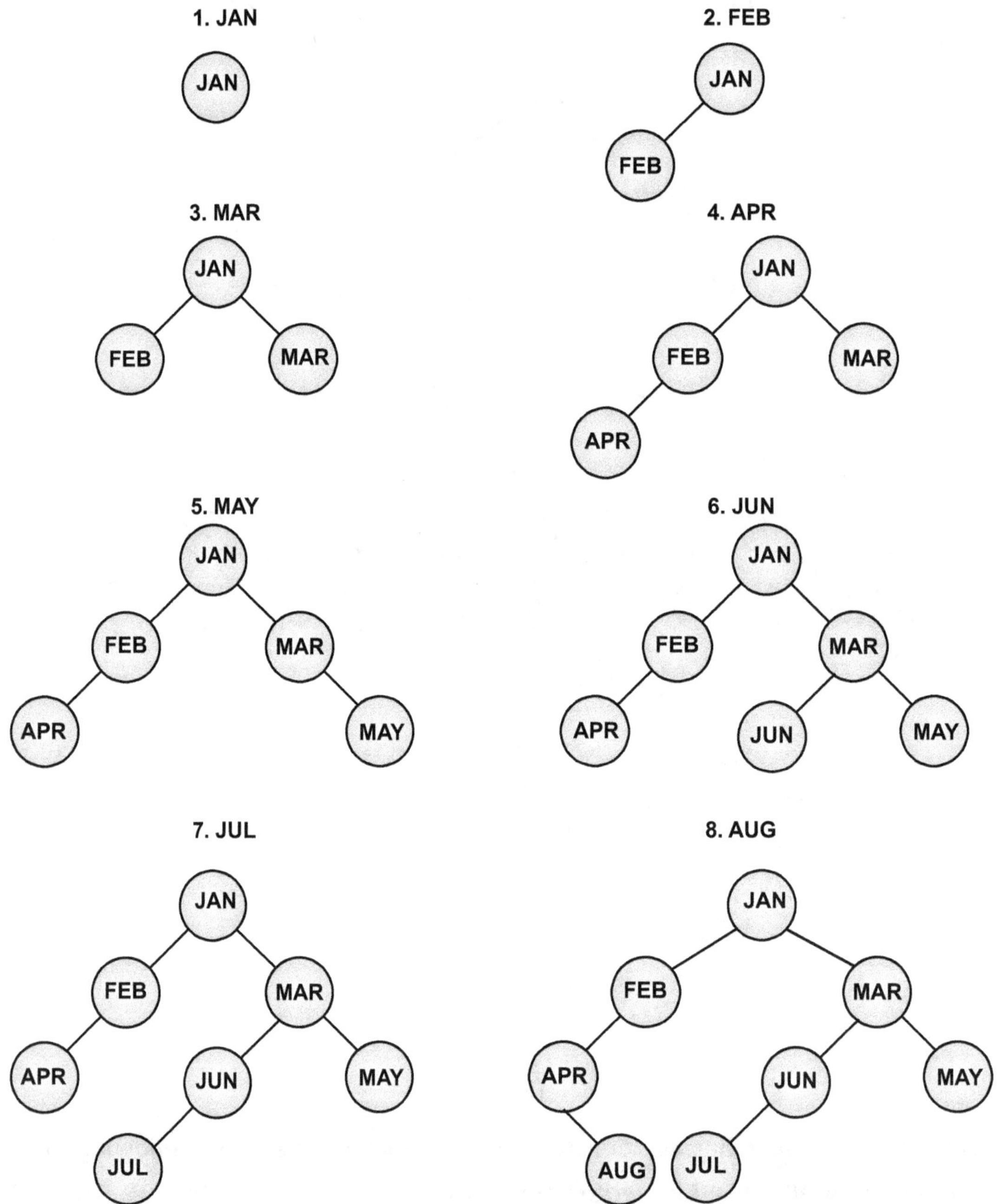

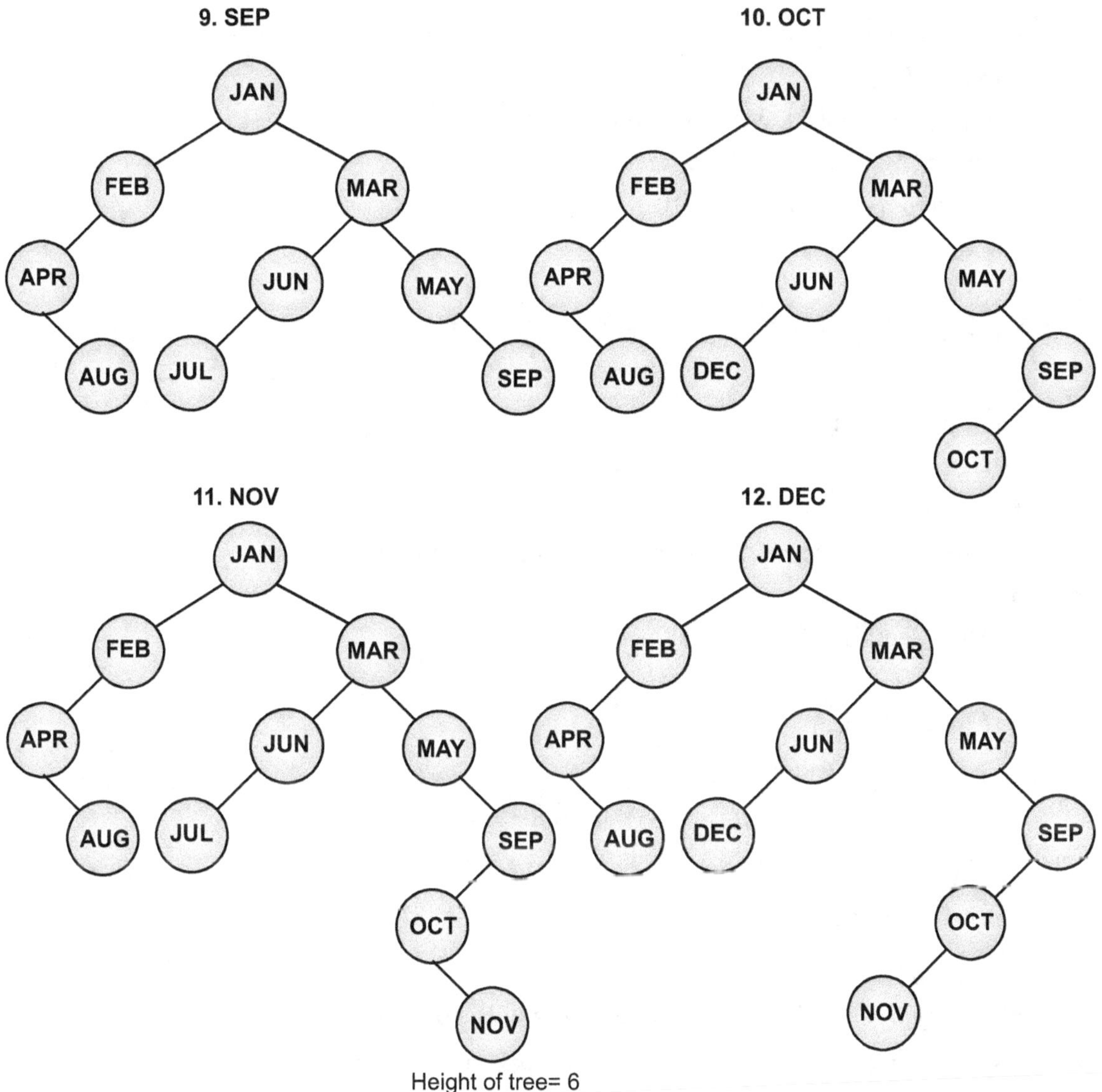

Height of tree= 6

Fig. 3.69

7. **Write a recursive function to find.**

   (i) **Height of a binary tree.**

   (ii) **To count and print leaf nodes of binary tree.**

Solution :

```
(i)   int height(NODE *root)
      {
            int c;
```

```
        if (root== NULL)
            return(0);
        if (root->lchild==NULL & root->rchild==NULL)
            return(0);
        hl=height(root->lchild);
        hr=height(root->rchild);
        if(hl>hr)
            return(1 + hl);
        else
            return(1 + hr);
        }
```

(ii) Refer solved problem 3.

8. Give pseudo code to print the leaves of tree using any traversal.

Solution :

```
    void print_leaves(NODE *root)
    {
        if (root!=NULL)
            print_leaves(root->lchild);
        if (root->lchild == NULL & root->rchild == NULL)
        printf("%d \n", root->data);
        print_leaves(root->rchild);
    }
```

9. Explain any one application of binary tree with suitable example.

Solution : There are two applications of binary tree that we can list out.

    (i)   Binary search tree.

    (ii) Expression tree.

(i) Binary Search Tree :

We can use binary tree to store data in such a way that it will be easier to search required data. We can store the binary search tree such that at each node on the left side we will have smaller numbers and on right side we will have larger numbers than the data at node.

(ii) Expression Tree :

Another application can be expression tree. We can store an infix expression into the binary tree so that we can have its prefix or postfix conversion using preorder or postorder traversal.

10. Write a non-recursive function to count number of leaf nodes in a binary tree.

Solution :

We can use non-recursive inorder traversal function. In place of print statement, we can use following statement.

```
if (temp->lchild==NULL&&temp->rchild==NULL)
    count=count + 1;
int count_leaves(NODE *root)
{   NODE *temp;   int count;
    temp=root;
    do
    {
        while(temp!=NULL)
        {
            push(temp);
            temp temp->lchild;
        }
        temp=pop( );
        if(temp-lchild==NULL && temp->rchild==NULL)
            count=count + 1;
        temp=temp->rchild;
    } while(!stack empty( ) || temp!=NULL);
    return(count);
}
```

EXERCISE

1. Define the following related to tree:
    1. Complete binary tree,
    2. Siblings,
    3. Non-terminals, (All non-leaf nodes are known as non-terminals)
    4. Forest,
    5. Height or Depth,
    6. Ancestors. (All nodes on the path joining the current node and the root node are ancestors of the current node.)
2. Define following terms with example.
    (i) Complete binary tree.
    (ii) Siblings.

    (iii) Height.

    (iv) Binary search tree.

    (v) Forest.

3. Define the following terms.

    1. Binary tree,

    2. Complete Binary tree,

    3. Threaded Binary Tree.

    4. What is binary tree?

5. Define the following:

    (a) Binary tree,

    (b) Complete binary tree,

    (c) Full binary, tree,

    (d) Sibling.

6. Define the following terms with respect to tree.

    (i) Complete binary tree.

    (ii) Forest.

    (iii) Height of binary tree.

    (iv) Skewed binary tree.

    (v) Full binary tree.

7. Explain the sequential representation of binary tree with example.

8. Define the term binary search tree. Give a 'C' declaration to define a node structure for the same. Write a function in 'C' to insert a node in a binary search tree.

9. What do you mean by binary search tree? Write a C function to search an element from a given binary search tree.

10. What is binary search tree? Explain its application.

11. What is binary search tree? Explain its application.

12. What is Binary search tree? Explain the application of BST.

13. Define binary search tree. Write a function to delete a node from a BST. Consider all possible cases.

14. Write necessary 'C' functions to search given data in BST.

15. Write a function to search an element in BST.

16. Traverse the tree built in Q. 47 in inorder, postorder and preorder and display the sequence of numbers.

17. Write a 'C' function (non-recursive) for deleting a node from binary search tree.

18. Write a C function to delete a node from binary search tree. Consider all cases.

19. Write necessary 'C' functions to delete a node in BST.

20. Write a non-recursive function to delete a node from BST. Explain all cases with suitable example.

21. Define binary search tree. Write a function to delete a node from BST.
22. Write a C function to insert a node in binary search tree.
23. Write a function to insert an element in BST.
24. Write necessary 'C' functions to implement inorder traversal in a binary tree non-recursively.
25. Write a non-recursive C function to traverse a binary tree in in-order traversal.
26. Write a non-recursive function in 'C' to perform a pre-order traversal on a binary tree.
27. Write necessary 'C' functions to implement preorder traversal in a binary tree non-recursively.
28. Write a pseudo code to traverse a given binary tree in preorder without recursion.
29. Write a non-recursive 'C' function to traverse binary tree in preorder. Explain with suitable example.
30. Explain non-recursive inorder traversal of binary tree.
31. Write an algorithm to implement non-recursive inorder traversal of binary tree.
32. Comment on "Threaded binary tree can be traversed without using stack".
33. What is threaded binary tree? State its advantage and disadvantages.
34. What is threaded binary tree? State its advantages and disadvantages.
35. State and explain the advantages of threaded binary tree.
36. Explain the term threaded binary tree. Give a 'C declaration to define the node structure of a threaded binary tree. What are the advantages of threaded binary trees over normal binary trees?
37. What do you mean by threaded binary tree? Also write pseudo code to perform non-recursive preorder traversal of TBT without using stack.
38. What is threaded binary tree? Explain its application.
39. What is threaded binary tree? Explain the application of threaded binary tree.
40. (i)   Give declaration in 'C' for TBT.
    (ii) Write a function in 'C' to perform traversal of threaded binary tree.
    (iii) Compare traversal of TBT with binary tree.
41. List the advantages of using a threaded binary tree. Give node structure for defining a threaded binary tree. Write a function in 'C' to find the pre-order successor of any node pointed by P in a threaded binary tree.
42. List advantages of threaded binary tree. Give its node structure. Write a function in 'C' to find preorder successor of any node pointed by 7 in TBT.
43. What is threaded binary tree? Explain its advantages/applications.
44. Comment on "Threaded binary tree can be traversed without stack".
45. Write a non-recursive algorithm for pre-order traversal of a binary tree.
46. What is AVL tree? Explain RR and LL rotations with example.
47. Build a binary search tree from the following set of elements: -
    100, 50, 200, 300, 20, 150, 70, 180, 120, 30

48. Construct binary search tree from the following set of strings:
    JAN, FEB, MAR, APR, MAY, JUN, JUL, AUG, SEP, OCT, NOV and DEC.

49. Construct Binary tree if following traversals are give.

    Inorder   :   D, F, E, G, A, H, I, C
    Postorder   :   D, F, G, E, B, I, H, C, A

50. Construct BST from following elements:
    (i)   MAT, TAN, BAN, BAT, SUN, CAT, RAT Show all steps.
    (ii) 100, 50, 200, 300, 20, 150, 70, 180, 120, 30

51. Construct binary search tree from the following set of strings:
    MAR, MAY, NOV, AUG, APR, JAN, DEC, JUL, FEB, JUN, OCT and SEP. Show all steps.

52. Create Binary Search Tree for the following data and print the tree using all tree traversals.
    MAR, OCT, JAN, APR, NOV, FEB, MAY, DEC, JUN, AUG, JUL, SEP.

53. Write a recursive function to count and print leaf nodes of binary tree.

54. Write a recursive function to find height of binary tree.

55. Write recursive functions to obtain:
    (i)   Height of a binary tree,
    (ii) To count and print the leaf nodes of a binary tree.

56. Explain any one application of binary tree with suitable example.

57. Construct a threaded binary search tree for the following set of elements:
    100, 50, 200, 300, 20, 150, 150, 70, 180, 120, 30 show all steps

CHAPTER 4
GRAPHS

4.1 INTRODUCTION

Graph is a nonlinear data structure used in many applications. These applications include finding shortest path in a network analysis of electrical circuits, project planning, genetics, identification of chemical compounds etc. Many problems can be modeled as graph and solved.

4.2 GRAPH THEORY AND TERMINOLOGY

Definition : A graph can be defined as set of nodes or vertices or points (V) and set of arcs or edges (E), such that each edge e is identified with unique ordered pair [u, v] of nodes in V.

A graph is denoted as G ≡ (V, E), where V is set of vertices and E is set of edges.

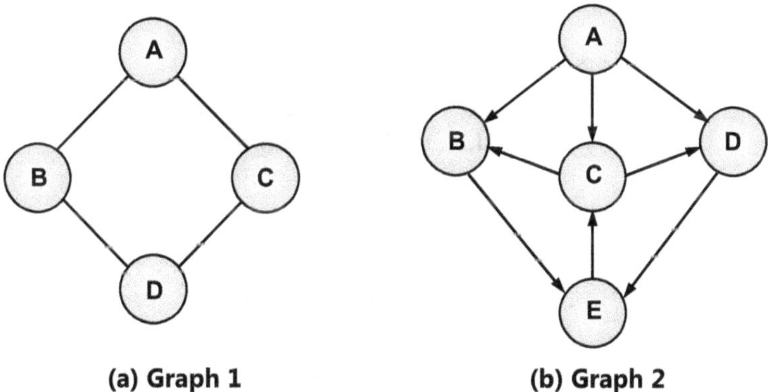

(a) Graph 1   (b) Graph 2

Fig. 4.1 : Example of graph

Graph 1 consists of vertices {A, B, C, D} and edges {(A, B), (A, C), (B, D), (C, D) }

Graph 2 consists of set of vertices {A, B, C, D, E} and set of edges {<A, B>, <A, D>, <A, C>, <C, D>, <C, B>, <B, E>, <E, C>, <D, E>}

If e = [u, v] is an edge, then the nodes u and v are called end points of e. Also u and v are said to be adjacent nodes or neighbours.

A graph can be of two types.

- Directed graph or digraph.
- Undirected graph.

Directed graph is a graph in which each edge has direction or we say that the pair of vertices in the graph is ordered Fig. 4.1 (b) is a directed graph.

The set of edges in such graph are written in < > sign.

Suppose G is directed graph with edge e = <v, u>, then e is also called an arc.
Following terminology is used.

- e begins at u and ends at v.
- u is origin and v is destination of e.
- u is predecessor and v is successor or neighbour of e.
- u is adjacent to v and v is adjacent to u.

Undirected graph is a graph in which the edges do not have direction. The flow between two edges can be in both directions. In undirected graph, the set of edges are written in ( ) sign. Fig. 4.1 (a) is an undirected graph.

The vertices in undirected graph are said to be unordered. If (v, u) is an edge and (u, v) represents same edge.

A graph sometimes has weight or cost specified for each edge as shown in Fig. 4.2. Such graph is said to be labelled or weighted graph.

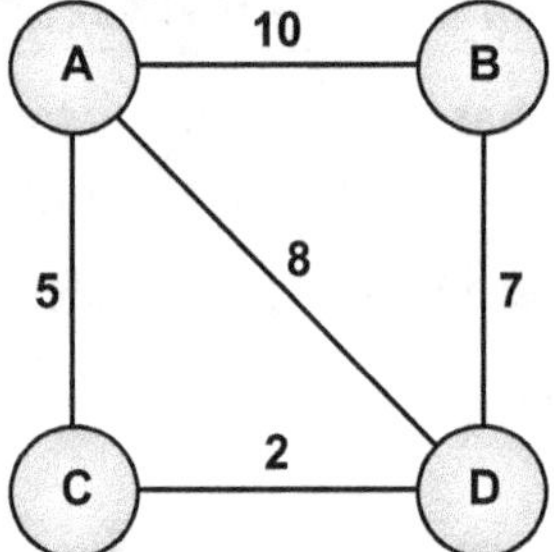

Fig. 4.2 : Weighted graph

Tree also can be termed as graph as it has set of edges and vertices.

There are some terms used with graph. Let us understand them.

- A graph is said to be complete if it has n(n − 1)/2 number of district unordered pairs, where n is number of vertices. For a directed graph maximum number of edges will be n(n − 1).
- If (u, v) is an edge of graph, we say that u and v are adjacent (vertices) and we say that edge (u, v) is incident on vertices u and v.
- A graph G1 is a subgraph of Graph G, in which all vertices of G1 belong to G and all edges of G1 belong to G.

Following Fig. 4.3 show graph G and its sub-graph.

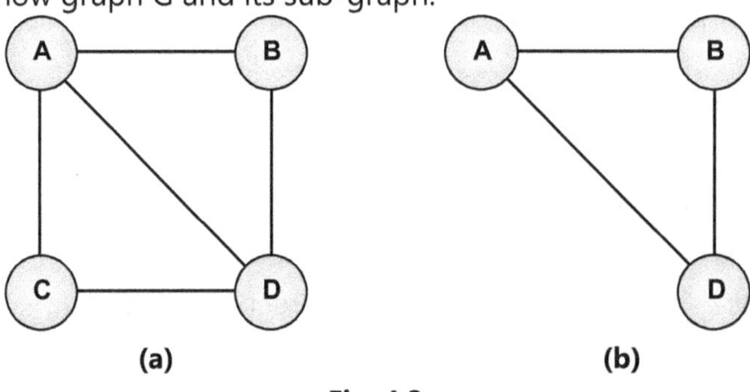

(a)   (b)

Fig. 4.3

- A path in a graph (G) is a sequence of vertices v_1, v_2, v_3, ... v_m, v_n where (v_1, v_2) (v_2, v_3) ... (v_m, v_n) are edges in the graph.

- A simple path is a path such that all vertices are distinct except first and last which could be same.

- A graph can have an edge from a vertex to same vertex called self edge as shown in Fig. 4.4. The path from A to A is called loop.

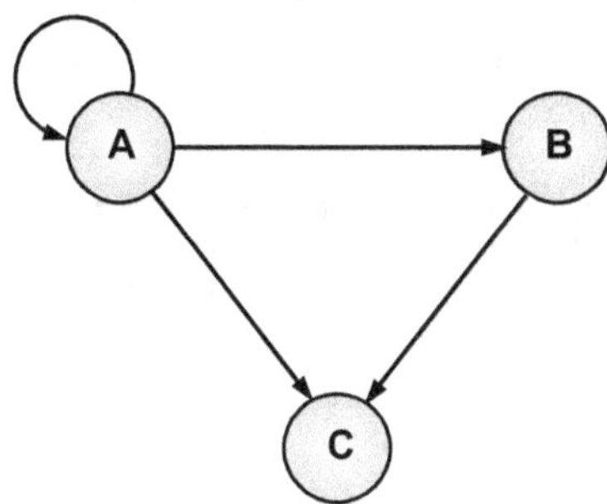

Fig. 4.4 : Graph with self edge node

- A cycle in a directed graph is a path of length at least 1 such that $v_1 = v_n$ i.e. the first and last vertex is same.

- In undirected graph for a cycle, the edges are to be distinct. Otherwise edge (u, v) will also be cycle.

- A directed graph is called acyclic if it has no cycles. It is denoted as DAG.

- An undirected graph is said to be connected if there is path from every vertex to all other vertices.

- A directed graph is said to be connected or strongly connected if for every pair of distinct vertices in graph G there is directed path in both direction i.e. v_i to v_j and v_j to v_i.

- Strongly connected component of undirected graph (G) is maximal connected sub-graph of G.

- Indegree of vertex in a graph is number of incoming edges at that vertex.

- Out-degree of vertex is the number of outgoing edges from that vertex.

- Total degree of vertex is sum of indegree and outdegree.

- A graph is said to be complete if every node in G is adjacent to every other node. A complete graph with n nodes will have n (n − 1)/2 edges.

- A graph without any cycle is called tree graph or free tree or simply tree.

- Distinct edges e and e' are called multiple edges if they connect same end points, that is, if e = [u, v] and e' = [u, v].

- An edge e is called a loop if it has identical endpoints, that is, if e = [u, u].

- A graph having multiple edges and loops is called multigraph.
- A multigraph with finite number of edges is called finite multigraph.
- A directed graph is said to be simple if G has no parallel edges. It means a simple graph can have loops but it cannot have more than one loop at a given node.
- A directed Acyclic Graph (DAG) can be used to solve problems like critical path analysis, expression free evaluation etc. A sink vertex is a vertex with only single edge ending on it. A source vertex is a vertex having edges starting from it.
- A Biconnected graph is a connected graph which cannot be broken down further by deletion of any single vertex (and incident edges).

4.3 REPRESENTATION OF GRAPH USING ADJACENCY MATRIX

[May 06, 07, 08, Dec. 05, 06, 07, 08, 10]

A graph can be represented using two different ways :
- Adjacency matrix
- Adjacency list.

The choice of particular representation depends on application or function to be performed. The adjacency matrix representation is the simplest representation in which we use a two-dimensional array of integers. The elements in the two-dimensional array represent the information about edges and vertices in the graph. Suppose, a graph has an edge (v_1, v_2) then the element in the matrix in row number v_1 and column number v_2 will be 1. If there is no edge between v_1 and v_2 the element will be 0.

Let us consider two graphs as shown in Fig. 4.5.

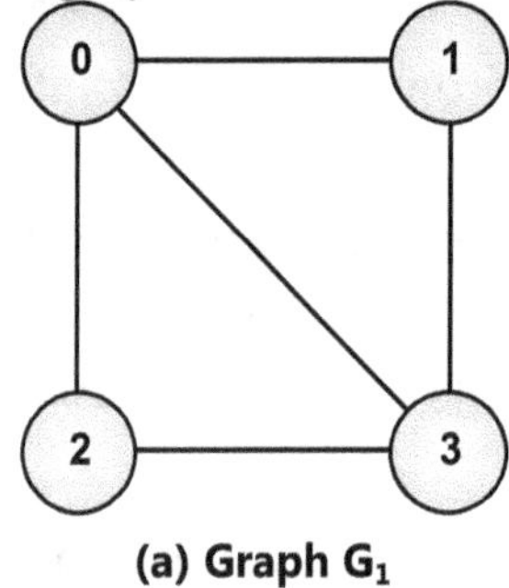

(a) Graph G₁

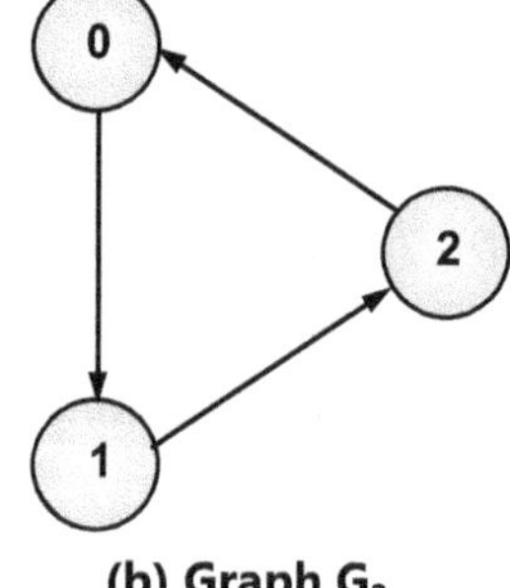

(b) Graph G₂

Fig. 4.5

The adjacency matrix for graph G_1 will have 4 rows and 4 columns as there are 4 vertices. The elements in the matrix will be as shown in Fig. 4.6.

$$
\begin{array}{c c}
 & \begin{matrix} 0 & 1 & 2 & 3 \end{matrix} \\
\begin{matrix} 0 \\ 1 \\ 2 \\ 3 \end{matrix} &
\begin{bmatrix}
0 & 1 & 1 & 1 \\
1 & 0 & 0 & 1 \\
1 & 0 & 0 & 1 \\
1 & 1 & 1 & 0
\end{bmatrix}
\end{array}
$$

Fig. 4.6 : Adjacency matrix for graph G₁

Note that the graph G_1 is undirected graph. Hence, the matrix is symmetric. We can store only upper or lower triangular matrix to reduce the space requirements. The adjacency matrix for graph G_2 is shown in Fig. 4.7.

$$\begin{array}{c} \quad\ 0 \ \ 1 \ \ 2 \\ \begin{array}{c}0\\1\\2\end{array}\left[\begin{array}{ccc} 0 & 1 & 0 \\ 0 & 0 & 1 \\ 1 & 0 & 0 \end{array}\right] \end{array}$$

Fig. 4.7 : Adjacency matrix for graph G_2

From adjacency matrix, we can find whether there is an edge between given two vertices or not.

We can find indegree of vertices by counting number of 1's in corresponding column and out-degree by counting number of 1's in corresponding row.

For example, Indegree of vertex 1 in G_1 = 2

Outdegree of vertex 1 in G_1 = 2

If the cost or weight is specified on the edges of graph, we can put the cost or weight in place of 1.

The advantage of adjacency matrix representation is its simplicity but requires more space of the order of n^2.

Let us write a program to represent a graph in adjacency matrix format. The program accepts from user number of vertices and edges in the graph and prints the matrix. It also calculates indegree, outdegree and total degree of a given vertex.

Explanation :

int g[MAX] {MAX} is the 2-D array for storing matrix.

n is number of vertices.

There are three functions used

- create_graph( )

  It accepts the number of vertices of n. If the graph is undirected, their reverse edge corresponding to two vertices is also stored.

- disp( )

  This function displays the matrix.

- calc( )

  This function calculates indegree, outdegree and total degree of a given vertex.

Program 4.1 : To represent graph using adjacency matrix, display it and calculate indegree - outdegree of nodes.

```
#define MAX 10,
int g[MAX] [MAX];
int n;
void create_graph( );
```

```c
void disp( );
void calc( );
void main( )
{
    create_graph( );
    disp( );
    calc( );
}
void create_graph( )
{
    char ch, type;
    printf("How many vertices\n");
    scanf("%d", &n);
    printf("Enter type of graph directed or undirected \n");
    type = getch( );
    do
    {
        printf("Enter edge");
        scanf("%d %d", &v1, &v2);
        g[v1] [v2] = 1;
        if(type=='u'||type=='U')
        g[v2] [v1] = 1;
        printf("Do you want to continue? \n");
        ch = getch( );
    }   while (ch=='y'||ch=='y');
}
void disp( )
{
    int i, j;
    for(i=0; i<n; i++)
```

```c
        {
            for(j=0; j<n; j++)
            {
                    printf("%d", g[i][j]);
            }
            printf("\n");

        }
    }
    void calc( )
    {
        int c1 = 0, c2 = 0, c3 = 0, v;
        printf("Enter vertex \n");
        scanf("%d", &v);
        for (i=0; i<n; i++)
        {
            if (g[i][v]==1)
            c1++;

        }
        for(i=0; i<n; i++)
        {
            if(g[v] [i] ==1)
            c2++;

        }
        c3 = c1 + c2;
        printf("Indegree =%d\n", c1);
        printf("outdegree=%d\n", c2);
        printf("Total degree = %\n", c3);

    }
```

If A is adjacency matrix of a graph G, then the element a_{ij} in the matrix A^k will be equal to number of paths of length k between vertex v_i to v_j.

Similarly, the matrix $B_r = A + A^2 + A^3 + ... A^r$ will have element b_{ij} equal to number of paths of length less than or equal to r from node v_i to v_j.

Consider a graph as given below.

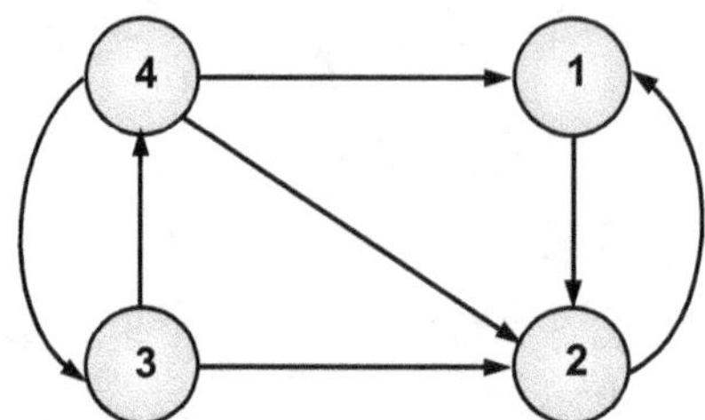

Fig. 4.8 : Graph G

The adjacency matrix for the graph will be

$$A = \begin{bmatrix} 0 & 1 & 1 & 1 \\ 0 & 0 & 1 & 0 \\ 1 & 1 & 1 & 0 \\ 1 & 0 & 1 & 0 \end{bmatrix}$$

$$\therefore \qquad A^2 = \begin{bmatrix} 1 & 0 & 2 & 0 \\ 1 & 1 & 0 & 0 \\ 0 & 1 & 1 & 0 \\ 1 & 2 & 0 & 1 \end{bmatrix}$$

$$A^3 = \begin{bmatrix} 2 & 3 & 0 & 1 \\ 0 & 1 & 1 & 1 \\ 2 & 1 & 2 & 0 \\ 1 & 1 & 3 & 1 \end{bmatrix}$$

We can see from A^2 there is one path of length 2 from 0 to 0 i.e. $0 - 3 - 0$. There is no path of length 2 from 0 to 1. There are two paths of length 2 from 0 to 2. i.e. $0 - 1 - 2$ and $0 - 3 - 2$ etc.

From A^3 we can observe that there are 2 paths of length 3 from 0 to 0 i.e. $0 - 1 - 2 - 0$ and $0 - 3 - 2 - 0$. There are 3 paths of length 3 from 0 to 1 i.e. $0 - 3 - 2 - 1, 0 - 3 - 0 - 1, 0 - 1 - 2 - 1$.

Path Matrix : Let G be a simple directed graph with n vertices $v_1, v_2, \dots v_n$, then the path matrix or reachability matrix of G is $n \times n$ matrix P such that the elements P_{ij} are.

$$P_{ij} = 1 \qquad \text{if there is a path between } v_i \text{ and } v_j$$

$$= 0 \qquad \text{otherwise}$$

The path matrix can be obtained from adjacency matrix. If A is adjacency matrix of graph G than the path matrix P will have a entry $P_{ij} = 1$ if and only if there is non-zero member in the ij entry of the matrix.

$$B_{nxn} = A + A^2 + A^3 + \dots A^n$$

Consider the graph shown in Fig. 4.8. There are 4 vertices i.e. n = 4.

$$\therefore \qquad B_4 = A + A^2 + A^3 + A^4$$

$$= \begin{bmatrix} 0 & 1 & 0 & 1 \\ 0 & 0 & 1 & 0 \\ 1 & 1 & 0 & 0 \\ 1 & 0 & 1 & 0 \end{bmatrix} + \begin{bmatrix} 1 & 0 & 2 & 0 \\ 1 & 1 & 0 & 0 \\ 0 & 1 & 1 & 1 \\ 1 & 2 & 0 & 1 \end{bmatrix} + \begin{bmatrix} 2 & 3 & 0 & 1 \\ 0 & 1 & 1 & 1 \\ 2 & 1 & 2 & 0 \\ 1 & 1 & 3 & 1 \end{bmatrix} + \begin{bmatrix} 1 & 2 & 4 & 2 \\ 2 & 1 & 2 & 0 \\ 2 & 4 & 1 & 2 \\ 4 & 4 & 2 & 1 \end{bmatrix}$$

$$= \begin{bmatrix} 4 & 6 & 6 & 4 \\ -3 & 3 & 4 & 1 \\ 5 & 7 & 4 & 3 \\ 7 & 7 & 6 & 3 \end{bmatrix}$$

Since all entries in B_4 are non zero, the path matrix will also have all 1's as below.

$$P = \begin{bmatrix} 1 & 1 & 1 & 1 \\ 1 & 1 & 1 & 1 \\ 1 & 1 & 1 & 1 \\ 1 & 1 & 1 & 1 \end{bmatrix}$$

It means the graph is strongly connected i.e. for any pair of nodes u and v in G, there is path from u to v and from v to u also.

A transitive closure of graph G is a graph G' such that G' has same number of nodes as G and there is an edge (v_i, v_j) in G' whenever there is path from v_i to v_j in G. Thus, path matrix of G is adjacency matrix of its transitive closure G'.

4.4 REPRESENTATION OF GRAPH USING ADJACENCY LIST

[Dec. 05, 06, 07, 08, 10, May 06, 08]

This is linked list representation of graph. The n rows of adjacency matrix are represented as n linked lists. For each vertex, there will be one list. The list contains adjacent vertices of that vertex. Let us consider two graphs and their adjacency list representations.

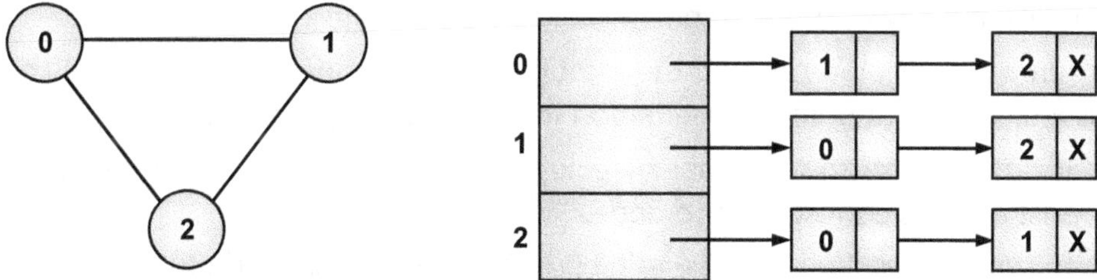

Fig. 4.9 : Graph and its adjacency list

As seen in the graph, vertex 0 has adjacent vertices 1 and 2. Hence, the list corresponding to vertex 0 has two nodes with 1 and 2 in its list and list 2 has vertices 0 and 1.

Another example is directed graph.

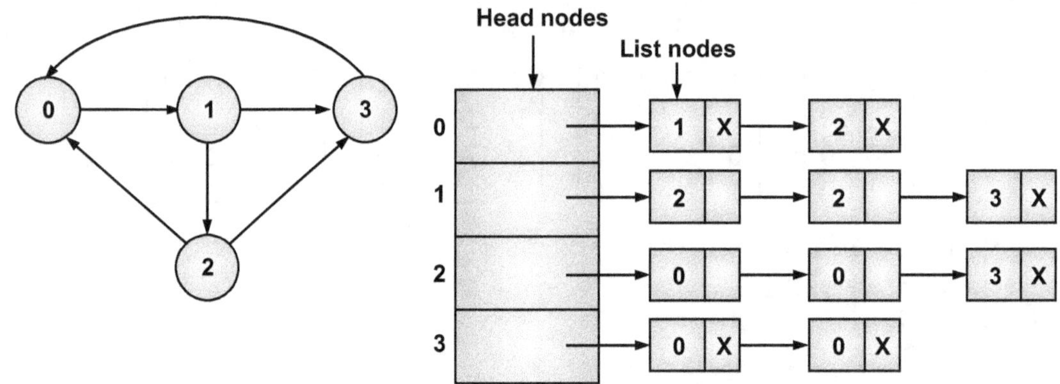

Fig. 4.10 : Graph and its adjacency list

Each list has head node which stores the address of the list. For directed graph, if there are n vertices and e edges, the adjacency list will have n head nodes and e list nodes.

For undirected graph if there are n vertices and e edges the list will have n head nodes and 2e list nodes.

The indegree of a vertex in undirected graph is number of nodes in the corresponding list.

The outdegree of a vertex in undirected graph is number of nodes in list.

The outdegree of a vertex in directed graph is number of nodes in the corresponding list.

The indegree of a vertex is calculated by examining the entire adjacency list. The number of nodes of that vertex in adjacency list is the indegree of that vertex.

The comparison of adjacency list with adjacency matrix is

- The adjacency list consists of dynamic allocation. Hence, space requirement for adjacency list will be less compared to matrix representation.
- The adjacency list is complex structure and difficult to implement whereas adjacency matrix is simple and easy to implement.

Operations on Graph : There are various operations such as searching, inserting and deleting nodes and edges in the graph.

Searching in a Graph : We can find the location, loc of a node N in a graph G. This can be accomplished easily with both representation that is adjacency matrix or adjacency list.

In adjacency matrix, the row number or column number responds to node. In adjacency matrix, the list address corresponds to node.

We can also find the location, loc of a edge (v_i, v_j) in the graph. In adjacency matrix if the ij^{th} entry in the matrix is 1 the edge is present otherwise absent.

In adjacency list representation, we can search the edge, (v_i, v_j) in the ith row of the list.

Inserting a Graph : To insert a node N in the graph, in adjacency matrix, we can increase row number and column number in the matrix. In the adjacency list, we can increase one more element in the list of pointers.

To insert an edge (v_i, v_j) we can enter 1 in the ith row and j^{th} column of the adjacency matrix. In case of adjacency list we can append one more node at the end (append) in the ith row of the list.

Deleting from a Graph : To delete a node from the graph, we can insert all zeros in the corresponding row and column, in case of adjacency matrix. In case of adjacency list, we can delete entire list corresponding to the node. We also must delete all nodes in the other lists corresponding this vertex.

4.5 TRAVERSALS OF GRAPH (DFS AND BFS)
[May 05, 06, 07, 08, 09, Dec. 05, 06, 07, 08]

The graph can be traversed in two different ways :

*   Depth first search,

*   Breadth first search.

Traversal means visiting each vertex in the graph once. The tree traversals were studied in chapter 3. In the starting point of the traversals, there was root node. In case of graph, starting point may be any vertex. Now traversing in case of graph means, visiting all vertices that are reachable from the starting vertex because every vertex may not be reachable from a given vertex.

4.5.1 Depth First Search (DFS) Traversal

[Dec. 05, 07, 08, 10, May 07, 09]

As the name suggests, starting from a given vertex we go till the depth of the vertex and then go back to traverse another path till its depth.

Suppose we start at a vertex v1, process it, we go to its adjacent vertex say v2, process it, then we move to adjacent vertex of v2 say v3. Like this, we continue till there is no vertex left with adjacent vertex. After this we come back to the previous vertex (last but one processed). If there is any other adjacent vertex, we move to that vertex, process and keep on going forward. When we have reached a vertex with no adjacent vertices, we keep coming back. Thus, when we start with a vertex we keep on going forward to its descendants. While doing this, every vertex should be processed only once in the entire traversal.

Let us take a graph and see the DFS traversal of it.

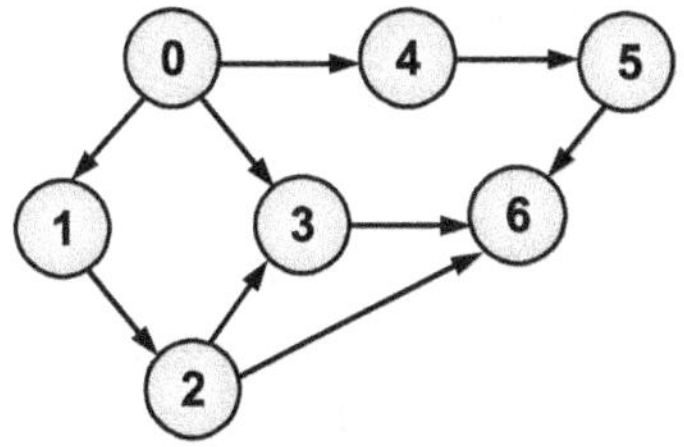

Fig. 4.11 : Graph

Suppose our starting vertex is 0 (process it)

From 0 we can go to 1 or 3 or 4 (Adjacent vertex).

Let us select 1 (process it)

From 1 we can go to 2 (process it)

From 2 we can go to 3 or 6.

Let us select 3 (process it).

From 3 we can go to 6 (process it)

From 6 you cannot reach any node, which is not processed or visited.

Hence, go back to 3 (previous vertex)

There is no other vertex connected to 3.

Go back to 2.

From 2 we can go to 6 but it is already processed.

Go back to 0.

From 0 we can go to 3 but it is already processed.

From 0 we can go to 4. (Process it)

From 4 we can go to 5. (Process it).

From 5 we can go to 6 but it is already processed.

Go back to 0.

There is no other vertex left out

Hence the Traversal is 0, 1, 2, 3, 6, 4, 5.

The traversal is shown in Fig. 4.12.

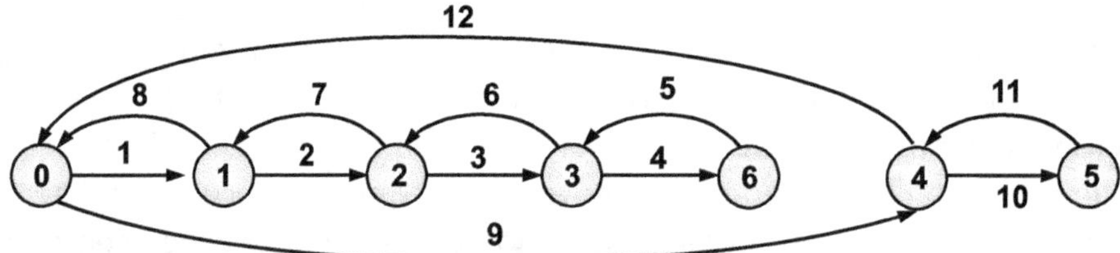

Fig. 4.12 : DFS traversal of graph in Fig. 4.11

Let us take one more graph and see its DFS Traversal.

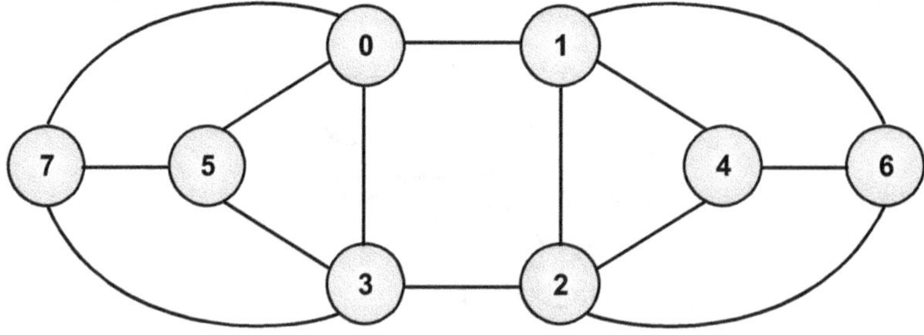

Fig. 4.13 : Graph

The traversal path is shown in Fig. 4.14.

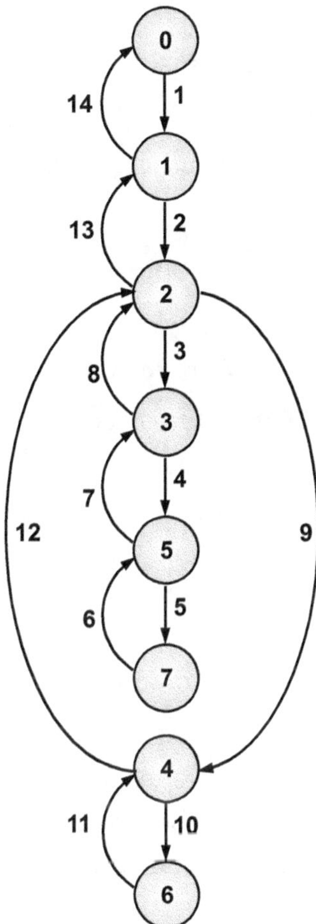

Fig. 4.14 : DFS traversal of graph in Fig. 4.13

The DFS traversal is 0 1 2 3 5 7 4 6.

Algorithm for DFS Traversal :

DFS is a recursive process. We can either use recursive function or stack to implement DFS. The algorithm we are going to write is for adjacency matrix representation. The create_graph( ) function which we have already written will be used here for storing graph in the 2-D array int g[MAX] [MAX] and n is number of vertices. We require an additional array to store the information about status of each vertex whether it is visited or not. Let us have the array int visited[MAX]. Initially, the elements of this array will be 0. Whenever a vertex is visited the corresponding element will be made 1. The algorithm is as follows :

```
    void dfs(int v1)
    {
        print v1;          // visit or process
        visited [v1] = 1; // mark as visited
        for(v2=0; v2<n; v2++)// check all adjacent vertices edge for a (v1, v2)
        {
            if (g[v1] [v2]==1)
            {
                if(visited [v2]==0)   // if not visited
                    dfs (v2);// Repeat dfs again
            }
        }
    }
```

Explanation :

- We start with source vertex v1 in the graph. It is processed (display) and marked as visited.

- In the loop, we are finding an adjacent vertex of v1 (verifying g[v1] [v2] ==) say v2 and if it is not visited yet, the function DFS will be called to process visit that node. This process continues recursively as explained in through example.

Analysis :

The total time to determine adjacent vertices of a vertex is n and for each vertex we must do this. Hence time complexity of this algorithm is $O(n^2)$. The space required for this algorithm is the array visited and stack (of program) a part from the $n \times n$ array.

Let us consider DFS traversal of the following graph.

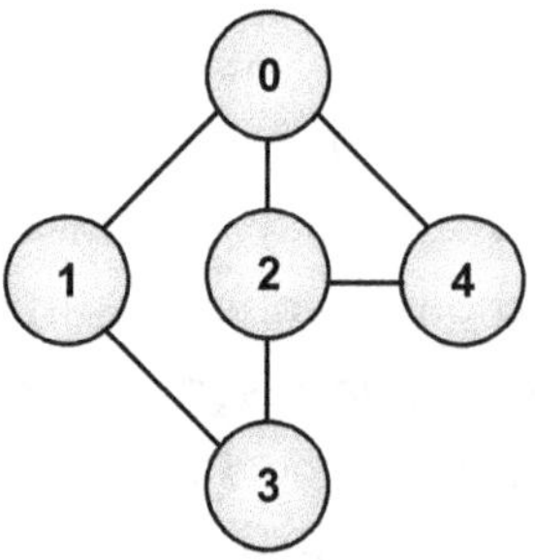

Fig. 4.15

Table 4.1

Call No.	V_1	Output	Visited array	V_2
1	0	0	0 1 2 3 4	
			1 0 0 0 0	0
				1
2	1	1	0 1 2 3 4	
			1 1 0 0 0	0
				1
				2
			0 1 2 3 4	3
3	3	3	1 1 0 1 0	0
				1
			0 1 2 3 4	2
4	2	2	1 1 1 1 0	0
				1
				2
				3
			0 1 2 3 4	4
5	4	4	1 1 1 1 1	0
				1
				2
				3
				4
				5 →

After call number 5, control goes back to 4 $V_2 = 5$

Control goes back to call 3 $V_2 = 3, 4, 5$

Control goes back to call 2 $V_2 = 4, 5$

Control goes back to call 1 $V_2 = 2, 3, 4, 5$

Following is the algorithm for non-recursive traversal of DFS.

```
void dfs(int v1)
{
    push v1;              // Store v1 in stack

    visited [v1] = 1;     // Mark it as visited

    while(stack not empty)
```

```
{
    v1 =pop( );      // Remove the vertex in stack
    print v1;        // Process or visit
    for(v2=0;v2<n;v2++)   // Check all adjacent vertices
    {
        if (g[v1][v2]==1 && visited [v2]==0)
                              // If there is edge v1 – v2 and V2 is not visited
        {
            visited [v2] == 1;      // Mark it as visited
            push (v2);              // Store the vertex on stack
        }
    }
}
}
```

4.5.2 Breadth First Search (BFS) Traversal

[May 06, 08, 09, 10, Dec. 06, 07, 08]

In BFS, we go to the breadth of the current vertex every time we come to a new vertex and then take up the next vertex.

Suppose we start with vertex v_1, process it, then we visit all the adjacent vertices of v_1 say v_{11}, v_{12}, v_{13} ... v_{1n}. Then we visit all the adjacent vertices of v_{11}, then of v_{12} so on upto v_{1n}. This is continued till there is not vertex left out to be visited. Let us consider a graph given in Fig. 4.16.

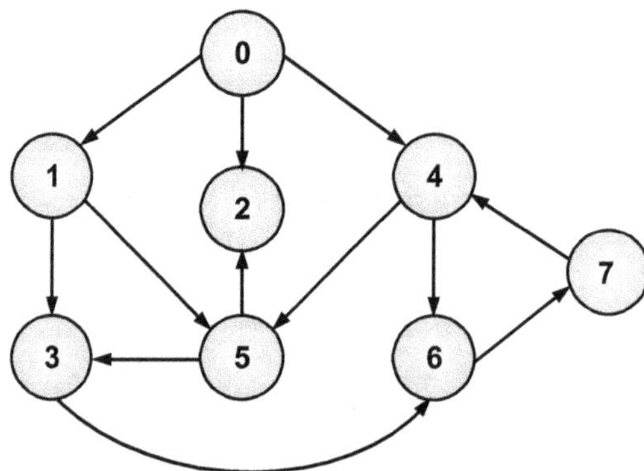

Fig. 4.16 : Graph

For the graph, we start with say vertex 0.

Mark it as visited.

The adjacent vertices are 1, 2 and 4.

Mark them as visited

The adjacent vertices of 1 are 3, 5

Mark them as visited

The adjacent vertices of 2 is 5 (already visited)

The adjacent vertices of 3 is 6

Mark it as visited.

The adjacent vertices of 5 is 2 and 3 already visited

The adjacent vertices of 6 is 7

Mark it as visited.

The adjacent vertices 7 is 4

Mark it as visited

The adjacent vertices of 4 are 0, 5 (already visited)

Hence, the BFS traversal is 0, 1, 2, 3, 5, 6, 7, 4.

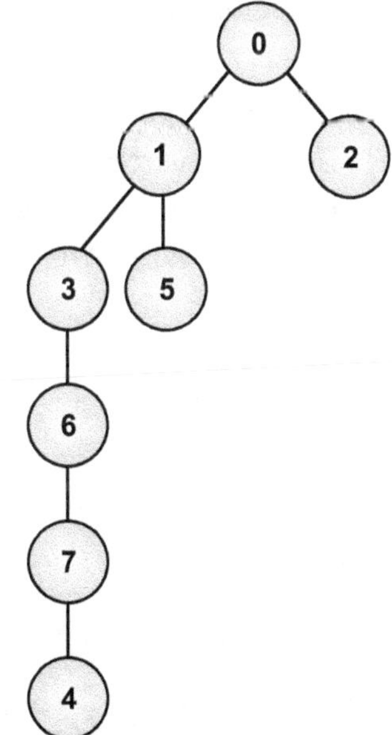

Fig. 4.17 : BFS traversal of graph in Fig. 4.16

Now consider an undirected graph shown in Fig. 4.18.

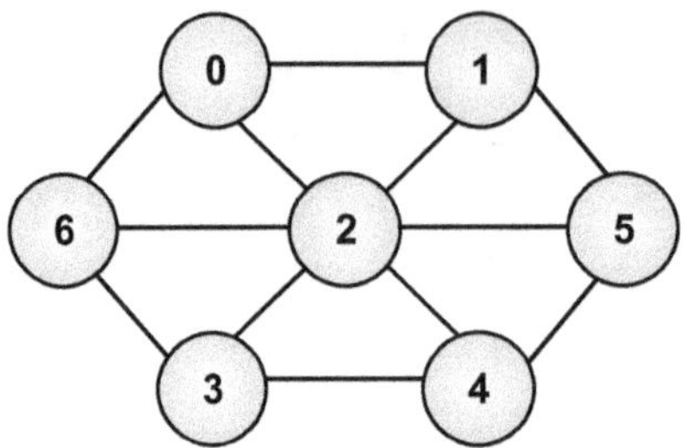

Fig. 4.18 : Graph

If starting vertex is 0.

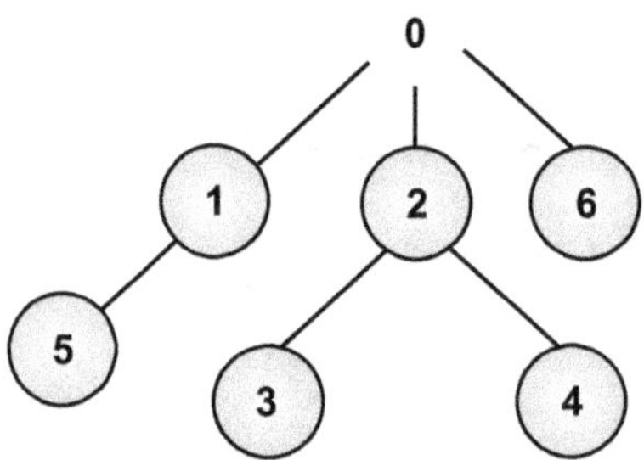

Fig. 4.19 : BFS traversal of graph in Fig. 4.18

Hence, the BFS Traversal is 0, 1, 2, 6, 5, 3, 4.

Algorithm for BFS Traversal :   **[May 05, 06, 09, Dec. 07]**

For implementing BFS traversal, we must use queue for storing the adjacent vertices of current vertex being visited.

The create_graph( ) function which was written earlier will be used here for storing graph in 2-D array int g[MAX] [MAX] and n is number of vertices. An additional array int visited [MAX] is used to store the information about status of each vertex whether it is visited or not. Initially, the elements of this array will be 0. Whenever a vertex is visited corresponding element will be made 1.

The algorithm is as below.

```
void bfs(int v1)
{
    insertq(v1);
    visited[v1] = 1;
    while (Queue is not empty)
    {
        v1=delq( );
        print v1;
```

```
            for(v2=0;v2<n;v2++)
            {
                    if(g[v1] [v2]==1)                // If there is edge v1 – v2
                    {
                            if(visited [v2]==0)      // If there is not yet visited
                            {
                                    insertq (v2)
                                    visited[v2] = 1;
                            }
                    }
            }
        }
}
```

Explanation :

- In above function, it is assumed that the queue is defined with an array of int, along with two functions insertq and delq. The detailed program is given at the end of this section.

- We start with source vertex v1 in the graph. It is inserted in the queue and marked as visited.

- A vertex in the queue is removed and it is processed i.e. displayed.

  All adjacent vertices of this current vertex are inserted in the queue and marked them as visited.

  This process is repeated until the queue becomes empty.

  Let us consider a graph given in Fig. 4.20.

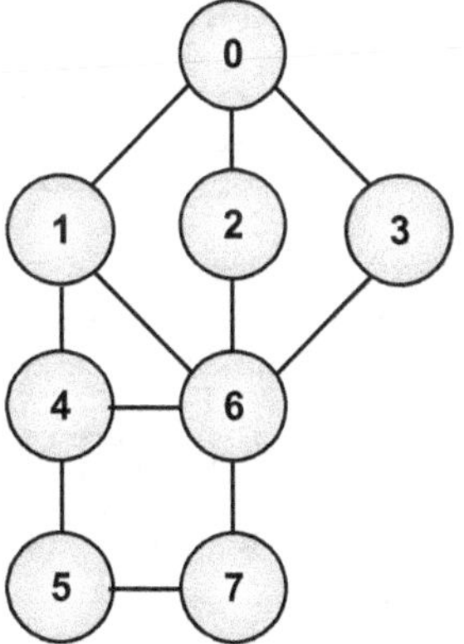

Fig. 4.20 : Graph

Step	q	visited
(0) Suppose our starting vertex is 0, it is inserted in queue and marked as visited.	q: 0	visited: 1 0 0 0 0 0 0 0 (indices 0 1 2 3 4 5 6 7)
(1) Remove 0 from queue and display. Output is 0. Insert adjacent vertices of 0 i.e. 1, 2, 3 on queue and mark them as visited.	q: X 1 2 3	visited: 1 1 1 1 0 0 0 0 (indices 0 1 2 3 4 5 6 7)
(2) Remove 1 from queue and display. Output is 1. Insert adjacent vertices of 1 i.e. 4 and 6 on queue and mark them as visited.	q: X X 2 3 4 6	visited: 1 1 1 1 1 0 1 0 (indices 0 1 2 3 4 5 6 7)
(3) Remove 2 from queue and display. Output is 2. There is no adjacent vertex of 2 not yet visited.	q: X X X 3 4 6	visited: 1 1 1 1 1 0 1 0 (indices 0 1 2 3 4 5 6 7)
(4) Remove 3 from queue and display. Output is 3. There is no adjacent vertex of 3 not yet visited.	q: X X X X 4 6	visited: 1 1 1 1 1 0 1 0 (indices 0 1 2 3 4 5 6 7)
(5) Remove 4 from queue and display. Output is 4. Insert 5 on queue. Mark it as visited.	q: X X X X X 6 5	visited: 1 1 1 1 1 1 1 0 (indices 0 1 2 3 4 5 6 7)
(6) Remove 6 from queue and display. Output is 6. Insert adjacent vertex of 6 i.e. 7 on queue and mark it as visited.	q: X X X X X X 5 7	visited: 1 1 1 1 1 1 1 1 (indices 0 1 2 3 4 5 6 7)

(7) Remove 5 from queue and display. Output is 5. There is no adjacent vertex of 3 not yet visited.	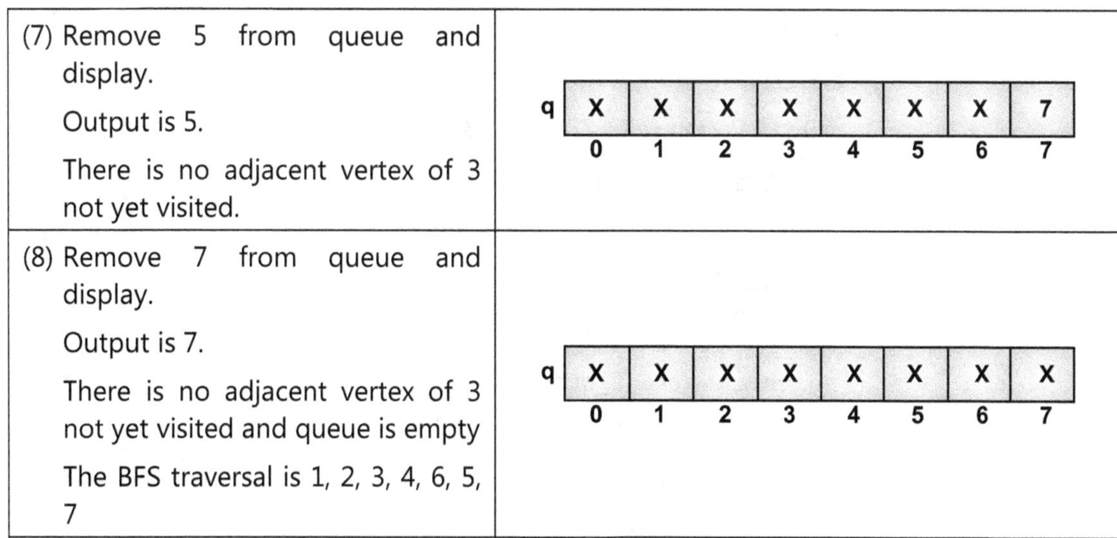
(8) Remove 7 from queue and display. Output is 7. There is no adjacent vertex of 3 not yet visited and queue is empty The BFS traversal is 1, 2, 3, 4, 6, 5, 7	

Following is the menu drive program to create a given graph using adjacency matrix and display BFS and DFS traversals.

```
# define MAX 10
int g[MAX] [MAX]
int n;
void create_graph( );
void disp( );
void bfs (int);
void dfs (int);
int q[MAX];
int rear = -1, front = -1;
void insertq (int);
int delq (int);
int visited [MAX];
void main( )
    {
        int ch, v1;
        do
        {
            for(i=0; i<n;i++)
```

```c
            visited [v1] = 0;
            clrscr();
            printf("1. create\n 2. Disp\n3. DFS\n4. BFS\n5. Exit\n")
            printf("Enter your choice\n");
            scanf("%d", &ch);
            switch(ch)
            {
                    case1 :  creat_graph();
                             break;
                    case2 :  disp( );
                             break;
                    case3 :  printf("Enter starting vertex\n");
                             scanf("%d, &v1);
                             dfs(v1);
                             break;
                    case4 :  printf("Enter starting vertex");
                             scan("%d", &v2);
                             bfs(v2);
            }
            getch( );
        } while (ch!=5);
}
void create_graph ()
{
    int v1, v2, i;
    char type, ch;
    printf("Enter type of graph\n");
    type = getch( );
    printf("Enter number of vertices\n");
    scanf("%d", &n);
```

```c
        do
        {
            printf("Enter edge\n");
            scanf("%d%d", &v1, &v2);
            g [v1] [v2] = 1;
            if(type=='u'||type=='u')
            g[v2] [v1] = 1;
            printf("Do you want to continue ?\n");
            ch = getch( );
        }   while(ch=='y'||ch=='Y')
}
void disp( )
{
    int i;
    printf("Adjacency matrix is\n");
    for(i=0;i<n;i++)
    {
        for(j=0;j<n;j++)
        {
            printf("%d",g[i][j]);
        }
        printf("\n");
    }
}
void dfs (int v1)
{
    int i, v2;
    printf("%d\n", v1);
    visited [v1] = 1;
    for (v2=0; v2<n; v2++)
```

```c
            {
                if (g[v1] [v2]==1)
                {
                    if (visited [v2]==0)
                    dfs (v2);
                }
            }
    }
    void bfs (int v1)
    {
        int v2;
        insertq (v1);
        visited[v1] = 1;
        while (front ! = rear)
        {
            v1 = delq ();
            printf("%d\n", v1);
            for(v2=0; v2<n; v2++)
            {
                if (g[v1] [v2]==1)
                {
                    if(visited [v2]==0)
                    {
                    insertq(v2);
                    visited [v2] = 1;
                    }
                }
            }
        }
    }
```

```c
void insertq(int v1)
{
        if (rear==MAX - 1)
        printf("Q full\n");
        else
        {
            rear++;
            q[rear] = v1;
        }
}
int delq( )
{
        int v1;
        if (front==rear)
        printf("Q empty\n");
        else
        {
            front ++;
            v1 = q[front];
            return(v1);
        }
}
```

Explanation :

- Most of the variables in the program are declared as global because they are required in at least one of function.

- The initialization of array visited[ ] is required because it is going to be modified in BFS and DFS functions.

- The variables front and rear of the queue are global and can be used directly in BFS to check whether q is empty or full.

- We can write separate functions for insertq, delq etc.

4.6 TOPOLOGICAL SORTING

We can represent the activities related to a task or project in the form of a graph. The activities in the task are interrelated. Suppose certain project has 5 activities to be completed in order to complete the project. They are represented by graph. The order of completion of the activities is also important, for example, unless we complete activities A and D we cannot start activity C.

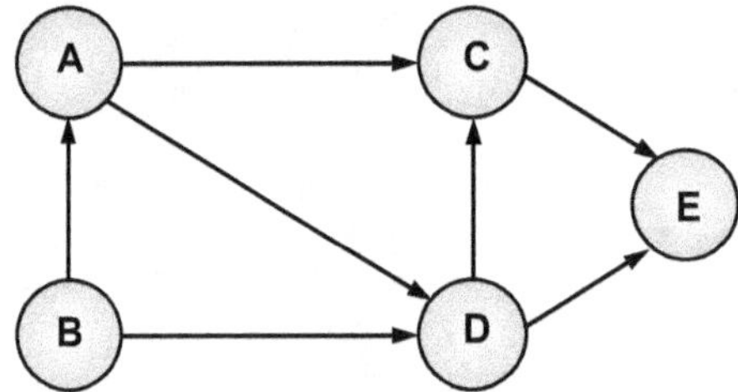

Fig. 4.21 : Activity graph

The topological sort is a process of assigning a linear ordering to the vertices of DAG (Directed Acyclic Graph), so that if there is an arc from vertex i to vertex j, than i appears before j in the linear ordering.

The topological sort for graph in Fig. 4.21 will be B, AD, C, E.

Note that the graph must be directed acyclic graph.

The directed graph has vertices representing activities and the edges represent precedence relationship between the activities is called Activity on Vertex Network (AOV).

The algorithm for topological sort is as below.

- Input AOV network.
- Let n be number of vertices.
- For i = 1 to n do

   If every vertex has predecessor stop (exit)
- Pick a vertex v which has no predecessor.
- Print v.
- Delete all edges starting from v.
- End (of for)
- Stop.

The topological sort for graph in Fig. 4.22 will be as below.

- We start with vertex B which has no predecessor.

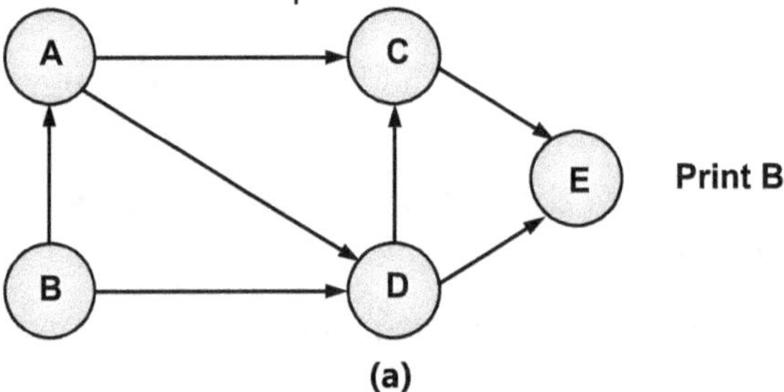

(a)

- Output B- delete the two outgoing edges from B.

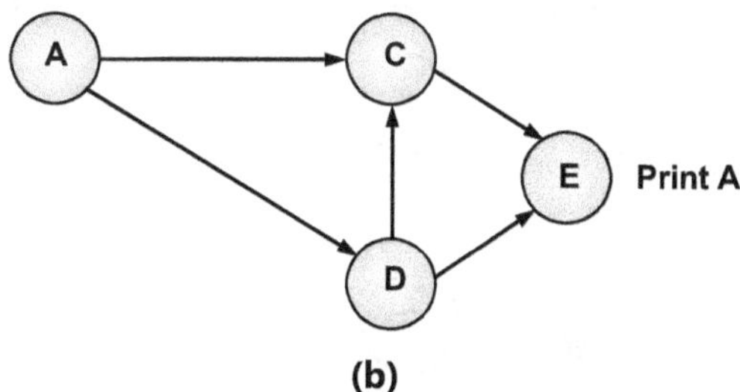

(b)

- We select vertex A which has no predecessor and delete outgoing edges from A.

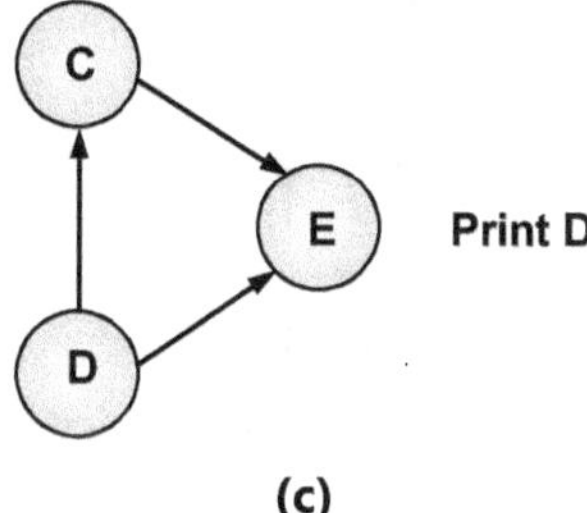

(c)

- We select vertex D and delete the outgoing edges.

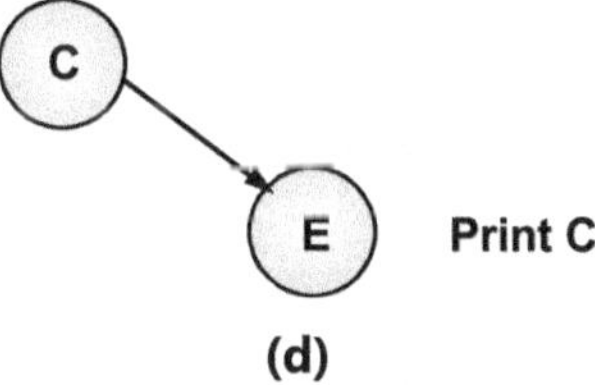

(d)

- We select vertex C and delete outgoing edges.

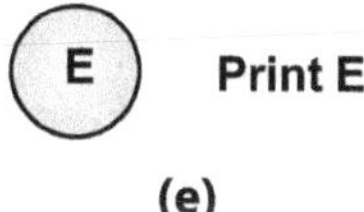

(e)

Thus, the topological sort can be represented as

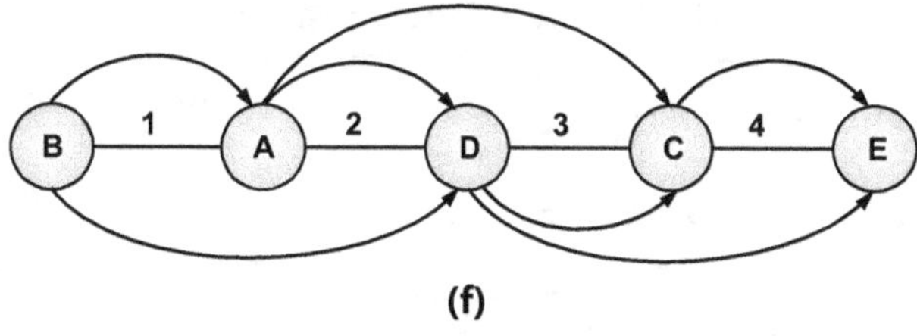

(f)

Fig. 4.22

Note : For a graph, there can be multiple topological sort order.

SOLVED EXAMPLES

Example 4.1 : Find topological sort for the graph given in Fig. 4.23.

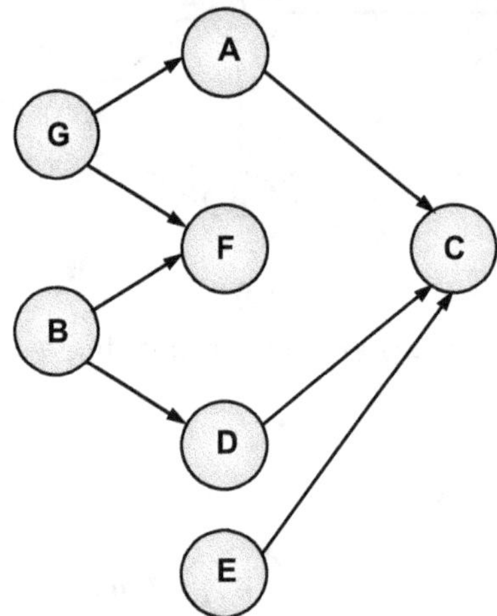

Fig. 4.23

Solution : We can start with either B, E or G. Hence there can be 3 different topological sorts.

If we start with B. It will be

B, D, G, A, F, E, and C. It is shown in Fig. 4.24 (a)

If we start with E it will be

E, G, B, A, D, F and C. It is shown in Fig. 4.24 (b)

If we start with G it can be

G, B, A, F, D, E and C

It is shown in Fig. 4.24 (c)

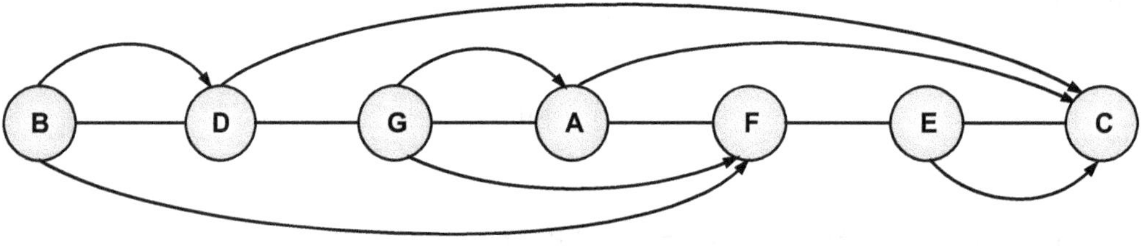

Fig. 4.24 (a) : Topological sort

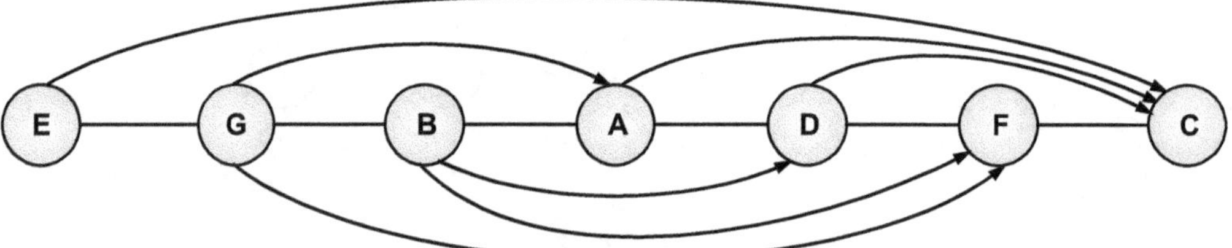

Fig. 4.24 (b) : Topological sort

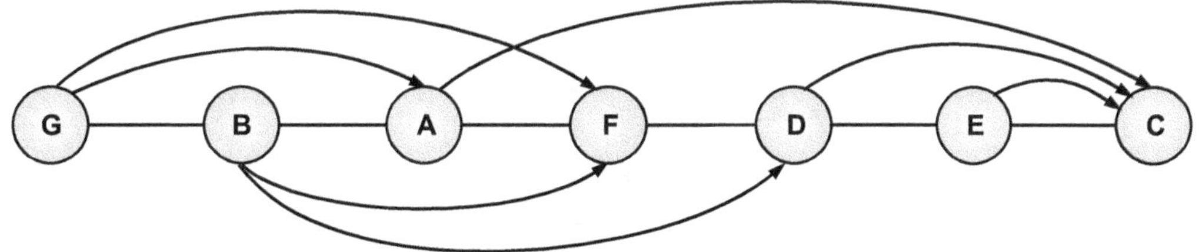

Fig. 4.24 (c) : Topological sort

4.7 MINIMAL SPANNING TREE   [May 06, Dec. 06, May 07, 08, 10]

An undirected graph is said to be connected if for every pair of distinct vertices there is a path.

For a connected undirected graph if we carry out DFS traversal from any vertex as source, all the vertices in the graph can be traversed.

Hence, for a connected undirected graph we can form set of edges which will include all the vertices. Moreover, it is possible for trees with the edges that include all the vertices. A tree is a graph in which there is no cycle (closed path).

Any tree that has set of edges in the graph and includes all the vertices is called spanning Tree.

Consider a graph given in Fig. 4.25 with cost/weights.

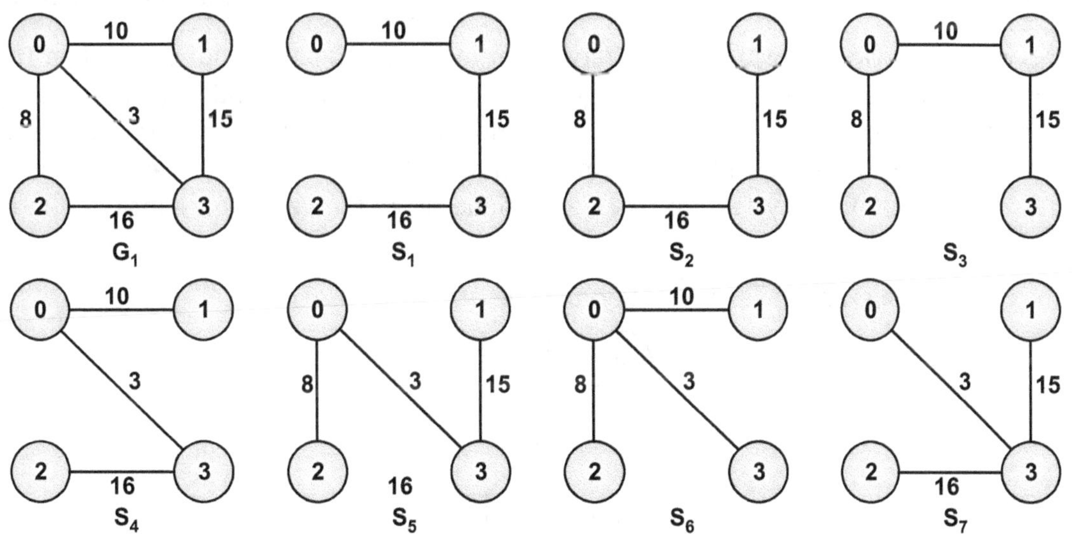

Fig. 4.25 : Graph G_1 and its spanning Trees

The cost of spanning tree is total weights of all the edges in the spanning tree.

The cost of spanning trees shown in the graph of Fig. 4.25 are

$S_1 \rightarrow 41$

$S_2 \rightarrow 39$

$S_3 \rightarrow 33$

$S_4 \rightarrow 29$

$S_5 \rightarrow 26$

$S_6 \rightarrow 21$

$S_7 \rightarrow 34$

The minimum cost is 21 for spanning tree S_6. It is called as minimal cost spanning tree or minimal spanning tree.

Definition :

The spanning tree of a graph whose sum of the costs or weights is minimum is called minimum spanning tree.

There are two algorithms which are used to find minimum spanning tree.

1.   Prim's algorithm

2.   Kruskal's algorithm

4.7.1 Prim's Algorithm   [May 06, 10, Dec. 06]

In this algorithm, we start with any arbitrary vertex in the graph as the root of the tree. Then we find the vertex adjacent to this root vertex which has an edge with minimum cost or weight. Now we have two vertices in the tree. Find all the out-going edges from these two vertices and select an edge with minimum cost among these such that the addition of this edge should not form a cycle. Like this we continue till all the vertices are included in the tree.

Let us consider an example i.e. the same graph we had in Fig. 4.26 (a).

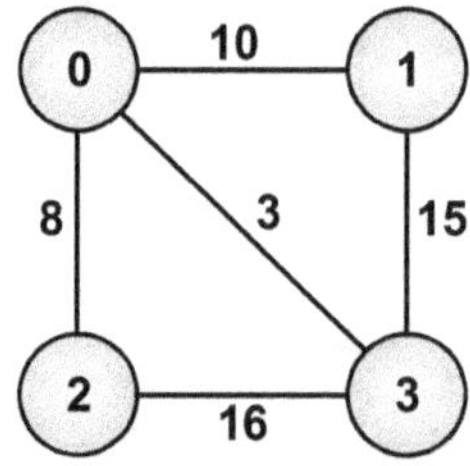

Fig. 4.26 (a) : Graph

Let us start with vertex 0.

The outgoing edges from this vertex and selected vertex is shown in Fig. 4.26 (b).

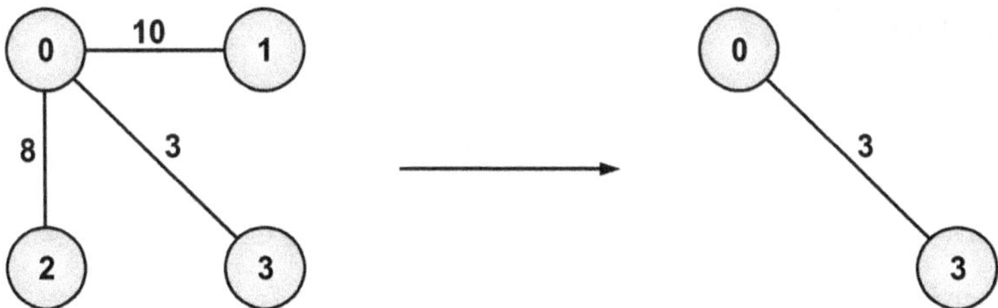

Fig. 4.26 (b) : Step 1 for MST

Now find the outgoing edges of 0 and 3 and select minimum of the edges.

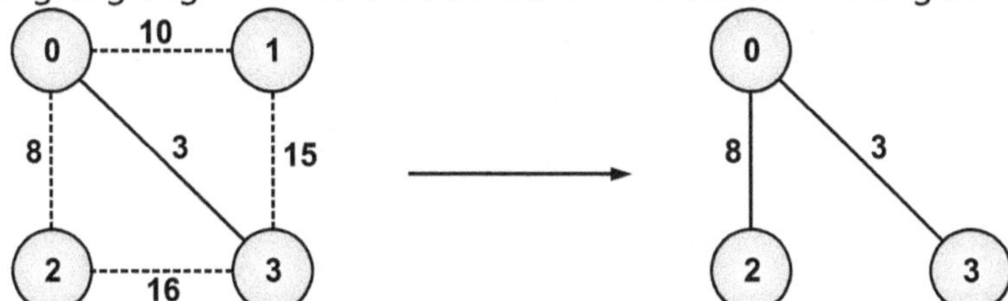

Fig. 4.26 (c) : Step 2 for MST

Now find the outgoing edges of 0, 2, and 3.

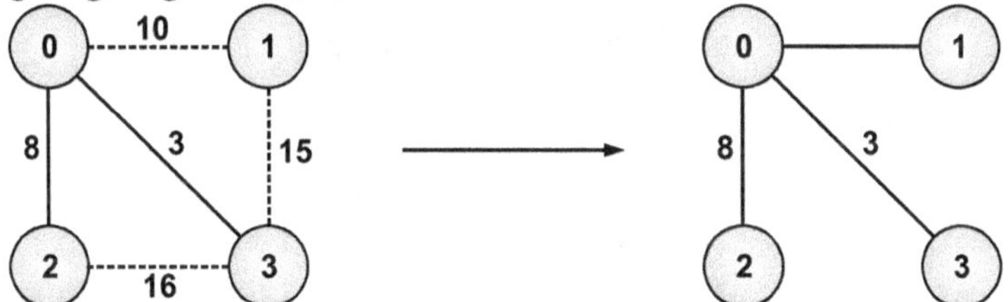

Fig. 4.26 (d) : Step 3 for MST

Since above graph includes all vertices it is the MST.

Example 4.2 : Show the stepwise construction of minimum spanning tree for the given graph using Prim's algorithm. [Fig. 4.27 (a)]

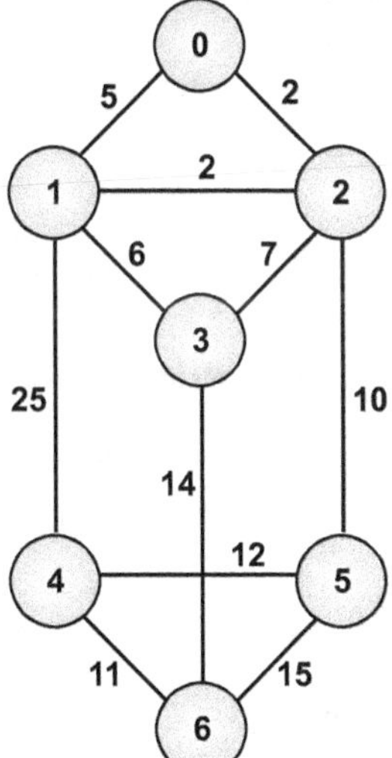

Fig. 4.27 (a) : Graph

Step 1 : Let us start from vertex 0

Fig. 4.27 (b) : Prim's algorithm

Step 2 : The adjacent vertices with cost are

$$0 - 1 \rightarrow 5$$

$$0 - 2 \rightarrow 2 \text{ (minimum)}$$

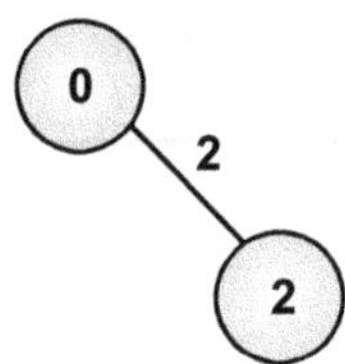

Fig. 4.27 (c) : Prim's algorithm

Step 3 : The adjacent vertex of 0 and 2 not forming cycle are

$$0 - 1 \rightarrow 5$$

$$0 - 2 \rightarrow 2 \text{ (minimum)}$$

$$2 - 3 \rightarrow 7$$

$$2 - 5 \rightarrow 10$$

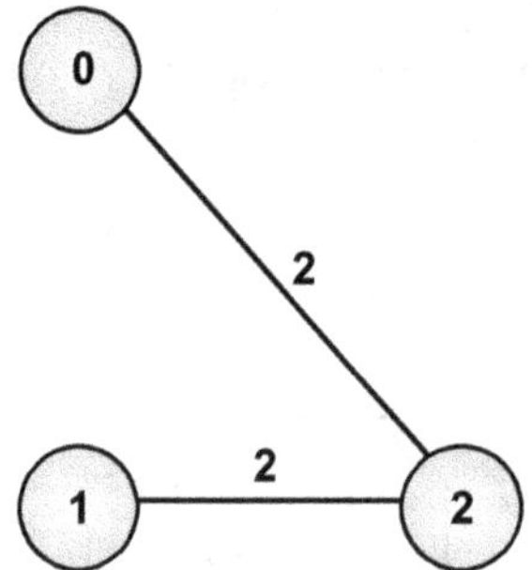

Fig. 4.27 (d) : Prim's algorithm

Step 4 : The adjacent vertex of 0, 1, 2 not forming cycle are

$$2 - 5 \rightarrow 10$$

$$2 - 3 \rightarrow 7$$

$$1 - 3 \rightarrow 6 \text{ (minimum)}$$

$$1 - 4 \rightarrow 25$$

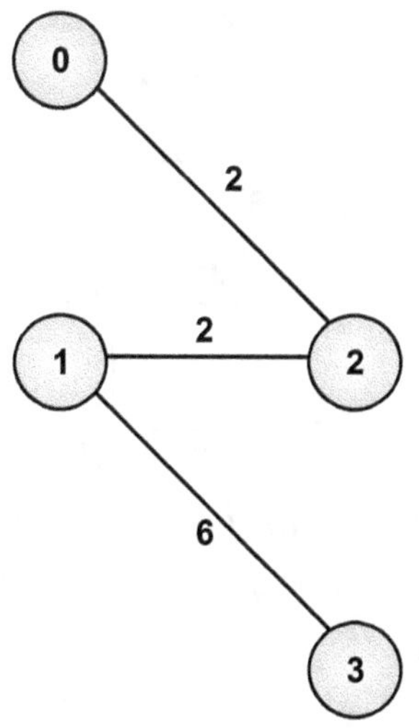

Fig. 4.27 (e) : Prim's algorithm

Step 5 : The adjacent vertex of 0, 1, 2, 3 are

$$2 - 5 \ -> 10 \ (minimum)$$
$$1 - 4 \ -> 25$$
$$3 - 6 \ -> \ 14$$

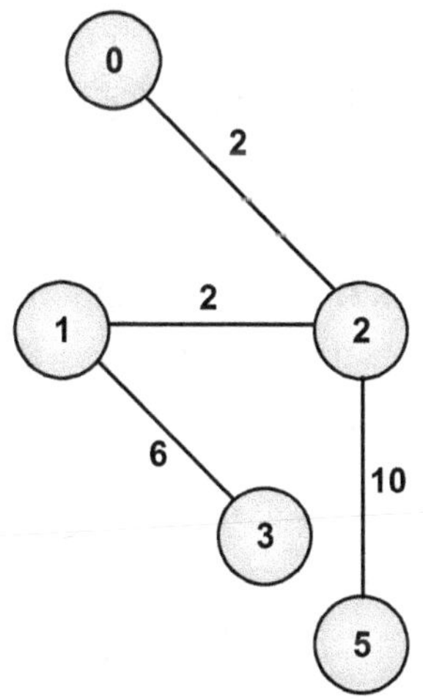

Fig. 4.27 (f) : Prim's algorithm

Step 6 : The adjacent vertex of 0, 1, 2, 3, 5 are

$$1 - 4 \ -> 25$$
$$5 - 4 \ -> 12 \ \ (minimum)$$
$$3 - 6 \ -> 14$$
$$5 - 6 \ -> 15$$

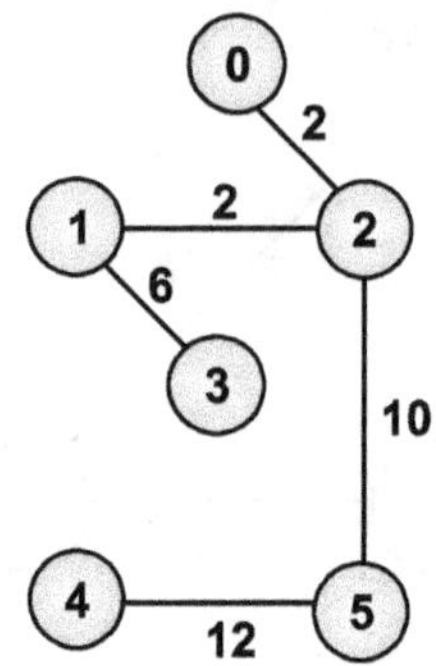

Fig. 4.27 (g) : Prim's algorithm

Step 7 : The adjacent vertex of 0, 1, 2, 3, 4, are

$$5 - 6 \rightarrow 15$$

$$4 - 6 \rightarrow 11 \quad (\text{minimum})$$

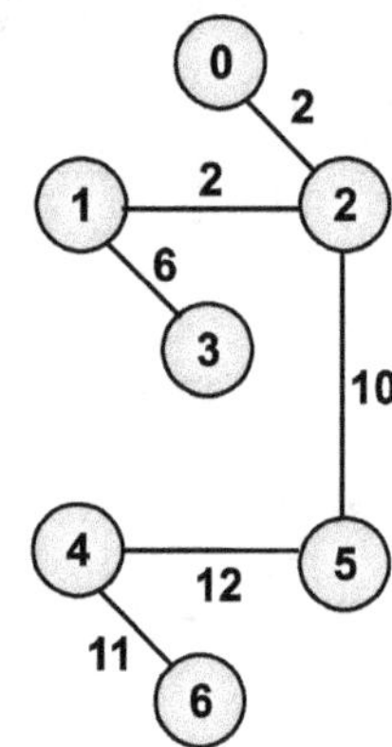

Fig. 4.27 (h) : Prim's algorithm

This is spanning tree of given graph the total cost is 2 + 2 + 6 + 10 + 12 + 11 = 43.

The algorithm can be written as below.

Prim's algorithm :

```
1.   T = {φ }
2.   S = {0}
3.   While(u≠v)
     {
             Let (u, v) be lowest cost edge such that u is in S and v is in V – S
             T = T ∪ { (c, v) }
             S = S ∪ {v}
     }
4.   Stop
```

Explanation :

1. T is the set of edges of the minimum spanning tree to be constructed. Initially, it will be empty set.

2. S is the set of vertices of the minimum spanning tree. Initially, it will be having starting vertex say 0.

3. At each step we find shortest edge (u, v) that connects S and remaining vertices of the graph G i.e. V − S. The edge is added to T and vertex to S.

This process is continued until S becomes V (i.e. all vertices of graph are included in the tree).

Analysis :

When we start with particular vertex, we examine the edges connected to it. For this we have to check connectivity to all vertices and then select minimum cost edge. This process is repeated for all vertices. Hence, it is nested loop where outer, and inner loop will run for n times; where n is number of vertices. Hence, time complexity of algorithm will be $O(n^2)$.

4.7.2 Kruskal's Algorithm   [May 06, 07, 09, 10]

This algorithm also finds minimum spanning tree. If we are given a graph $G \equiv (V, E)$, we start taking all vertices of the graph initially and no edges. We keep on adding the edges to the spanning tree in order of increasing cost in the MST, till all vertices are in one component.

Algorithm :

1. $G \equiv (V, E)$.

2. We start with a graph $T \equiv (V, \varphi)$ consisting of n vertices of G and no edges.

3. Examine edges from E. Repeat 4 and 5 in increasing order of cost of edges.

4. Add edge e_i to T if it connects two vertices in two different connected components of T. Otherwise discard e_i.

5. Take next edge and go to 3, if the vertices are not in one connected component.

Analysis :

A priority queue can be used to store the edges and taking them in increasing cost order. The formation of priority queue of e edges will require $O(e\log_2 e)$. Hence, there are n vertices and e edges assuming n < e. This algorithm will have time complexity $O(e\log_2 e)$.

Consider following example :   [May 06]

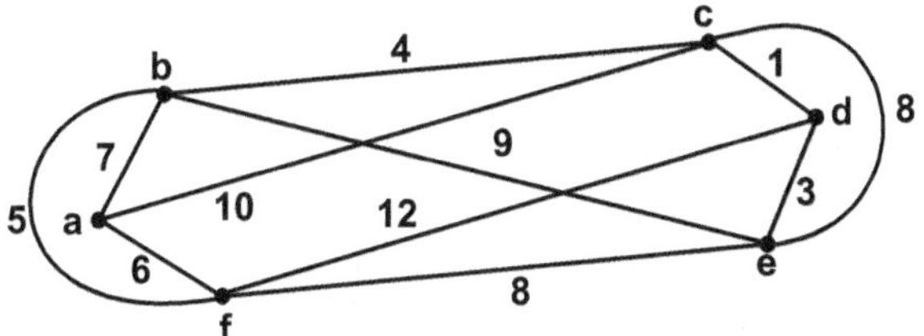

Fig. 4.28 (a) : Graph

We start with all vertices in the graph a, b, c, d, e, f as follows :

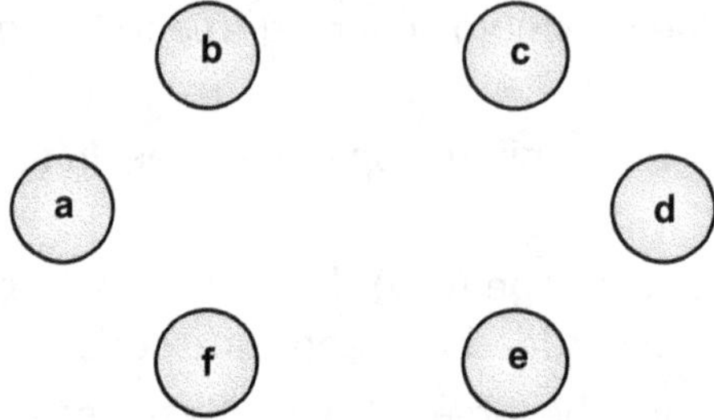

Fig. 4.28 (b) : Kruskal's algorithm

Step 1 : The edges with cost 1 are c – d include it in MST.

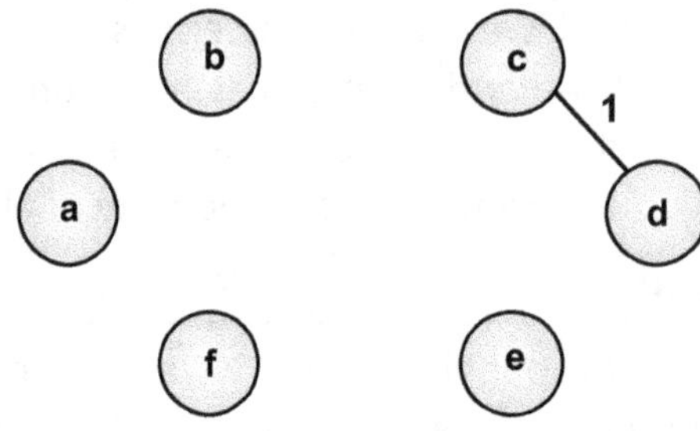

Fig. 4.28 (c) : Kruskal's algorithm

Step 2 : Edges with cost 2 Nil

Edges with cost 3 d – e

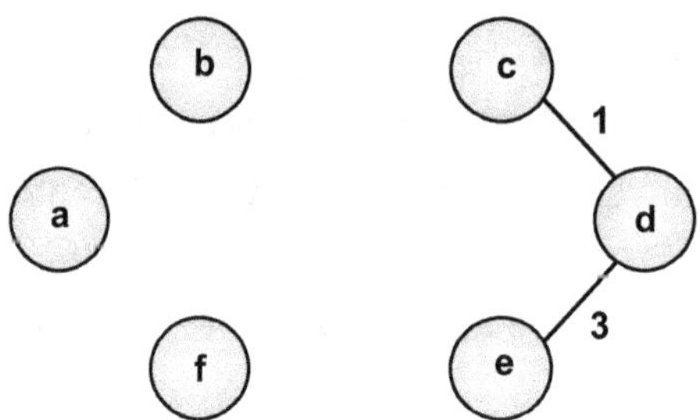

Fig. 4.28 (d) : Kruskal's algorithm

Step 3 : Edges with cost 4 : b – c

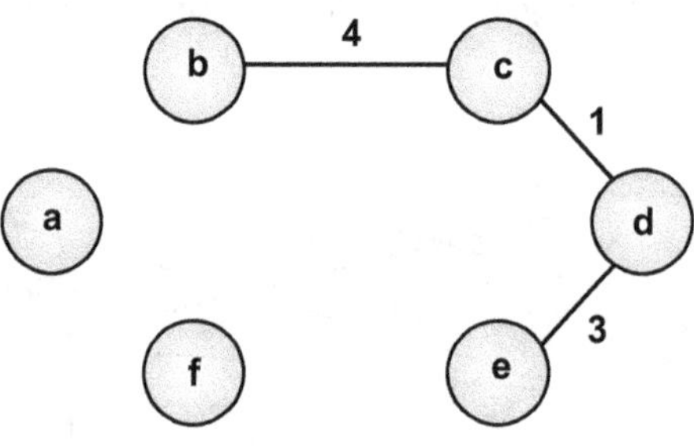

Fig. 4.28 (e) : Kruskal's algorithm

Step 4 : Edges with cost 5 : b – f

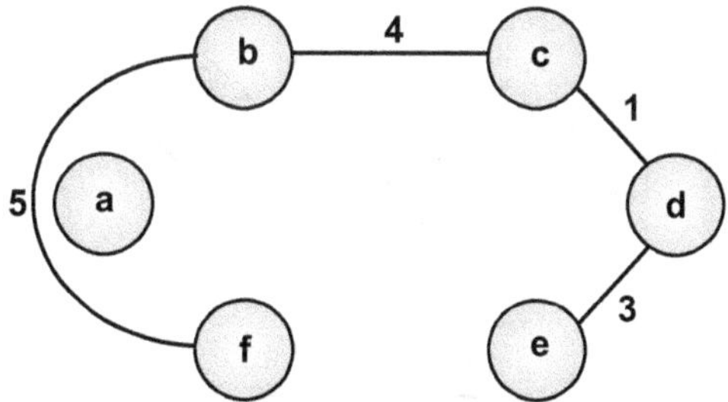

Fig. 4.28 (f) : Kruskal's algorithm

Step 5 : Edges with cost 6 : f – a

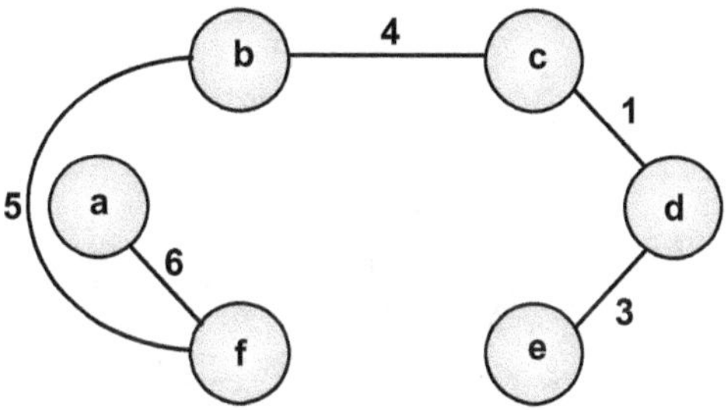

Fig. 4.28 (g) : Kruskal's algorithm

This is minimum spanning tree. Total cost is 19.

Example 4.3 : Find minimum spanning tree for following graph using *Kruskal's* algorithm.

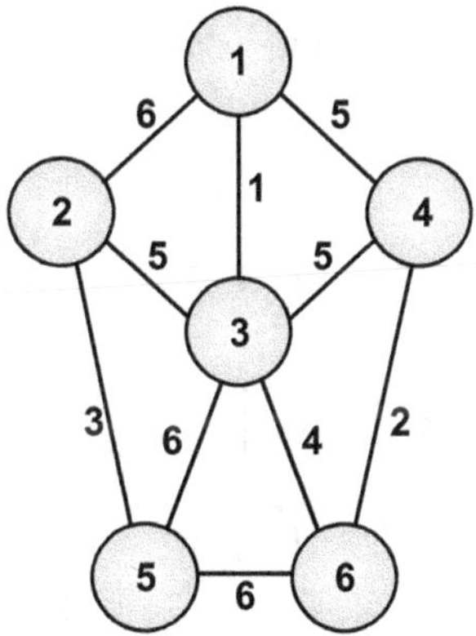

Fig. 4.29 (a) : Graph

Solution :

We start with all vertices in the graph.

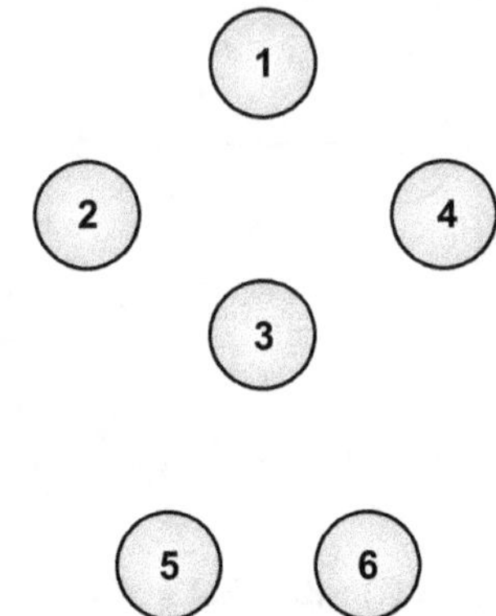

Fig. 4.29 (b) : Kruskal's algorithm

Step 1 : Edges with cost = 1 are 1 – 3

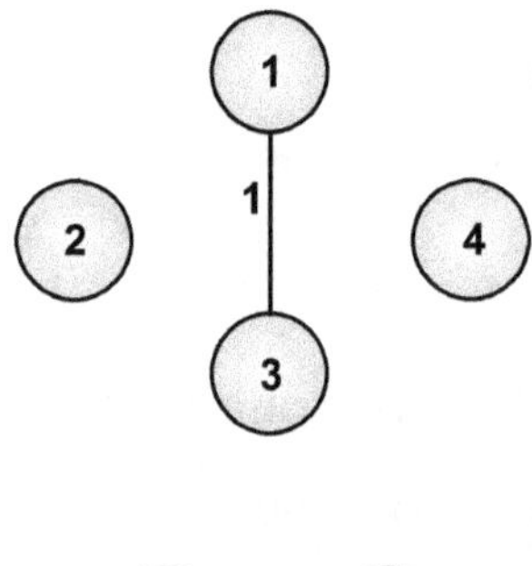

Fig. 4.29 (c) : Kruskal's algorithm

Step 2 : Edges with cost = 2 are 4 – 6

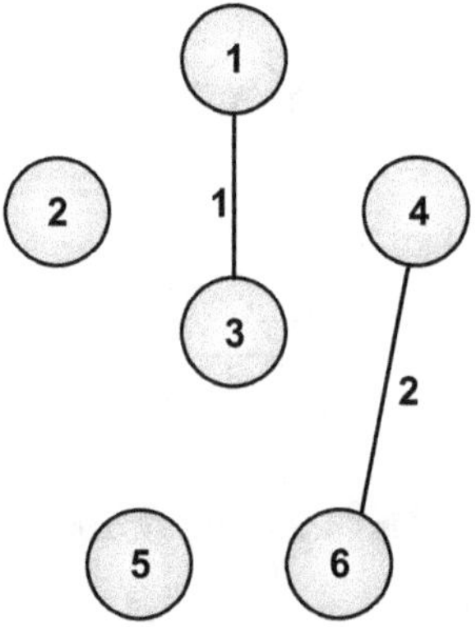

Fig. 4.29 (d) : Kruskal's algorithm

Step 3 : Edges with cost = 3 are 2 – 5

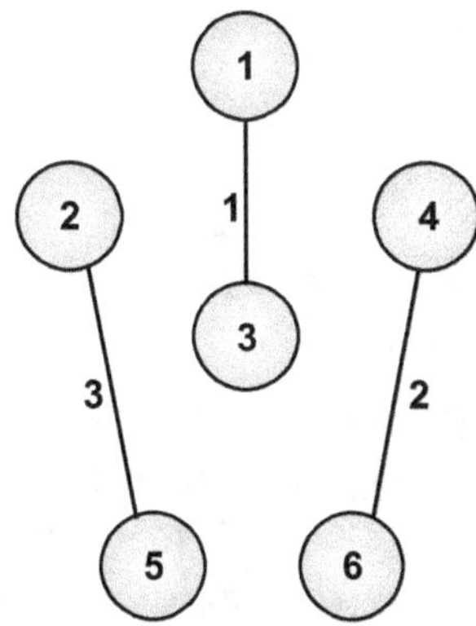

Fig. 4.29 (e) : Kruskal's algorithm

Step 4 : Edges with cost = 4 are 3 – 6

Vertices are not in one component.

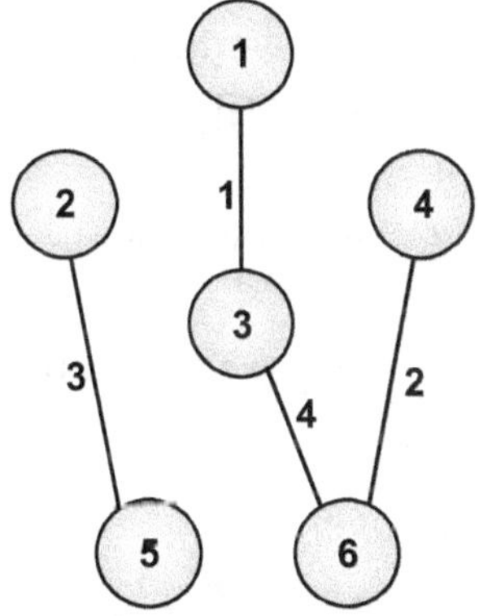

Fig. 4.29 (f) : Kruskal's algorithm

Step 5 : Edges with cost = 5 are 2 – 3 and 3 – 4

3, 4 are in same connected component hence exclude.

2, 3 are in different connected component hence include.

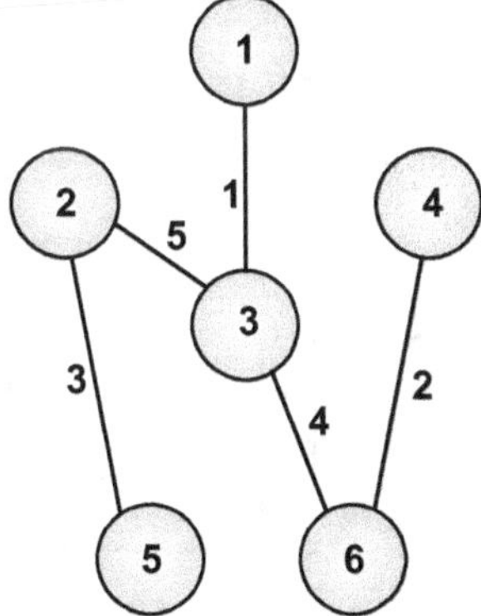

Fig. 4.29 (g) : Kruskal's algorithm

All vertices are in are connected component.

Hence this is minimum spanning tree.

The cost of MST is 15.

Shortest Paths :

The shortest path between two nodes of a graph is a sequence of connected nodes so that the sum of the edges that inter-connect them is minimal.

Shortest Path using Dijkstra's Algorithm :

Dijkstra's algorithm solves the single-source shortest-path problem when all edges have non-negative weights. It is a greedy algorithm and similar to Prim's algorithm. Algorithm starts at the source vertex, s, it grows a tree, T, that ultimately spans all vertices reachable from S. Vertices are added to T in order of distance i.e., first S, then the vertex closest to S, then the next closest, and so on. Following implementation assumes that graph G is represented by adjacency lists.

DIJKSTRA (G, w, s)

- INITIALIZE SINGLE-SOURCE (G, s)
- S ← { }   // S will ultimately contains vertices of final shortest-path weights from s
- Initialize priority queue Q i.e., Q ← V[G]
- while priority queue Q is not empty do
- u ← EXTRACT_MIN(Q)   // Pull out new vertex
- S ← S E {u}

    // Perform relaxation for each vertex v adjacent to u
- for each vertex v in Adj[u] do
- Relax (u, v, w)

Analysis

Like Prim's algorithm, Dijkstra's algorithm runs in O(|E|lg|V|) time.

Example 4.4 : Step by Step operation of Dijkstra algorithm.

Step 1 : Given initial graph G = (V, E). All nodes have infinite cost except the source node, s, which has 0 cost.

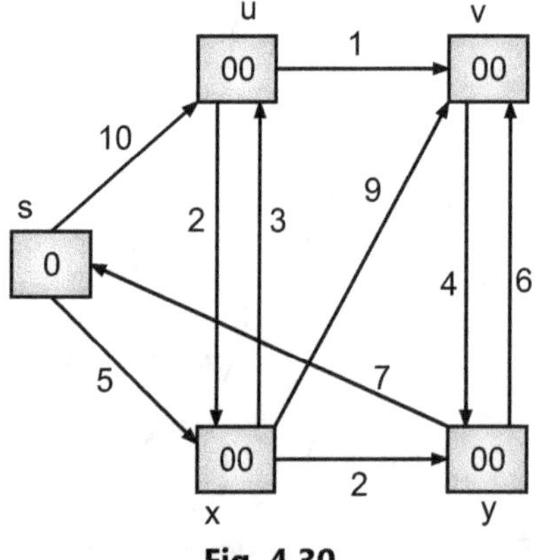

Fig. 4.30

Step 2 : First we choose the node, which is closest to the source node, s. We initialize d[s] to 0. Add it to S. Relax all nodes adjacent to source, s. Update predecessor (see red light arrow in diagram below) for all nodes updated.

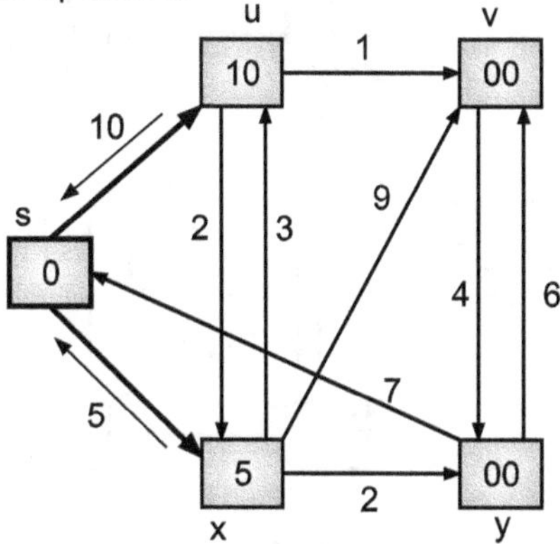

Fig. 4.31

Step 3 : Choose the closest node, x. Relax all nodes adjacent to node x. Update predecessors for nodes u, v and y (again notice red light arrows in diagram below).

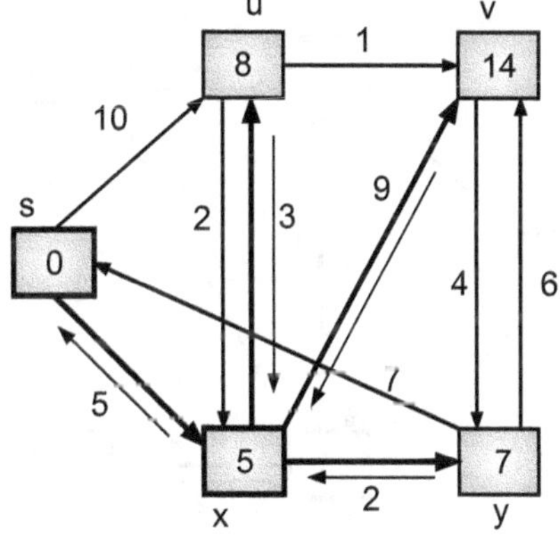

Fig. 4.32

Step 4 : Now, node y is the closest node, so add it to S. Relax node v and adjust its predecessor (red light arrows remember!).

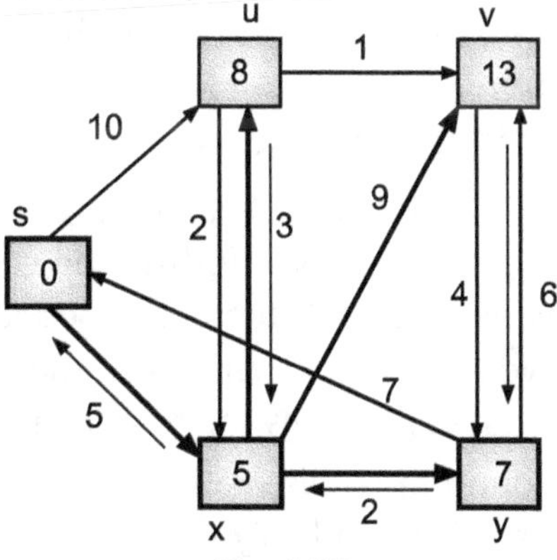

Fig. 4.33

Step 5 : Now we have node u that is closest. Choose this node and adjust its neighbor node v.

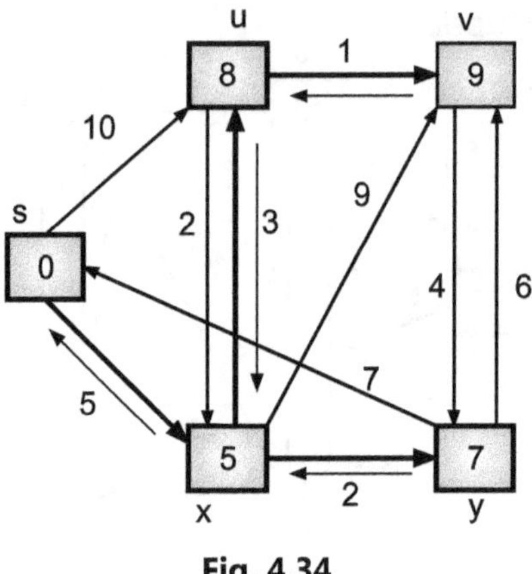

Fig. 4.34

Step 6 : Finally, add node v. The predecessor list now defines the shortest path from each node to the source node, s.

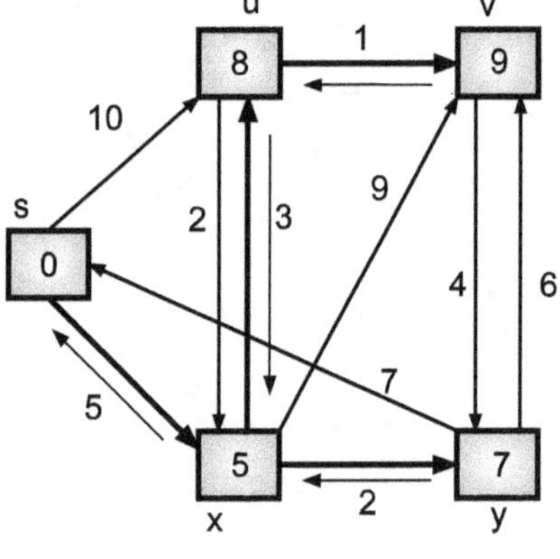

Fig. 4.35

Shortest Path using Warshall's Algorithm

Warshall algorithm is a procedure, which is used to find the shortest (longest) paths among all pairs of nodes in a graph, which does not contain any cycles of negative length. The main advantage of Warshall algorithm is its simplicity.

Warshall algorithm uses a matrix of lengths D_0 as its input. If there is an edge between nodes i and j, then the matrix D_0 contains its length at the corresponding coordinates. The diagonal of the matrix contains only zeros. If there is no edge between edges i and j, then the position (i, j) contains positive infinity. In other words, the matrix represents lengths of all paths between nodes that does not contain any intermediate node.

In each iteration of Warshall algorithm is this matrix recalculated, so it contains lengths of paths among all pairs of nodes using gradually enlarging set of intermediate nodes. The matrix D_1, which is created by the first iteration of the procedure, contains paths among all nodes using exactly one (predefined) intermediate node. D_2 contains lengths using two predefined intermediate nodes. Finally, the matrix D_n uses n intermediate nodes.

This transformation can be described using the following recurrent formula :

$$D^n_{ij} = \min \left(D^{n-1}_{ij}, D^{n-1}_{ik}, D^{n-1}_{kj} \right)$$

Because this transformation never rewrites elements, which are to be used to calculate the new matrix, we can use the same matrix for both D^i and D^{i+1}.

Take this graph,

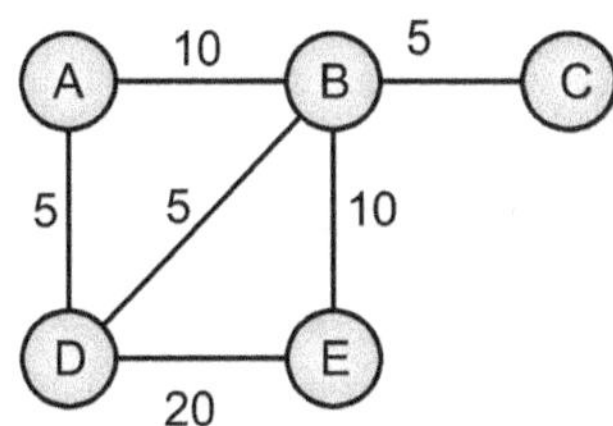

Fig. 4.36

There are several paths between A and E :

Path 1 : A -> B -> E 20

Path 2 : A -> D -> E 25

Path 3 : A -> B -> D -> E 35

Path 4 : A -> D -> B -> E 20

There are several things to notice here :

- There can be more then one route between two nodes.
- The number of nodes in the route isn't important (**Path 4** has 4 nodes but is shorter than **Path 2**, which has 3 nodes).
- There can be more than one path of minimal length.

Something else that should be obvious from the graph, is that, any path worth considering is simple. That is, you only go through each node **once**.

Unfortunately, this is not always the case. The problem appears when you allow negative weight edges. This isn't by itself bad. But if **a loop of negative weight appears**, then **there is no shortest path**. Look at this example :

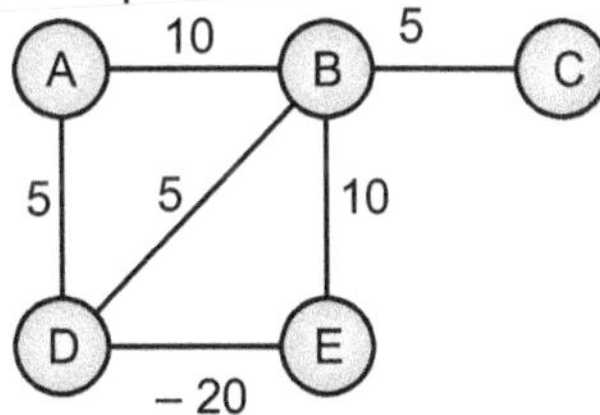

Fig. 4.37

Look at the path B -> E -> D -> B. This is a loop, because the starting node is also the end. What's the cost? It's 10 – 20 + 5 = -5. This means that adding this loop to a path once lowers the cost of the path by 5. Adding it twice would lower the cost by 2 * 5 = 10. So, whatever shortest path you may have come up with, you can make it smaller by going through the loop one more time. BTW there's no problem with a negative cost path.

Warshall Algorithm :

This algorithm calculates the length of the shortest path between all nodes of a graph in O(V3) time. Note that it doesn't actually find the paths, only their lengths.

Let's say you have the adjacency matrix of a graph. Assuming no loop of negative values, at this point you have the minimum distance between any two nodes which are connected by an edge.

A B C D E

A 0 10 0 5 0

B 10 0 5 5 10

C 0 5 0 0 0

D 5 5 0 0 20

E 0 10 0 20 0

The graph is the one shown above (the first one).

The idea is to try to interspace A between any two nodes in hopes of finding a shorter path.

A B C D E

A 0 10 0 5 0

B 10 0 5 5 10

C 0 5 0 0 0

D 5 5 0 0 20

E 0 10 0 20 0

Then try to interspace *B* between any two nodes :

A B C D E

A 0 10 **15** 5 **20**

B 10 0 5 5 10

C **15** 5 0 **10** **15**

D 5 5 **10** 0 **15**

E **20** 10 **15** **15** 0

Do the same for *C* :

A B C D E

A 0 10 15 5 20

B 10 0 5 5 10

C 15 5 0 10 15

D 5 5 10 0 15
E 20 10 15 15 0
Do the same for D :
A B C D E
A 0 10 15 5 20
B 10 0 5 5 10
C 15 5 0 10 15
D 5 5 10 0 15
E 20 10 15 15 0
And for E :
 A B C D E
A 0 10 15 5 20
B 10 0 5 5 10
C 15 5 0 10 15
D 5 5 10 0 15
E 20 10 15 15 0

SUMMARY

- Graph is a non-linear data structure consisting of set of nodes or vertices or points and set of arcs or edges (E).
- A graph can be of two types :
  (i) Directed graph,
  (ii) Undirected graph.
- Directed graph has ordered edges whereas undirected graph does not have ordered edges.
- A graph can be represented using :
  (i) Adjacency matrix,
  (ii) Adjacency list.
- In adjacency matrix representation, if there is edge between two vertices of graph v_1 and v_2, the element in row v_1 and column v_2 is 1, otherwise it will be 0.
- In adjacency list representation, a list of nodes adjacent to each vertex is stored in an array of head nodes.
- A graph can be traversed using two ways :
  (i) Depth First Search (DFS),
  (ii) Breadth First Search (BFS).
- DFS traversal involves visiting vertices such that every time we visit a new vertex adjacent to it.
- BFS traversal involves visiting all the adjacent vertices of current vertex then move to the next.
- Shortest path algorithm (Dijkstra's algorithm) is used to find shortest path from a vertex to all other vertices of the graph.

- A spanning tree of a graph is a tree which includes all the vertices of the graph.
- Minimum spanning tree of a graph is a spanning tree of the graph whose sum of costs is minimum.
- Two algorithm can be used to find minimum spanning tree :
    (i)   Prim's algorithm,
    (ii) Kruskal's algorithm.

SOLVED PROBLEMS

1.　**Find minimum spanning tree for following graph using Prim's algorithm.**

[(4m) Dec. 05, Dec. 10]

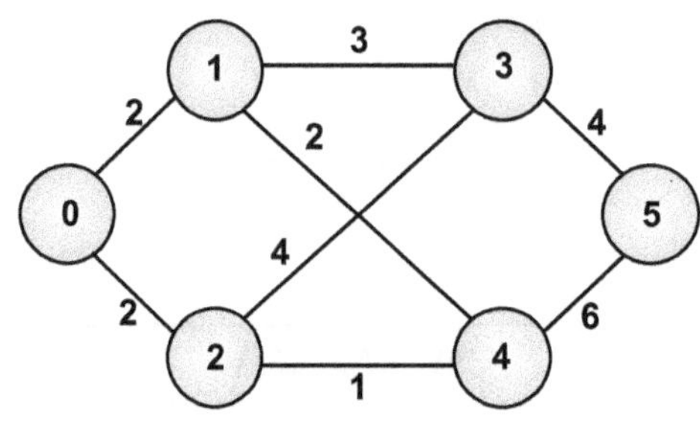

Fig. 4.38

Solution : We start with vertex 0.

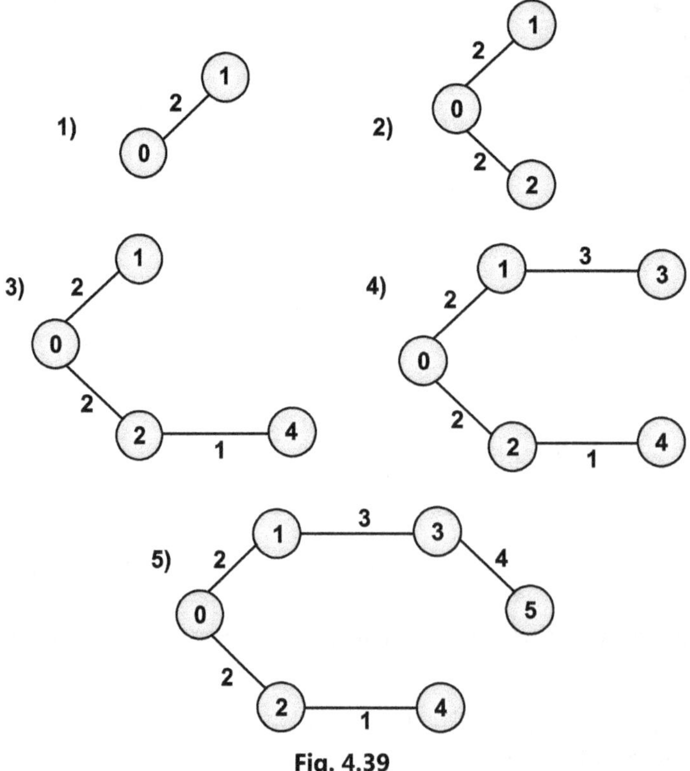

Fig. 4.39

2. **Find minimum spanning tree for the graph given in solved problem 1 (Fig. 4.38) using Kruskal's algoritm.** **[May 05, 06, Dec. 05, 07, 10]**

Solution :

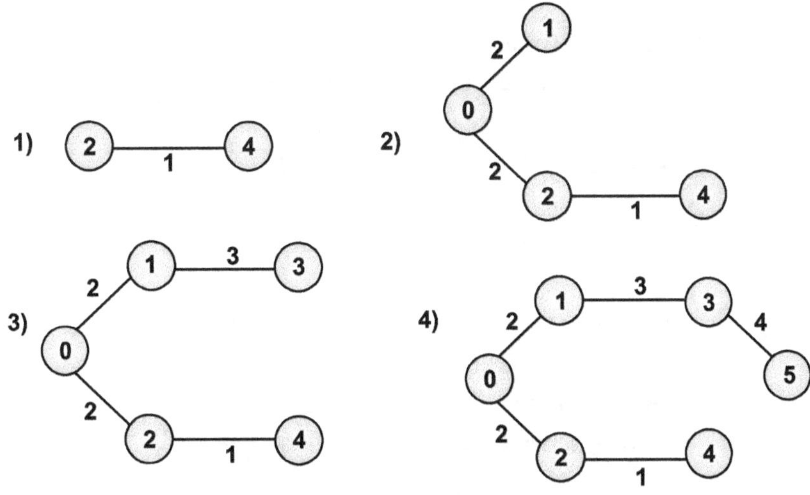

Fig. 4.40

$$\text{Total cost} = 1 + 2 + 2 + 3 + 4$$
$$= 12$$

3. **Represent following graph using adjacency matrix and adjacency list.**

[(6m) May 10]

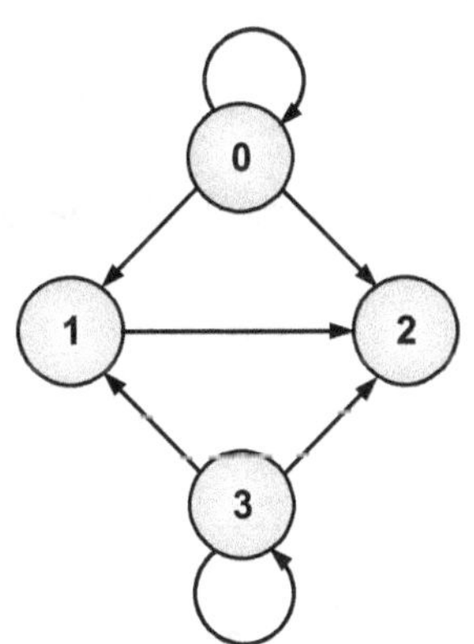

Fig. 4.41

Solution :

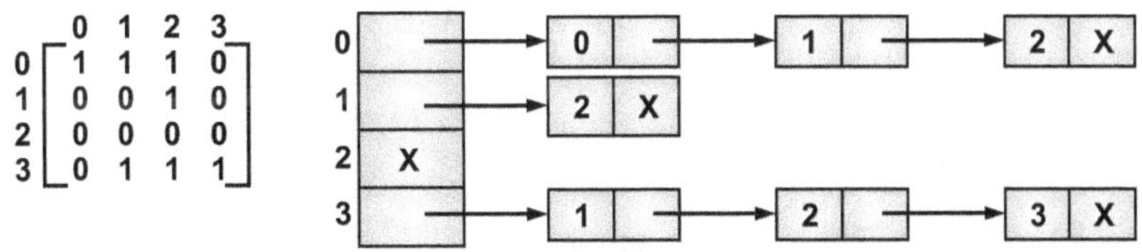

Fig. 4.42

4. Write DFS and BFS traversal for given graph in solved problem 3 (Fig. 4.41)

[(4m) May 08, 10]

Solution :

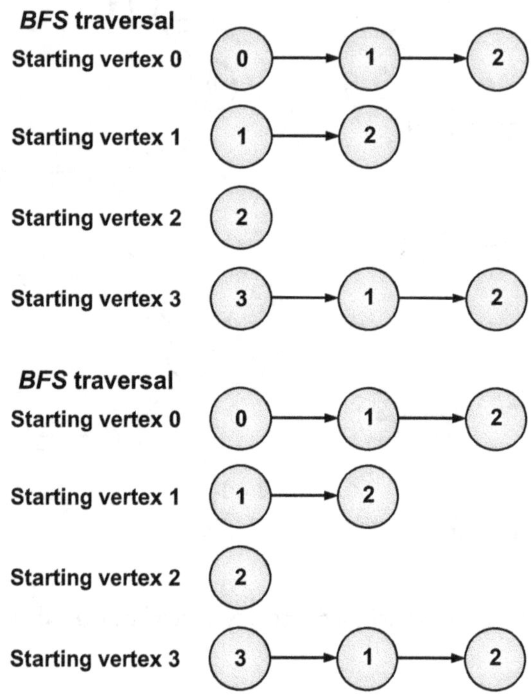

Fig. 4.43

5. What do you mean by adjacency matrix and adjacency list of the following graph :

[(8m) May 07]

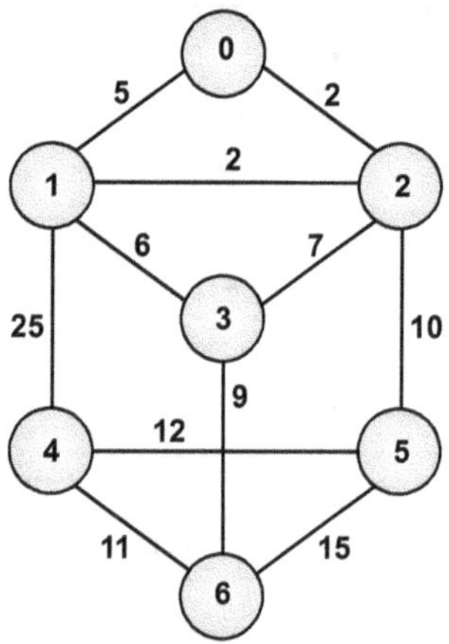

Fig. 4.44

Solution :

1. 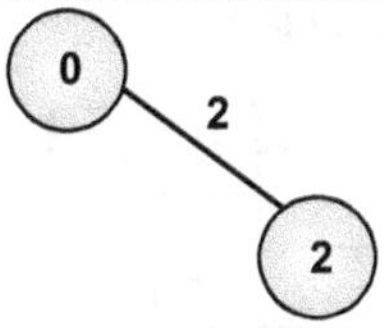 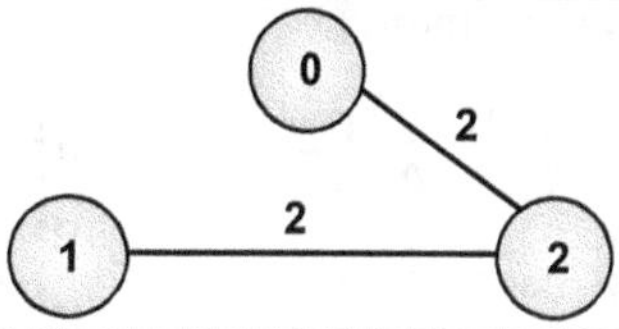	
2. 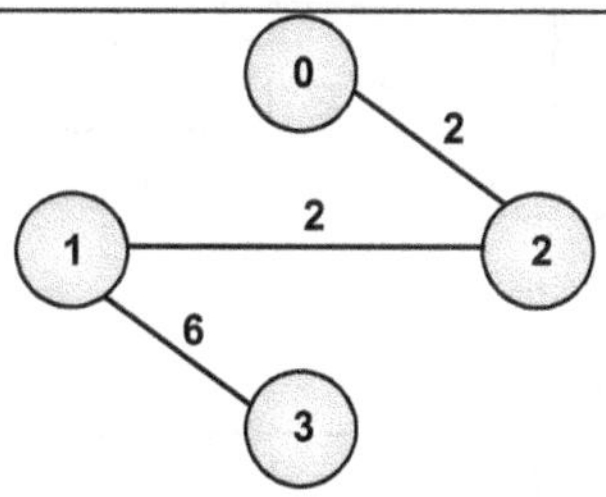 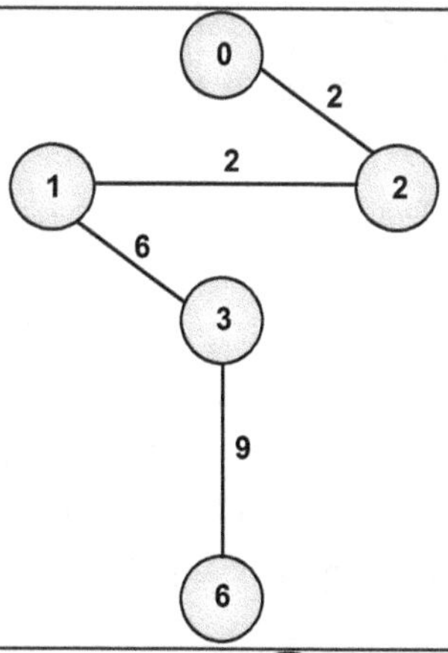	
3. 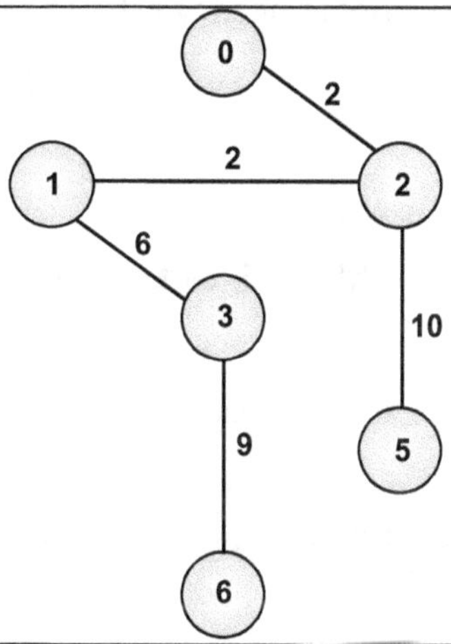 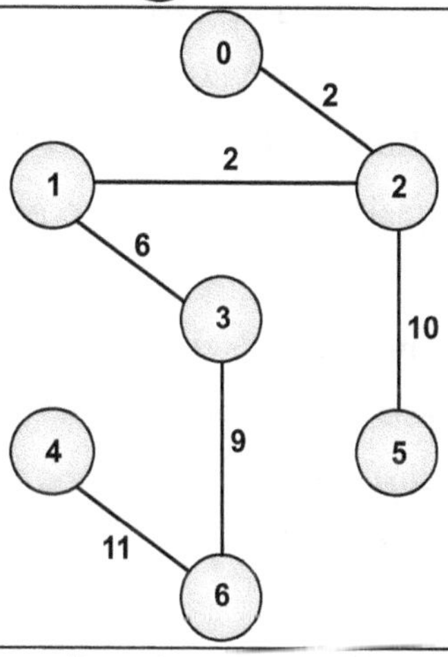	

6. **What do you mean by adjacency matrix and adjacency list of the following graph :**

[(8m) May 07]

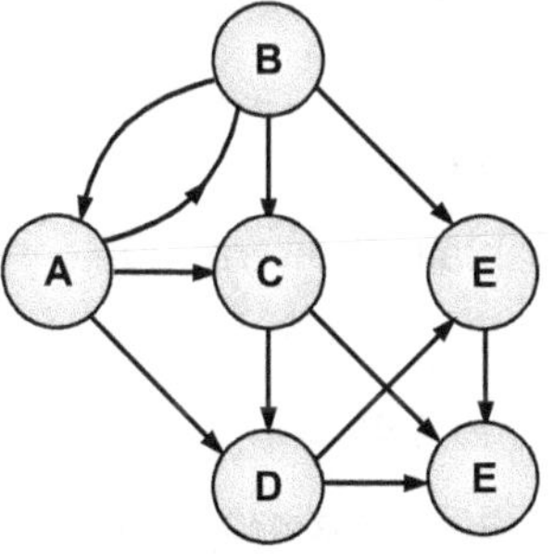

Fig. 4.45

Solution :

Adjacency matrix

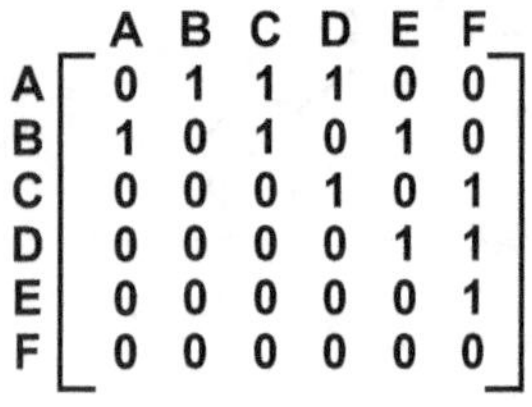

Adjacency list

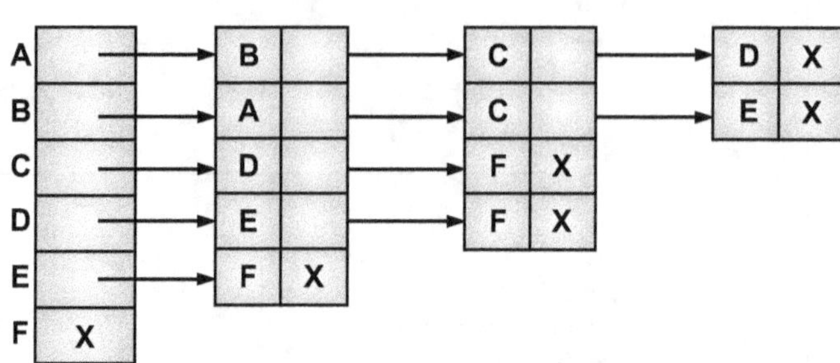

Fig. 4.46

EXERCISE

1. Define the term graph. With the help of suitable example give adjacency matrix representation and adjacency list representation for the same.　　**[(8M) Dec. 06]**

   Solution : (Refer Sections 4.2, 4.3 and 4.4)

2. What is graph? Explain how to represent graph using adjacency list and matrix.

   　　[(8m) Dec. 07]

   Solution : (Refer Sections 4.2, 4.3, 4.4)

3. Explain how graph is represented using suitable example.

   　　[May 06, Oct. 07, May 08, Oct. 08]

   Solution : (Refer Sections 4.3 and 4.4)

4. Describe the methods of representing graph with suitable example.　　**[(10m) Dec. 05]**

   Solution : (Refer Sections 4.3 and 4.4)

5. What are the different ways of representing graph? Explain with suitable example.

   　　[(6m) May 06]

   Solution : (Refer Sections 4.3 and 4.4)

6. What are the different ways of representing a graph? Explain with suitable example.

   　　[(6m) May 06]

   Solution : (Refer Sections 4.3 and 4.4)

7. With the help of any graph, explain the term adjacency list and adjacency matrix.

   　　[(4m) Dec. 05, 08, May 06, 08]

   Solution : (Refer Section 4.3 and 4.4)

8. Take your own example of graph and represent it using matrix and adjacency linked list. Give 'C' declaration for the above mentioned representation.　　**[(8m) May 08]**

Solution : (Refer Sections 4.3 and 4.4)

9. With the help of any graph, explain the terms adjacency list and adjacency matrix.

[(4m) Dec. 08]

Solution : (Refer Sections 4.3 and 4.4)

10. How can a graph be represented? Explain with suitable example.

[(6m) May 06, 08 Dec. 07, 08, 10]

Solution : (Refer Section 4.3)

11. Write non-recursive pseudo-c algorithm for depth first search of a graph.

[(6m) May 05]

Solution : (Refer Section 4.5.1)

12. Write non-recursive pseudo-c algorithm for BFS of a graph.   **[(6m) May 05]**

Solution : (Refer Section 4.5.2)

13. Describe the following with suitable examples.   **[(10m) Dec. 05]**

    (i) Depth first search (Refer Section 4.5.1)

14. Write a non-recursive pseudo-c function for breadth first search of a graph.

[(6m) May 06]

Solution : (Refer Section 4.5.2)

15. Write a non-recursive pseudo-c function for depth-first search of a graph.

[(6m) May 06]

Solution : (Refer Section 4.5.1)

16. Write an algorithm for Depth First Search for a graph.   **[(8m) Dec. 06]**

Solution : (Refer Section 4.5.1)

17. What is Depth First Search? What are the advantages and disadvantages of DFS? Give pseudo-code to implement DFS on any graph.   **[(8m) May 07]**

Solution : (Refer Section 4.5.1)

18. Explain what are BFS and DFS. Write a pseudo-c to traverse a graph using BFS.

[(8m) Dec. 07]

Solution : (Refer Section 4.5 and 4.5.2)

19. Write necessary C functions to implement BFS of graph.   **[May 06; Oct. 07, 08]**

Solution : (Refer Section 4.5.2)

20. Define DFS and BFS for graph.   **[May 08]**

Solution : (Refer Section 4.5)

21. Write recursive C functions to find DFS of graph.   **[Oct. 05, 07, 08]**

Solution : (Refer Section 4.5.1)

22. What is DFS? Write a function for DFS for a graph.   **[(6m) Dec. 05, 07, 08, 10]**

Solution : (Refer Section 4.5.1)

23. Write recursive function to find DFS of a graph.   **[(4m) Dec. 08]**

Solution : (Refer Section 4.5.1)

24. Write non-recursive pseudo-c algorithm for DFS of graph and explain with suitable example.   **[(8m) May 09]**

Solution : (Refer Section 4.5.1)

25. Write non-recursive pseudo-c algorithm for BFS of graph and explain with suitable example.   **[(8m) May 09]**

Solution : (Refer Section 4.5.2)

26. What is BFS? Write a function for BFS for a graph.

[(6m) May 06, 10, Oct. 07, 08]

Solution : (Refer Section 4.5.2)

27. What do you mean by spanning tree? Explain Kruskal's algorithm to find minimum spanning tree with the help of suitable example.   **[(8m) May 07]**

Solution : (Refer Section 4.7 and 4.7.2)

28. What is spanning tree? What is minimal spanning tree?   **[May 08]**

Solution : (Refer Section 4.7)

29. What is minimal spanning tree? Explain Prim's algorithm.   **[(6m) May 06, 10]**

Solution : (Refer Sections 4.7, 4.7.1)

30. Explain Prim's algorithm.

Solution : (Refer Section 4.7.1)

31. What do you mean by spanning tree? Explain Kruskal's algorithm to find minimum spanning tree with suitable example.   **[May 06]**

Solution : (Refer Section 4.7 and 4.7.2)

32. Explain Kruskal's algorithm.   **[May 07]**

Solution : (Refer Section 4.7.2)

33. Write pseudo-c code to find minimum spanning tree using Kruskal's algorithm. Explain all steps with suitable example. What is time complexity of algorithm?   **[(8m) May 09]**

   Solution : (Refer Section 4.7.2)

34. Explain Kruskal's algorithm.   **[(4m) May 10]**

   Solution : (Refer Section 4.7.2)

35. Find the minimum spanning tree for the graph shown in Fig. 4.38 using Prim's algorithm. Show all necessary steps.   **[(8m) Dec. 05]**

   Solution : (Similar to solved problem 1)

36. Construct minimum spanning tree (step-by-step) from the following graph using Kruskal's algorithm.   **[(6m) May 05]**

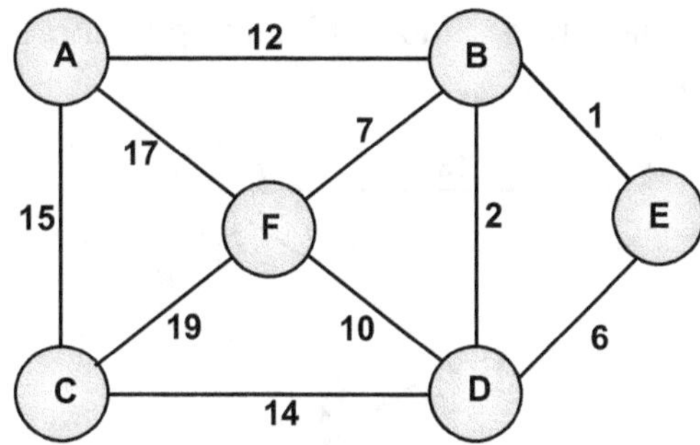

Fig. 4.47 : Graph

   Solution : (Similar to solved problem 2)

37. Determine minimum spanning tree for the following graph using Kruskal's algorithm. Show all the steps.   **[(8m) Dec. 05]**

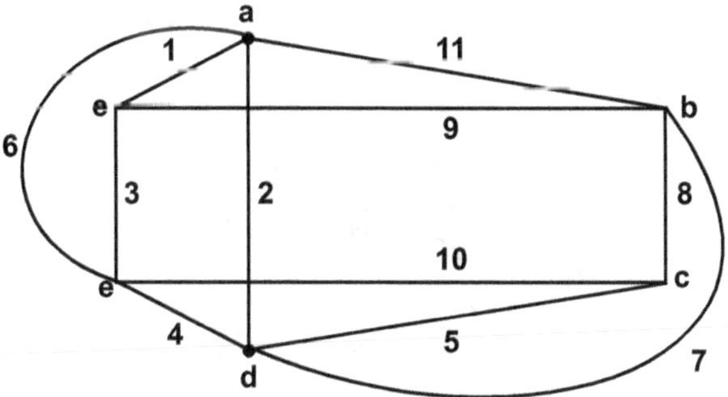

Fig. 4.48

   Solution : (Similar to solved problem 2)

38. Construct minimum spanning tree using Kruskal's algorithm for the following graph :

[May 06]

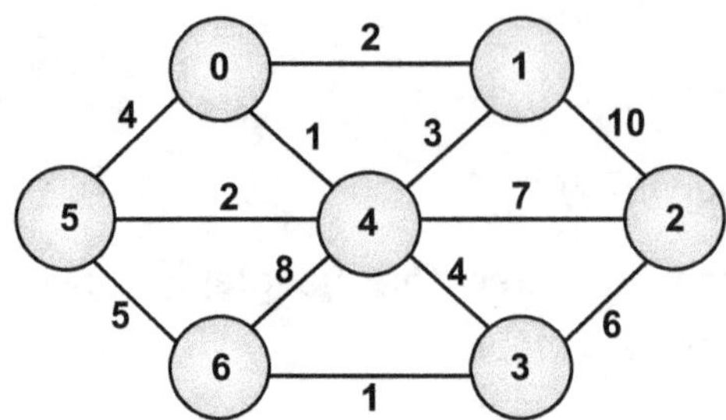

Fig. 4.49 : Graph

Solution : (Similar to solved problem 2)

39. What is minimum spanning tree? Find minimum spanning tree of the following graph using Kruskal's algorithm.   **[Oct. 07]**

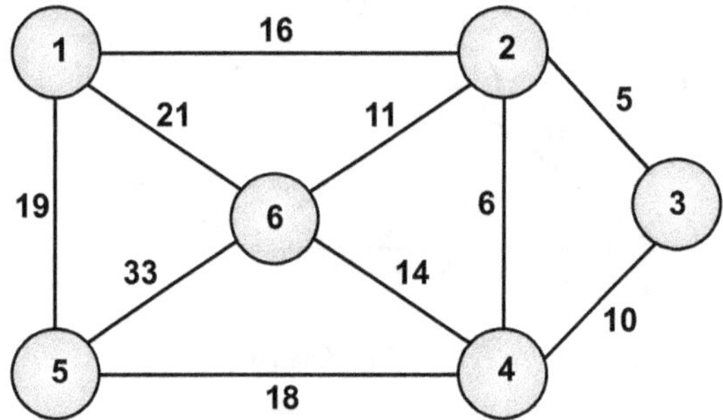

Fig. 4.50 : Graph

Solution : (Similar to solved problem 2)

40. What is minimum spanning tree? Find minimum spanning tree of the following graph using Kruskal's algorithm.   **[(8m) Dec. 07]**

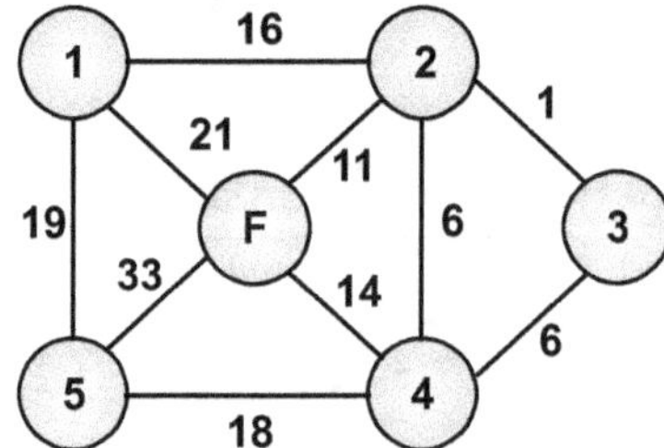

Fig. 4.51 : Graph

Solution : (Similar to solved problem 2)

41. Define DFS and BFS for graph. Show DFS and BFS for the graph given below :

[(6m) May 08]

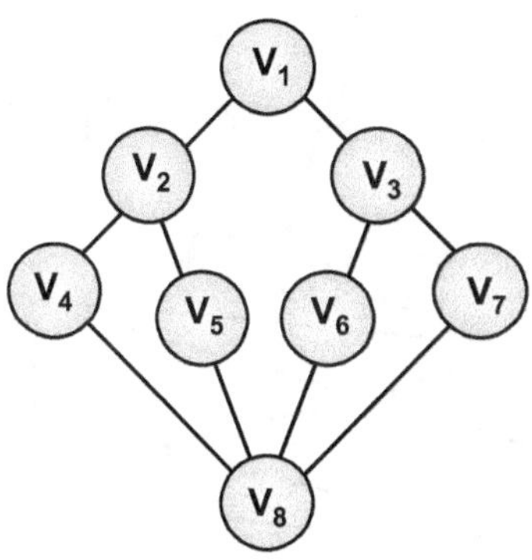

Fig. 4.52 : Graph

Solution : (Similar to solved problem 4)

42. Construct minimum spanning tree using Prim's algorithm for the Fig. 4.47.

Solution : (Similar to solved problem 5)

43. What do you mean by adjacency matrix and adjacency list? Give the adjacency matrix and adjacency list of the following graph :   **[(8m) May 07]**

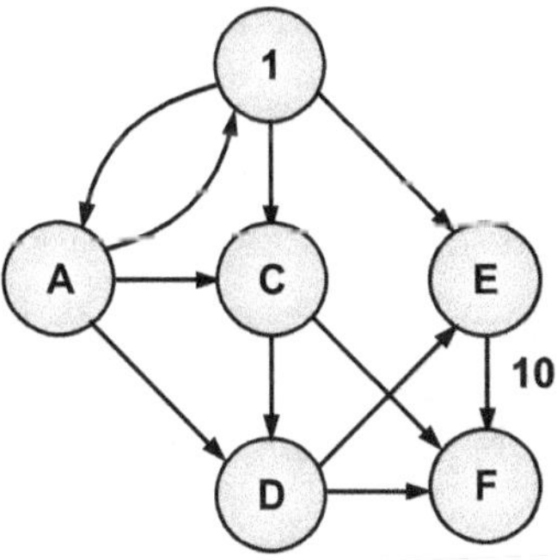

Fig. 4.53 : Graph

Solution : (Similar to solved problem 6)

DRILL PROBLEMS

1. Construct adjacency matrix and adjacency list for the graph of Fig. 4.47.

[(6m) May 05]

2. Construct minimum spanning tree using Prim's algorithm for the following graph :

[(6m) May 06]

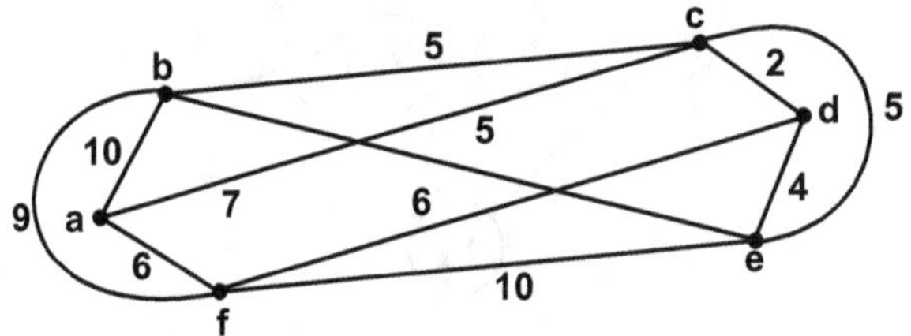

Fig. 4.54

3. What do you mean by spanning tree? Construct minimum spanning tree using Kruskal's algorithm for the graph given below. **[(8m) May 08]**

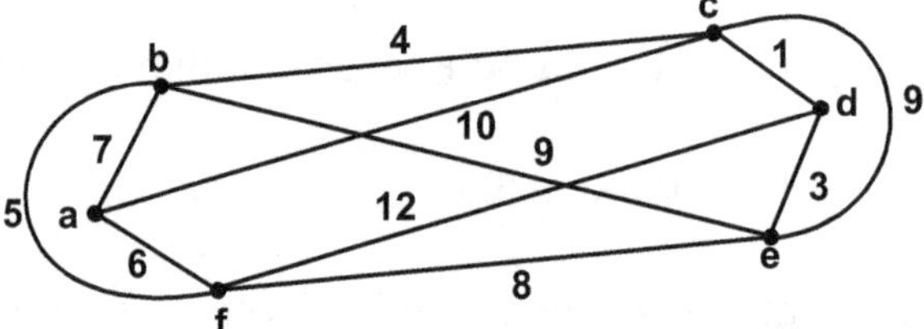

Fig. 4.55

CHAPTER 5
TABLES

5.1 SYMBOL TABLE

While compilers and assemblers scan a program, each identifier must be examined to determine if it is a keyword. This information concerning the keywords in a programming language is stored in a **symbol table.**

Keyed tables are very useful structures of the same. The keyed table stores **<key, information>** pairs with no additional logical structure.

The operations on symbol tables are :

* The pairs <key, information> are inserted into the collection.

* The pair <key, information> removed by specifying the key.

* Search for particular key.

* Retrieve the information associated with a key.

For Example :

Symbol	Information
A	------
B	------
Sum	------

Any time compiler wants to store information that can be retrieved by some unique key value, it means we are using a keyed table. The field that contains the value by which we want to retrieve the information is the key field.

Keyed tables are used in assemblers, where the key (the symbol) is the programmers identifier and the information is the location assigned by the assembler to that identifier. The keyed tables are also called as symbol tables.

Representation of Symbol Table :

There are two different techniques for implementing the keyed tables; symbol table and tree tables.

Static Tree Tables : Static tree tables are used when symbols are known in advance and no insertion and deletion is allowed. An example of this type of table is reserved word table in a compiler. This table is searched once for every occurrence of an identifier in a program. If an identifier is not in the reserved word table, then it is looked for in another table. To optimize a table knowing what keys are in the table and what the probable distribution is of those that are not in the table, we build an Optimal Binary Search Tree (OBST).

- Stored as sorted sequential list and binary search ($O(\log_2 n)$)can be used to search a symbol.

- Balanced BST can be used to find symbols having equal probabilities.

- OBST (Optimal Binary Search Tree) is used when different symbols are searched with different probabilities.

- Hash tables can be used to store symbol table having search time O(1).

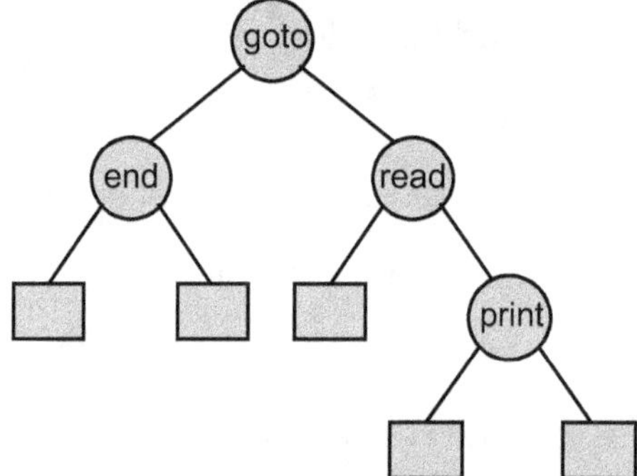

Fig. 5.1 : Optimal binary search tree

Dynamic Tree Table : Dynamic tree tables are used when symbols are not known in advance and inserted as they come and deleted if not required. Dynamic keyed tables are those that are built on the fly. The keys have no history associated with their use. As we know nothing about them, not even how many symbols are there, so balanced binary search tree is a good choice for Dynamic tree tables.

AVL tree is an example of dynamic tree table.

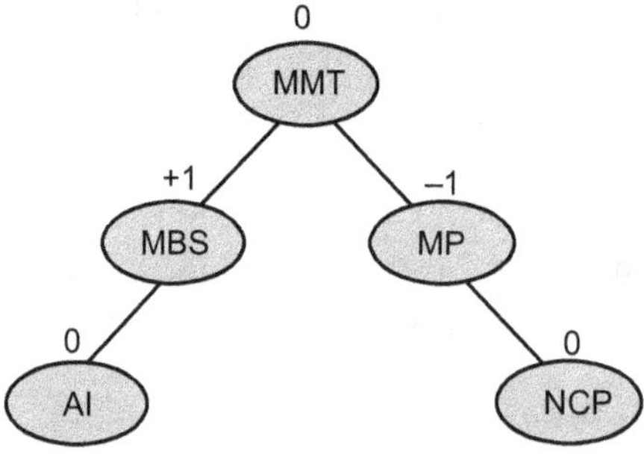

Fig. 5.2 : AVL tree (Balance Factor (0 or -1 or 1))

5.2 OPTIMAL BINARY SEARCH TREES

A binary search tree is one of the most important data structures in computer science. When array is used to store ordered data, we can use very efficient searching technique binary search, but insertion and deletion algorithms are inefficient. They require shifting of data in the array. The alternative is use of linked list to store ordered data, which provide efficient insertion and deletion algorithms, but now searching algorithm used should be sequential search which is inefficient. The binary search tree is a data structure that has an efficient searching algorithm and efficient insertion and deletion algorithms.

BST Definition : A binary search tree is a binary tree. It may be empty. If not, then it satisfies the following properties :

- Every element has a key and no two elements have the same key (i.e. the keys are distinct).
- The keys (if any) in the left subtree are smaller than the key in the root.
- The keys (if any) in the right subtree are greater than or equal to the key in the root.
- Each subtree is itself a binary search tree.

For example, consider the following binary search tree.

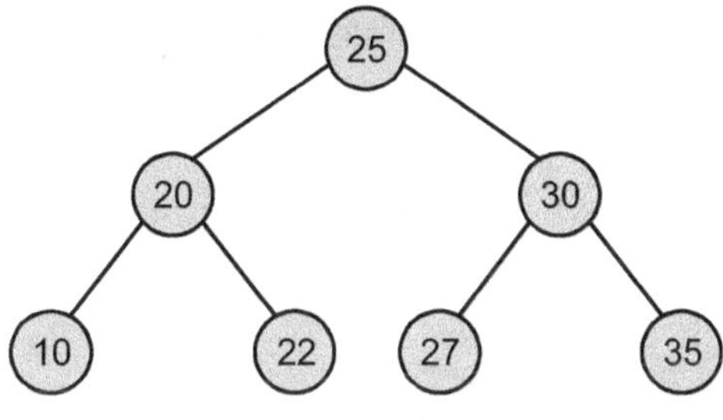

Fig. 5.3

The inorder traversal of the above binary search tree produces an ordered list – 10, 20, 22, 25, 27, 30, 35.

One of the important application of binary search tree is to arrange a set of keys from some linear ordered set to minimize the average search time. If probabilities of searching for elements of a set are known from some previous searches, then an optimal binary search tree can be obtained for which the average number of comparisons in a search is the smallest possible.

For Example : If four keys P, Q, R, S are to be searched with probabilities 0.1, 0.2, 0.4, and 0.3 respectively, then there are 14 possible binary search trees. Few of them are shown in the figure given below. Out of these 14 we have to find out which is optimal. One way is to construct all possible binary search trees and find the optimal one. But as the number of keys n increases, the total number of search trees also increases. So, this approach is unrealistic for large n. Therefore, the alternative is to use a general algorithm.

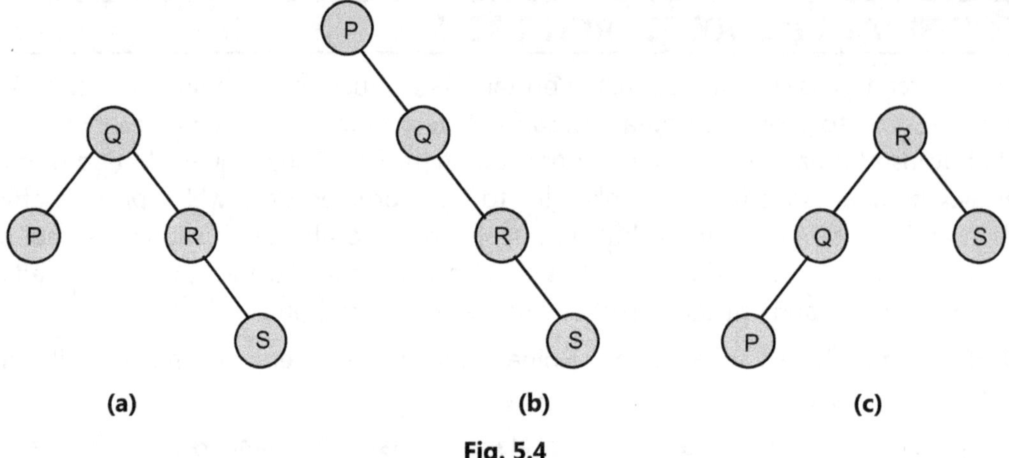

(a)   (b)   (c)

Fig. 5.4

Let $a_1, a_2, ..., a_n$ be distinct keys ordered with a_1 being smallest and a_n being largest. Let $p_1, p_2, ..., p_n$ be the probabilities for searching them. Let $C[i,j]$ be the smallest average number of comparisons made in a successful search in a binary tree T_i^j having keys $a_i, ..., a_j$, where i, j are integer indices, $1 \leq i \leq j \leq n$.

First using the dynamic programming algorithm, we shall find values of $C[i,j]$ for all smaller instances of the problem. Consider all possible ways to choose a_k as the root among the keys $a_i, ..., a_j$. See the following Fig. 5.5.

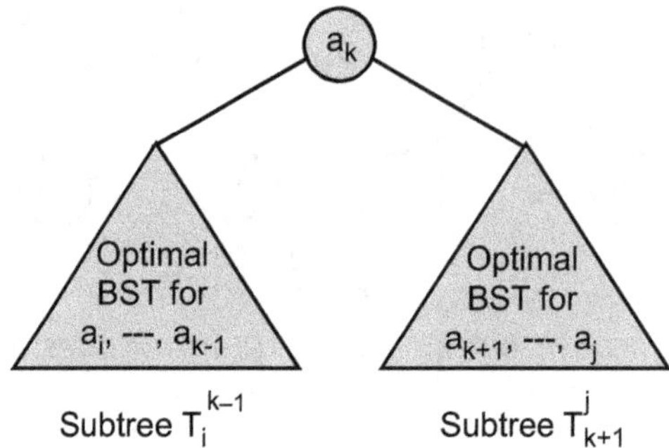

Fig. 5.5

In such a binary search tree, a_k is the root, T_i^{k-1} is the left subtree which contains $a_i, ..., a_{k-1}$ keys optimally arranged and T_{k+1}^j is the right subtree which contains $a_{k+1}, ..., a_j$ keys optimally arranged. Let, tree levels are counted from 1. Assume that $C[i, i-1] = 0$ for $1 \leq i \leq n+1$, which means that number of comparisons is 0 in the empty tree. The recurrence relation is,

$$C[i,j] = \min_{i \leq k \leq j} \{C[i,k-1]+C[k+1,j]\} + \sum_{s=i}^{j} P_s \text{ for } 1 \leq i \leq j \leq n$$

From this formula, we can obtain formula for a one-mode binary tree containing key a_i, as given below :

$$C[i,i] = P_i \text{ for } 1 \le i \le n.$$

The initial cost table of the dynamic programming algorithm for constructing optimal binary search tree is shown below :

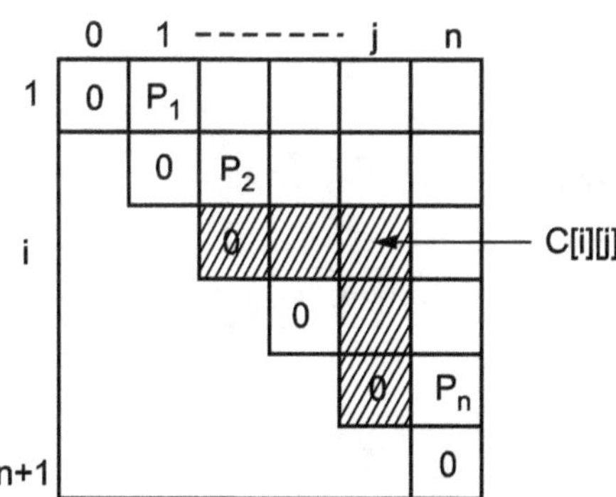

Fig. 5.6

The values needed for computing C[i][j] are shaded in the above table. They are in row i and the columns to the left of column j, and the values in column j and the rows below row i.

The pseudocode of the dynamic programming algorithm to find an optimal binary search tree is given below :

Algorithm OptBST(P[1...n])

Input : An array P[1...n] of search probabilities for a sorted list of n keys.

Output : Two dimensional arrays C and R of size $(n + 2) \infty (n + 1)$, 0 based. For the subrange of key a_i, ..., a_j C[i,j] gives the minimum weighted search cost and R[i,j] gives the best choice of the root for the binary search tree on this subrange of keys. The optimal cost for whole tree is C[1,n].

Algorithm for OBST :

```
    for i=1 to n do
    begin
        C[i,i-1]=0
        C[i,i]=P[i]
        R[i,i]=i
    end
    C[n+1,n]=0
    for d=1 to n-1 do        // diagonal count
```

```
begin
    for i=1 to n-d do
    begin
                j=i+d
             minval=∞
         for k=i to j do
             begin
                    if C[i,k-1]+C[k+1,j]<minval
                    begin
                        minval=C[i,k-1]+C[k+1,j]
                        kmin=k
                    end
        end
    R[i,j]=k
    sum=P[i]
    for s=i+1 to j do
    begin
        sum=sum+P[s]
    end
    C[i,j]=minval+sum
    end
end
return C[1,n],R
```

Let us see one example to illustrate the above algorithm.

For the 4 keys

Keys	P	Q	R	S
Probabilities	0.1	0.2	0.4	0.3

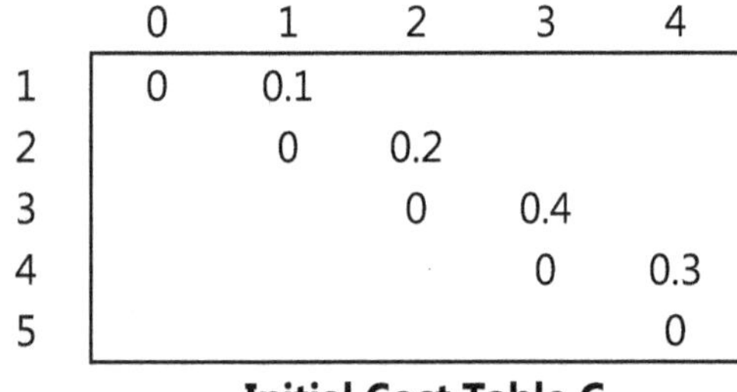

	0	1	2	3	4
1	0	0.1			
2		0	0.2		
3			0	0.4	
4				0	0.3
5					0

Initial Cost Table C

	0	1	2	3	4
1		1			
2			2		
3				3	
4					4
5					

Initial Root Table R

Diagonal count 'd' will vary from 1 to 3. i will vary from 1 to n–d.

Initially d=1, i will vary from 1 to 3.

[A] For i = 1, j = i + d = 1 + 1 = 2

Let us find C[1,2] for k=1 and k=2.

For k = 1,

$$C[i,j] = C[i,k-1] + C[k+1,j] + \sum_{s=i}^{j} Ps$$

$$C[1,2] = C[1,0] + C[2,2] + \sum_{s=1}^{2} Ps$$

$$= 0 + 0.2 + (P_1 + P_2)$$

$$= 0 + 0.2 + (0.1 + 0.2)$$

$$= 0 + 0.2 + 0.3$$

$$= 0.5$$

Similarly for k=2

$$C[1,2] = C[1,1] + C[3,2] + \sum_{s=1}^{2} Ps$$

$$= 0.1 + 0 + (0.1 + 0.2)$$

$$= 0.4$$

Select minimum value.

$$\therefore \qquad C[1,2] = 0.4 \text{ for } k=2$$

$$\therefore \qquad \text{Put } R[1,2] = k=2$$

[B] For i=2, j−i+d=2+1=3

Let us find C[2,3] for k=2,3.

For k=2,

$$C[2,3] = C[2,1] + C[3,3] + \sum_{s=2}^{3} Ps$$

$$= 0 + 0.4 + (P2 + P3)$$

$$= 0 + 0.4 + (0.2 + 0.4)$$

$$= 1.0$$

For k=3,

$$C[2,3] = C[2,2]+C[4,3]+ \sum_{s=2}^{3} Ps$$

$$= 0.2+0+(0.2+0.4)$$

$$= 0.8$$

∴ Select minimum value.

$$C[2,3] = 0.8 \text{ for } k=3$$

∴ $R[2,3] = 3$

[C] For i=3,j=i+d=3+1=4

Let us find C[3,4] for k=3,4.

For k=3,

$$C[3,4] = C[3,2]+C[4,4]+ \sum_{s=3}^{4} Ps$$

$$= 0+0.3+(P3+P4)$$

$$= 0+0.3+(0.4+0.3)$$

$$= 1.0$$

$$C[3,4] = C[3,3]+C[5,4]+ \sum_{s=3}^{4} Ps$$

$$= 0.4+0+(0.4+0.3)$$

$$= 1.1$$

Select minimum value.

∴ $C[3,4] = 1.0 \text{ for } k=3$

∴ $R[3,4] = 3$

	0	1	2	3	4
1	0	0.1	0.4		
2		0	0.2	0.8	
3			0	0.4	1.0
4				0	0.3
5					0

Cost Table C

	0	1	2	3	4
1		1	2		
2			2	3	
3				3	3
4					4
5					

Root Table R

[D] Now d=2 and i will vary from 1 to 2.

For i=1, j=i+d=1+2=3.

Let us find C[1,3] for k=1,2,3.

For k=1,

$$C[1,3] = C[1,0]+C[2,3]+ \sum_{s=1}^{3} Ps$$

$$= 0+0.8+(P1+P2+P3)$$

$$= 0+0.8+(0.1+0.2+0.4)$$

$$= 1.5$$

For k=2,

$$C[1,3] = C[1,1]+C[3,1]+C[3,3]+ \sum_{s=1}^{3} Ps$$

$$= 0.1+0.4+(0.1+0.2+0.4)$$

$$= 1.2$$

For k=3,

$$C[1,3] = C[1,2]+C[4,3]+ \sum_{s=1}^{3} Ps$$

$$= 0.4+0+(0.1+0.2+0.4)$$

$$= 1.1$$

Select minimum value

$\therefore$ C[1,3] = 1.1 for k=3

$\therefore$ Set R[1,3] = 3

[E] Now i=2, j=i+d=2+2=4.

Let us find C[2,4] for k=2,3,4

For k=2,

$$C[2,4] = C[2,1]+C[3,4] + \sum_{s=2}^{4} Ps$$

$$= 0+1.0+(P2+P3+P4)$$

$$= 0+1.0+(0.2+0.4+0.3)$$

$$= 1.9$$

For k=3,

$$C[2,4] = C[2,2]+C[4,4] + \sum_{s=2}^{4} Ps$$

$$= 0.2+0.3+(0.2+0.4+0.3)$$

$$= 1.4$$

For k=4,

$$C[2,4] = C[2,3]+C[5,4] + \sum_{s=2}^{4} Ps$$

$$= 0.8+0+(0.2+0.4+0.3)$$

$$= 1.7$$

Select minimum value.

$\therefore \qquad C[2,4] = 1.4$ for k=3

$\therefore \qquad$ Set $R[2,4] = 3$

	0	1	2	3	4
1	0	0.1	0.4	1.1	
2		0	0.2	0.8	1.4
3			0	0.4	1.0
4				0	0.3
5					0

Cost Table C

	0	1	2	3	4
1		1	2	3	
2			2	3	3
3				3	3
4					4
5					

Root Table R

[F] Now d=3, i=1, j=i+d=1+3=4.

Let us find C[1,4] for k=1 to 4.

For k=1,

$$C[1,4] = C[1,0]+C[2,4] + \sum_{s=1}^{4} Ps$$

$$= 0+1.4+(P1+P2+P3+P4)$$

$$= 0+1.4+(0.1+0.2+0.4+0.3)$$

$$= 2.4$$

For k=2,

$$C[1,4] = C[1,1]+C[3,4]+ \sum_{s=1}^{4} Ps$$

$$= 0.1+1.0+(0.1+0.2+0.4+0.3)$$

$$= 2.1$$

For k=3, $$C[1,4] = C[1,2]+C[4,4]+ \sum_{s=1}^{4} Ps$$

$$= 0.4+0.3+(0.1+0.2+0.4+0.3)$$

$$= 1.7$$

For k=4, $$C[1,4] = C[1,3]+C[5,4]+ \sum_{s=1}^{4} Ps$$

$$= 1.1+0+(0.1+0.2+0.4+0.3)$$

$$= 2.1$$

Select minimum value.

$$\therefore \qquad C[1,4] = 1.7 \text{ for k=3}$$

$$\therefore \qquad \text{Set } R[1,4] = 3$$

	0	1	2	3	4
1	0	0.1	0.4	1.1	1.7
2		0	0.2	0.8	1.4
3			0	0.4	1.0
4				0	0.3
5					0

Final Cost Table C

	0	1	2	3	4
1			1	2	3	3
2				2	3	3
3					3	3
4						4
5						

Final Root Table R

Finally, C[1,4]=1.7 and R[1,4]=3

So, for the four keys P, Q, R, S, the optimal BST has root at index 3 (i.e. key R) and the average number of comparisons in a successful search in this tree is 1.7. The following figure shows the optimal BST for the above example.

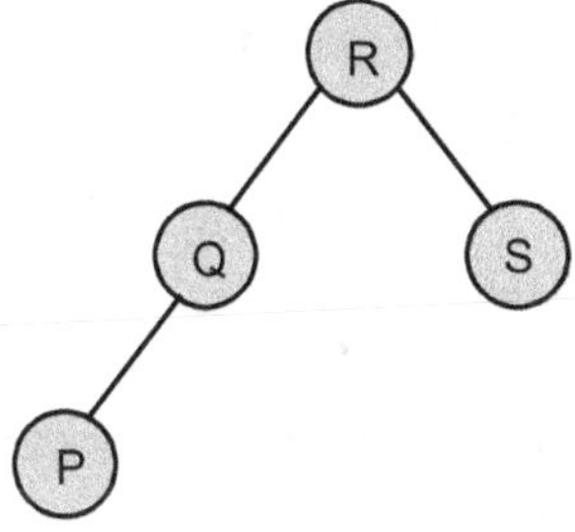

Fig. 5.7

The algorithm given above has quadratic space efficiency and cubic time efficiency.

5.3 HUFFMAN'S ALGORITHM

Why Huffman Coding??

- Huffman coding is a technique used to compress files before transmission.
- Uses statistical coding
  - ➢ More frequently used symbols have shorter code words by making the use of prefix codes.
- Works well for text and fax transmissions.

One of the most important applications of binary tree is in communication (sending and receiving data).

Consider an example of transmitting an English text made up from a, b, c, d, e, f, g, h.

We are going to represent these characters in binary numbers.

As there are 8 characters, we can use three bits for generating unique codes for them, which are shown in the following table.

Table 5.1

Character	Code/Seq.
a	000
b	001
c	010
d	011
e	100
f	101
g	110
h	111

Let us consider that sequence of 1000 character is to be send. Hence total bits transmitted will be 1000*3=3000 (as every character in the sequence will be represented by 3 bits).

It may happen that, among these 1000 characters, the letters b, d and f are appeared maximum number of times in the sequence.

So, in such transmissions, we represent the letters having more frequent occurrence with shorter sequences (using less no. of bits) and less frequently used letters with longer sequences (using more no. of bits). So, that the overall length of the string will be reduced.

In the above example, if b, d and f are represented by sequence of 2 bits and each of them appeared in the sequence 150 times then, $3 \times 150 \times 2 = 900$ bits will be formed for transmission. But before shortening them, each letter we were representing by 3 bits that time we would have required $3 \times 150 \times 3 = 1350$ bits.

It means that after shortening the sequence of letters b, d and f, we are transmitting 1350–900=450 less bits. This means we have done data compression compared to the first regular technique.

Such a coding is called as 'variable length coding', even though variable length coding reduces the overall length of the sequence to be transmitted, the interesting problem arises :

Problem Due to Variable Length Coding :

Lets us consider the following sequences :

Table 5.2

Character	Sequence/code
a	00
n	01
t	0001

- We will transmit 'an' letters by sending the sequence 0001.
- At receiving end, it is difficult to determine whether the transmitted sequence is 'an' or 't'.
- This is because 00 is a prefix of code 0001.
- For that while assigning the variable sequence to letters, we must take care that no code should be prefix of the other.

Prefix Code :

A set of sequence is said to be a prefix code, if no sequence in the set is a prefix of another sequence in the set. For Example, see the following table,

Table 5.3

Character	Sequence/code
a	000
b	001
c	01
d	10

The sequence codes in the above table are called as prefix codes.

Now see the following table

Table 5.4

Character	Sequence/Code
a	1
b	00
c	000
d	0001

The sequence codes in the above table are not prefix codes. Huffman had given a very elegant procedure to construct optimal binary tree for generating the prefix codes of variable lengths for the letters from the point of unambiguous data transmission.

5.3.1 Huffman's Algorithm

- Organize the data into a row as ascending order of their frequency of occurrence in the given sequence of letters.

- Find two nodes with smaller weights, join them to form the third node. This will form a new two level tree. The weight of new third node is addition of weights of two nodes.

- Repeat step 2 till all nodes on every level are combined to form a single tree.

Huffman's Coding :

SOLVED EXAMPLES

Example 5.1 : For the given data, build the Huffman's tree and find out prefix code for each letter.   **[IT 08]**

Table 5.5

Data	Weight
A	22
B	5
C	11
D	19
E	2
F	11
G	25
H	5

Solution :

Step 1 :

Step 2 :

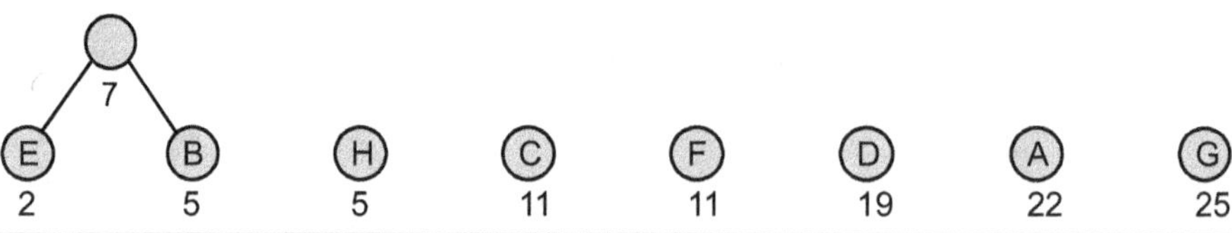

Step 3 : Sort the list in ascending order.

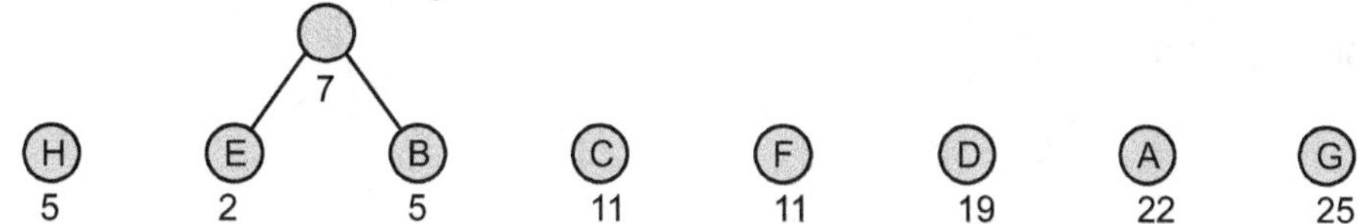

Step 4 :

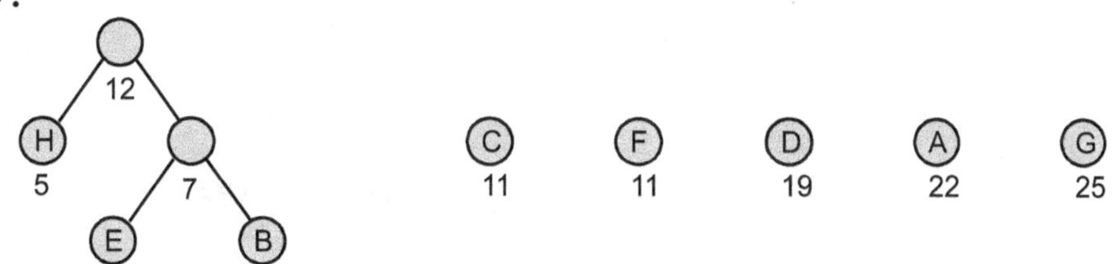

Step 5 : Arrange the list in ascending order

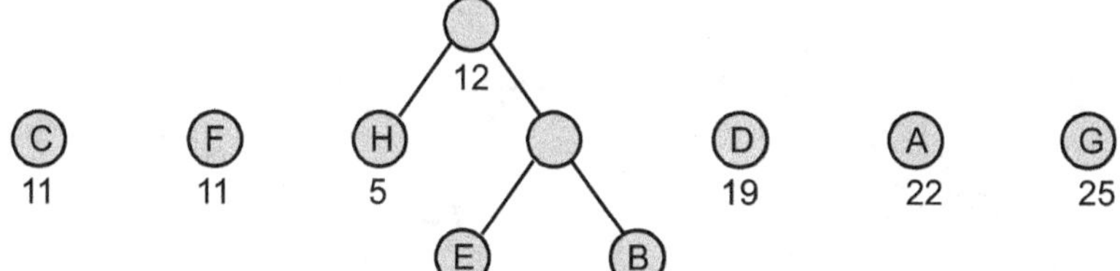

Step 6 :

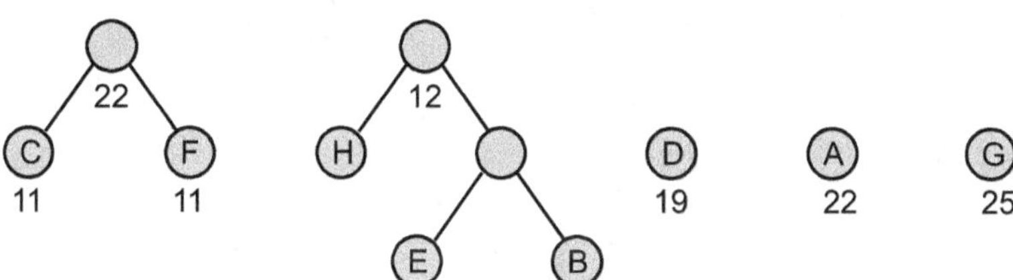

Step 7 :

Sort the list in ascending order.

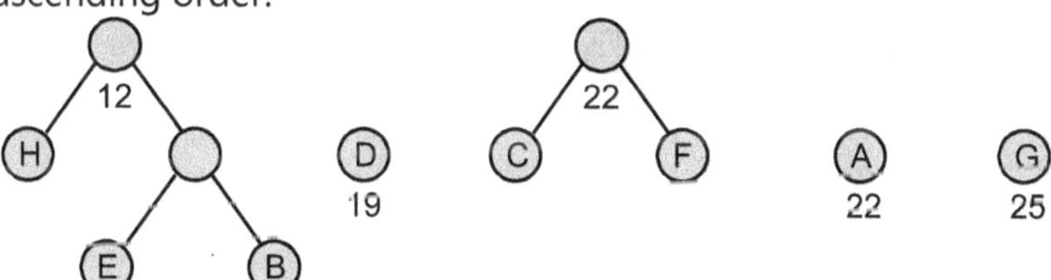

Step 8 :

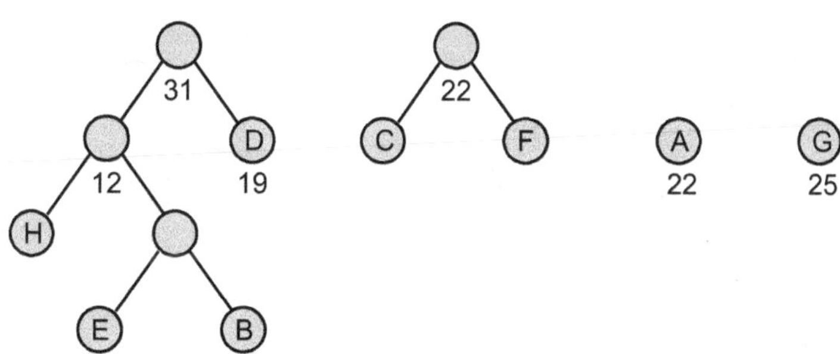

Step 9 :

Sort the list in ascending order.

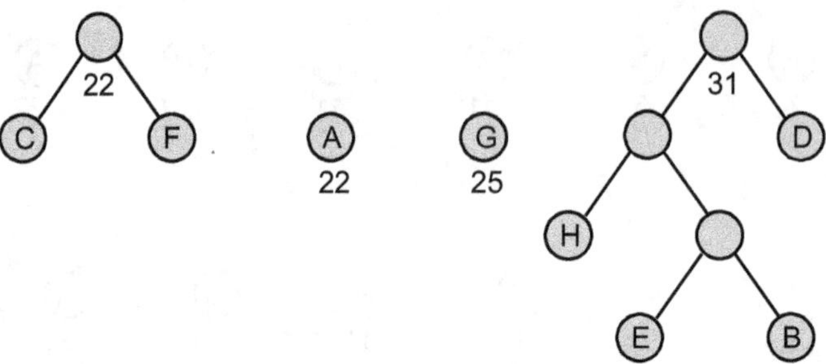

Step 10 :

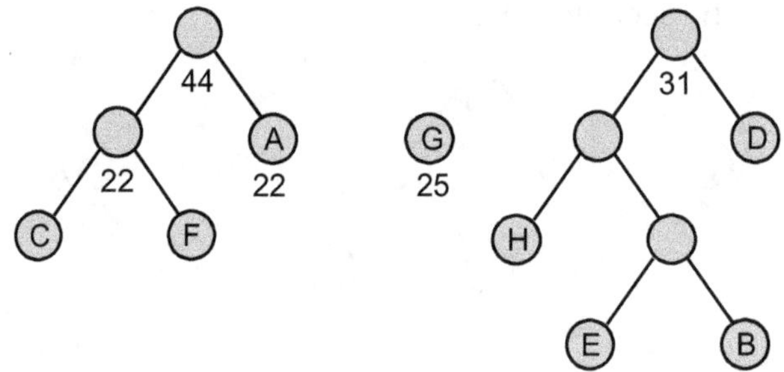

Step 11 :

Sort the list in ascending order

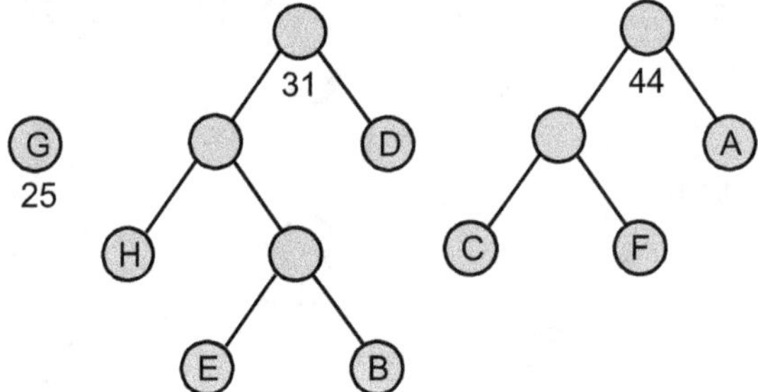

Step 12 :

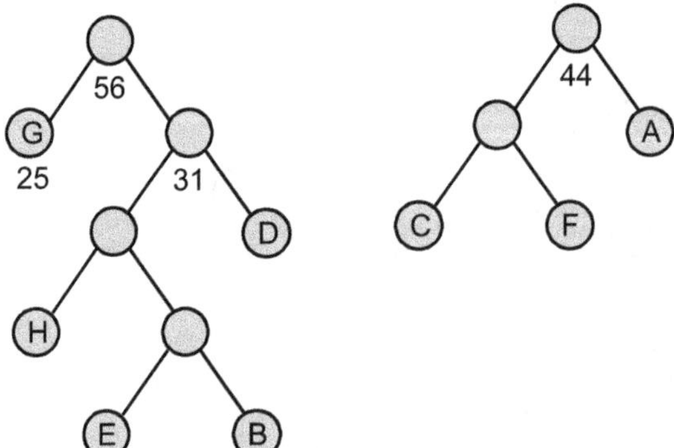

Step 13 :

Sort the list according to its ascending order.

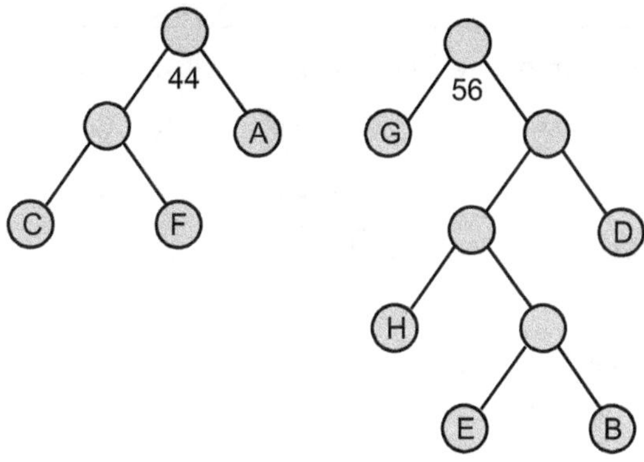

Step 14 :

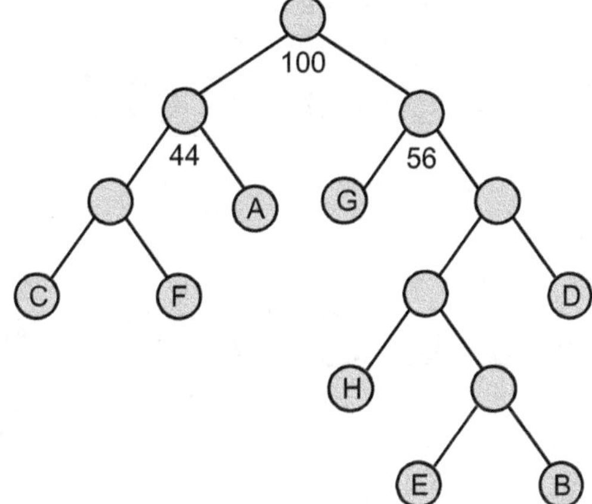

Huffman's codes will be as follows :

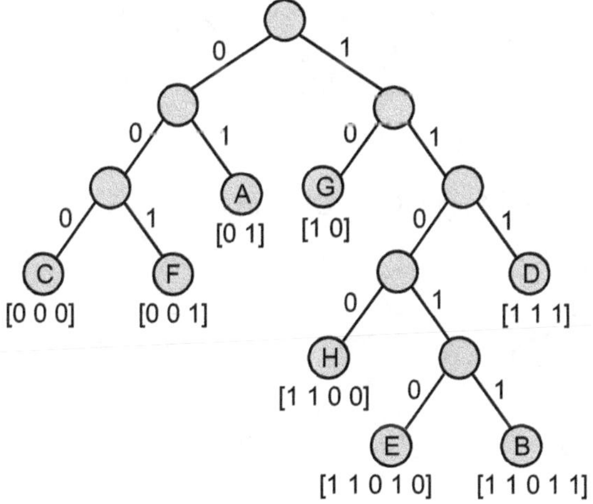

Note : See the Huffman codes carefully, the number of bits required to represent A and G (having weights 22 and 25 respectively) are only 2, while that of E and B (having weights 2 and 5) are 5.

Example 5.2 : Construct Huffman tree based on the following character weights :   **[Dec. 11]**

E = 15	T = 12	A = 10	O = 08	R = 07	N = 06	S = 05
U = 05	I = 04	D = 04	M = 03	C = 03	G = 02	K = 02

Also give Huffman code assignment at each node.

Solution :

Step 1 : Each node is represented as tree

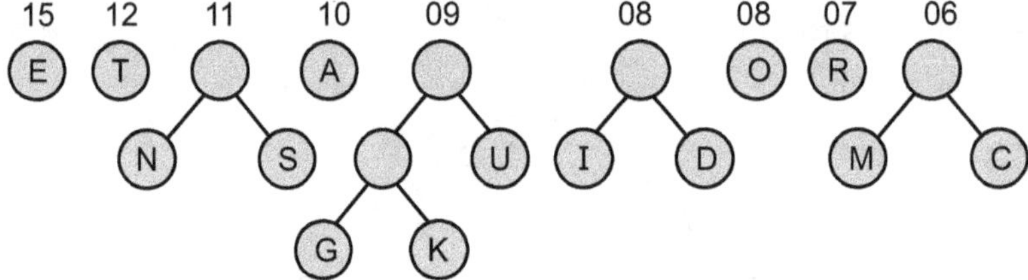

Step 2 : Merge G.K. (Trees of minimum weights)

Step 3 : Merge M, C and I, D

Step 4 : Merge (U, (G, K)) and Merge (N, S)

Step 5 : Merge (R, (M, C)) and Merge (O, (I, D)) and merge (A, (G, K, U))

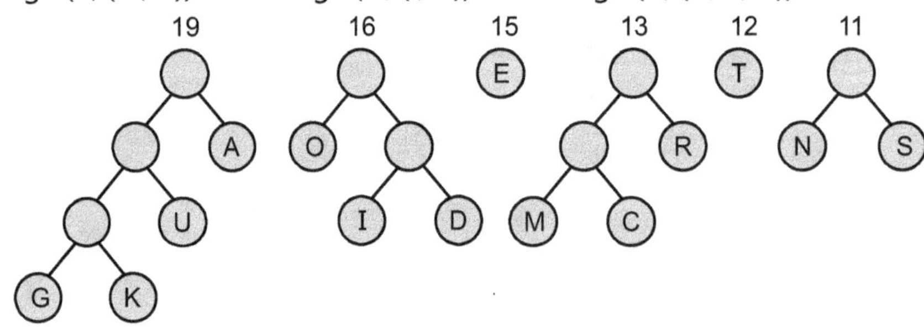

Step 6 : Merge (T, (N, S)) and Merge (E, (M, C, R)) and Merge ((G, K, U, A), (O, I, D))

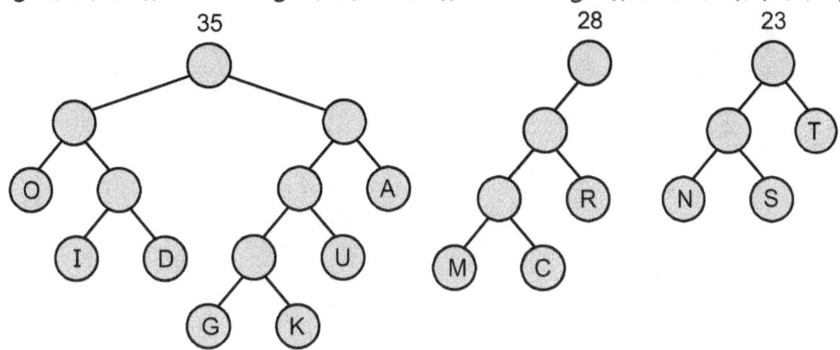

Step 7 : Merge ((M, C, R, E), (N, S, T))

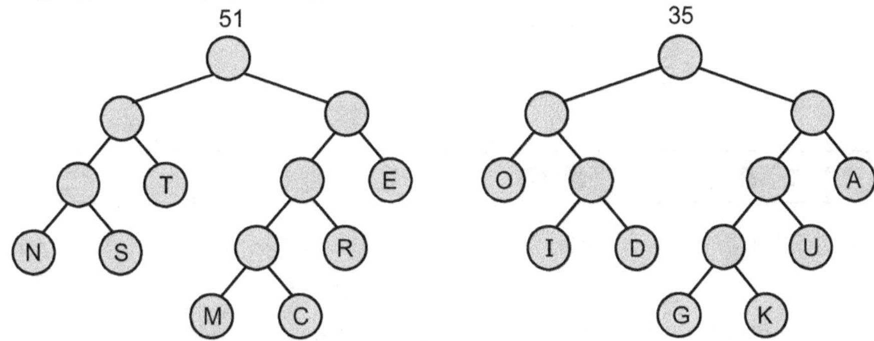

Step 8 : Merge ((N, S, T, M, C, R, E), (O, I, D, G, K, U, A))

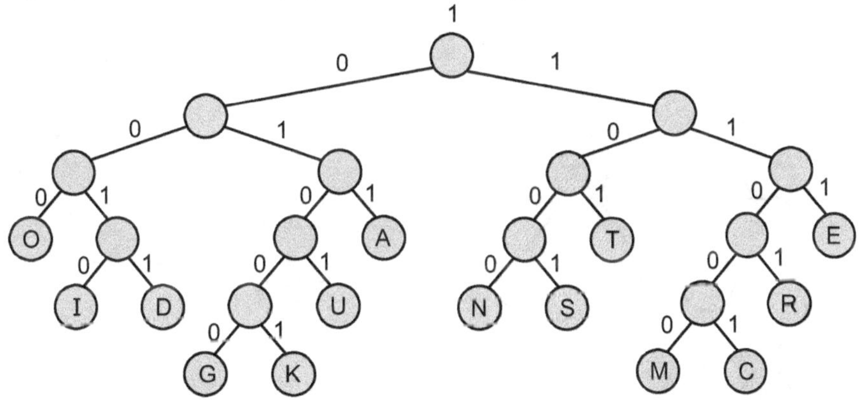

Table 5.6

Symbol	Huffman Code
E	111
T	101
A	011
O	000

...Conti.

R	1101
N	1000
S	1001
U	0101
I	0010
D	0011
M	11000
C	11001
G	01000
K	01001

5.4 HEAP DATA STRUCTURE

Heap is a special tree-based data structure, that satisfies the following special heap properties :

- **Shape Property :** Heap data structure is always a Complete Binary Tree, which means all levels of the tree are fully filled.

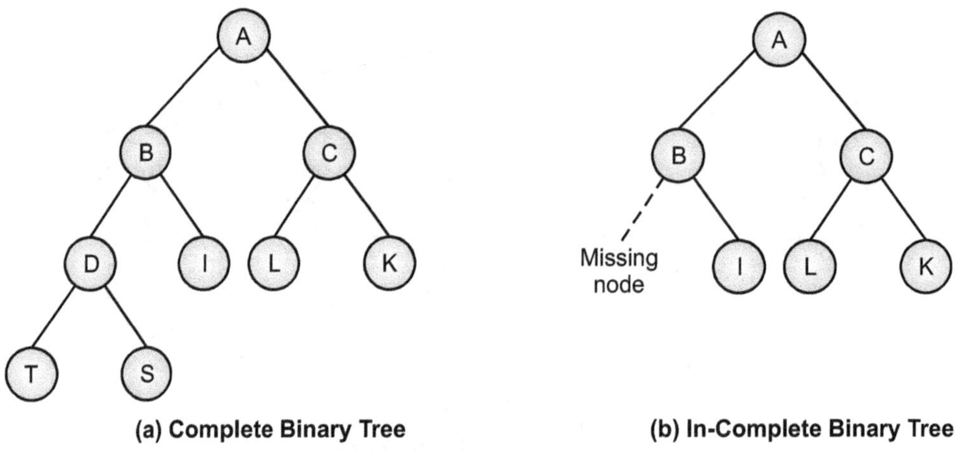

(a) Complete Binary Tree   (b) In-Complete Binary Tree

Fig. 5.8

- **Heap Property :** All nodes are either [greater than or equal to] or [less than or equal to] each of its children. If the parent nodes are greater than their children, heap is called a **Max-Heap**, and if the parent nodes are smaller than their child nodes, heap is called **Min-Heap**.

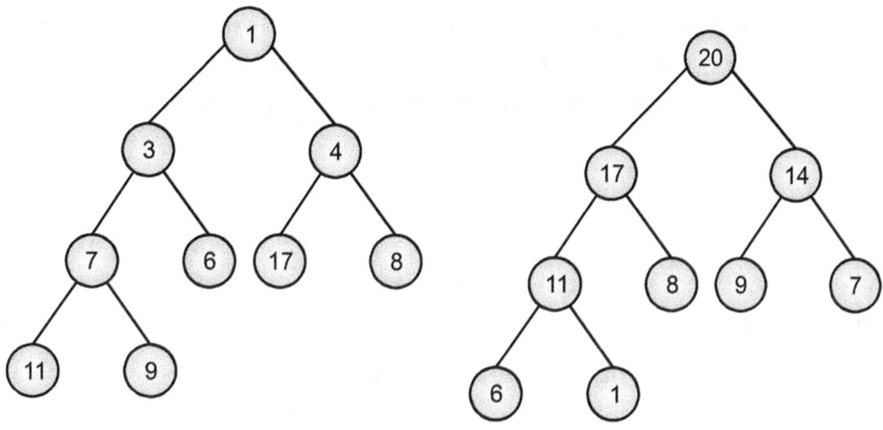

Fig. 5.9

Min-Heap	Max-Heap
In min-heap, first element is the smallest. So when we want to sort a list in ascending order, we create a min-heap from that list, and picks the first element, as it is the smallest, then we repeat the process with remaining elements.	In max-heap, the first element is the largest, hence it is used when we need to sort a list in descending order.

How Heap Sort Works?

Initially on receiving an unsorted list, the first step in heap sort is to create a heap data structure (Max-Heap or Min-Heap). Once heap is built, the first element of the Heap is either largest or smallest (depending upon Max-Heap or Min-Heap), so we put the first element of the heap in our array. Then we again make heap using the remaining elements, to again pick the first element of the heap and put it into the array. We keep on doing the same repeatedly until we have the complete sorted list in our array.

Heap Sort is one of the best sorting methods being in-place and with no quadratic worst-case scenarios. Heap sort algorithm is divided into two basic parts :

- Creating a Heap of the unsorted list.
- Then a sorted array is created by repeatedly removing the largest/smallest element from the heap, and inserting it into the array. The heap is reconstructed after each removal.

Heap Sort :

Heap sort is a comparison based sorting technique based on Binary Heap data structure. It is similar to selection sort where we first find the maximum element and place the maximum element at the end. We repeat the same process for remaining element.

What is Binary Heap?

Let us first define a Complete Binary Tree. A complete binary tree is a binary tree in which every level, except possibly the last, is completely filled, and all nodes are as far left as possible.

A Binary Heap is a Complete Binary Tree where items are stored in a special order such that value in a parent node is greater (or smaller) than the values in its two children nodes. The former is called as max heap and the latter is called min heap. The heap can be represented by binary tree or array.

Why Array Based Representation for Binary Heap?

Since a Binary Heap is a Complete Binary Tree, it can be easily represented as array and array based representation is space efficient. If the parent node is stored at index I, the left child can be calculated by 2 * I + 1 and right child by 2 * I + 2 (assuming the indexing starts at 0).

Heap Sort Algorithm for Sorting in Increasing Order :

- Build a max heap from the input data.

- At this point, the largest item is stored at the root of the heap. Replace it with the last item of the heap followed by reducing the size of heap by 1. Finally, heapify the root of tree.

- Repeat above steps until size of heap is greater than 1.

How to Build the Heap?

Heapify procedure can be applied to a node only if its children nodes are heapified. So, the heapification must be performed in the bottom up order.

Let's understand with the help of an example :

Input data : 4, 10, 3, 5, 1

```
        4(0)
       /  \
    10(1)  3(2)
     / \
   5(3)  1(4)
```

The numbers in bracket represent the indices in the array representation of data.

Applying heapify procedure to index 1 :

```
        4(0)
       /  \
    10(1)   3(2)
     / \
   5(3)   1(4)
```

Applying heapify procedure to index 0 :

```
      10(0)
      / \
   5(1)  3(2)
    / \
  4(3)  1(4)
```

The heapify procedure calls itself recursively to build heap in top down manner.

```cpp
// C++ program for implementation of Heap Sort
#include <iostream.h>
using namespace std;
// To heapify a subtree rooted with node i which is
// an index in arr[]. n is size of heap
void heapify(int arr[], int n, int i)
{
    int largest = i;  // Initialize largest as root
    int l = 2*i + 1;  // left = 2*i + 1
    int r = 2*i + 2;  // right = 2*i + 2
    // If left child is larger than root
    if (l < n && arr[l] > arr[largest])
        largest = l;
    // If right child is larger than largest so far
    if (r < n && arr[r] > arr[largest])
        largest = r;
    // If largest is not root
    if (largest != i)
    {
        swap(arr[i], arr[largest]);
        // Recursively heapify the affected sub-tree
        heapify(arr, n, largest);
    }
}
```

```cpp
// main function to do heap sort
void heapSort(int arr[], int n)
{
    // Build heap (rearrange array)
    for (int i = n / 2 - 1; i >= 0; i--)
        heapify(arr, n, i);
    // One by one extract an element from heap
    for (int i=n-1; i>=0; i--)
    {
        // Move current root to end
        swap(arr[0], arr[i]);
        // call max heapify on the reduced heap
        heapify(arr, i, 0);
    }
}
/* A utility function to print array of size n */
void printArray(int arr[], int n)
{
  for (int i=0; i<n; ++i)
      cout << arr[i] << " ";
    cout << "\n";
}
// Driver program
int main()
{
    int arr[] = {12, 11, 13, 5, 6, 7};
    int n = sizeof(arr)/sizeof(arr[0]);
    heapSort(arr, n);
    cout << "Sorted array is \n";
    printArray(arr, n);
}
```

Output :

Sorted array is

5 6 7 11 12 13

Notes :

- Heap sort is an in-place algorithm.

- Its typical implementation is not stable, but can be made stable.

Time Complexity : Time complexity of heapify is O(Logn). Time complexity of create And Build Heap() is O(n) and overall time complexity of Heap Sort is O(nLogn).

Heap Sort Implementation

Heap sort algorithm starts by building a heap from the given elements,and then heap removes its largest element from the end of partially sorted array. After removing the largest element, it reconstructs the heap, removes the largest remaining item, and places it in the next open position from the end of the partially sorted array. This is repeated until there are no items left in the heap and the sorted array is full. Elementary implementations require two arrays – one to hold the heap and the other to hold the sorted elements.

```c
Implementation in C
#include<stdio.h>
void heapsort(int[],int);
void heapify(int[],int);
void adjust(int[],int);
main() {
    int n,i,a[50];
    system("clear");
    printf("\nEnter the limit:");
    scanf("%d",&n);
    printf("\nEnter the elements:");
    for (i=0;i<n;i++)
      scanf("%d",&a[i]);
    heapsort(a,n);
    printf("\nThe Sorted Elements Are:\n");
    for (i=0;i<n;i++)
      printf("\t%d",a[i]);
```

```c
        printf("\n");
}
void heapsort(int a[],int n) {
    int i,t;
    heapify(a,n);
    for (i=n-1;i>0;i--) {
        t = a[0];
        a[0] = a[i];
        a[i] = t;
        adjust(a,i);
    }
}
void heapify(int a[],int n) {
    int k,i,j,item;
    for (k=1;k<n;k++) {
        item = a[k];
        i = k;
        j = (i-1)/2;
        while((i>0)&&(item>a[j])) {
            a[i] = a[j];
            i = j;
            j = (i-1)/2;
        }
        a[i] = item;
    }
}
void adjust(int a[],int n) {
    int i,j,item;
```

```
    j = 0;
    item = a[j];
    i = 2*j+1;
    while(i<=n-1) {
        if(i+1 <= n-1)
          if(a[i] <a[i+1])
            i++;
        if(item<a[i]) {
            a[j] = a[i];
            j = i;
            i = 2*j+1;
        } else
          break;
    }
    a[j] = item;
}
```

5.5 MIN MAX HEAP

A binary heap is a heap data structure created using a binary tree.

Binary tree has two rules :

- Binary Heap must be complete binary tree at all levels except the last level. This is called **shape property**.

- All nodes are either greater than equal to (**Max-Heap**) or less than equal to (**Min-Heap**) to each of its child nodes. This is called **heap property**.

Implementation :

- Use array to store the data.

- Start storing from index 1, not 0.

- For any given node at position i :

- Its **Left Child** is at **[2*i]** if available.

- Its **Right Child** is at **[2*i+1]** if available.

- Its **Parent Node** is at **[i/2]** if available.

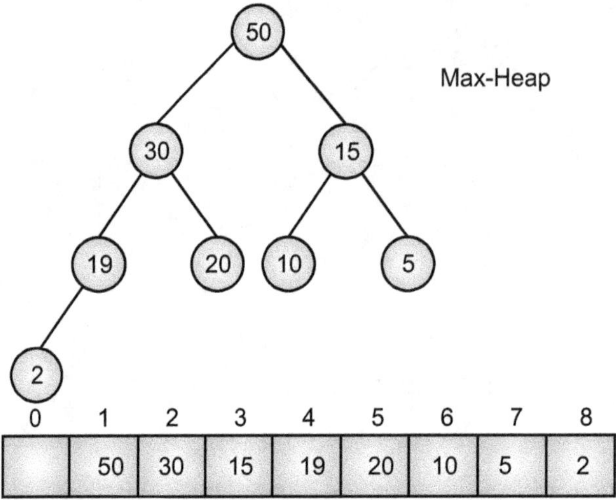

For node at i : Left child will be 2i right child will
be at 2i + 1 and parent node will be at [i/2].

Fig. 5.10

Max-Heap :

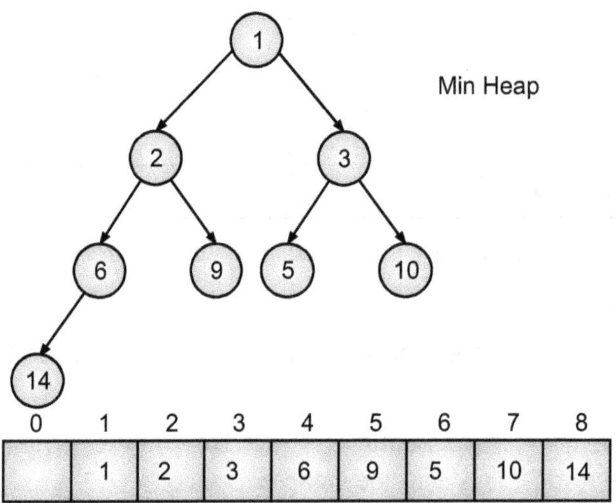

For node at i : Left child will be 2i right child will
be at 2i + 1 and parent node will be at [i/2].

Fig. 5.11

Min-Heap :

Heap majorly has 3 operations :

- Insert Operation
- Delete Operation
- Extract-Min (OR Extract-Max)

Insert Operation :

- Add the element at the bottom leaf of the Heap.

- Perform the Bubble-Up operation.

- All Insert Operations must perform the **bubble-up** operation (**it is also called as up-heap, percolate-up, sift-up, trickle-up, heapify-up, or cascade-up**)

Bubble-up Operation :

- If inserted element is smaller than its parent node in case of Min-Heap or greater than its parent node in case of Max-Heap, swap the element with its parent.

- Keep repeating the above step, if node reaches its correct position, STOP.

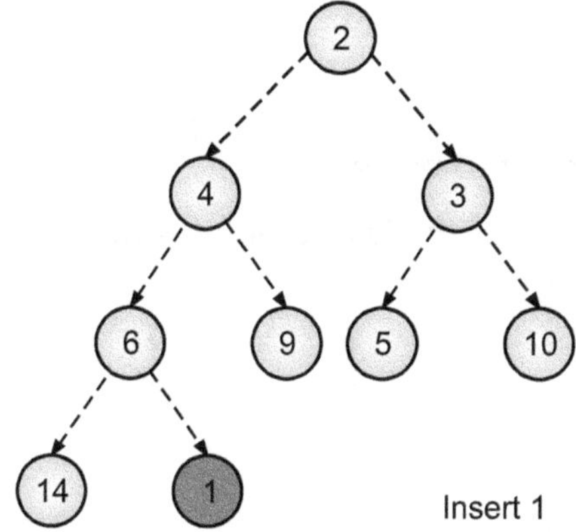

Fig. 5.12 : Insert() — Bubble-Up Min-Heap

Extract-Min or Extract-Max Operation :

- Take out the element from the root. (it will be minimum in case of Min-Heap and maximum in case of Max-Heap).

- Take out the last element from the last level from the heap and replace the root with the element.

- Perform **Sink-Down.**

- All delete operations must perform Sink-Down Operation (also known as bubble-down, percolate-down, sift-down, trickle down, heapify-down, cascade-down).

Sink-Down Operation :

- If replaced element is greater than any of its child node in case of Min-Heap or smaller than any if its child node in case of Max-Heap, swap the element with its smallest child(Min-Heap) or with its greatest child(Max-Heap).

- Keep repeating the above step, if node reaches its correct position, STOP.

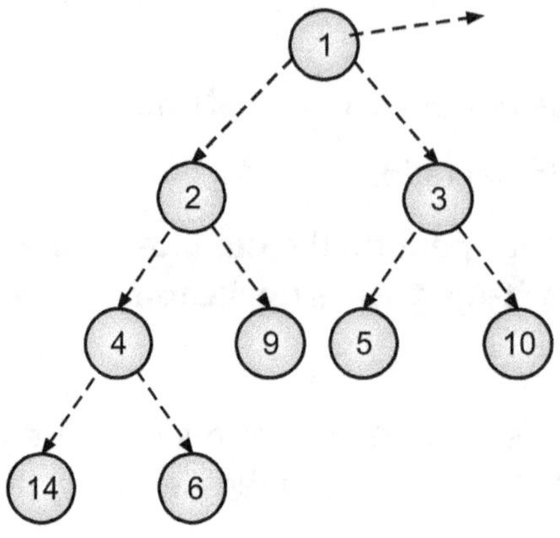

Fig. 5.13

Delete or Extract Min from Heap :

Delete Operation :

- Find the index for the element to be deleted.

- Take out the last element from the last level from the heap and replace the index with this element.

- Perform **Sink-Down**

Time and Space Complexity :

Space	O(n)
Search	O(n)
Insert	O(log n)
Delete	O(log n)

5.6 APPLICATIONS OF HEAP

Heap Data Structure is generally taught with Heapsort. Heapsort algorithm has limited uses because Quicksort is better in practice. Nevertheless, the Heap data structure itself is enormously used. Following are some uses other than Heapsort.

- **Priority Queues :** Priority queues can be efficiently implemented using Binary Heap because it supports insert(), delete() and extractmax(), decreaseKey() operations in O(log n) time. Binomial Heap and Fibonacci Heap are variations of Binary Heap. These variations perform union also in O(log n) time which is a O(n) operation in Binary Heap. Heap implemented priority queues are used in Graph algorithms like Prim's Algorithm and Dijkstra's algorithm.

- **Order Statistics :** The Heap data structure can be used to efficiently find the kth smallest (or largest) element in an array.

5.7 HASH TABLES

Hash tables are the data structures which favor efficient storage and retrieval of data elements which are **linear** in nature.

Dictionaries :

Dictionaries is a collection of data elements uniquely identified by a field called **key**. A dictionary supports operations of search, insert and delete.

A dictionary supports both **sequential and random access**. A sequential access is the process in which the data elements of the dictionary are **ordered** and accessed according to the order of the keys (ascending/descending). A random access is the process in which the data elements of the dictionary are not accessed according to a particular order.

Hash tables are ideal data structures for dictionaries.

Hash Search :

Hash search is a search in which the key, through an algorithmic function, determines the location of the data. Hashing is a key to address transformation in which the keys map to addresses in a list.

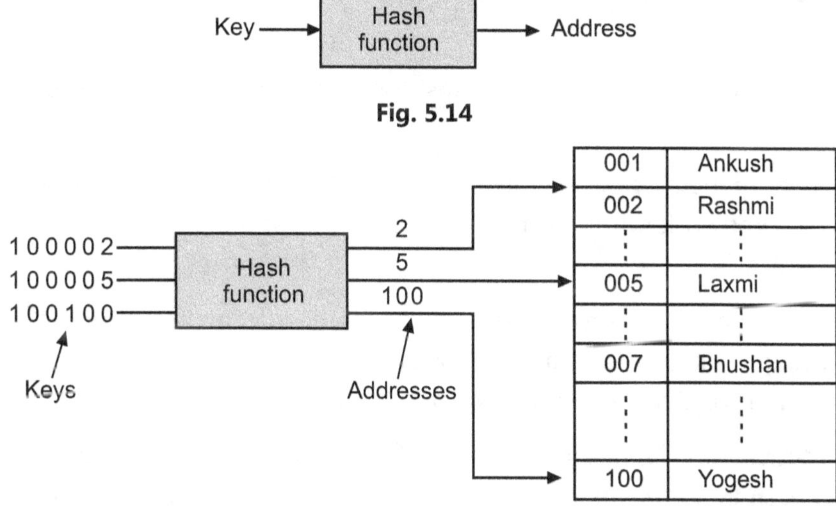

Fig. 5.14

Fig. 5.15

Hash Functions :

A hash function is a mathematical function which maps a given key of the dictionary to its corresponding location in the storage table (known as hash table).

The process of mapping the keys to their respective position in the hash table is called as hashing.

The choice of the hash function plays a significant role in the performance of the hash table. It is therefore essential that a hash function satisfies following characteristics :

Characteristics of Hash Functions :

- Easy and quick to compute.

- Even distribution of keys across the hash table.

- A hash function must minimize collisions.

Basic Definitions of Hashing :

- **Synonyms :** The set of **keys** that hash to the **same location** in our list is called as synonyms.

- **Collision :** Collision is the event that occurs when a hashing algorithm produces an address for an insertion key and that address is already occupied.

- **Home Address :** The address produced by the hashing algorithm is known as home address.

- **Prime Area :** The memory that contains all the home addresses is known as the prime area.

Probe : Each calculation of an address and test for success is known as a probe.

Scattered table

We have seen both pointer-based and array-based implementations for all of the data structures considered so far and hash tables are no exception. Array-based hash tables are called scatter tables .

The essential idea behind a scatter table is that all of the information is stored within a fixed size array. Hashing is used to identify the position where an item should be stored. When a collision occurs, the colliding item is stored somewhere else in the array.

One of the motivations for using scatter tables can be seen by considering again the pointer-based hash table shown in Figure. Since most of the linked lists are empty, much of the array is unused. At the same time, for each item that is added to the table, dynamic memory is consumed. Why not simply store the data in the unused array positions?

The elements of a chained scatter table are ordered pairs. Each array element contains a key and a pointer. All keys are stored in the table itself. Consequently, there is a fixed limit on the number of items that can be stored in a scatter table.

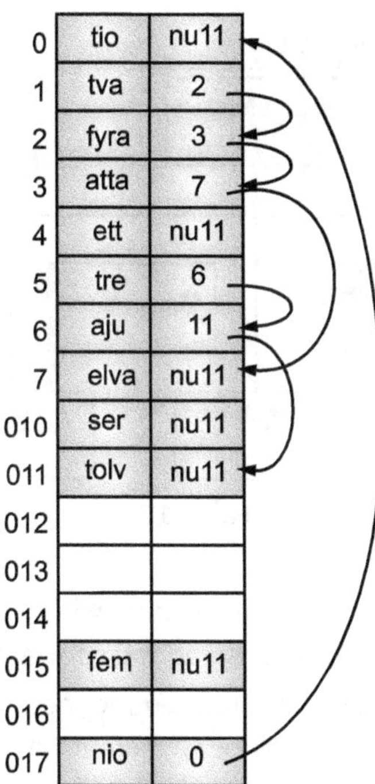

Fig. 5.16 : Chained Scatter Table

Since the pointers point to other elements in the array, they are implemented as integer-valued array subscripts rather than as address-valued pointer variables. Since valid array subscripts start from the value zero, the null pointer must be represented not as zero, but by an integer value that is outside the array bounds.

To find an item in a chained scatter table, we begin by hashing that item to determine the location from which to begin the search. E.g., to find the string "åtta", which hashes to the value 01406565418, we begin the search in array location 18. The item at that location is "två", which does not match. So we follow the pointer in location 18 to location 28. The item there, "fyra", does not match either. We follow the pointer again, this time to location 38 where we ultimately find the string we are looking for.

we see that the chained scatter table has embedded within it the linked lists which appear to be the same as those in the separately chained hash table. However, the lists are not exactly identical. When using the chained scatter table, it is possible for lists to coalesce .

For example, when using separate chaining, the keys "tre" and "sju" appear in a separate list from the key "tolv". This is because both "tre" and "sju" hash to position 58, whereas "tolv" hashes to position 68. The same keys appear together in a single list starting at position 58 in the chained scatter table. The two lists have coalesced.

5.7.1 Basic Hashing Techniques

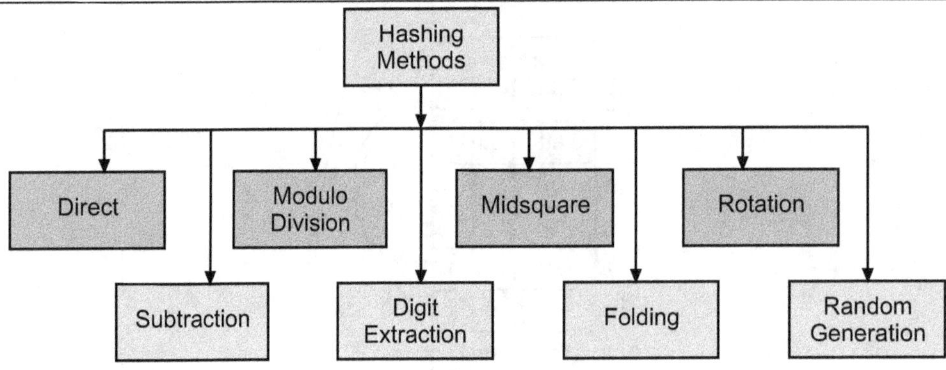

Fig. 5.17

(1) Direct Hashing :

In direct hashing, address for a key is generated without any algorithmic manipulation. Therefore, the data structure must contain an address for every possible key.

For Example, A small organization has 100 employees. Each employee is assigned an employee number between 1 to 100. Hence, we create an array of 100 employee records, the employee number can be directly used as the address of any individual record.

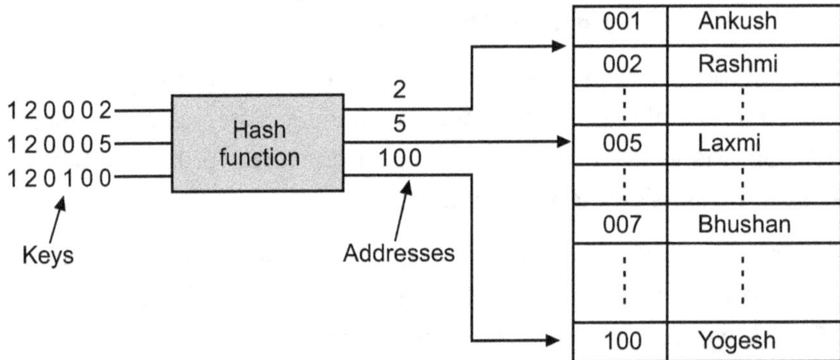

Fig. 5.18

(2) Subtraction Method :

Sometimes we have keys that are consecutive but do not start from one. This method is simple and it guarantees no collisions. Limitation is this method can be used for small lists in which the keys map to a densely filled list.

For Example, Consider a company has 100 employees, but their employee number starts from 1000 up to 1100 consecutively. Then we use a very simple hashing function that subtracts 1000 from the key to determine the address.

(3) Modulo-Division Method/Division Remainder :

This method divides the key by an array or bucket size and uses the remainder plus one for the address.

$$\therefore \quad \text{Address} = (\text{key} \% \text{list size}) + 1$$

A list size that is a prime number produces fewer collisions than other list sizes.

For Example, Suppose, we have 300 employees. The first prime number greater than 300 is 307. We therefore choose 307 as our list size.

$$\therefore \quad \text{Employee number} - 121267$$

$$\therefore \quad (121267 \% 307) + 1 = 2 + 1 = 3$$

(4) Digit Extraction Method :

Using digit extraction, selected digits are extracted from the key and used as the address.

For Example,

$$\underline{3}7\underline{94}52 \rightarrow 394$$
$$\underline{121}267 \rightarrow 112$$
$$\underline{378}845 \rightarrow 388$$
$$1\underline{60}252 \rightarrow 102$$
$$\underline{0}4\underline{51}28 \rightarrow 051$$

(5) Midsquare Method :

Key is squared and the address is selected from the middle of the squared no.

For Example, $9452 * 9452 = 89\underline{3403}04$

Address is 3403

(6) Folding Method :

There are 2 folding methods :

(a) Fold Shift :

The key value is divided into parts whose size matches with the size of the required address. Then the left and right parts are shifted and added with middle part.

For Example, suppose we have 3-digit addresses and key is 123456789

```
    1 2 3
  + 4 5 6
  + 7 8 9
  -------
 (1) 3 6 8
```

Discard (1) so address is 368.

(b) Fold Boundary :

Left and right numbers are folded on a fixed boundary between them and the center number. This results in the two outside values being reversed.

For Example, suppose we have 3 digit addresses and key is 123456789

$$3\ 2\ 1 \rightarrow \text{Reversed digits of } 123$$
$$+\ 4\ 5\ 6$$
$$\underline{+\ 9\ 8\ 7} \rightarrow \text{Reversed digits of } 789$$
$$(1)\ 7\ 6\ 4$$

Discard (1). So address is 764.

(7) Rotation Method :

Rotation method is incorporated in combination with other hashing methods. It is most useful when keys are assigned serially, such as we often see in employee numbers and part numbers.

For Example,

Original Key	Rotation	Rotated Key
6 0 0 1 0 1	6 0 0 1 0 $\boxed{1}$	$\boxed{1}$ 6 0 0 1 0
6 0 0 1 0 2	6 0 0 1 0 $\boxed{2}$	$\boxed{2}$ 6 0 0 1 0
6 0 0 1 0 3	6 0 0 1 0 $\boxed{3}$	$\boxed{3}$ 6 0 0 1 0
6 0 0 1 0 4	6 0 0 1 0 $\boxed{4}$	$\boxed{4}$ 6 0 0 1 0

(8) Pseudorandom Method :

The key is used as the seed in pseudorandom number generator and the resulting random number then scaled into the possible address range using modulo division. Common random generator is Y = ax + c.

For Example, Consider a = 17 and c = 7. Also, consider list size is 307. Key is 121267.

$$\therefore \quad y = ((17 * 121267) + 7)\ \%\ 307 + 1$$
$$y = (2061539 + 7)\ \%\ 307 + 1$$
$$y = (2061546\ \%\ 307) + 1$$
$$y = 41 + 1$$
$$y = 42$$

$\therefore$ Address is 42.

5.7.2 Forms of Hashing Data Structure

(1) Linear Open Addressing : It allows any number of records to be stored, because the space is dynamic.

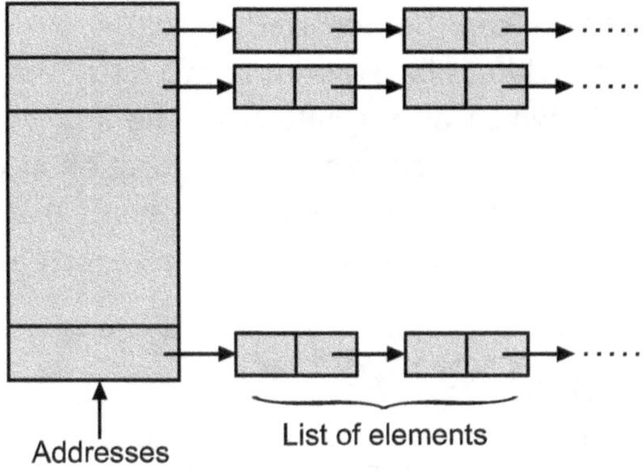

Fig. 5.19

(2) Linear Closed Addressing : It uses a fixed space for storage and hence this limits the size of hash table.

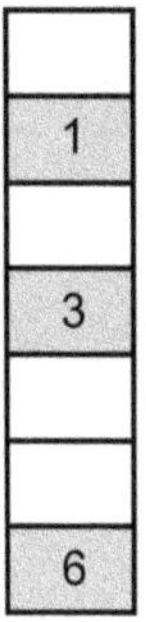

Fig. 5.20

In this case, maximum 7 elements can be stored as array size is only 7 and that is fixed.

Synonym or Collision

Overflow: Sometimes new data are to be inserted into the data structure but there is no available space, i.e. the free storage list is empty. This situation is usually called overflow.

If there are no enough buckets to handle the data then overflow happens in buckets.

Collision: In the small number of cases, where multiple keys map to the same integer, then elements with different keys may be stored in the same "slot" of the hash table. It is clear that when the hash function is used to locate a potential match, it will be necessary to compare the key of that element with the search key. But there may be more than one element which should be stored in a single slot of the table. This is called as a Collision.

For almost all hash functions, it is possible that more than one key is assigned to the same table address. For example, if the hash function computes the address just based on the first letter of the key, then all keys starting with the same letter will be hashed to the same location, resulting in a collision.

Collision Resolution: Collision can be resolved partially, by choosing another hash function, which computes the address based on first two letters of the key. However, even if a hash function is chosen in which all the letters of the key participate, there is still a possibility that number of keys may hash to the same location in the hash table. Another factor that can be used to avoid collision of multiple keys is the size of the hash table. A larger size will result in fewer collisions, but that would also increase the access time during retrieval.

5.8 COLLISION RESOLUTION METHODS

To avoid the collision we can use different collision resolution methods which are :

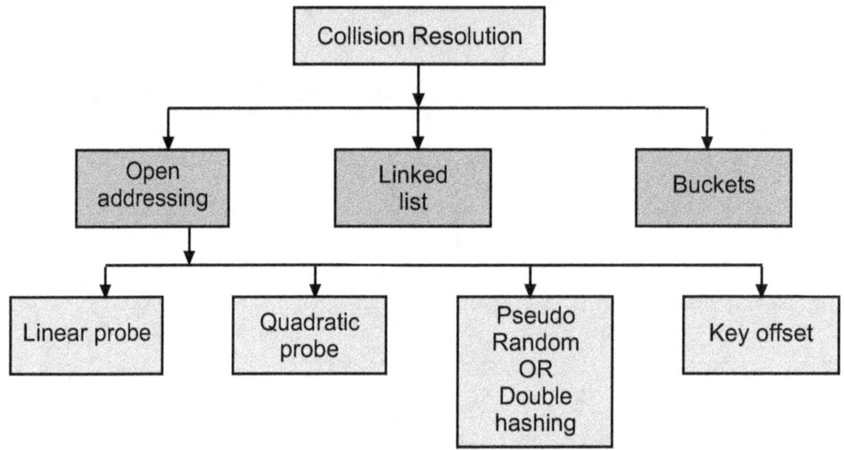

Fig. 5.21

Open Addressing :

In open addressing when a collision occurs, the home area addresses are searched for an unoccupied element where the new data can be placed.

(1) Linear Probe

(a) Linear Probing without Chaining :

When collision occurs, we resolve the collision by finding the next empty cell.

For Example, 3, 33, 42, 63, 89, 45, 93

Hash function = Key % 10

	Empty	After 3	After 33	After 42	After 63	After 89	After 45	After 93
0	-	-	-	-	-	-	-	-
1	-	-	-	-	-	-	-	-
2	-	-	-	**42**	42	42	42	42
3	-	**3**	3	3	3	3	3	3

...Conti

4	-	-	**33**	33	33	33	33	33
5	-	-	-	-	**63**	63	63	63
6	-	-	-	-	-	-	**45**	45
7	-	-	-	-	-	-	-	**93**
8	-	-	-	-	-	-	-	-
9	-	-	-	-	-	**89**	89	89

(b) Linear Probing with Chaining (without Replacement) :

Excessive collisions can be dealt by means of chaining. All the records mapped to same location are stored in a chain.

For Example, **Keys** – 3, 33, 42, 63, 89, 45, 93

Hash function $\Rightarrow$ key % 10.

Index	Key	Chain
0	-	-1
1	-	-1
2	-	-1
3	-	-1
4	-	-1
5	-	-1
6	-	-1
7	-	-1
8	-	-1
9	-	-1

-1 shows there is no chaining yet.

Index	Key	Chain
0	-	-1
1	-	-1
2	42	-1
3	3	4
4	33	5
5	63	7
6	45	-1
7	93	-1
8	-	-1
9	**89**	-1

Here 3, 33, 63 and 93 are supposed to be mapped at location 3. Hence all these are chained by index number at chain column.

index of 33
index of 63
index of 93

(c) Linear Probing with Chaining (with Replacement) :

In above example, key 45 has misplaced its starting location is at index 5. So to overcome this issue we replace key at index 5 by 45 and shift 63 to another subsequent empty location.

For Example, Keys – 3, 33, 42, 63, 89, 45, 93.

Hash function = key % 10.

Index	Key	Chain
0	-	– 1
1	-	– 1
2	**42**	– 1
3	**3**	4
4	**33**	5
5	**63**	– 1
6	-	– 1
7	-	– 1
8	-	– 1
9	**89**	– 1

Now to insert 45, we have shift 63 to next index 6 and place 45 at index 5.

(index 3 chain 4 → index of 33)
(index 4 chain 5 → index of 63)

After arrival of 45 and 93 :

Index	Key	Chain
0	-	– 1
1	-	– 1
2	42	– 1
3	3	4
4	33	**6**
5	**45**	– 1
6	63	7
7	**93**	– 1
8	-	– 1
9	89	– 1

(index 3 chain 4 → index of 33)
(index 4 chain 6 → new index of 63)
(index 6 chain 7 → index of 93)

Program to implement Direct Access File, collision handling through linear probing with chaining and without replacement.

Program on Hash Table-Linear Probing without Chaining :

```
/*   To implement Direct Access File ,Collision handling through linear probing with
chaining and without replacement.  */


#include <iomanip.h>
#include <iostream.h>
#include <fstream.h>
#include <conio.h>
#include <string.h>
#define SIZE 10
#define h(x) x%SIZE
struct student
{
    int rollno;
    char name[20];
    float marks;
    int status;
    int link;
};

class lin_probe
{
  char table[30];
  fstream tab;
  student rec;
  public :
    lin_probe(char *a);

    void displayall();
    void insert(student rec1);
    void  Delete(int rollno);
```

```cpp
    int  search(int rollno);
    void display(int recno)
     {
        int i=recno;
        tab.open(table,ios : :binary  | ios : :in | ios : :nocreate);
        tab.seekg(recno*sizeof(student),ios : :beg);
        tab.read((char*)&rec,sizeof(student));
        if(rec.status==0)
         {
            cout<<"\n"<<i<<") "<<rec.rollno<<"  "<<rec.name<<"
"<<setprecision(2)<<rec.marks;
            cout<<" "<<rec.link;
         }
        else
            cout<<"\n"<<i<<" ***** Empty  ********";
        tab.close();
     }
    void read(int recno)
     {
        tab.open(table,ios : :binary | ios : :in);
        tab.seekg(recno*sizeof(student),ios : :beg);
        tab.read((char*) &rec,sizeof(student));
        tab.close();
     }
    void write(int recno)
     {
        tab.open(table,ios : :binary | ios : :nocreate | ios : :out | ios : :in);
        tab.seekp(recno*sizeof(student),ios : :beg);
        tab.write((char*)&rec,sizeof(student));
```

```cpp
        tab.close();
    }


};
void lin_probe : :lin_probe(char *a)
{
    int i;
    strcpy(table,a);
    rec.status=1;rec.link=-1;
    tab.open(table,ios : :binary | ios : :out);
    tab.close();
    for(i=0;i<SIZE;i++)
        write(i);
}
void lin_probe : :displayall()
{
    int i=1,n;
    cout<<"\n*********Data File*********\n";
    for(i=0;i<SIZE;i++)
        display(i);
}
void lin_probe : :insert(student rec1)
{
    int n,i,j,start,k;
    rec1.status=0;
    rec1.link=-1;
    start=h(rec1.rollno);
    for(i=0;i<SIZE;i++)
    {
        j=(start+i)%SIZE;
```

```
        read(j);
        if(rec.status==0 && h(rec.rollno)==start)
          break;
   }
  if(i<10)
   {
       while(rec.link!=-1)
     {
     j=rec.link;
     read(j);
     }
      for(i=0;i<SIZE;i++)
      {
       k=(start+i)%SIZE;
       read(k);
      if(rec.status==1)
        {
          rec=rec1;
          write(k);
          read(j);
          rec.link=k;
          write(j);
          return;
        }
      }
     cout<<"\nTable is full ";
  }
  else
   {
    for(i=0;i<SIZE;i++)
```

```
        {
         k=(start+i)%SIZE;
         read(k);
        if(rec.status==1)
          {
            rec=rec1;
            write(k);
            return;
          }
        }
      cout<<"\nTable is full ";
    }


}

void lin_probe : :Delete(int rollno)
{
    student rec1;
    int recno;
    int i,j,start,k;
    start=h(rollno);
    for(i=0;i<SIZE;i++)
      {
        j=(start+i)%SIZE;
        read(j);
        if(rec.status==0 && h(rec.rollno)==start)//synonim found
          break;
      }
    if(i<10)
    {
```

```cpp
    if(rec.rollno==rollno )
     {
         rec.status=1;
         write(j);
     }
     else
     {
         while(rec.rollno !=rollno && rec.link!=-1)
           {
               k=j;
               j=rec.link;
               read(j);
           }

         if(rec.rollno==rollno)
           { rec.status=1;
               write(j);
               int nextlink=rec.link;
               read(k);
               rec.link=nextlink;
               write(k);
           }
         else
         cout<<"\nElement not found";
     }
    }
    else
      cout<<"\nRecord Not Found ";
}
int lin_probe : :search(int rollno)
```

```c
{
    int start,i,j;
    start=h(rollno);
    for(i=0;i<SIZE;i++)
     {
        j=(start+i)%SIZE;
        read(j);
        if(rec.status==0 && h(rec.rollno)==start)//synonim found
          break;
     }
    if(i<10)
    {
        while(rec.rollno !=rollno && rec.link!=-1)
          {
                j=rec.link;
                 read(j);
          }

        if(rec.rollno==rollno)
                return(j);

        else
                return -1;
    }
    else
      return -1;
}

void main()
```

```cpp
{
  lin_probe object("table.txt");
  int rollno,op,recno;
  student rec1;
  clrscr();
  do
   {
      cout<<"\n\n1)Print\n2)Insert\n3)Delete";
      cout<<"\n4)Search\n5)Quit";
      cout<<"\nEnter Your Choice :";
      cin>>op;
      switch(op)
      {
       case 1 :object.displayall();
          break;
       case 2 :
          cout<<"\nEnter a record to be inserted(roll no,name,marks) : ";
          cin>>rec1.rollno>>rec1.name>>rec1.marks;
          object.insert(rec1);
           break;
       case 3 :
          cout<<"\nEnter the roll no. :";
          cin>>rollno;
          object.Delete(rollno);
           break;
        case 4 :
          cout<<"\nEnter a roll no. : ";
          cin>>rollno;
          recno=object.search(rollno);
          if(recno>=0)
```

```
            {
                cout<<"\n Record No. :  "<<recno;
                object.display(recno);
            }
        else
                cout<<"\nRecord Not Found ";
            break;
        }
    }while(op!=5);
}


/**************OUTPUT***************/
1)  Print
2)  Insert
3)  Delete
4)  Search
5)  Quit
Enter Your Choice :2


Enter a record to be inserted(roll no,name,marks) : 155 ABC 76


1)  Print
2)  Insert
3)  Delete
4)  Search
5)  Quit


Enter Your Choice :2


Enter a record to be inserted(roll no,name,marks) : 45 LMN 88
```

1) Print
2) Insert
3) Delete
4) Search
5) Quit

Enter Your Choice :2

Enter a record to be inserted(roll no,name,marks) : 90 XYZ 70

1) Print
2) Insert
3) Delete
4) Search
5) Quit

Enter Your Choice :4

Enter a roll no. : 45

Record No. : 6

6) 45 Komal 88 -1

1) Print
2) Insert
3) Delete
4) Search
5) Quit
Enter Your Choice :1

*********Data File*********

0) 90 XYZ 70 -1

1) ***** Empty ********

2) ***** Empty ********

3) ***** Empty ********

4) ***** Empty ********

5) 155 ABC 76 6

6) 45 LMN 88 -1

7) ***** Empty ********

8) ***** Empty ********

9) ***** Empty ********

1) Print

2) Insert

3) Delete

4) Search

5) Quit

Enter Your Choice :3

Enter the roll no. :45

1) Print

2) Insert

3) Delete

4) Search

5) Quit

Enter Your Choice :1

*********Data File*********

```
0)  90 XYZ 70 -1
1)  ***** Empty ********
2)  ***** Empty ********
3)  ***** Empty ********
4)  ***** Empty ********
5)  155 ABC 76 -1
6)  ***** Empty ********
7)  ***** Empty ********
8)  ***** Empty ********
9)  ***** Empty ********


1)  Print
2)  Insert
3)  Delete
4)  Search
5)  Quit


Enter Your Choice :5
```

(2) Quadratic Probe :

In quadratic probe, the increment is the collision probe number squared. Thus for 1st probe we add 1^2; for 2nd probe we add 2^2; for 3rd probe we add 3^2; and so forth until we find an empty element or we exhaust the possible elements.

This probe does not ensure that all cells will be examined to find empty cell. Thus, it may be possible that key won't be inserted even if there is an empty cell in the table.

Probe Number	Collision Location	$(Probe)^2$ and Increment	New Address
1	1	$(1)^2 = 1$	1 + 1 = 2
2	2	$(2)^2 = 4$	2 + 4 = 6
3	6	$(3)^2 = 9$	6 + 9 = 15
4	15	$(4)^2 = 16$	15 + 16 = 31
5	31	$(5)^2 = 25$	31 + 25 = 56

Quadratic collision resolution increments.

For Example, 4371, 1323, 6173, 4199, 4344, 9679, 1989.

Hash function = Key % 10.

<table>
<tr><td>

Index	Key
0	9679
1	4371
2	–
3	1323
4	6173
5	4344
6	–
7	–
8	1989
9	4199

</td><td>

i)   4371 % 10 = 1   (1st location is empty, put the element directly)

ii)   1323 % 10 = 3   (3rd location is empty, put the element directly)

iii)   6173 % 10 = 3   (3rd location is not empty)

∴ $6173 \% 10 = 3 + (1)^2 = 4$ (4th location is empty, put the element directly)

iv)   4199 % 10 = 9   (9th location is empty, put the element directly)

v)   4344 % 10 = 4   (4th location is not empty)

∴ $4344 \% 10 = 4 + (1)^2 = 5$ (5th location is empty, put the element directly)

vi)   9679 % 10 = 9   (9th location is not empty)

∴ $9679 \% 10 = 9 + (1)^2 = 10 \% 10 = 0$ (0th location is empty, So put the element directly)

vii)   1989 % 10 = 9   (9th location is not empty)

∴ $1989 \% 10 = 9 + (1)^2 = 10 \% 10 = 0$ (0th location is not empty)

∴ $1989 \% 10 = 9 + (2)^2 = 9 + 4 = 13 \% 10 = 3$ (3rd location is not empty)

∴ $1989 \% 10 = 9 + (3)^2 = 9 + 9 = 18 \% 10 - 8$ (8th location is empty. So put the element there)

</td></tr>
</table>

(3) Pseudorandom / Double Hashing :

Rather than using an arithmetic probe function, the address is rehashed. This means if first hash function yields an address which is already occupied then apply second hash function to get the different address for a key.

For Example, keys – 4371, 1323, 6173, 4199, 4344, 9679

First hash function = key % 10

Second hash function = 7 – (key % 7)

Index	Key	To insert
0		(a) 6173 →
1	4371	$7 - (6173 \% 7) = 7 - 6 = 1$
2		$\therefore 6173 \% 10 = 3 + (1)^{\times 1} = 4$
3	1323	(b) 4344 →
4	6173	$7 - (4344 \% 7) = 7 - 4 = 3$
5	9679	$\therefore 4344 \% 10 = 4 + (3)^{\times 1} = 7$
6		(c) 9679 →
7	4344	$7 - (9679 \% 7) = 7 - 5 = 2$
8		$\therefore 9679 \% 10 = 9 + (2)^{1} = 11 \% 10 = 1$
9	4199	Again $9679 \% 10 = 9 + (2)^{2} = 13 \% 10 = 3$
		Again $9679 \% 10 = 9 + (2)^{3} = 15 \% 10 = 5$

(4) Key Offset :

Key offset is a double hashing method that produces different collision paths for different keys. Key offset calculates the new address as a function of the old address and the key.

Offset = [Key / Listsize]

Address = [(Offset + Old address) % List size] + 1

For Example, key → 166702

size → 307

1st hash function = key % 10

$\therefore$ $166702 \% 10 = 2$

$\therefore$ Offset = $(166702/307) = 543$

Address = $[(543 + 002) \% 307] + 1 = 239$

If at 239 there is also a collision, then repeat the process to locate next address.

$\therefore$ Offset = $(166702/307) = 543$

Address = $[(543 + 239) \% 307] + 1 = 169$

(5) Linked List Resolution/Dynamic Hashing :

Linked list is an ordered collection of data in which each element contains the location of the next element.

Linked list resolution uses a separate area to store collisions and chairs all synonyms together in a linked list. It uses two storage areas, prime area and overflow area.

When a collision occurs one element is stored in prime area and chained to its corresponding linked list in overflow area.

For Example, **Keys** - 3, 33, 42, 63, 89, 45, 93.

Hash function = key % 10.

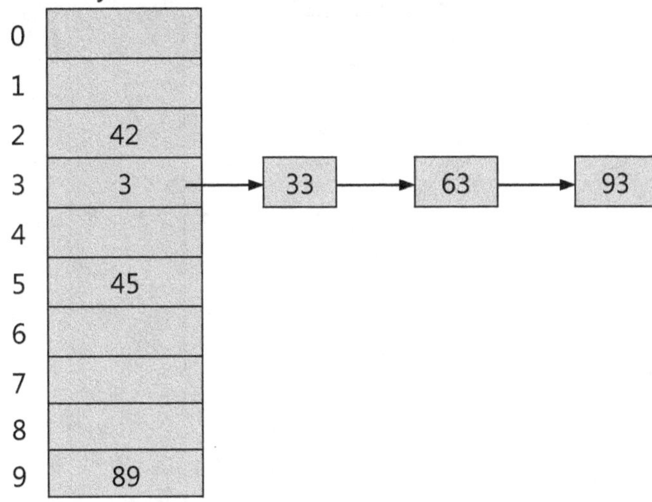

(6) Bucket Hashing :

Bucket nodes that accommodate **multiple data occurrences**. Because a bucket can hold multiple pieces of data, collisions are postponed until the bucket is full.

For Example, **Keys** - 3, 33, 42, 63, 89, 45

Hash function = key % 10.

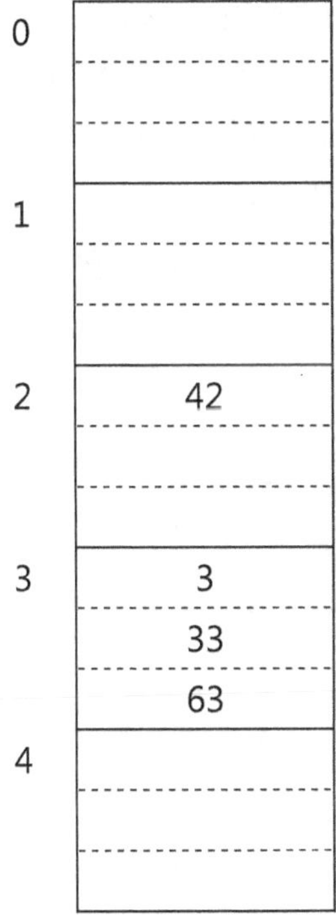

...Conti

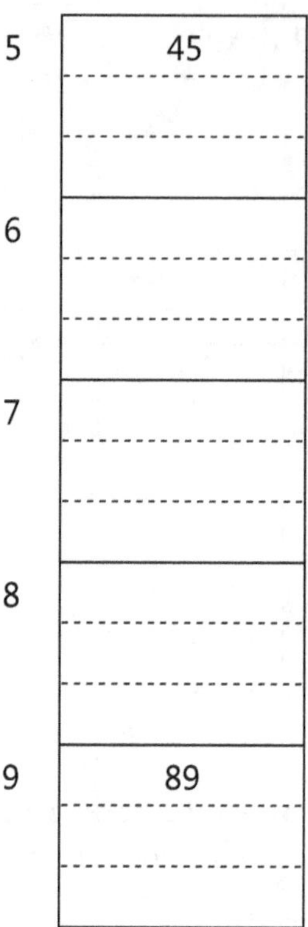

Example 5.3 : Explain linear probing with and without replacement using the following data : 12, 01, 04, 03, 07, 08, 10, 02, 05, 14, 06, 28. Assume buckets from 0 to 9 and each bucket has one slot. Calculate average cost or number of comparison for both.

Solution : (a) Linear probing without replacement.

Index	Key	Chain
0	**10**	- 1
1	**01**	- 1
2	**12**	- 1
3	**03**	- 1
4	**04**	- 1
5	-	- 1
6	-	- 1
7	07	- 1
8	08	- 1
9	-	- 1

After insertion of 1st 7 keys.

Total comparisons = 7 × 1 = 7

Index	Key	Chain
0	10	- 1
1	01	- 1
2	12	5
3	03	- 1
4	04	- 1
5	02	- 1
6	05	- 1
7	07	- 1
8	08	- 1
9	-	- 1

After insertion of 02 and 05

For 2 Total comparisons are = 4

For 5 Total comparisons are = 2

Index	Key	Chain
0	10	- 1
1	01	- 1
2	12	5
3	03	- 1
4	04	9
5	02	- 1
6	05	- 1
7	07	- 1
8	08	- 1
9	14	- 1

After insertion of 14

(6 comparisons - 1st at 4, 2nd at 5, 3rd at 6 and 4th at 7, 5th at 8 and 6th at 9th position)

Keys 06 and 28 cannot be inserted as the bucket size of hash table is full.

So, therefore total number of comparisons.

$$= (7 \times 1) + 4 + 2 + 6$$

$$= 19$$

(b) Linear Probing with Replacement :

Index	Key	Chain
0	10	- 1
1	01	- 1
2	12	- 1
3	03	- 1
4	04	- 1
5	-	- 1
6	-	- 1
7	07	- 1
8	08	- 1
9	-	- 1

After insertion of 1st 7 keys which are
12, 01, 04, 03, 07, 08, 10.
(Each with 1 comparison only
at 2, 1, 4, 3, 7, 8, and 0 respectively)

Index	Key	Chain
0	10	- 1
1	01	- 1
2	12	5
3	03	- 1
4	04	- 1
5	02	- 1
6	-	- 1
7	07	- 1
8	08	- 1
9	-	- 1

After insertion of 02
(4 comparisons – 1st at 2, 2nd at 3,
3rd at 4 and 4th at 5th position)

Index	Key	Chain
0	10	- 1
1	01	- 1
2	12	6
3	03	- 1
4	04	9
5	05	- 1
6	02	- 1
7	07	- 1
8	08	- 1
9	14	- 1

After insertion of 5
(3 comparisons – 1st at 5, 2nd at 6 to
remove 2 at 6th position
3rd at 2nd to change chain number)
and After insertion of 14
(6 comparisons – 1st at 4, 2nd at 5,
3rd at 6, 4th at 7, 5th at 8, and 6th at 9th
position)

Keys 06 and 28 cannot be inserted as the bucket size 9 of hash table is full.

So, therefore total number of comparisons.

$$= 7 \times 1 + 4 + 3 + 6$$
$$= 20$$

Example 5.4 : Given the input {4371, 1323, 6173, 4199, 4344, 9679, 1989} and hash function $h(x) = (x \bmod 10)$, show the results for the following :

(a) Open addressing hash table using linear probing.

(b) Open addressing hash table with quadratic probing.

(c) Open addressing hash table with second hash function.

which is $h2(x) = 7 - (x \bmod 7)$.

Solution :

(a) Open Addressing Hash Table with Linear Probing.

Index	4371	1323	6173	4199	4344	9679	1989
0	-	-	-	-	-	9679	9679
1	**4371**	4371	4371	4371	4371	4371	4371
2	-	-	-	-	-	-	**1989**
3	-	**1323**	1323	1323	1323	1323	1323
4	-	-	**6173**	6173	6173	6173	6173
5	-	-	-	-	**4344**	4344	4344
6	-	-	-	-	-	-	-
7	-	-	-	-	-	-	-
8	-	-	-	-	-	-	-
9	-	-	-	4199	4199	4199	4199

(b) Open Addressing Hash Table with Quadratic Probing.

Index	4371	1323	6173	4199	4344	9679	1989
0	-	-	-	-	-	**9679**	9679
1	**4371**	4371	4371	4371	4371	4371	4371
2	-	-	-	-	-	-	-
3	-	**1323**	1323	1323	1323	1323	1323
4	-	-	**6173**	6173	6173	6173	6173
5	-	-	-	-	**4344**	4344	4344
6	-	-	-	-	-	-	-
7	-	-	-	-	-	-	-
8	-	-	-	-	-	-	**1989**
9	-	-	-	**4199**	4199	4199	4199

-    Key 6173 to be mapped to

$$(6173 \% 10 + (1)^2) = 3 + 1 = 4$$

- Key 4344 to be mapped to

    $(4344 \% 10 + (1)^2) = 4 + 1 = 5$

- Key 9679 to be mapped to

    $(9679 \% 10 + (1)^2) = 9 + 1 = 10 \% 10 = 0$

- Key 1989 to be mapped to

    $(1989 \% 10 + (1)^2) = 9 + 1 = 10 \% 10 = 0$

    0th position not available

    So $(1989 \% 10 + (2)^2) = 9 + 4 = 13 \% 10 = 3$

    3rd position not available

    So $(1989 \% 10 + (3)^2) = 9 + 9 = 18 \% 10 = 8.$

    8th position is empty. So insert 1989 at 8th position.

(c) Open Addressing Hash Table with 2nd Hash Function :

$$h2(x) = 7 - (x \bmod 7)$$

Index	4371	1323	6173	4199	4344	9679	1989
0	-	-	-	-	-	-	-
1	**4371**	4371	4371	4371	4371	4371	4371
2	-	-	-	-	-	-	**1989**
3	-	**1323**	1323	1323	1323	1323	1323
4	-	-	**6173**	6173	6173	6173	6173
5	-	-	-	-	-	**9679**	9679
6	-	-	-	-	-	-	-
7	-	-	-	-	**4344**	4344	4344
8	-	-	-	-	-	-	-
9	-	-	-	4199	4199	4199	4199

Here 1989 is not mapped.

- $h2 (6173) = 7 - 6173 \% 7 = 7 - 6 = 1$

    So 6173 to be mapped to $6173 \% 10 + (1 \times h2(6173)) = 3 + 1 = 4$

- $h2 (4344) = 7 - 4344 \% 7 = 7 - 4 = 3$

    So 4344 to be mapped to $4344 \% 10 + (1 \times h2 (4344)) = 4 + 3 = 7$

- $h2 (9679) = 7 - 9679 \% 7 = 7 - 5 = 2$

So 9679 to be mapped to $9679 \% 10 + (1 \times h2\,(9679)) = 9 + 2 = 11 \% 10 = 1$

$$9679 \% 10 + (2 \times h2\,(9679)) = 9 + 4 = 13 \% 10 = 3$$

$$9679 \% 10 + (3 \times h2\,(9679)) = 9 + 6 = 15 \% 10 = 5$$

- $h2\,(1989) = 7 - 1989 \% 7 = 7 - 1 = 6$

This key cannot be inserted as any location of $(9 + 6 \times i) \% 10$ is not empty.

Example 5.5 : Assume a has table of size 19 and hash function $H(x) = x \bmod 10$ performs linear probing with and without replacement for the given set of values.

0, 1, 4, 72, 65, 85, 87, 90, 58

Solution :

(a) Linear Probing without Replacement :

Index	Key	Chain
0	**0**	- 1
1	**1**	- 1
2	**72**	- 1
3	-	- 1
4	**4**	- 1
5	**65**	- 1
6	-	- 1
7	-	- 1
8	-	- 1
9	-	- 1

After insertion of 1st 5 keys,

Index	Key	Chain
0	0	- 1
1	1	- 1
2	72	- 1
3	-	- 1
4	4	- 1
5	65	- 1
6	**85**	6
7	**87**	- 1
8	-	- 1
9	-	- 1

After insertion of 85 and 87

Index	Key	Chain
0	0	3
1	1	- 1
2	72	- 1
3	**90**	- 1
4	4	- 1
5	65	6
6	85	- 1
7	87	- 1
8	**58**	- 1
9	-	- 1

After insertion of 90 and 58

Linear probing with replacement

Index	Key	Chain
0	**0**	- 1
1	**1**	- 1
2	**72**	- 1
3	-	- 1
4	**4**	- 1
5	**65**	- 1
6	-	- 1
7	-	- 1
8	-	- 1
9	-	- 1

After insertion of 1st 5 keys.

Index	Key	Chain
0	0	- 1
1	1	- 1
2	72	- 1
3	-	- 1
4	4	- 1
5	65	6
6	**85**	- 1
7	**87**	- 1
8	-	- 1
9	-	- 1

After insertion of 85 and 87

Index	Key	Chain
0	0	- 1
1	1	- 1
2	72	- 1
3	**90**	- 1
4	4	- 1
5	65	6
6	85	- 1
7	87	- 1
8	**58**	- 1
9	-	- 1

After insertion of 90 and 58

Example 5.6 : Explain linear probing, chaining with replacement and chaining without replacement using the following data :

10, 12, 22, 23, 14, 6, 5, 3, 9, 11

Assume buckets from 0 to 9 and each bucket has one slot. Hash function is key % 10. Calculate average number of comparisons for all.

Solution :

(a) Linear Probing, Chaining without Replacement :

Index	Key	Chain
0	**10**	- 1
1	-	- 1
2	**12**	- 1
3	-	- 1
4	-	- 1
5	-	- 1
6	-	- 1
7	-	- 1
8	-	- 1
9	-	- 1

After insertion of 1st 2 keys which are 10 and 12. (Each with 1 comparison only at 0th and 2nd index position)

Index	Key	Chain
0	10	- 1
1	-	- 1
2	12	3
3	**22**	- 1
4	**23**	- 1
5	**14**	- 1
6	**6**	- 1
7	-	- 1
8	-	- 1
9	-	- 1

After insertion of 22, 23 24 and 6. (2 comparisons for 22 at 2nd and 3rd position, for 23 at 3rd and 4th position, for 14 at 4th and 5th position and 1 comparison for 6 at 6th position only)

Index	Key	Chain
0	10	- 1
1	**11**	- 1
2	12	3
3	22	- 1
4	23	**8**
5	14	- 1
6	6	- 1
7	**5**	- 1
8	**3**	- 1
9	**9**	- 1

After insertion of 5, 3, 9, and 11. (3 comparisons for 5 at 5th, 6th and 7th position, for 6 comparisons for 3 at 3, 4, 5, 6, 7 and 8th position, 1 comparison each for 9 and 11)

So therefore total number of comparisons

$$= 2 + 6 + 1 + 3 + 6 + 2$$

$$= 20$$

(b) Linear Probing Chaining with Replacement

Index	Key	Chain
0	**10**	- 1
1	-	- 1
2	**12**	3
3	**22**	- 1
4	-	- 1
5	-	- 1
6	-	- 1
7	-	- 1
8	-	- 1
9	-	- 1

After insertion of 10, 12 and 22. (1 comparison for 10 and 12 at 0 and 2nd position respectively. 2 comparisons for 22 at 2nd and 3rd position)

Index	Key	Chain
0	10	- 1
1	-	- 1
2	**12**	4
3	**23**	- 1
4	22	- 1
5	-	- 1
6	-	- 1
7	-	- 1
8	-	- 1
9	-	- 1

After insertion of 23 (3 comparisons at 3rd, at 4th to shift 22 and at 2nd to change chain number)

Index	Key	Chain
0	10	- 1
1	-	1
2	12	5
3	23	- 1
4	**14**	- 1
5	22	- 1
6	**6**	- 1
7	-	- 1
8	-	- 1
9	-	- 1

After insertion of 14 and 6. (3 comparisons for inserting 14 and one comparison for inserting 6)

Index	Key	Chain
0	10	- 1
1	**11**	- 1
2	12	7
3	23	8
4	14	- 1
5	**5**	- 1
6	6	- 1
7	22	- 1
8	**3**	- 1
9	**9**	- 1

After insertion of 5, 3, 9 and 11 (4 comparisons for inserting 5 6 comparisons for inserting 3 1 comparison each for inserting 9 and 11)

So, therefore total number of comparisons

$$= 2 + 2 + 3 + 3 + 1 + 4 + 6 + 2$$

$$= 23.$$

O(1) access to files means that no matter how big the file grows, access to a record always takes the same, small number of seeks. By contrast, sequential searching gives us O(N) access, where in the number of seeks grow in proportion to the size of the files. As we shall study in preceding chapters, B trees improve on this greatly, providing $O(\log_k N)$ access, the number of seeks increases as the logarithm to the base k of the number of records, where k is a measure of the leaf size. $O(\log_k N)$ access provide very good retrieval performance, even for very large files, but it is still not O(1) access. In this chapter, we shall study how to achieve this.

Re-hashing:

Rehashing is a computer programming technique used in hash tables to resolve hash collisions, cases when two different values to be searched for produce the same hash key. It is a popular collision-resolution technique in open-addressed hash table.

EXERCISE

1. What is a Hashing function ? Explain any 4 types of Hashing functions.   **(6m)**

2. What is an optimal binary search tree ? What is its use ?   **(4m)**

3. Give any 3 points of comparison between Binary search tree, OBST, Huffman's tree and AVL tree.   **(6m)**

4. Obtain the height balance tree for the following sequence of data December, January, April, March, July, August, October, November, May, June. Show all steps.   **(6m)**

5. What is collision? What are different collision resolution techniques? Explain any two methods in detail.   **(Dec. 10,8m)**

6. Explain static and dynamic tree tables.   **(Dec. 10, 4m)**

7. Write a Pseudo 'C' algorithm for LL, RR, LR and RL rotations for AVL tree. **(Dec. 10, 4m)**

8. What is hashing ? What are the characteristics of good hash function ? Explain any two types of hash functions.   **(May 11, 6m)**

9. Explain linear probing, chaining with replacement and chaining without replacement using the following data 10, 12, 22, 23, 14, 6, 5, 3, 9, 11. Assume buckets from 0 to 9 and each bucket has one slot. Hash function is key % 10. Calculate average number of comparisons for all.   **(May 11, 10m)**

10. What is symbol table? What are operations on symbol table? Give complete specification off symbol table ADT.   **(May 11, 8m)**

11. What is collision? Explain any two methods of handling collision.   **(May 11, 8m)**

12. What is hash function ? What are issues in hashing ? What are rules for designing hash function? Give types of uniform hash functions.   **(May 11, 8m)**

13. What is bucket hashing? Explain with example.   **(May 12, 8m)**

14. What is hash function? Explain the following hash function :   **(May 12, 8m)**

    (i) Mid-square   (ii) Modulo Division

    (iii) Folding Method   (iv) Digit Analysis.

15. Write and explain algorithm to delete node form AVL tree.   **(Dec. 12, 8m)**

16. What is hash function? Explain the different types of hash functions.   **(Dec. 12, 8m)**

17. Explain different types of rotation for AVL tree with suitable example.   **(Dec. 12, 8m)**

18.   What are hashing methods? Explain in brief.   **(Dec. 12, 8m)**

19.   What is the use of hash tables? Explain the characteristics of a good hash function.

(May 13)

20.   Enlist various static and dynamic tree tables. Explain when to select the static tree tables and dynamic tree tables.   **(May 13)**

21.   Write a pseudo C/C++ code for LL, RR, LR and RL rotations for AVL tree.   **(May 13)**

22.   Assume a hash table of size 10 and hash function H(X)=X mod 10 performs linear probing with and without replacement for the given set of values. 0, 1, 2, 4, 72, 65, 85, 87, 90, 58.   **(May 13)**

CHAPTER 6
ADVANCE TREES

6.1 THREADED BINARY TREE   [May 04, 07, 08, 09, 10, Dec. 06, 07, 08]

- Almost every operation performed on binary tree requires traversing a binary tree. We have seen recursive traversals are not that efficient. It is because the recursive calls take place even for NULL values of leaf nodes.

- Another problem with binary tree is that, the *l*child and *r*child of leaf nodes store nothing. The space of *l*child and *r*child is wasted. If the height of tree is more this is a serious issue because there will be more number of leaf nodes.

- Both these problems have a single solution and it is threaded binary tree i.e. we can utilize the space of *l*child and *r*child of leaf nodes and speed up the traversal by eliminating recursion.

- The idea of threaded binary tree is to replace NULL links with addresses of the nodes in the binary tree itself.

- Now which node's address is to be stored in the NULL field? We can store the address of the node which is next node in inorder traversal. For example, for inorder traversal, we will be storing the inorder successor's addresses in rchild. Such a pointer is called thread. The tree so designed is called right-in-threaded binary tree.

- If the NULL pointer in *l*child is replaced by the pointers to inorder predecessor then the tree is called left-in-threaded binary tree.

- If both NULL pointers in *l*child and rchild are replaced by pointers to inorder predecess or and successor respectively, it is called in-threaded binary tree or inorder-threaded binary tree.

- If the NULL pointer in *l*child and rchild are replaced by pointers to preorder predecessor and successor respectively, then it is called pre-threaded or preorder thereaded binary tree.

- If the NULL pointers in *l*child and rchild are replaced by pointers to postorder predecessor and successor respectively, then it is called post-threaded or post-order threaded binary tree.

- Now one important point about the threaded binary tree is how to distinguish between the thread and normal pointers? Because threads are not the natural pointers in the binary tree, they are created and are to be distinguished in traversal algorithms from normal pointers. For this, an extra field is added in each node to indicate whether the rchild or *l*child is a thread or not. For these two threads, we will require two logical fields say rt and lt. The values of rt and *l*t will be equal to 1 if the *l*child or rchild is thread otherwise it will be 0.

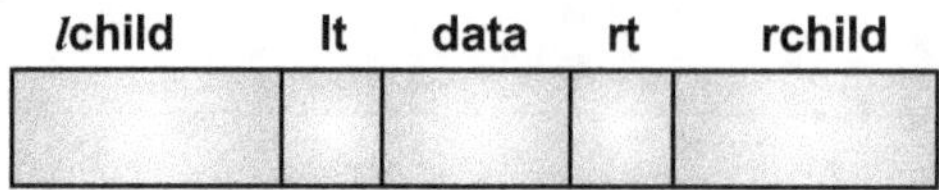

Fig. 6.1 : Node in a threaded binary tree

The node structure for threaded binary tree will be as follows :   **[May 08; Dec. 08]**

```
typedef struct node
{
    int data;
    int rt, lt;
    struct node *lchild, *rchild;
}NODE;
```

Following figures show some threaded binary trees.

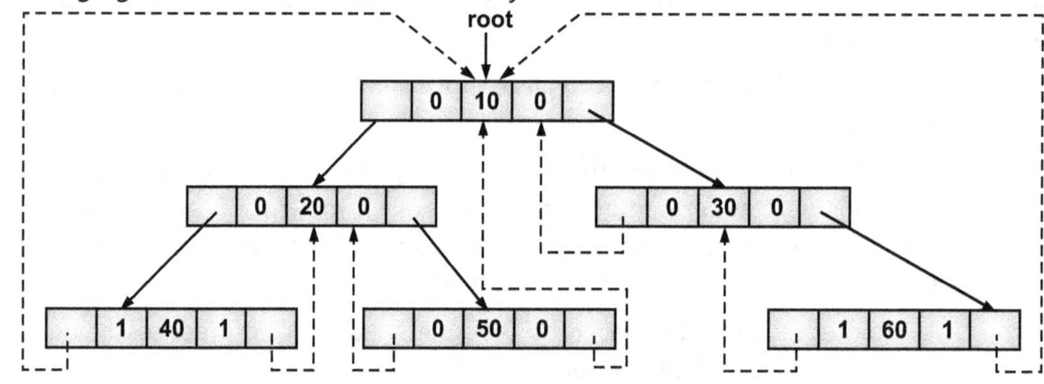

Fig. 6.2 : Threaded binary tree

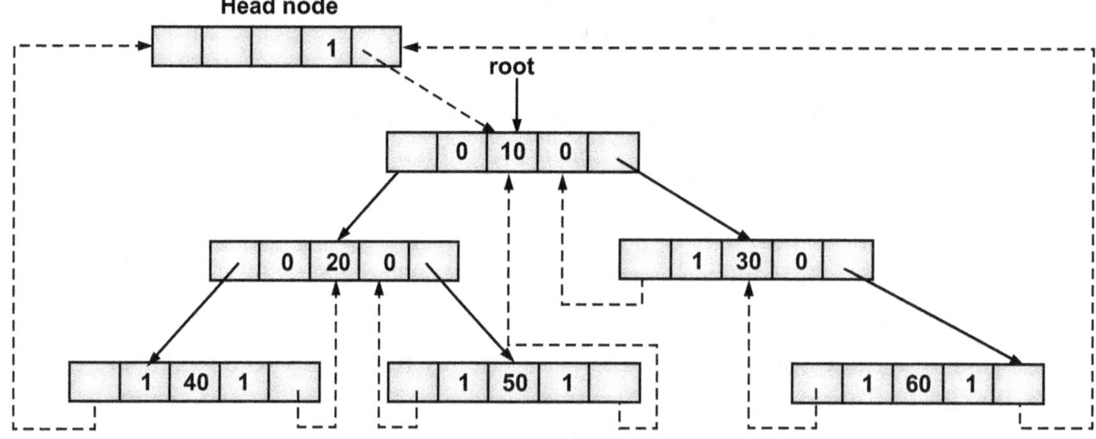

Fig. 6.3 : Threaded binary tree with header node

Note : Threads are shown with dotted lines.

Some more threaded binary trees are as shown in Figs. 6.4, 6.5, 6.6.

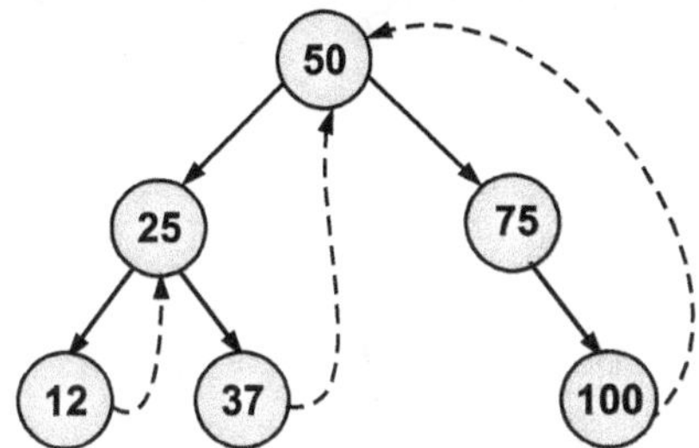

Fig. 6.4 : Right-in-threaded binary search tree

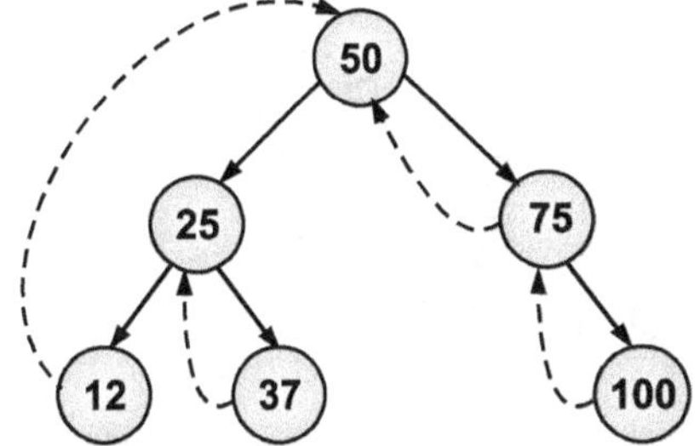

Fig. 6.5 : Left-in-threaded binary search tree

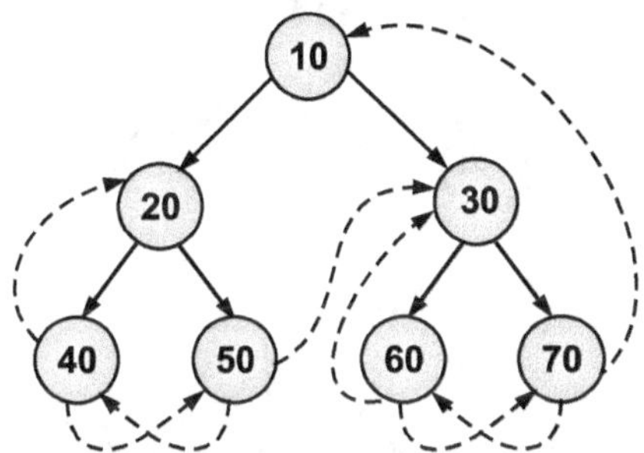

Fig. 6.6 : Pre-threaded binary tree

Note : To draw a threaded binary tree.

- Write the traversal for example in pre-threaded binary tree above, preorder traversal is 10 20 40 50 30 60 70.

- Find predecessor and successors of nodes whose *l*child or *r*child is NULL and draw the threads. For example, preorder successor of 40 is 50 and predecessor is 20.

  Hence, threads from 40 are going to 50 and 20.

  Now, let us consider the operations on threaded binary tree. For this we consider only inorder threaded binary tree. The primitive operations are create, insert and traversals.

6.1.1 Create/Insert Operation

Suppose we are given elements to be stored in a threaded binary tree as 10 20 30 40 50 60

The steps will be as follows :

Step 1 :

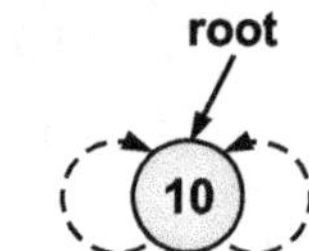

Step 2 :

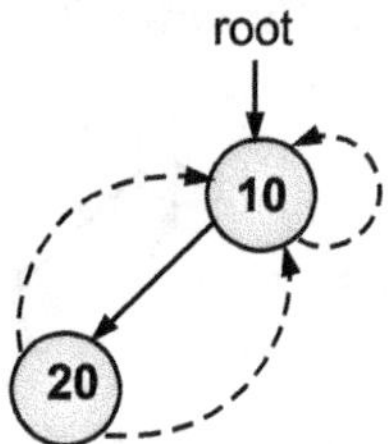

Step 3 :

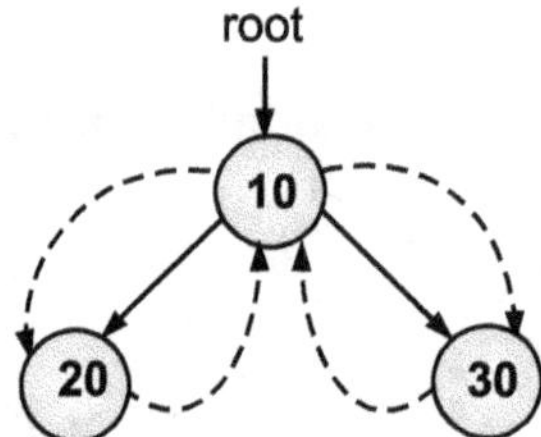

Step 4 :

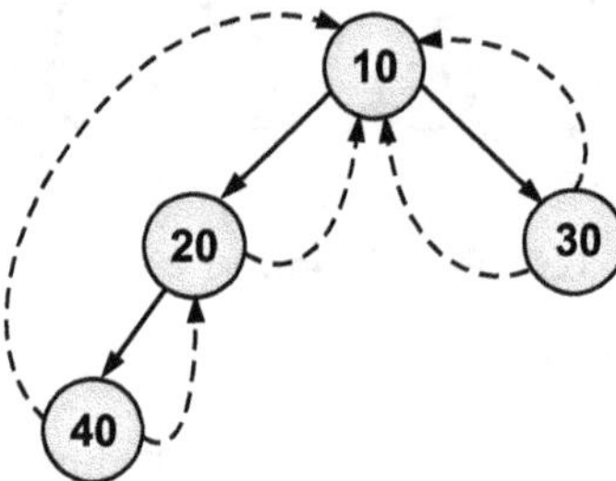

Step 5 :

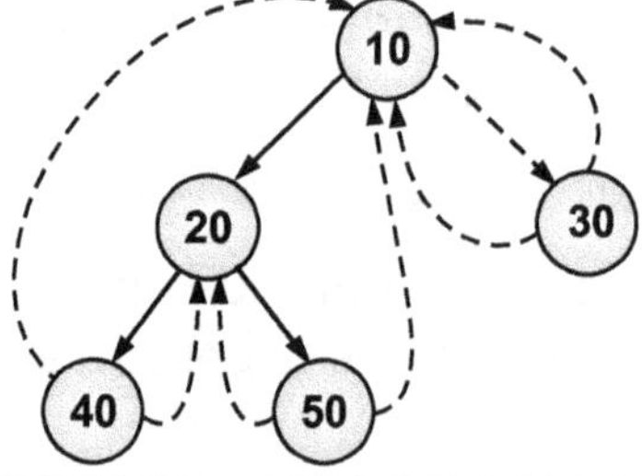

Step 6 :

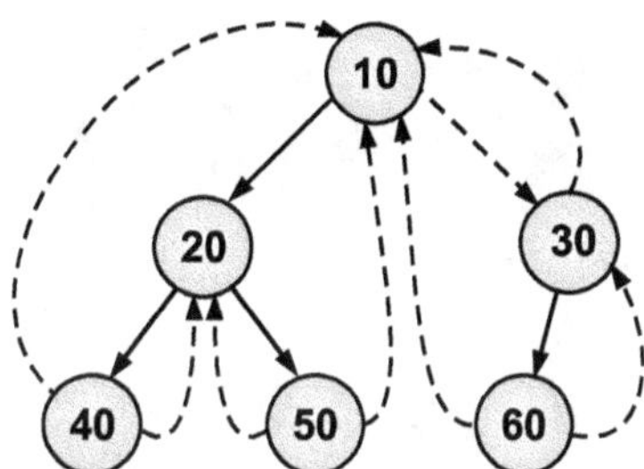

Fig. 6.7 : Create/Insert operation in threaded binary tree

When new node is added, threads are constructed as follows :

If the new node is added in left sub-tree of a node, point rchild to that node (parent) and point *l*child to a place where *l*child of parent was pointing earlier. Make *l*t and rt fields of the new node 1. Make it field of parent 0.

When new node is to be added in the right sub-tree of a node, point left child to that node (parent) and right child to a place where right child of parent was pointing earlier. Make lt and rt field of new node 1 and rt field of parent 0.

6.1.2 Non-Recursive Traversals   [May 05, 08, Dec. 08, 10)

The advantage of threaded binary tree is that, we don't have to use stack for traversing the tree. Let us look into non-recursive inorder and preorder traversals for in-threaded binary tree.

Algorithm 6.1 : Inorder traversal of in-threaded binary tree.

```
1.  temp=root

2.  curr=root

3.  do
    {
4.      if (temp!=root)
            temp=curr->rchild
5.      if(curr->rt==0)
        {
            while(temp->lt==0)
                temp=temp->lchild;
        }
6.      if (temp!=root)
```

```
              print temp ->data
7.       curr=temp
     }   while (temp!=root)
8.  stop.
```

Explanation :

1,2. Two more pointers are used curr and temp.

3.   The process (steps 4, 5, 6, 7) of traversal continues until we come back to root.

4.   Except for the first time (when temp=root) more to right (R of LVR).

5.   If previous node was not thread (rt=0) then more to left side (L of LVR) till there is no left child.

6.   Print the data (V of LVR).

7.   Make it current node.

Algorithm 6.2 : Preorder traversal of in-threaded binary tree.

```
1.   temp=root, curr=root
2.   do
     {
3.       if (curr->rt==0)
         {
4.           while (temp->lt==0)
             {
                 printf("%d \n", temp->data);
                 temp=temp->lchild;
             }
5.           printf("%d \n", temp->data);
         }
6.           curr=temp;
7.           temp=curr->rchild;
     }       while(temp! =root)
8.           stop
```

Explanation :

1.   Start with two pointers, curr and temp at root.

2.   Repeat the process of traversal until we come back to root.

3,5. If the current node has right child then till we get a thread move to left and display the data.

6,7. Move to the right side and repeat.

Concept of Red and Black Trees :

Note : Red – Refer to light portion in Fig.

Black – Refer to dark portion in Fig.

A red-black tree is a binary search tree with one extra attribute for each node : the colour, which is either red or black. We also need to keep track of the parent of each node, so that a red-black tree's node structure would be :

```
struct t_red_black_node {
   enum { red, black } colour;
   void *item;
   struct t_red_black_node *left,
             *right,
             *parent;
}
```

For the purpose of this discussion, the NULL nodes which terminate the tree are considered to be the leaves and are coloured black.

Definition of a Red-Black Tree :

A red-black tree is a binary search tree which has the following *red-black properties* :

- Every node is either red or black.

- Every leaf (NULL) is black.

- If a node is red, then both its children are black.

- Every simple path from a node to a descendant leaf contains the same number of black nodes. Implies that on any path from the root to a leaf, red nodes must not be adjacent. However, any number of black nodes may appear in a sequence.

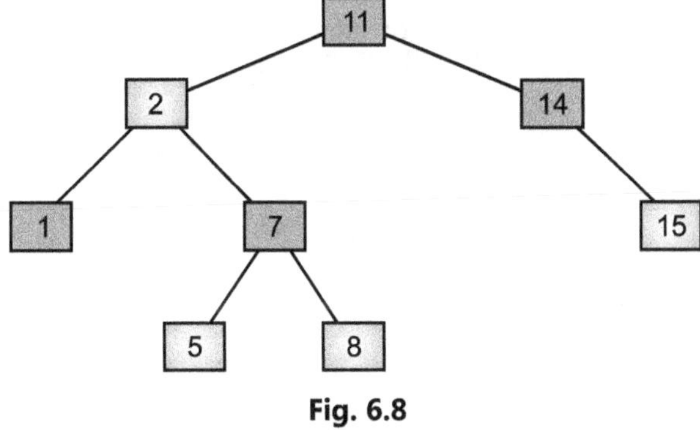

Fig. 6.8

A Basic Red-Black Tree :

Basic red-black tree with the sentinel nodes added. Implementations of the red-black tree algorithms will usually include the sentinel nodes as a convenient means of flagging that you have reached a leaf node.

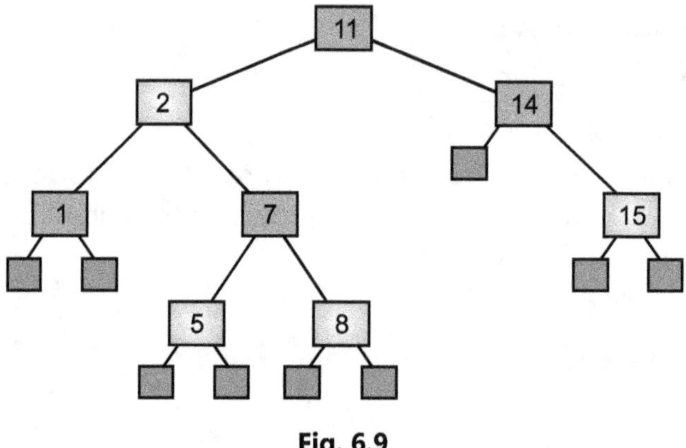

Fig. 6.9

They are the NULL black nodes of property 2.

The number of black nodes on any path from, but not including, a node **x** to a leaf is called the *black-height* of a node, denoted **bh(x)**. We can prove the following lemma :

Lemma :

A red-black tree with **n** internal nodes has height at most **2log(n+1)**. (For a proof, see Cormen, p 264)

This demonstrates why the red-black tree is a good search tree : it can always be searched in **O(log n)** time.

As with heaps, additions and deletions from red-black trees destroy the red-black property, so we need to restore it. To do this we need to look at some operations on red-black trees.

Rotations :

A rotation is a local operation in a search tree that preserves *in-order* traversal key ordering.

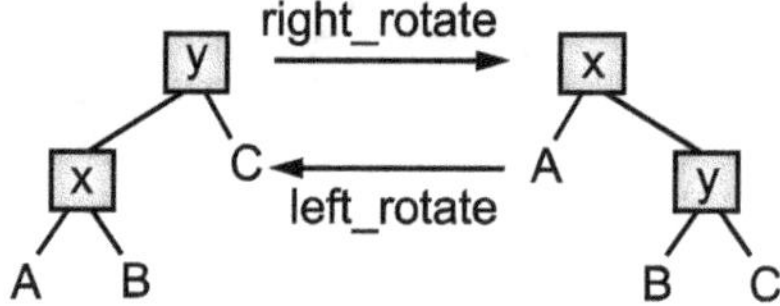

Fig. 6.10

Note that in both trees, an in-order traversal yields :

$$A \times B\,y\,C$$

The left_rotate operation may be encoded :

```
left_rotate( Tree T, node x ) {
    node y;
    y = x->right;
    /* Turn y's left sub-tree into x's right sub-tree */
    x->right = y->left;
    if ( y->left != NULL )
        y->left->parent = x;
    /* y's new parent was x's parent */
    y->parent = x->parent;
    /* Set the parent to point to y instead of x */
    /* First see whether we're at the root */
    if ( x->parent == NULL ) T->root = y;
    else
        if ( x == (x->parent)->left )
            /* x was on the left of its parent */
            x->parent->left = y;
        else
            /* x must have been on the right */
            x->parent->right = y;
    /* Finally, put x on y's left */
    y->left = x;
    x->parent = y;
}
```

Insertion :

Insertion is somewhat complex and involves a number of cases. Note that we start by inserting the new node, x, in the tree just as we would for any other binary tree, using the tree_insert function. This new node is labelled red, and possibly destroys the red-black property. The main loop moves up the tree, restoring the red-black property.

```
rb_insert( Tree T, node x ) {
    /* Insert in the tree in the usual way */
```

```
tree_insert( T, x );
/* Now restore the red-black property */
x->colour = red;
while ( (x != T->root) && (x->parent->colour == red) ) {
  if ( x->parent == x->parent->parent->left ) {
    /* If x's parent is a left, y is x's right 'uncle' */
    y = x->parent->parent->right;
    if ( y->colour == red ) {
      /* case 1 - change the colours */
      x->parent->colour = black;
      y->colour = black;
      x->parent->parent->colour = red;
      /* Move x up the tree */
      x = x->parent->parent;
      }
    else {
      /* y is a black node */
      if ( x == x->parent->right ) {
        /* and x is to the right */
        /* case 2 - move x up and rotate */
        x = x->parent;
        left_rotate( T, x );
        }
      /* case 3 */
      x->parent->colour = black;
      x->parent->parent->colour = red;
      right_rotate( T, x->parent->parent );
      }
    }
  else {
```

```
      /* repeat the "if" part with right and left
         exchanged */
      }
   }
/* Colour the root black */
T->root->colour = black;
}
```

6.2 HEIGHT BALANCE TREE (AVL TREE)

A binary search tree (BST) is used to store and retrieve data. The maximum number of comparisons required for searching in a binary search tree depends on how data is stored in a tree. If tree is well balanced as shown in Fig. 6.11, the number of comparisons will be minimum.

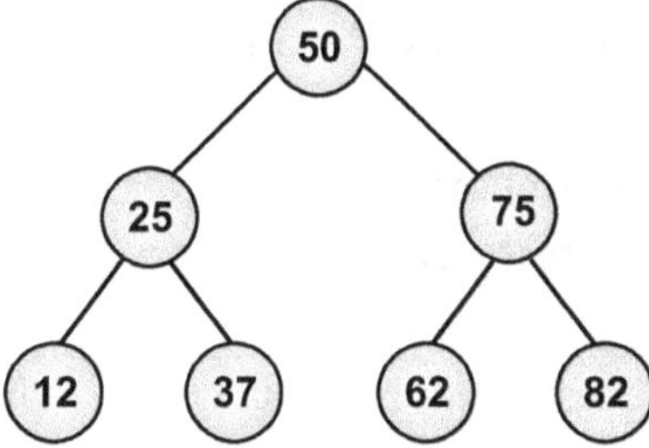

Fig. 6.11 : Balanced binary tree

If the tree is right or left skewed it will require same number of comparison as that of sequential search.

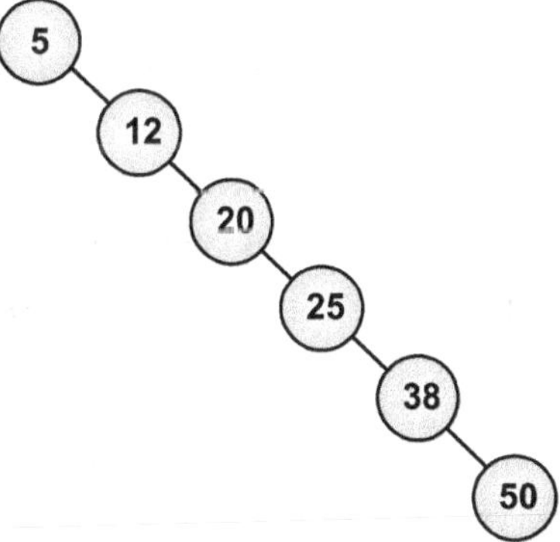

Fig. 6.12 : Unbalanced binary tree

Imagine a situation where the BST is dynamic means the elements of the tree are getting deleted or new elements getting added to it. Average and maximum search time will be minimized, if tree is maintained as complete binary tree at all times. It will require restructuring of tree to accumulate new entry, so that both average and worst case search time will be $O(\log_2 n)$ for the tree of n nodes.

Adelson-Velskii and Landis (AVL) in 1962 introduced a Binary Tree that is balanced with respect to height of sub-trees.

Definition : An empty tree is height balanced. If T is non-empty binary tree with T_l and T_r as left and right sub-tree, then T is said to be height balanced if and only if.

1. T_l and T_r is height balanced.

2. $|h_l - h_r| \leq 1$.

    Where, h_f and h_r are heights of T_l and T_r.

The tree in Fig. 6.13 is height balanced.

Restructuring of BST is done so that tree becomes height balanced. When we add a node to a particular tree its height may change. This change can disturb the balancing also. In order to verify whether a tree is height balanced or not, we need to find out balanced factor of every node.

Balanced Factor : Balanced factor of a node is defined as $h_l - h_r$ where h_l and h_r are heights of T_l and T_r.

When a new node is added in BST one of the four types of situations can arise in the tree. In other words, there are 4 ways in which rebalancing can be done. These are called Rotations. They are RR, LL, RL, LR rotations.

1. **RR Rotation :** If the newly inserted node (say Y) is in right sub-tree of right sub-tree of the nearest ancestor (say A) whose | balanced factor | >= 2.

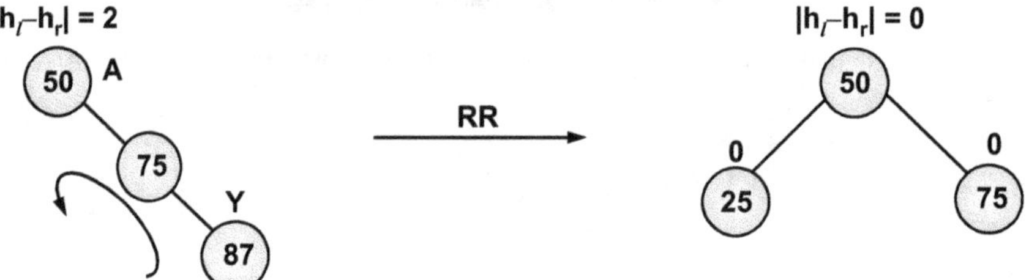

Fig. 6.13 : RR rotation

2. **LL Rotation :** The newly inserted node Y is the left sub-tree of left sub-tree of A.

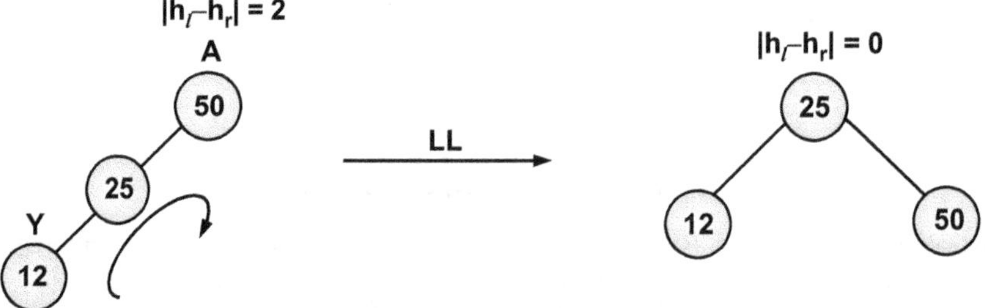

Fig. 6.14 : LL rotation

3. **LR Rotation :** Y is inserted in right sub-tree of left sub-tree of A.

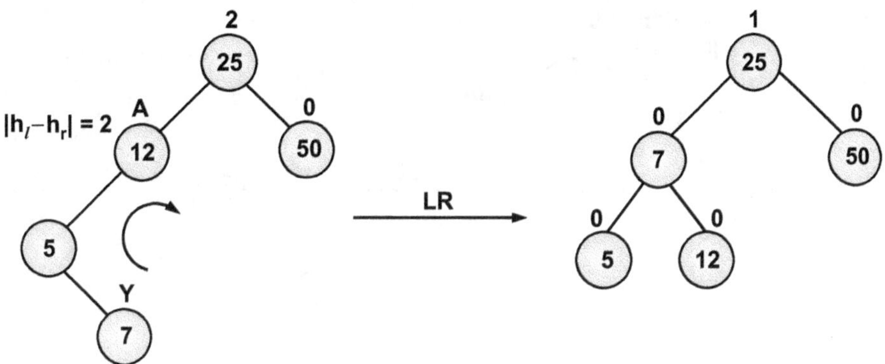

Fig. 6.15 : LR rotation

4. **RL Rotation :** Y is inserted in left sub-tree of right sub-tree of A.

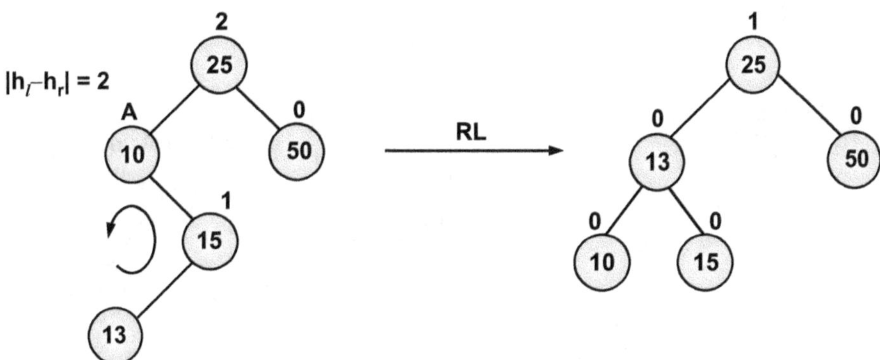

Fig. 6.16 : RL rotation

Let us look into some more examples. Each rotation type has two different situations. First is the simple and the other is complex.

Case I : LL Rotation

Situation 1

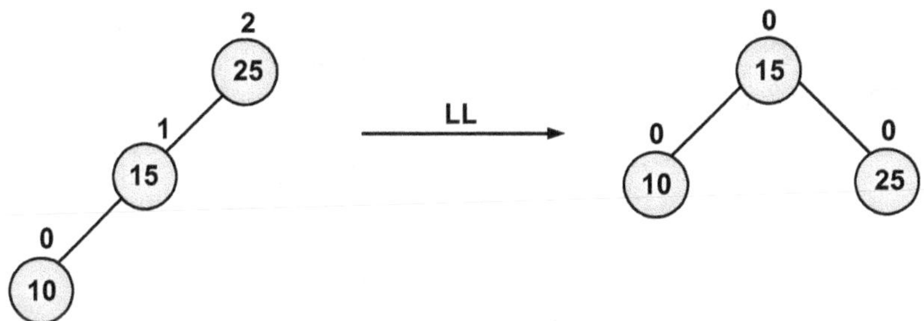

Fig. 6.17 (a) : LL rotation

Situation 2

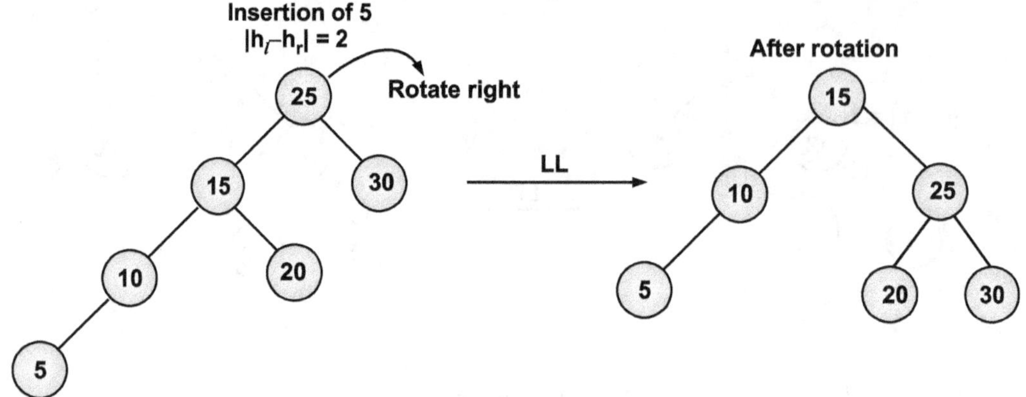

Fig. 6.17 (b) : LL rotation

Case II : RR Rotation

Situation 1

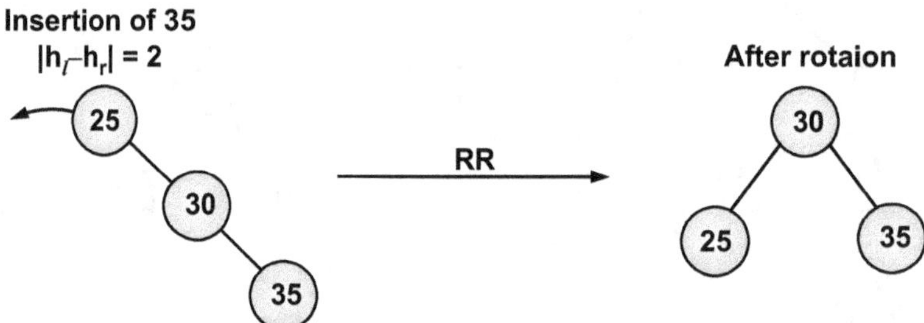

Fig. 6.17 (c) : RR rotation

Situation 2

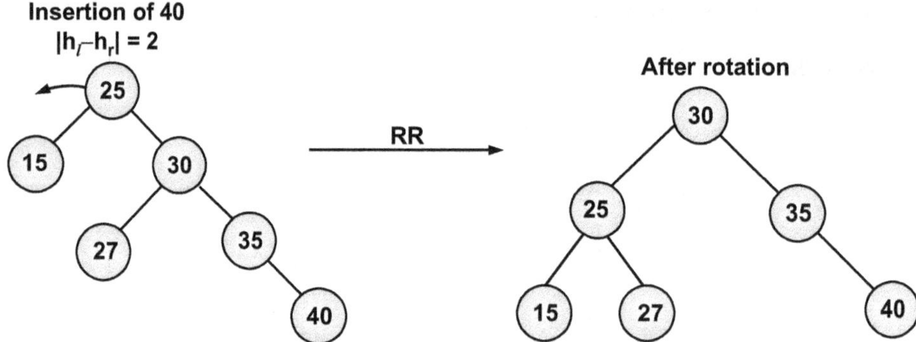

Fig. 6.17 (d) : RR rotation

Actually, the RL and LR rotations are carried out in two steps. Following examples illustrate how exactly these rotations are done.

Case III : LR Rotation

Situation 1

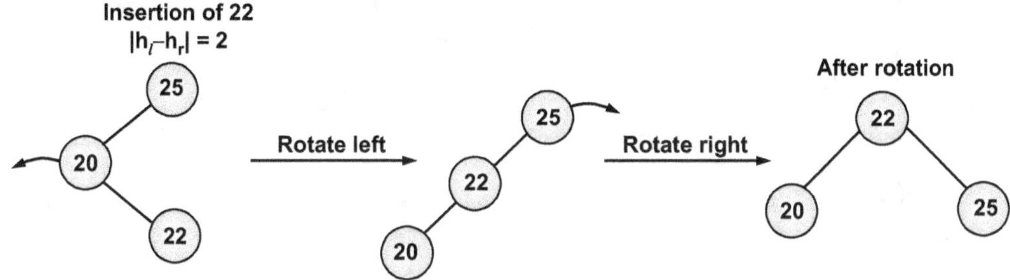

Fig. 6.17 (e) : LR rotation

Situation 2

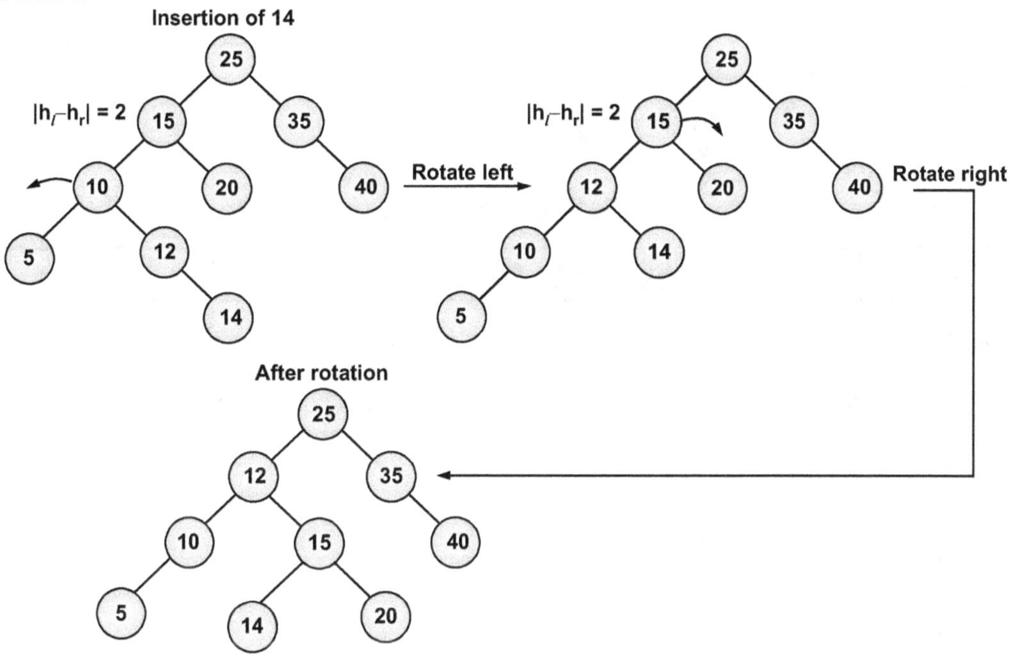

Fig. 6.17 (f) : LR rotation

Case IV : RL Rotation

Situation 1

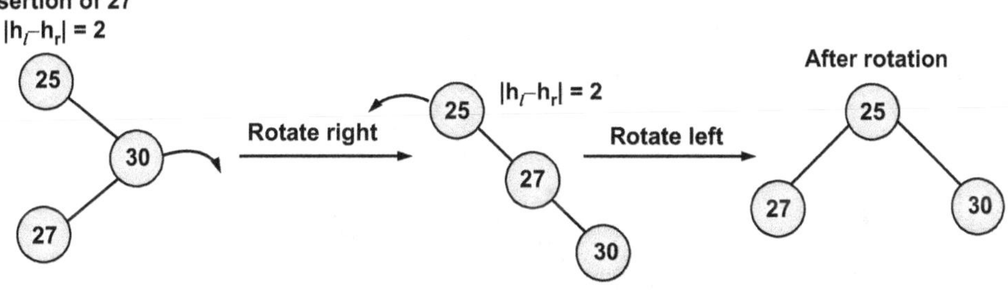

Fig. 6.17 (g) : RL rotation

Situation 2

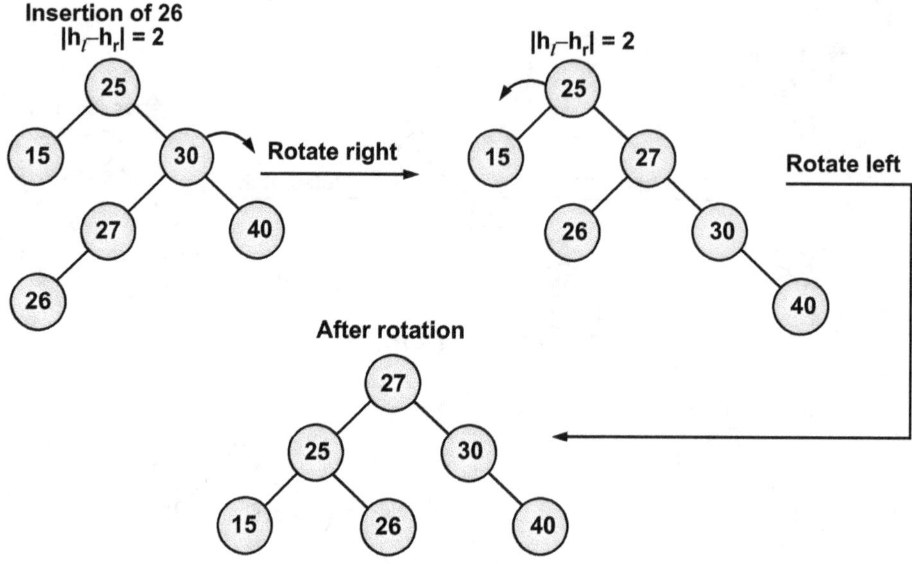

Fig. 6.17 (h) : RL rotation

SOLVED EXAMPLES

Example 6.1 : Create AVL tree for the following elements :

BAG CAR MAN SAD TAN FAN

Solution :

Note : The figures shown in nodes are balance factors.

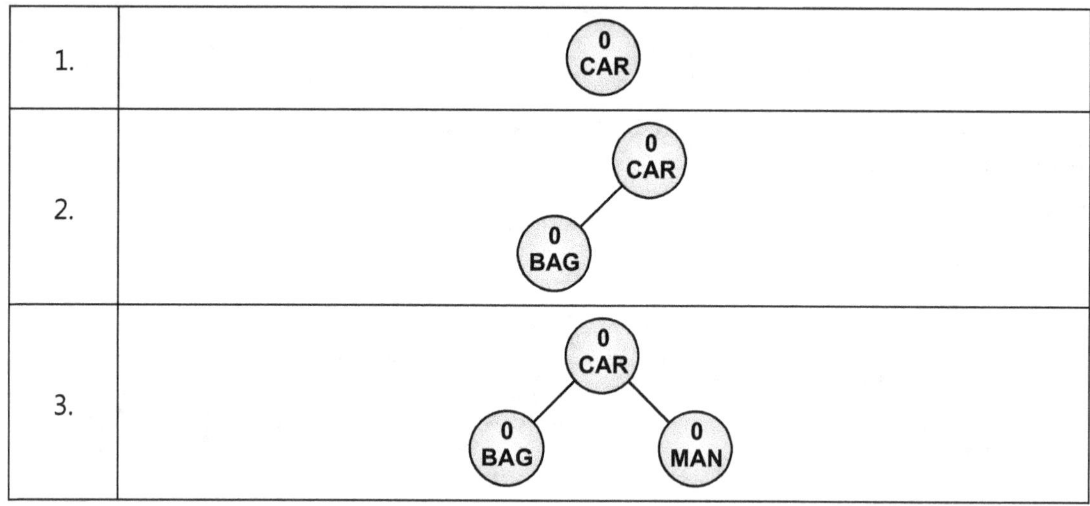

...Conti.

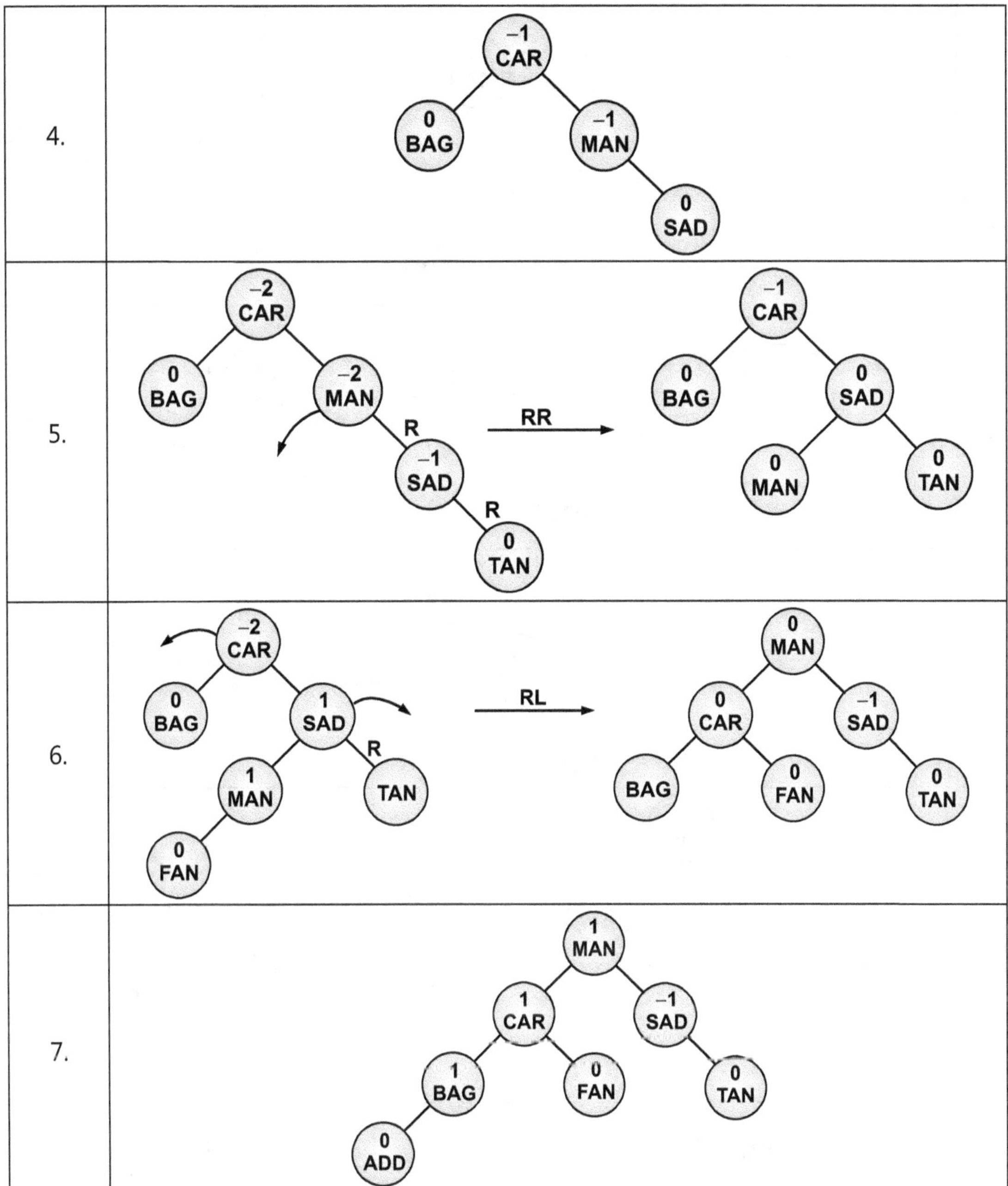

Fig. 6.18 : Creating height balance (AVL) binary tree

Example 6.2 : Create AVL tree for the following elements :

MAR MAY NOV AUG APR JAN DEC JUL FEB

Solution :

Note : The figures shown in nodes are balance factors.

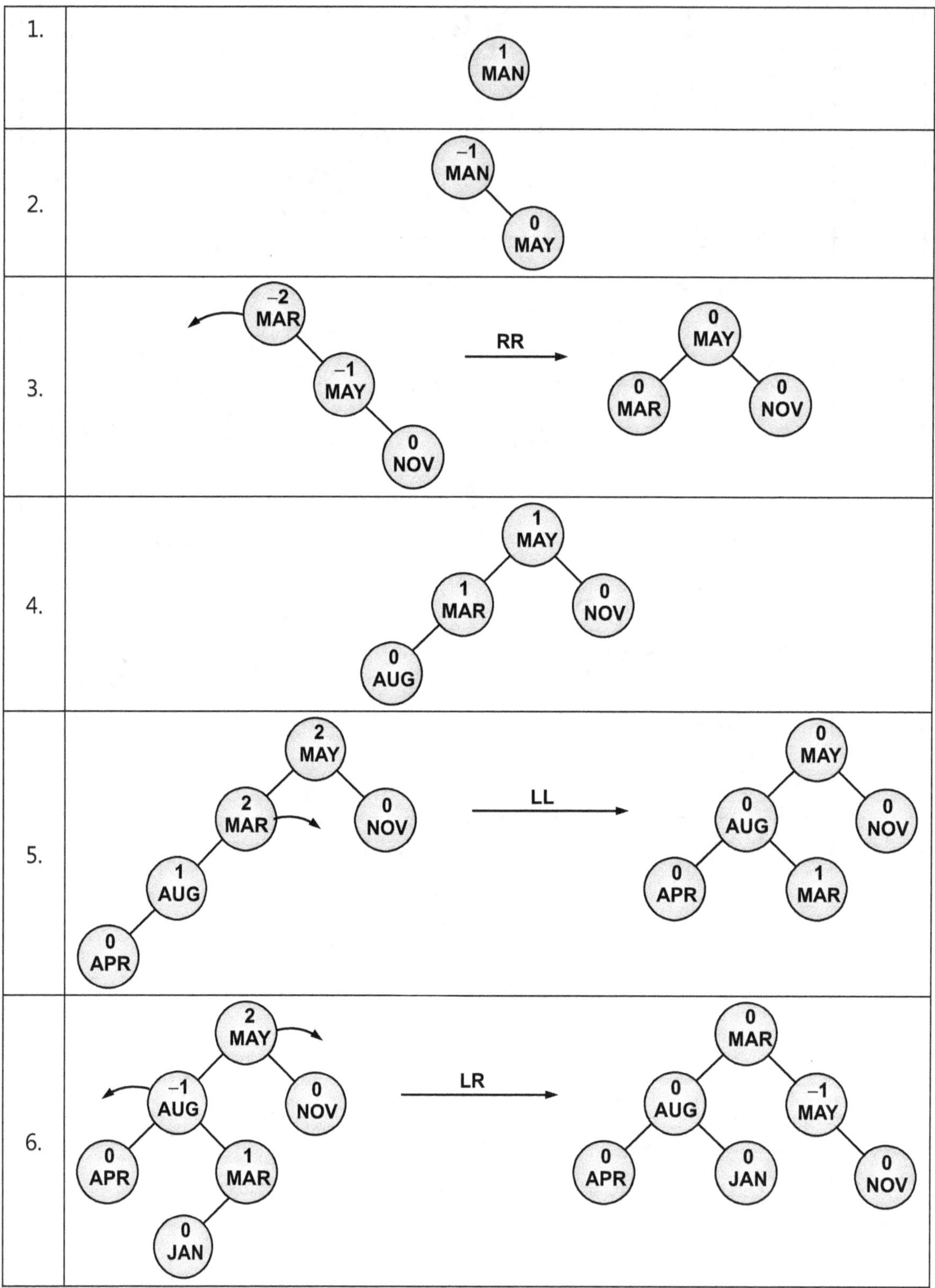
1.
1
MAN

2.
−1
MAN
0
MAY

3.
−2
MAR
−1
MAY
0
NOV
RR
0
MAY
0
MAR
0
NOV

4.
1
MAY
1
MAR
0
NOV
0
AUG

5.
2
MAY
2
MAR
0
NOV
1
AUG
0
APR
LL
0
MAY
0
AUG
0
NOV
0
APR
1
MAR

6.
2
MAY
−1
AUG
0
NOV
0
APR
1
MAR
0
JAN
LR
0
MAR
0
AUG
−1
MAY
0
APR
0
JAN
0
NOV

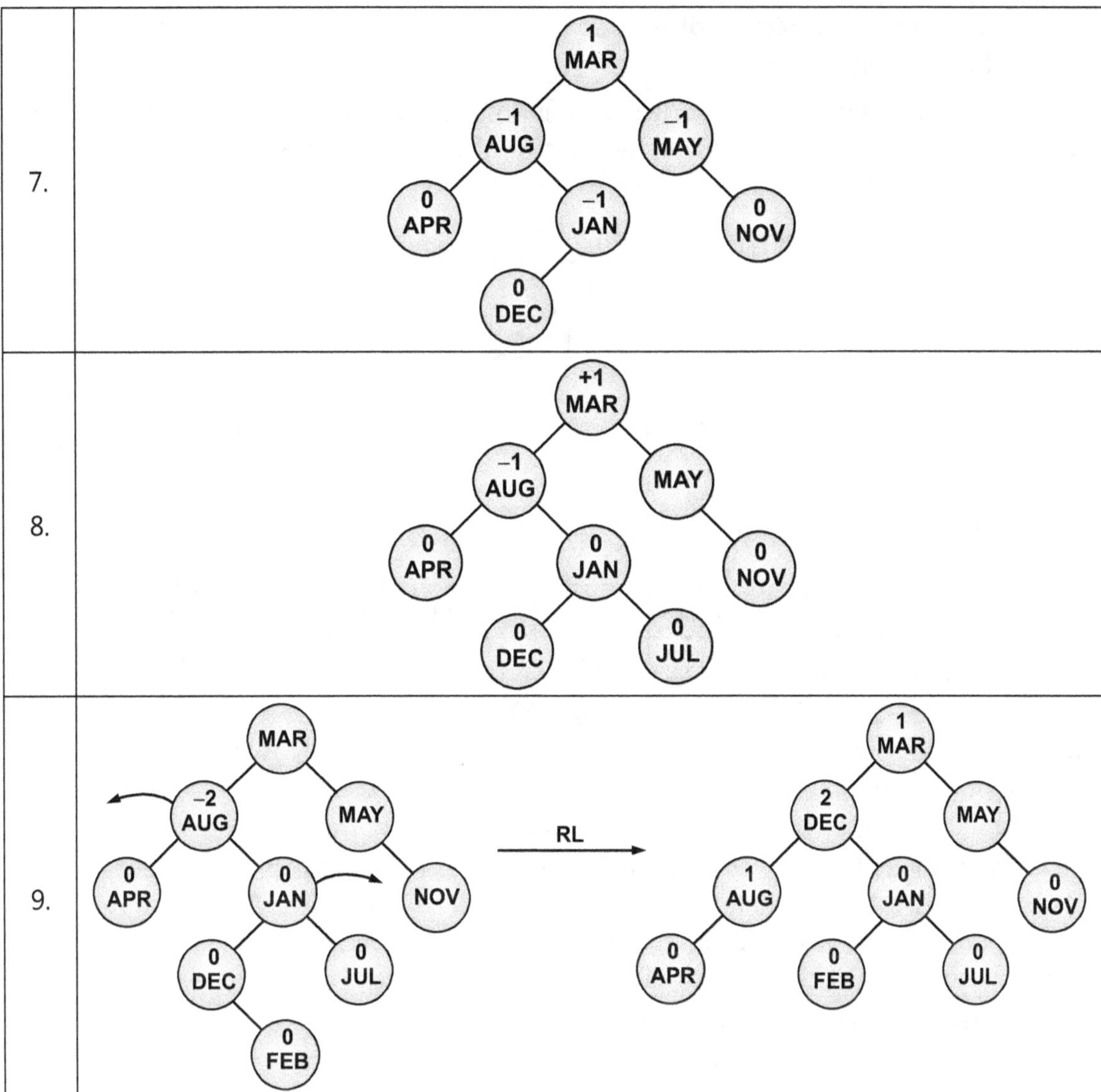

Fig. 6.19 : Creating height balance (AVL) binary tree

1. B+Tree :

Most queries can be executed more quickly if the values are stored in order. But it's not practical to hope to store all the rows in the table one after another, in sorted order, because this requires rewriting the entire table with each insertion or deletion of a row.

This leads us to instead imagine storing our rows in a tree structure. Our first instinct would be a balanced binary search tree like a red-black tree, but this really doesn't make much sense for a database since it is stored on disk. You see, disks work by reading and writing whole blocks of data at once — typically 512 bytes or four kilobytes. A node of a binary search tree uses a small fraction of that, so it makes sense to look for a structure that fits more neatly into a disk block.

Hence the B+tree, in which each node stores up to d references to children and up to d − 1 keys. Each reference is considered "between" two of the node's keys; it references the root of a subtree for which all values are between these two keys.

Here is a fairly small tree using 4 as our value for *d*.

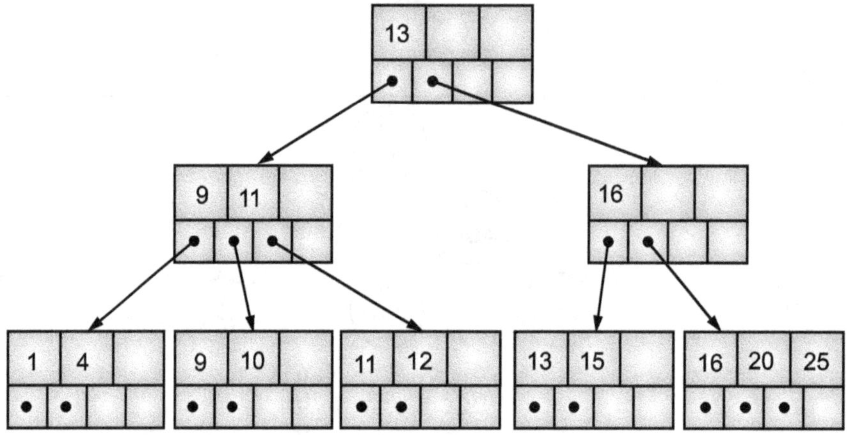

Fig. 6.20

A B+tree requires that each leaf be the same distance from the root, as in this picture, where searching for any of the 11 values (all listed on the bottom level) will involve loading three nodes from the disk (the root block, a second-level block, and a leaf).

In practice, *d* will be larger — as large, in fact, as it takes to fill a disk block. Suppose a block is 4KB, our keys are 4-byte integers, and each reference is a 6-byte file offset. Then we'd choose *d* to be the largest value so that $4(d − 1) + 6d \leq 4096$; solving this inequality for *d*, we end up with $d \leq 410$, so we'd use 410 for *d*. As you can see, *d* can be large.

A B+tree maintains the following invariants :

- Every node has one more references than it has keys.
- All leaves are at the same distance from the root.
- For every non-leaf node *N* with *k* being the number of keys in *N* : all keys in the first child's subtree are less than *N*'s first key; and all keys in the *i*th child's subtree $(2 \leq i \leq k)$ are between the $(i − 1)$th key of *n* and the *i*th key of *n*.
- The root has at least two children.
- Every non-leaf, non-root node has at least *floor(d / 2)* children.
- Each leaf contains at least *floor(d / 2)* keys.
- Every key from the table appears in a leaf, in left-to-right sorted order.

In our examples, we'll continue to use 4 for *d*. Looking at our invariants, this requires that each leaf have at least two keys, and each internal node to have at least two children (and thus at least one key).

2. Insertion Algorithm :

Descend to the leaf where the key fits.

- If the node has an empty space, insert the key/reference pair into the node.

- If the node is already full, split it into two nodes, distributing the keys evenly between the two nodes. If the node is a leaf, take a copy of the minimum value in the second of these two nodes and repeat this insertion algorithm to insert it into the parent node. If the node is a non-leaf, exclude the middle value during the split and repeat this insertion algorithm to insert this excluded value into the parent node.

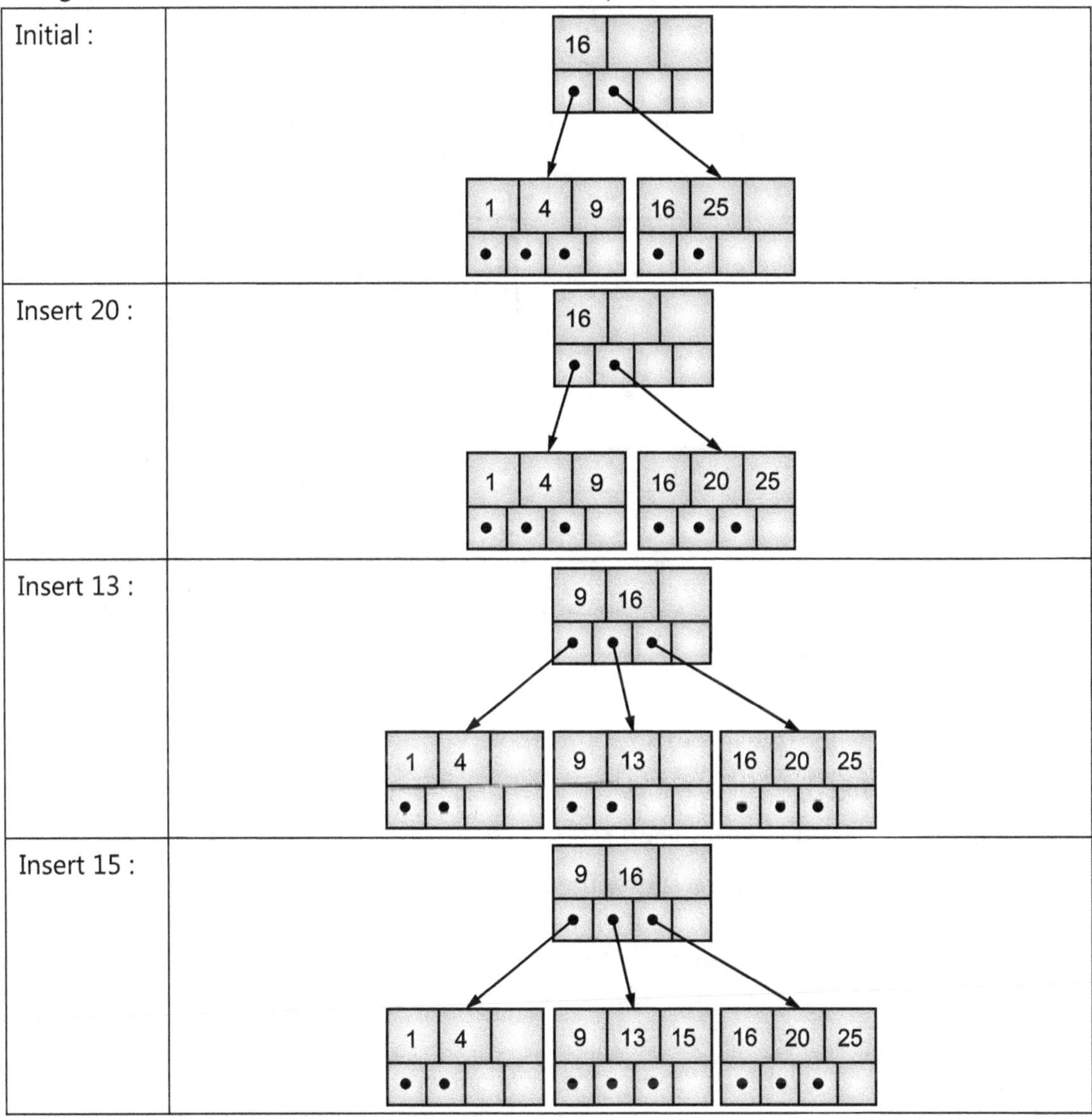

...Conti.

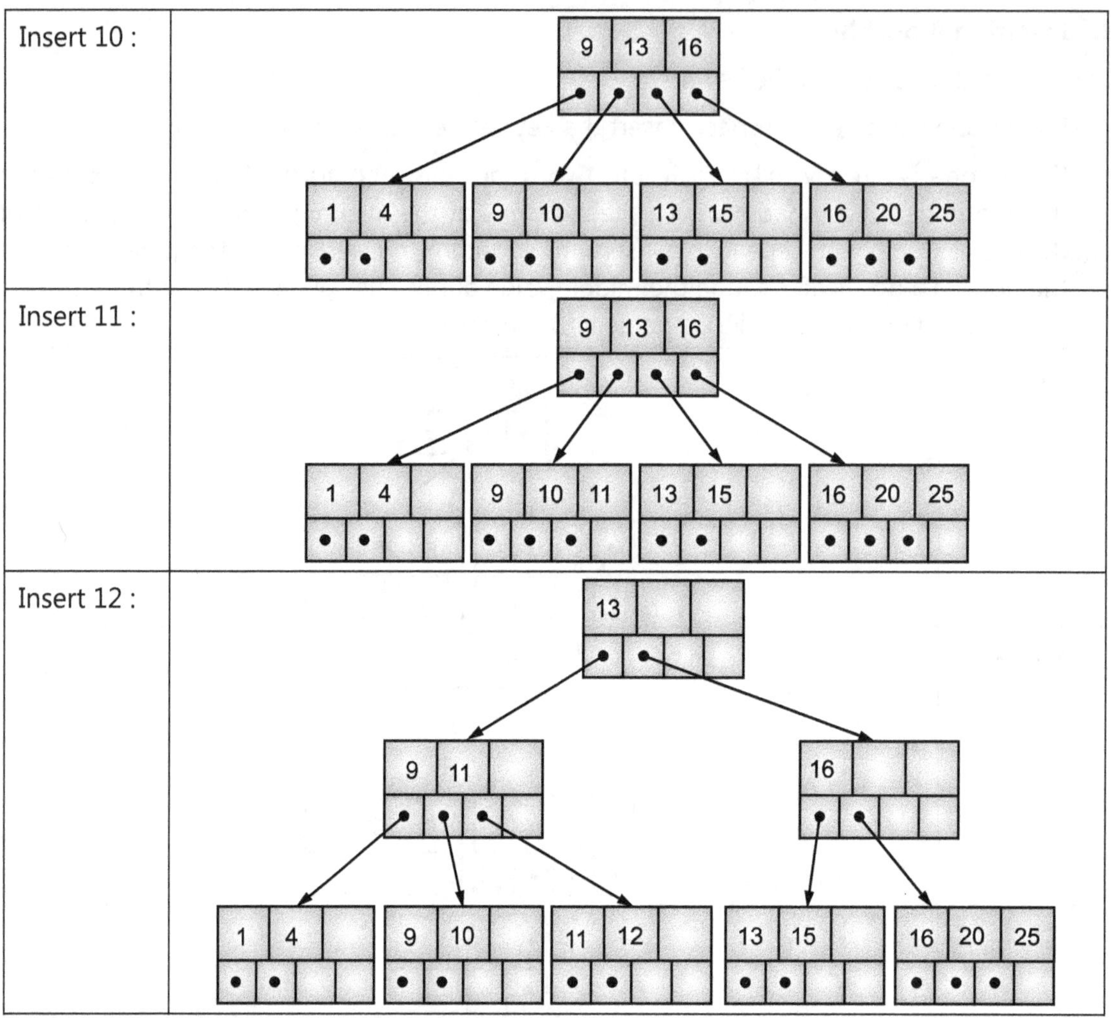

3. Deletion Algorithm :

Descend to the leaf where the key exists.

- Remove the required key and associated reference from the node.

- If the node still has enough keys and references to satisfy the invariants, stop.

- If the node has too few keys to satisfy the invariants, but its next oldest or next youngest sibling at the same level has more than necessary, distribute the keys between this node and the neighbor. Repair the keys in the level above to represent that these nodes now have a different "split point" between them; this involves simply changing a key in the levels above, without deletion or insertion.

- If the node has too few keys to satisfy the invariant, and the next oldest or next youngest sibling is at the minimum for the invariant, then merge the node with its sibling; if the node is a non-leaf, we will need to incorporate the "split key" from the parent into our merging. In either case, we will need to repeat the removal algorithm on the parent node to remove the "split key" that previously separated these merged nodes — unless the parent is the root and we are removing the final key from the root, in which case the merged node becomes the new root (and the tree has become one level shorter than before).

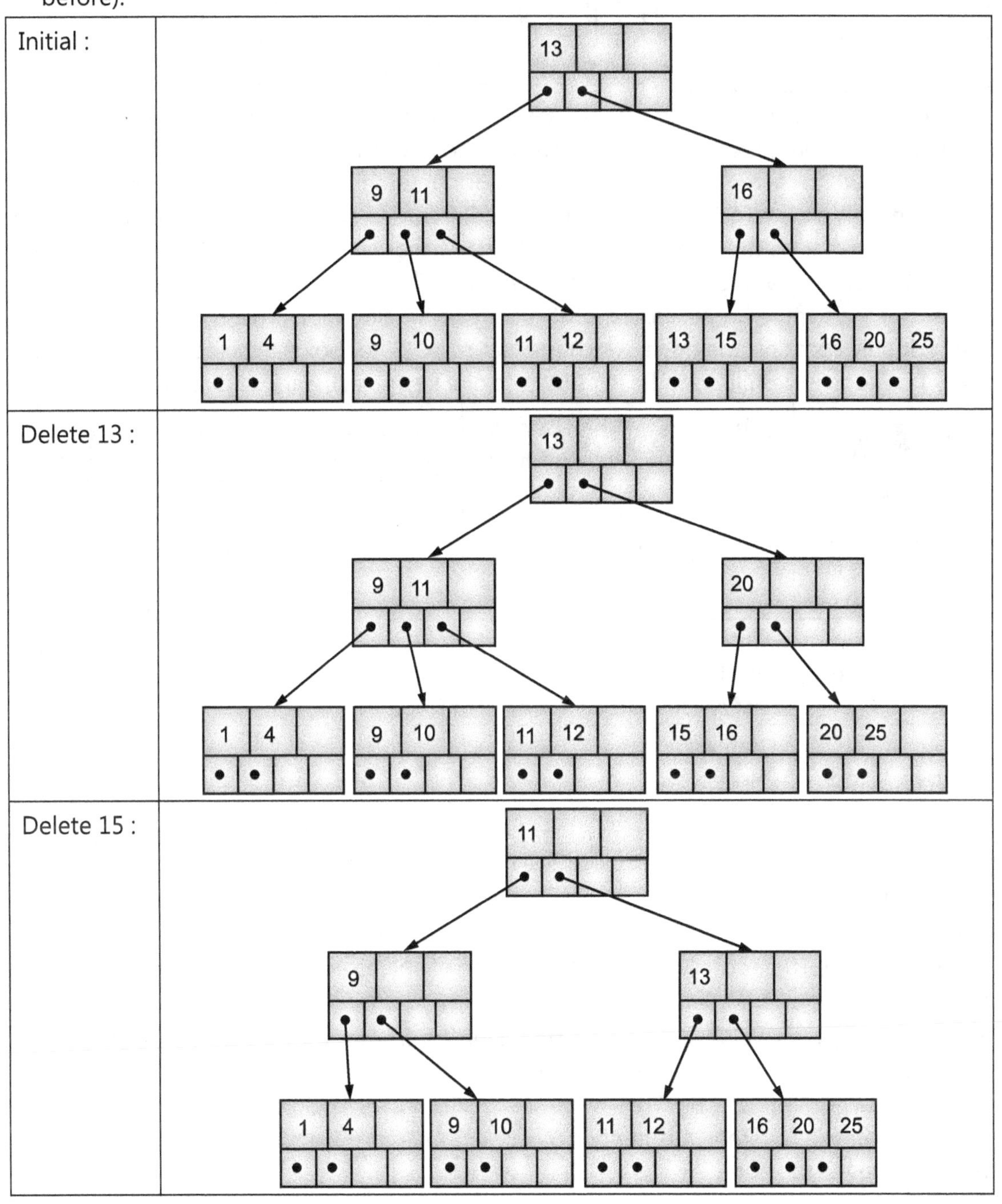

Delete 1 :	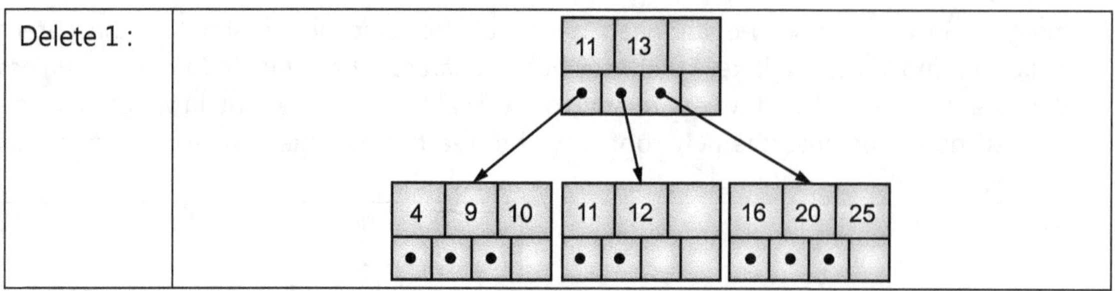

The order, or branching factor, *b* of a B+ tree measures the capacity of nodes (i.e., the number of children nodes) for internal nodes in the tree. The actual number of children for a node, referred to here as *m*, is constrained for internal nodes so that, the root is an exception : it is allowed to have as few as two children. For example, if the order of a B+ tree is 7, each internal node (except for the root) may have between 4 and 7 children; the root may have between 2 and 7. Leaf nodes have no children, but are constrained so that the number of keys must be at least and at most . In the situation where a B+ tree is nearly empty, it only contains one node, which is a leaf node. (The root is also the single leaf, in this case.) This node is permitted to have as little as one key if necessary, and at most b.

Node Type	Children Type	Min Number of Children	Max Number of Children	Example b = 7	Example b = 100
Root Node (when it is the only node in the tree)	Records	1	b - 1	1 - 6	1 - 99
Root Node	Internal Nodes or Leaf Nodes	2	b	2 - 7	2 - 100
Internal Node	Internal Nodes or Leaf Nodes		b	4 - 7	50 - 100
Leaf Node	Records		b - 1	3 - 6	49 - 99

Algorithms :

Search :

The root of a B+ Tree represents the whole range of values in the tree, where every internal node is a subinterval.

We are looking for a value k in the B+ Tree. Starting from the root, we are looking for the leaf which may contain the value k. At each node, we figure out which internal pointer we should follow. An internal B+ Tree node has at most d ≤ b children, where every one of them represents a different sub-interval. We select the corresponding node by searching on the key values of the node.

```
Function : search (k)
  return tree_search (k, root);
Function : tree_search (k, node)
  if node is a leaf then
    return node;
  switch k do
  case k < k_0
    return tree_search(k, p_0);
  case k_i ≤ k < k_{i+1}
    return tree_search(k, p_{i+1});
  case k_d ≤ k
    return tree_search(k, p_{d+1});
```

6.2.1 Binary Tree

In computer science, a **binary tree** is a tree data structure in which each node has at most two child nodes, usually distinguished as "left" and "right" children.

Nodes with children are called as parent nodes. Child nodes may contain references to their parents. Ancestor of all nodes is called as "root" node.

Any node in the data structure can be reached by starting at root node and repeatedly following references to either the left or right child.

A tree which does not have any node other than root node is called a null tree. In a binary tree a degree of every node is maximum two.

Definition of Binary Tree :

A binary tree is a finite set of nodes which is either empty or consists of a root node and two disjoint binary trees called as the left subtree and the right subtree.

Basic Tree Concepts :

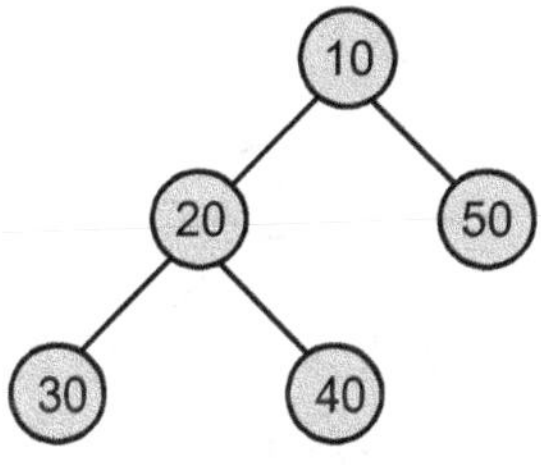

Fig. 6.21 : Binary tree

- **Root :** Root is a unique node in the tree to which further subtrees are attached in above Fig. 6.21. 10 is a root node.

- **Parent Node :** This is a node which is having sub-branches attached to it.

  In the above Fig. 6.21, 10 and 20 are parent nodes.

- **Child Nodes :** Child nodes are the Childs of there parents as shown in the following Fig. 6.22.

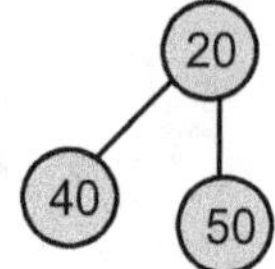

Fig. 6.22

Here 40 and 50 are child nodes of parent 20.

- **Leaves :** These are the terminal nodes of the tree.

  Consider a tree

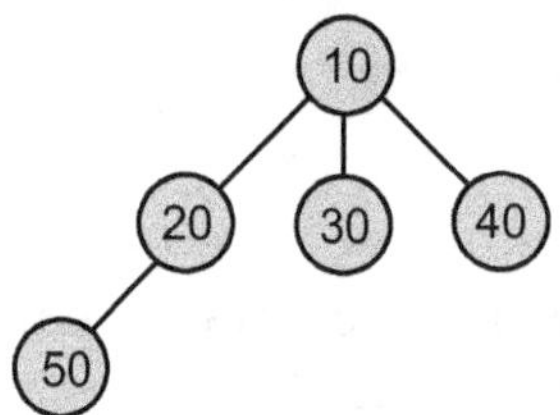

Fig. 6.23

In this tree 50, 30 and 40 are child nodes.

- **Degree of the Node :** Total number of subtrees attached to that node is called the degree of the node.

  For example,

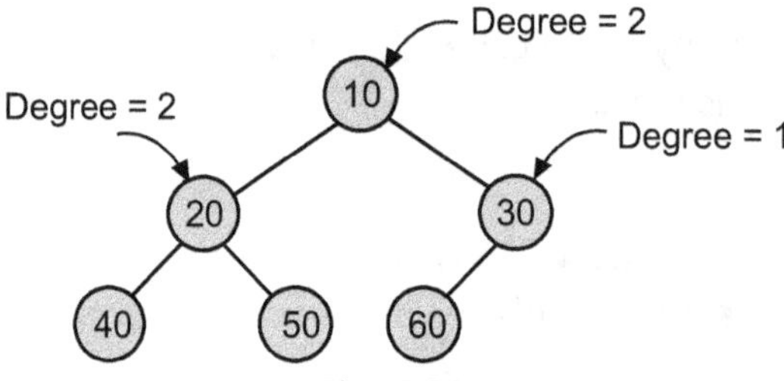

Fig. 6.24

- **Siblings :** The nodes which are having common parent are called as siblings. For example,

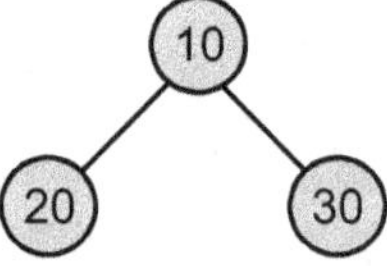

Fig. 6.25

20 and 30 are siblings as they are having common parent i.e. 10.

Binary Tree and its Properties :

Binary tree is one of the most commonly used classes of the tree. It is shown in the figure below.

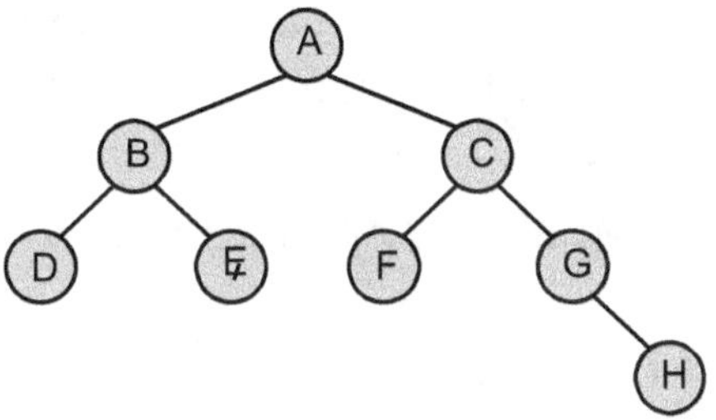

Fig. 6.26 : A Binary Tree

Every node of binary tree has a maximum degree of two, i.e. it has maximum two children.

Binary tree is either 1) an empty tree OR 2) a tree where every node is having either maximum two children (left and right) associated with it or it may be a leaf node.

All the internal nodes of a binary tree are themselves the root nodes of their respective sub-trees.

Properties of Binary Tree :

(a) Maximum Number of Nodes :

- The maximum number of nodes on level i of binary tree are 2^{i-1} where i>=1.

- The maximum number of nodes of depth d of binary tree are 2^{d-1} where d>=1.

Proof by Induction :

Assuming root is only one node at level 1.

Hence maximum number of nodes are 2^{i-1} i.e. 2^{1-1} is $2^0 = 1$

By Induction Hypothesis : Let i be any arbitrary positive integer greater than 1, then maximum number of nodes on level i-1 is 2^{i-1-1} (2^{i-2})

Hence it is proved that maximum nodes at level i are 2^{i-1}

Note : If we assume root at level 0 then this equation is 2^i

Since, each node in a binary tree has a maximum degree 2, so maximum nodes at level i is 2^{i-1}.

The maximum number of nodes of depth d of binary tree are :

$$\sum_{i=1}^{d} (\text{Maximum number of nodes at level i}) = \sum_{i=1}^{d} 2^{d-1}$$

(b) Relation between Number of Leaf Nodes and Degree-2 Nodes :

In any non empty tree T, if there are n_0 leaf nodes n_2 are the nodes of degree 2. then $n_0 = n_2 + 1$.

If n_1 are number of nodes of degree 1, n_0 are the number of nodes of degree 0, n_2 are the number of nodes of degree 2 and n be total number of nodes.

$$\therefore \qquad n = n_0 + n_1 + n_2 \qquad \text{... (1)}$$

If number of branches are B then n=B+1. All the branches stem from a node of degree 1 or 2. Thus,

$$B = n_1 + 2n_2$$

So
$$n = B + 1 = n_1 + 2n_2 + 1 \qquad \text{... (2)}$$

Subtracting Equation (2) from Equation (1) we get

$$n_0 = n_2 + 1$$

i.e.   no. of leaf nodes = no. of nodes of degree 2 + 1

(c) A Full Binary Tree with n Internal Nodes has n+1 External Nodes :

Taking base case as of tree of only one node that is root, it has two external nodes or null links. So, if n=1 then external nodes are n+1 i.e. 2.

From this base case if there are n internal nodes where left subtree has L internal nodes and right subtree has n − L − 1 internal nodes (1 is for root)

By Induction hypothesis.

External nodes of left subtree are L + 1.

External nodes of right subtree are (n − L − 1) + 1 = n − L

So total number of external nodes are L+ 1 + n − L = n + 1 that is proved.

6.2.2 Representation using Sequential and Linked Organization

6.2.1.1 Array (Sequential) Representation of a Binary Tree

A complete binary tree has a simple array representation. Suppose we number the nodes from left to right, beginning at the top and ending at the bottom.

Then we can store the various data items in the corresponding elements of an array.

(NOTE : Empty nodes are also numbered.)

For example :

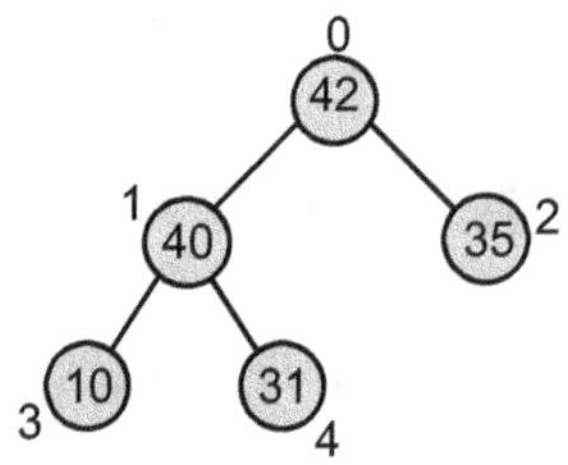

Can be represented by the array

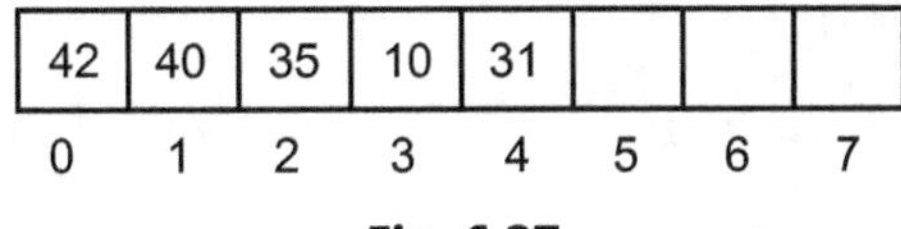

Fig. 6.27

Non existing children are represented by '\0' in the array. See the following representation of tree in the form of array which contains some non existing children.

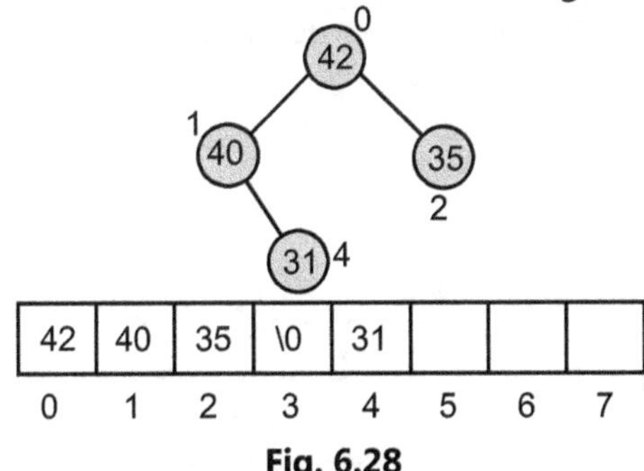

Fig. 6.28

Advantages of Array Representation of Binary Tree :

- Any node can be accessed from any other node by calculating the index.
- Use of pointer is avoided.
- It can be used in the programming languages such as BASIC and FORTRAN, where dynamic memory allocation is not possible.

Disadvantages of Array Representation of Binary Tree :

- Other than full binary trees, majority of array entries may be empty.
- It allows only static representation of binary tree as array size cannot be changed during execution.
- Inserting or deleting a new node to it is inefficient with this representation, because it requires excessive amount of processing time.

6.2.1.2 Linked Representation of a Binary Tree

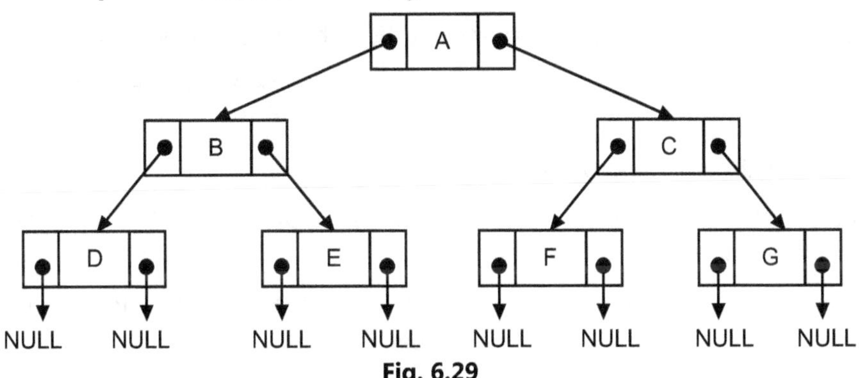

Fig. 6.29

A Linked representation of binary tree is shown in the above figure. Here every node is represented by using three fields :

- Address of Left child
- Data
- Address of Right child.

For forming a node, we can create our own user defined data type named as "node" and which is represented by using the following structure :

```
class tree
{
    private :

                    int data;              Fields of the  node
            class tree*left,*right;

    public :

            //various functions of tree.

};
```

As left, right and data are the fields in the class tree, so the data type of the node will be class tree.

LEFT	DATA	RIGHT

As left and right fields of every node are pointing the left and right nodes of the tree (whose data type is class tree), so their (left and right's) data types are considered as the class tree*.

Refer above class declaration, where the data type of left and right field of the class is class tree*.

Advantages of Linked Representation of Binary Tree :

- The drawbacks of sequential representation are overcome in this representation. Memory is not wasted in linked representation.
- Insertion and deletion operations are more efficient in this representation.

Useful in case of dynamic tree where we want to insert or delete new elements in the tree at run time.

Disadvantages of Linked Representation of Binary Tree :

In this representation, there is no direct access to any node. It has to be traversed from root to reach to a particular node.

- As compared to sequential representation memory needed per node is more; this is due to two links fields (left and right child pointers).

- Programming languages not supporting dynamic memory management would not be useful for this type of representation.

Important Observations of Linked Representation :

- Present of a node is not directly accessible.
- Each node requires two addition pointers to store addresses of left and right subtrees.
- Memory requirement is proportional to the number of data to be stored.
- The tree can grow or shrink dynamically.

6.2.2 Height of the Tree

Height of a tree is the length of the path from root of that tree to its farthest node (i.e. leaf node farthest from the root).

The height of the tree given in the Fig. 6.30 is 3.

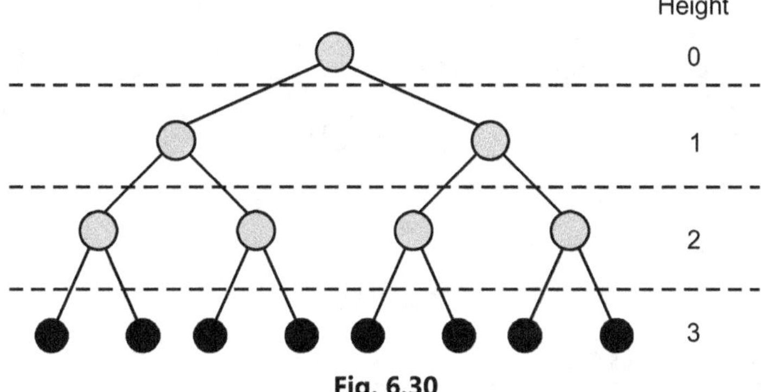

Fig. 6.30

For a tree with just one node, the root node, the height is defined to be 0, if there are 2 levels of nodes the height is 1 and so on. A null tree (no nodes except the null node) is defined to have a height of −1.

6.3 TYPES OF BINARY TREE

6.3.1 Full Binary Tree

A binary tree T is full if each node is either a leaf or possesses exactly two child nodes.

The numbers of nodes in any level are exactly equal to 2^{level}. For example, in the following diagram of the tree level 0 contains $2^0=1$ node, level 1 contains $2^1=2$ and level 2 contains $2^2=4$ nodes.

Every level in full binary tree is completely filled.

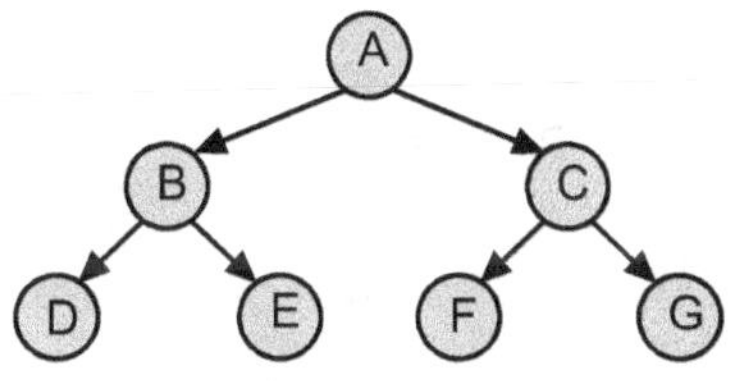

Fig. 6.31

Total number of nodes in full binary tree are= $2^{(h+1)}-1$

Where h is the height of the tree

In the above tree, height of the tree is 2. So the total number of nodes in the above tree are $2^{(2+1)}-1=7$

6.3.2 Complete Binary Tree

A complete binary tree is defined as a binary tree in which levels are filled from left to right and in which all leaf nodes are on level n or n–1. Following Fig. 6.32 (a) shows the complete binary tree.

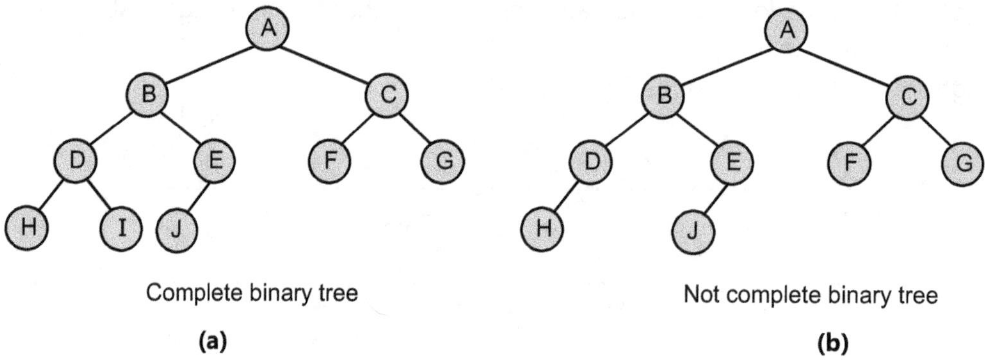

Complete binary tree   Not complete binary tree

(a)   (b)

Fig. 6.32

6.3.3 Skewed Binary Tree

The meaning of skewed is inclined or tilted or slanted.

The skewed binary trees could be skewed to left or right.

In left skewed binary tree, most of the nodes have left child without corresponding right child.

Similarly, in right skewed binary tree most of the nodes have right child without corresponding left child.

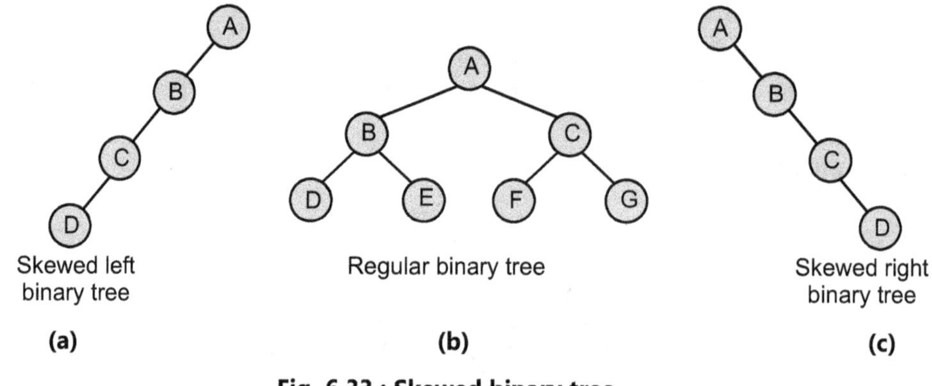

Skewed left   Regular binary tree   Skewed right
binary tree   binary tree

(a)   (b)   (c)

Fig. 6.33 : Skewed binary tree

6.3.4 Strictly Binary Tree

When every non-leaf node in binary tree is filled with left and right sub-trees, the tree is called strictly binary tree.

In the following tree, D, E, H, I and G are leaf nodes, while A, B, C and F are non-leaf nodes having both left and right children.

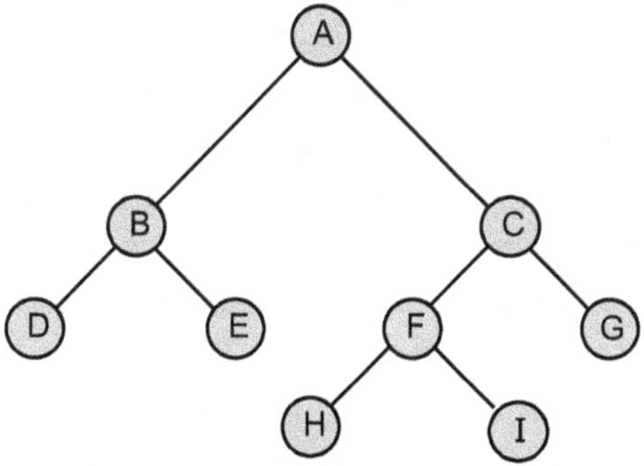

Fig. 6.34 : Strictly binary tree

6.3.5 Extended Binary Tree

An extended binary tree is a transformation of any binary tree into a complete binary tree.

This transformation consists of replacing every null sub tree of the original tree with "special nodes."

The nodes from the original tree are then internal nodes, while the ``special nodes'' are external nodes.

For instance, consider the following binary tree in Fig. 6.35.

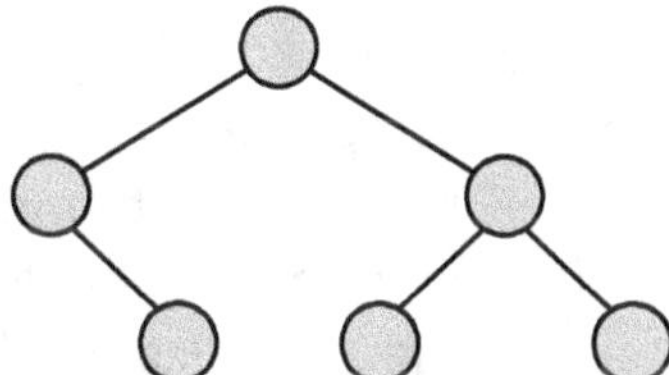

Fig. 6.35 : Binary tree

The following tree is its extended binary tree. Empty circles represent internal nodes, and filled circles represent external nodes.

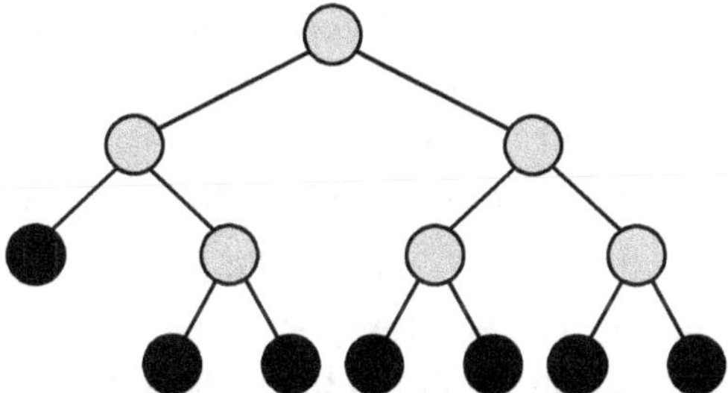

Fig. 6.36 : Extended binary tree

Every internal node in the extended tree has exactly two children, and every external node is a leaf. The result is a complete binary tree.

6.3.6 Splay Trees

- A **splay tree** is an efficient implementation of a balanced binary search tree that takes advantage of locality in the keys used in incoming lookup requests. For many applications, there is excellent key locality. A good example is a network router. A network router receives network packets at a high rate from incoming connections and must quickly decide on which outgoing wire to send each packet, based on the IP address in the packet. The router needs a big table (a map) that can be used to look up an IP address and find out which outgoing connection to use. If an IP address has been used once, it is likely to be used again, perhaps many times. Splay trees can provide good performance in this situation.

- Importantly, splay trees offer amortized $O(\lg n)$ performance; a sequence of M operations on an n-node splay tree takes $O(M \lg n)$ time.

- Splay tree is a self-balancing data structure where the last accessed key is always at root. The insert operation is similar to Binary Search Tree insert with additional steps to make sure that the newly inserted key becomes the new root.

- A splay tree is a self-adjusting search algorithm for placing and locating files (called records or keys) in a database. The algorithm finds data by repeatedly making choices at decision points called nodes.

- In a splay tree, as in a binary tree, a node has two branches (also called children). Records are stored in locations called leaves. This name derives from the fact that records always exist at end points; there is nothing beyond them. The starting point is called the root. The number of access operations required to reach the desired record is called the depth. In a practical tree, there can be thousands, millions, or billions of nodes, children, leaves, and records. Not every leaf necessarily contains a record, but more than half do. A leaf that does not contain data is called a null.

- The splay tree scheme is unique because the tree organization varies depending on which nodes are most frequently accessed. This structural change takes place by means of so-called splaying operations, also called rotations. (In general, to splay is to spread or extend out or apart.) There are several ways in which splaying can be done. It always involves interchanging the root with the node in question. One or more other nodes might change position as well. The purpose of splaying is to minimize the number of access operations required to recover desired data records over a period of time.

- A splay tree is a binary search tree. It has one interesting difference, however : whenever an element is looked up in the tree, the splay tree reorganizes to move that element to the root of the tree, without breaking the binary search tree invariant. If the next lookup request is for the same element, it can be returned immediately. In general, if a small number of elements are being heavily used, they will tend to be found near the top of the tree and are thus found quickly.

- We have already seen a way to move an element upward in a binary search tree : tree rotation. When an element is accessed in a splay tree, tree rotations are used to move it to the top of the tree. This simple algorithm can result in extremely good performance in practice. Notice that the algorithm requires that we be able to update the tree in place, but the abstract view of the set of elements represented by the tree does not change and the rep invariant is maintained. This is an example of a benign side effect, because it does not change the value represented by the data structure.

- There are three kinds of tree rotations that are used to move elements upward in the tree. These rotations have two important effects : they move the node being splayed upward in the tree, and they also shorten the path to any nodes along the path to the splayed node. This latter effect means that splaying operations tend to make the tree more balanced.

Rotation 1 : Simple Rotation

The simple tree rotation used in AVL trees is also applied at the root of the splay tree, moving the splayed node x up to become the new tree root. Here we have A < x < B < y < C, and the splayed node is either x or y depending on which direction the rotation is. It is highlighted in red.

```
        y                    x
       / \                  / \
      x   C    <->         A   y
     / \                      / \
    A   B                    B   C
```

Rotation 2 : Zig-Zig and Zag-Zag

Lower down in the tree rotations are performed in pairs so that nodes on the path from the splayed node to the root move closer to the root on average. In the "zig-zig" case, the splayed node is the left child of a left child or the right child of a right child ("zag-zag").

```
        z                 x
       / \               / \
      y   D             A   y
     / \                   / \
    x   C     <->         B   z          (A < x < B < y < C < z < D)
   / \                       / \
  A   B                     C   D
```

Rotation 3 : Zig-Zag

In the "zig-zag" case, the splayed node is the left child of a right child or vice-versa. The rotations produce a subtree whose height is less than that of the original tree. Thus, this rotation improves the balance of the tree. In each of the two cases shown, y is the splayed node :

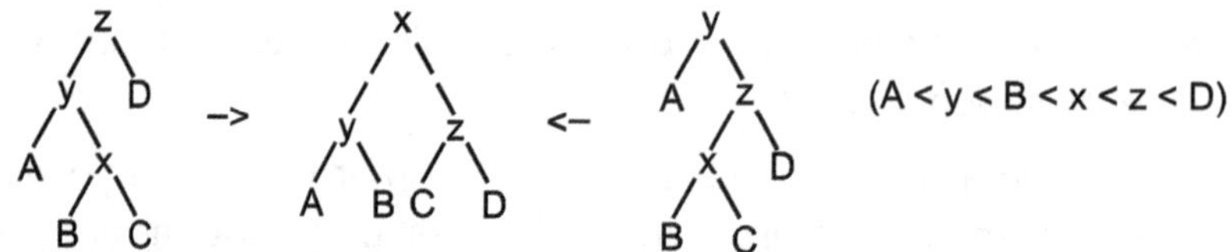

Following are different cases to insert a key k in splay tree.

- Root is NULL : We simply allocate a new node and return it as root.

- Splay the given key k. If k is already present, then it becomes the new root. If not present, then last accessed leaf node becomes the new root.

- If new root's key is same as k, don't do anything as k is already present.

- Else allocate memory for new node and compare root's key with k.

  - If k is smaller than root's key, make root as right child of new node, copy left child of root as left child of new node and make left child of root as NULL.

  - If k is greater than root's key, make root as left child of new node, copy right child of root as right child of new node and make right child of root as NULL.

- Return new node as new root of tree.

Example :

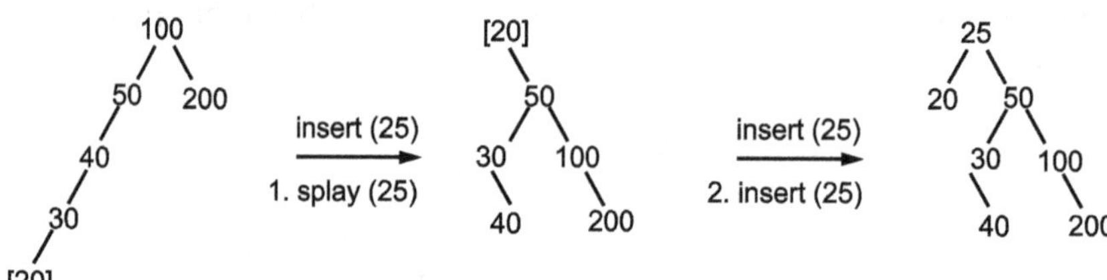


```c
#include<stdio.h>
#include<stdlib.h>
// An AVL tree node
struct node
{
    int key;
    struct node *left, *right;
};
/* Helper function that allocates a new node with the given key and
    NULL left and right pointers. */
struct node* newNode(int key)
{
```

```c
    struct node* node = (struct node*)malloc(sizeof(struct node));
    node->key  = key;
    node->left = node->right = NULL;
    return (node);
}
// A utility function to right rotate subtree rooted with y
// See the diagram given above.
struct node *rightRotate(struct node *x)
{
    struct node *y = x->left;
    x->left = y->right;
    y->right = x;
    return y;
}
// A utility function to left rotate subtree rooted with x
// See the diagram given above.
struct node *leftRotate(struct node *x)
{
    struct node *y = x->right;
    x->right = y->left;
    y->left = x;
    return y;
}
// This function brings the key at root if key is present in tree.
// If key is not present, then it brings the last accessed item at
// root.  This function modifies the tree and returns the new root
struct node *splay(struct node *root, int key)
{
    // Base cases : root is NULL or key is present at root
    if (root == NULL || root->key == key)
```

```c
        return root;
    // Key lies in left subtree
    if (root->key > key)
    {
        // Key is not in tree, we are done
        if (root->left == NULL) return root;
        // Zig-Zig (Left Left)
        if (root->left->key > key)
        {
            // First recursively bring the key as root of left-left
            root->left->left = splay(root->left->left, key);
            // Do first rotation for root, second rotation is done after else
            root = rightRotate(root);
        }
        else if (root->left->key < key) // Zig-Zag (Left Right)
        {
            // First recursively bring the key as root of left-right
            root->left->right = splay(root->left->right, key);
            // Do first rotation for root->left
            if (root->left->right != NULL)
                root->left = leftRotate(root->left);
        }
        // Do second rotation for root
        return (root->left == NULL)? root : rightRotate(root);
    }
    else // Key lies in right subtree
    {
        // Key is not in tree, we are done
        if (root->right == NULL) return root;
        // Zig-Zag (Right Left)
```

```c
        if (root->right->key > key)
        {
            // Bring the key as root of right-left
            root->right->left = splay(root->right->left, key);
            // Do first rotation for root->right
            if (root->right->left != NULL)
                root->right = rightRotate(root->right);
        }
        else if (root->right->key < key)// Zag-Zag (Right Right)
        {
            // Bring the key as root of right-right and do first rotation
            root->right->right = splay(root->right->right, key);
            root = leftRotate(root);
        }
        // Do second rotation for root
        return (root->right == NULL)? root : leftRotate(root);
    }
}
// Function to insert a new key k in splay tree with given root
struct node *insert(struct node *root, int k)
{
    // Simple Case : If tree is empty
    if (root == NULL) return newNode(k);
    // Bring the closest leaf node to root
    root = splay(root, k);
    // If key is already present, then return
    if (root->key == k) return root;
    // Otherwise allocate memory for new node
    struct node *newnode  = newNode(k);
    // If root's key is greater, make root as right child
```

```c
    // of newnode and copy the left child of root to newnode
    if (root->key > k)
    {
        newnode->right = root;
        newnode->left = root->left;
        root->left = NULL;
    }
    // If root's key is smaller, make root as left child
    // of newnode and copy the right child of root to newnode
    else
    {
        newnode->left = root;
        newnode->right = root->right;
        root->right = NULL;
    }
    return newnode; // newnode becomes new root
}
// A utility function to print preorder traversal of the tree.
// The function also prints height of every node
void preOrder(struct node *root)
{
    if (root != NULL)
    {
        printf("%d ", root->key);
        preOrder(root->left);
        preOrder(root->right);
    }
}
/* Drier program to test above function*/
int main()
```

```
{
    struct node *root = newNode(100);
    root->left = newNode(50);
    root->right = newNode(200);
    root->left->left = newNode(40);
    root->left->left->left = newNode(30);
    root->left->left->left->left = newNode(20);
    root = insert(root, 25);
    printf("Preorder traversal of the modified Splay tree is \n");
    preOrder(root);
    return 0;
}
```

Output :

Preorder traversal of the modified Splay tree is

25 20 50 30 40 100 200

Search Operation :

The search operation in Splay tree does the standard BST search, in addition to search, it also splays (move a node to the root). If the search is successful, then the node that is found is splayed and becomes the new root. Else the last node accessed prior to reaching the NULL is splayed and becomes the new root.

There are following cases for the node being accessed.

- **Node is Root :** We simply return the root, don't do anything else as the accessed node is already root.

- **Zig :** Node is child of root (the node has no grandparent). Node is either a left child of root (we do a right rotation) or node is a right child of its parent (we do a left rotation). T1, T2 and T3 are subtrees of the tree rooted with y (on left side) or x (on right side).

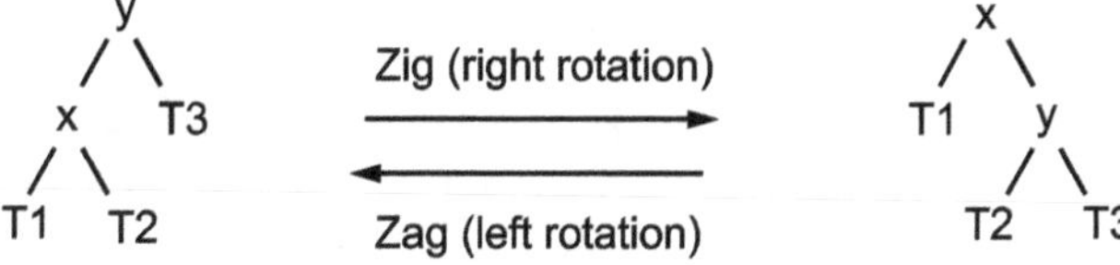

- **Node has both parent and grandparent.** There can be following subcases.

  - ➢ **Zig-Zig and Zag-Zag** Node is left child of parent and parent is also left child of grand parent (Two right rotations) OR node is right child of its parent and parent is also right child of grand parent (Two Left Rotations).

Zig-Zig (Left Left Case) :

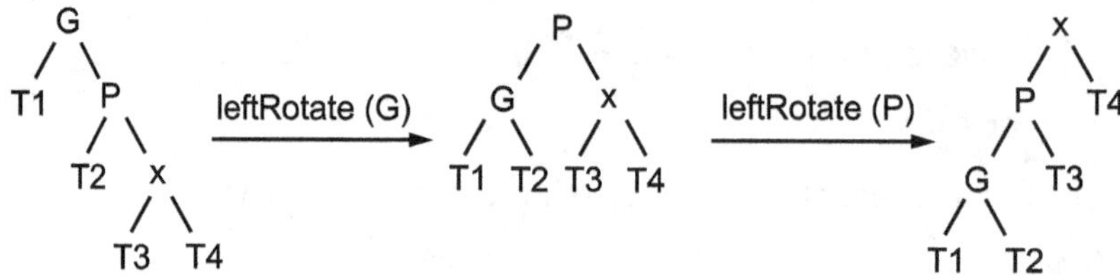

Zag-Zag (Right Right Case) :

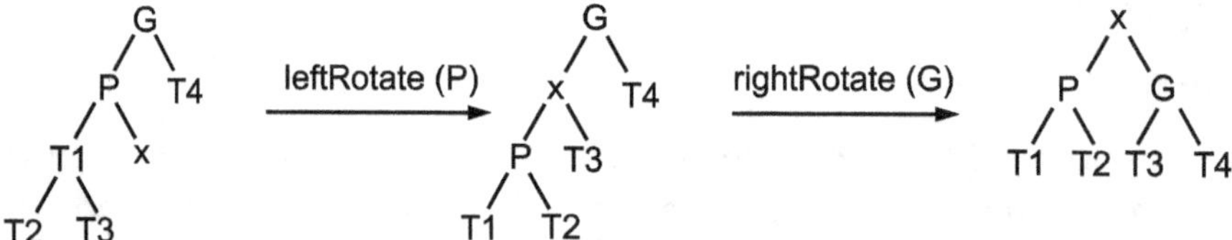

> **Zig-Zag and Zag-Zig** Node is left child of parent and parent is right child of grand parent (Left Rotation followed by right rotation) OR node is right child of its parent and parent is left child of grand parent (Right Rotation followed by left rotation).

Zig-Zag (Left Right Case) :

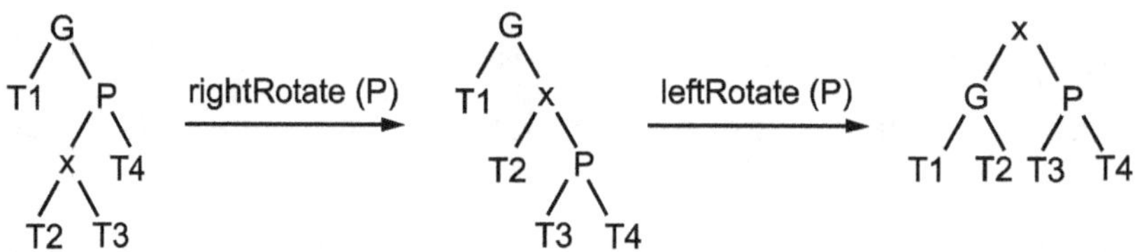

Zag-Zig (Right Left Case) :

Example :

The important thing to note is, the search or splay operation not only brings the searched key to root, but also balances the BST. For example, in above case, height of BST is reduced by 1.

Implementation :

```c
// The code is adopted from

#include<stdio.h>
#include<stdlib.h>
// An AVL tree node
struct node
{
    int key;
    struct node *left, *right;
};
/* Helper function that allocates a new node with the given key and
   NULL left and right pointers. */
struct node* newNode(int key)
{
    struct node* node = (struct node*)malloc(sizeof(struct node));
    node->key   = key;
    node->left  = node->right  = NULL;
    return (node);
}
// A utility function to right rotate subtree rooted with y
// See the diagram given above.
struct node *rightRotate(struct node *x)
{
    struct node *y = x->left;
    x->left = y->right;
    y->right = x;
    return y;
}
// A utility function to left rotate subtree rooted with x
// See the diagram given above.
```

```c
struct node *leftRotate(struct node *x)
{
    struct node *y = x->right;
    x->right = y->left;
    y->left = x;
    return y;
}

// This function brings the key at root if key is present in tree.
// If key is not present, then it brings the last accessed item at
// root.  This function modifies the tree and returns the new root
struct node *splay(struct node *root, int key)
{
    // Base cases : root is NULL or key is present at root
    if (root == NULL || root->key == key)
        return root;
    // Key lies in left subtree
    if (root->key > key)
    {
        // Key is not in tree, we are done
        if (root->left == NULL) return root;
        // Zig-Zig (Left Left)
        if (root->left->key > key)
        {
            // First recursively bring the key as root of left-left
            root->left->left = splay(root->left->left, key);
            // Do first rotation for root, second rotation is done after else
            root = rightRotate(root);
        }
```

```c
    else if (root->left->key < key) // Zig-Zag (Left Right)
    {
        // First recursively bring the key as root of left-right
        root->left->right = splay(root->left->right, key);
        // Do first rotation for root->left
        if (root->left->right != NULL)
            root->left = leftRotate(root->left);
    }
    // Do second rotation for root
    return (root->left == NULL)? root : rightRotate(root);
}
else // Key lies in right subtree
{
    // Key is not in tree, we are done
    if (root->right == NULL) return root;
    // Zag-Zig (Right Left)
    if (root->right->key > key)
    {
        // Bring the key as root of right-left
        root->right->left = splay(root->right->left, key);
        // Do first rotation for root->right
        if (root->right->left != NULL)
            root->right = rightRotate(root->right);
    }
    else if (root->right->key < key)// Zag-Zag (Right Right)
    {
        // Bring the key as root of right-right and do first rotation
        root->right->right = splay(root->right->right, key);
```

```c
        root = leftRotate(root);
    }
    // Do second rotation for root
    return (root->right == NULL)? root : leftRotate(root);
  }
}
// The search function for Splay tree.  Note that this function
// returns the new root of Splay Tree.  If key is present in tree
// then, it is moved to root.
struct node *search(struct node *root, int key)
{
   return splay(root, key);
}
// A utility function to print preorder traversal of the tree.
// The function also prints height of every node
void preOrder(struct node *root)
{
   if (root != NULL)
   {
     printf("%d ", root->key);
     preOrder(root->left);
     preOrder(root->right);
   }
}
/* Drier program to test above function*/
int main()
{
   struct node *root = newNode(100);
```

```
root->left = newNode(50);

root->right = newNode(200);

root->left->left = newNode(40);

root->left->left->left = newNode(30);

root->left->left->left->left = newNode(20);

root = search(root, 20);

printf("Preorder traversal of the modified Splay tree is \n");

preOrder(root);

return 0;

}
```

Output :

Preorder traversal of the modified Splay tree is

20 50 30 40 100 200

SUMMARY

- Splay trees have excellent locality properties. Frequently accessed items are easy to find. Infrequent items are out of way.

- All splay tree operations take O(log n) time on average. Splay trees can be rigorously shown to run in O(log n) average time per operation, over any sequence of operations (assuming we start from an empty tree).

- Splay trees are simpler compared to AVL and Red-Black Trees as no extra field is required in every tree node.

- Unlike AVL tree, a splay tree can change even with read-only operations like search.

EXERCISE

1. Explain the concept of threaded binary tree with suitable example

2. Explain the following traversals for threaded binary tree with suitable example

    a. Preorder

    b. Inorder

3. Explain the concept of red and black trees with suitable example

4. Create an AVL tree for the following data.

    40 20 10 30 70 60 55

5. Create an AVL tree for the following elements. Show all steps with rotation.

    CAR BAG MAN SAD TAN FAN ADD

6. Comment on "Threaded binary tree can be traversed without using stack".

7. Explain the concept of B tree with suitable examples.

8. Explain the concept of B+ tree with suitable examples

9. Differentiate between B tree and B+ tree.

10. Explain the concept of Splay tree with suitable examples

CHAPTER 7
FILE ORGANIZATION

7.1 INTRODUCTION TO FILES [Dec. 10, 11]

A file is a collection of records where each record consists of one or more fields. Files provide a mechanism for long term data storage in the computer. Hard disk, CD's, DVD's are generally used to store the files. All the data in the computer is stored in the form of files.

File organization can be defined as the method of storing data records in a file. The primary objective of file organization is to provide means for record retrieval and update.

The factors involved in selecting a particular file organization are :

- Economy of storage
- Ease of retrieval
- Convenience of update
- Reliability
- Security
- Integrity
- Volume of transaction

File management is one of the most visible services of an operating system. The operating system abstracts from physical properties of its storage devices to define a logical storage unit, the file. File is a collection of related information defined by its creator.

Following are the commonly used file types :

- **Sequential File :** In these files, data records are stored in a specific sequence. Records are physically ordered according to ordering key or they can be stored in order of their arrival.

- **Indexed Sequential File :** An index is added to a sequential file to provide random access.

- **Direct Access File :** This file is popularly known as a hashed file.

- **Relative File :** Each record is stored at a fixed place in the file. Each record is associated with an integer key value, which is mapped to a fixed slot in a file.

- **Index File :** Data records need not be sequenced. An index is maintained to improve access.

Many real life problems handle large volumes of data and in such situations we need to store this data on pen drive, hard disk etc. A file is a collection of related data, stored in a particular area on the disk. Programs can be designed to perform the read and write operations on these files. We prefer hard disk pen drives, CD's and DVD's (in short secondary memory devices) to store files because there are certain limitations of the main memory, which are given below.

Limitations of Main Memory :

- Limited in size

- Usually volatile

- Convenient only for small amount of data but not feasible where large amount of data which is stored permanently and is in repeated use and repeated modifications.

Thus, we need a storage that is non-volatile and is unlimited, as secondary memory.

For example, Magnetic tape floppy disk, Hard disk etc. Hence, when we organize data in 'files' data structure, the data is permanent (non-volatile), which means data is residing on storage after execution of program is over.

7.2 EXTERNAL STORAGE DEVICES

The external storage device is a device other than main memory on which information or data can be stored and from which it can be retrieved.

The storage and retrieval operations are called as writing and reading respectively. Capacity of external storage devices is larger than that of main memory and is less expensive than main memory.

External storage devices are mainly used for storage of programs for future use. We will discuss the most common external storage devices such as magnetic tape, drum and disk drives.

7.2.1 Magnetic Tape

A tape is **made up of a plastic material** coated with a **ferrite** substance which is easily magnetized.

The physical appearance of the tape is similar to the tape used for sound recording. Computer tapes are **wider**.

Several thousand feet of tape are wound on one reel, and information is encoded on the tape character by character.

A number of channels or **tracks** run the length of the tape. **One channel being** required for each bit position in binary coded representation of character.

Information is read or written on the tape through the use of a magnetic tape drive.

A limitation of magnetic tape devices is that records must be processed in the order in which they reside on the tape. Therefore, accessing a record requires the scanning of all records that precede it. This form of access is called as **sequential access.**

Magnetic tape is probably the cheapest form of external bulk storage. A reel of tape can be easily placed on and removed from a tape drive.

The magnetic tape device consists of two spindles. While one spindle holds the source reel and the other holds the take up reel. Following is the diagram of magnetic tape drive.

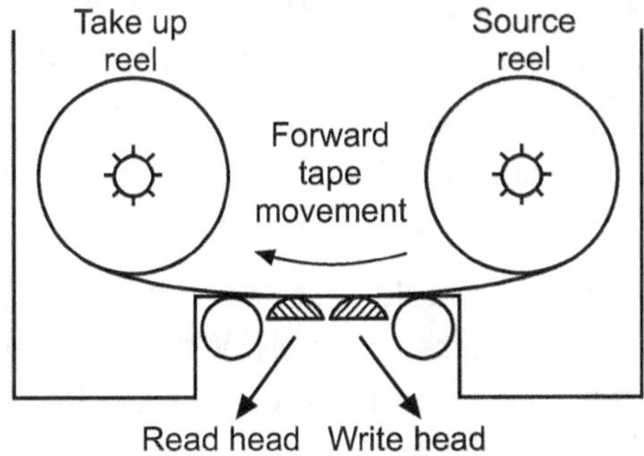

Fig. 7.1

The data to be stored on a tape is written on it in terms of blocks. These blocks may be fixed or variable size. A gap of ¾″ is left between the blocks, that is called Inter Block Gap (IBG).

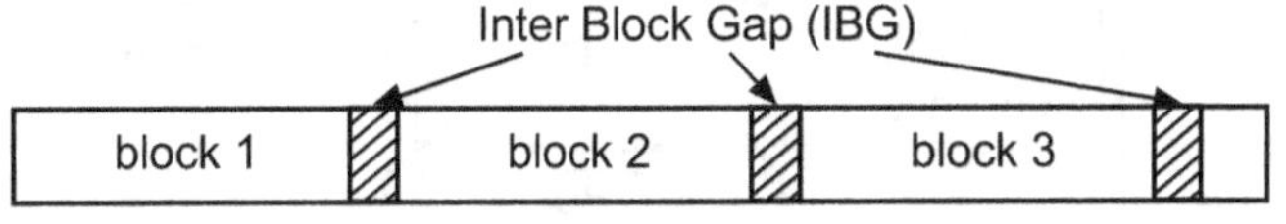

Fig. 7.2

7.2.2 Magnetic Drums

A magnetic drum is a metal cylinder, from 10 to 36 inches in diameter, which has an outside surface coated with a magnetic recording material.

The cylindrical surface of the drum is divided into a number of parallel bands called tracks.

The tracks are further divided into either sectors or blocks. The sector or block is the smallest addressable unit.

A particular sector or block is directly addressable. Hence, a drum is called as direct access storage devices.

Magnetic Tape Vs Magnetic Drum :

- The addressable units (sectors or blocks) on magnetic drums are rapidly accessed for data transfers, and no scanning of irrelevant data is required as with a magnetic tape.

- Also, unlike magnetic tape, a drum cannot be removed from its shaft or drive. Hence, the maximum storage capacity for a drum device is limited to the capacity of a single drum.

7.2.3 Magnetic Disks

The magnetic disk is a direct access storage device, which has become more widely used than the magnetic drum, mainly because of its lower cost.

Disk devices provide relatively low access times and high-speed data transfer.

There are two types of disk devices, namely, fixed disks and exchangeable disks. For both types, the disk unit or pack consists of a number of metal platters, which are stacked on the top of each other on a spindle. The upper and lower surfaces of each platter are coated with ferromagnetic particles that provide on information storage media.

The surfaces of each platter are divided into concentric bands called tracks. Each track is further divided into sectors (or blocks) which are addressable units. There are read/write heads floating just above or below the surface of disk while the disk is rotating.

An exchangeable disk device has movable read/write heads. The heads are attached to a movable arm to form a comb-like access assembly. When data on a particular track must be accessed, the whole assembly moves to position the read/write heads over the derived track. While many heads may be in position for a read/write transaction at a given point in time, data transmission can only take place through one head at a time.

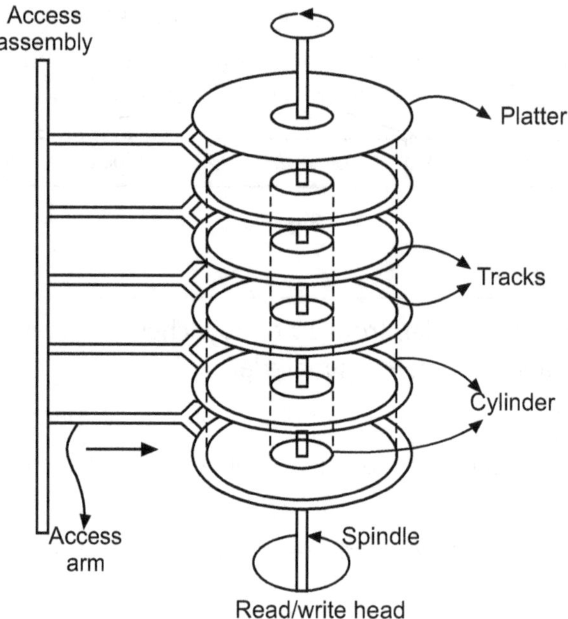

Fig. 7.3 : Diagram of a disk pack

Disk pack is viewed as a collection of cylinders. Each track is divided into sectors. The read/write head moves across the cylinder, to position it on the right cylinder.

Seek Time : The time taken to position read/write head on the correct cylinder is known as seek time.

Latency Time or Rotation Delay : The time taken for right sector to appear under the read/write head is latency time.

Access Time : The sum of seek time and latency time is access time.

Data Transmission Time : The time taken to transfer data to and from the disk is known as data transmission time.

7.3 FILE HANDLING IN C

We frequently use files for storing information which can be processed by our programs. In order to store information permanently and retrieve it, we need to use files.

Files are not only used for data storage but also to store our programs.

The editor which you use to enter your program and save it simply manipulates files for you.

In order to use files, we have to learn about *File I/O* i.e. how to write information to a file and how to read information from a file.

We will see that file I/O is almost identical to the terminal I/O that we have being using so far.

The primary difference between manipulating files and doing terminal I/O is that we must specify in our programs which files we wish to use.

As you know, you can have many files on your disk. If you wish to use a file in your programs, then you must specify which file or files you wish to use.

Specifying the file, you wish to use is referred to as **opening** the file.

When you open a file, you must also specify what you wish to do with it i.e. **Read** from the file, **Write** to the file, or both.

Because you may use a number of different files in your program, you must specify when reading or writing which file you wish to use. This is accomplished by using a variable called a **file pointer.**

Every file you open has its own file pointer variable. When you wish to write to a file you specify the file by using its file pointer variable.

You declare these file pointer variables as follows :

       FILE   *fp, *fp1, *fp2, *fp3;

The variables fp1, fp2, fp3 are file pointers. You may use any name you wish.

The file <stdio.h> contains declarations for the Standard I/O library and should always be **included** at the very beginning of C programs using files.

You should note that a file pointer is simply a variable like an integer or character.

It does **not** point to a file or the data in a file. It is simply used to indicate which file your I/O operation refers to.

The function **fopen** is one of the Standard Library functions and returns a file pointer which you use to refer to the file you have opened For Example,

$$fp = fopen(\text{"prog.c"}, \text{"r"}) ;$$

The above statement **opens** a file called prog.c for **reading** and associates the file pointer fp with the file.

When we wish to access this file for I/O, we use the file pointer variable fp to refer to it.

You can have about 20 files open in your program. You need one file pointer for each file you intend to use.

Note : All the 'C' programs are written using text file only.

File I/O

The Standard I/O Library provides similar routines for file I/O to those used for standard I/O.

The routine getc(fp) is similar to getchar() and putc(c,fp) is similar to putchar(c).

Thus, the statement

```
c = getc(fp);
```

reads the next character from the file referenced by fp and the statement

```
putc(c,fp);
```

writes the character c into file referenced by fp.

```
/* file.c : Display contents of a file on screen */
#include <stdio.h>
void main()
{
    FILE *fopen(), *fp;
    int c ;
    fp = fopen("prog.c", "r");
    c = getc(fp);
    while (c != EOF)
    {
        putchar(c);
        c = getc (fp);
    }
    fclose(fp);
}
```

In this program, we open the file prog.c for reading.

We then read a character from the file. This file must exist for this program to work.

If the file is empty, we are at the end, so getc returns EOF a special value to indicate that the end of file has been reached (Normally -1 is used for EOF).

The while loop simply keeps reading characters from the file and displaying them, until the end of the file is reached.

The function **fclose** is used to **close** the file. It indicates that we have finished the processing of this file.

We could reuse the file pointer fp by opening another file.

Consider the program given below. This program accepts filename from the user.

/* Prompt user for Filename and Display File on Screen */

```c
#include <stdio.h>


void main()
{
    FILE *fopen(), *fp;
    int c ;
    char filename[40];


    printf("Enter file to be displayed : ");
    gets(filename ;


    fp = fopen(filename, "r");



    c = getc(fp);


    while (c != EOF)
    {
        putchar(c);
        c = getc (fp);
    }
```

Filename is not fixed. It can be changed at runtime by the user.

```
    fclose(fp);
}
```

In this program, user specifies the name of the file which he wants to open and that name is stored in the array called filename.

The above program suffers a major limitation. It **does not** check whether the files to be used exist or not.

If you attempt to read from a non-existent file, your program will crash.

The fopen function was designed to cope with this eventuality. It checks if the file can be opened appropriately. If the file **cannot be opened**, it returns a **NULL** pointer.

Thus, by checking the file pointer returned by fopen, you can determine if the file was opened correctly and take appropriate action For Example,

```
fp = fopen (filename, "r");
if (fp==NULL)
{
    printf("Cannot open %s for reading \n", filename );
    exit(1);          /*Terminate program :!!*/
}
```

The above code fragment show how a program might check if a file could be opened appropriately.

The function **exit()** is a special function which terminates your program immediately.

In exit(0), zero indicates that your program terminated successfully whereas a nonzero value means that your program is terminating due to an error condition.

Alternatively, you could prompt the user to enter the filename again, and try to open it again :

```
fp = fopen (fname, "r");
while (fp==NULL)
{
    printf("Cannot open %s for reading \n", fname);
    printf("\n\nEnter filename :" );
    gets(fname);
    fp = fopen (fname, "r");
}
```

In this code fragment, we keep reading filenames from the user until a valid existing filename is entered.

Example 1 : Write a program to count the number of lines and characters in a file.

/*count.c : Count Characters in a File*/

```c
#include <stdio.h>
void main()   /* Prompt user for file and count number of characters  and lines in it*/
{
    FILE *fopen(), *fp;
    int c , nc, nlines;
    char filename[40];

    nlines = 0;
    nc = 0;

    printf("Enter file name : ");
    gets( filename );

    fp = fopen( filename, "r" );

    if ( fp == NULL )
    {
        printf("Cannot open %s for reading \n", filename );
        exit(1);    /* terminate program */
    }

    c = getc( fp);
    while (  c != EOF )
    {
        if ( c == '\n' )
        nlines++ ;
```

Counts the no. of lines of the file

```
        nc++ ;
        c = getc ( fp );
    }
    fclose( fp );
    if ( nc != 0 )
    {
        printf("There are %d characters in %s \n", nc, filename );
        printf("There are %d lines \n", nlines );
    }
    else
        printf("File : %s is empty \n", filename );
}
```

Counts the no. of characters of the file

Example 2 : Write a program to display file contents 20 lines at a time. The program pauses after displaying 20 lines until the user presses either Q to quit or Return to display the next 20 lines. (The Unix operating system has a command called **more** to do this)

As in previous programs, we read the filename from user and open it appropriately. We then process the file :

```
read character from file
while not end of file and not finished do
begin
    display character
    if character is newline then
        linecount = linecount + 1;
    if linecount == 20 then
    begin
        linecount = 1;
        Prompt user and get reply;
    end
    read next character from file
end
```

/* Program for displaying the content of the file (20 lines at a time) */

```c
#include <stdio.h>

void main( )
{
    FILE *fopen(), *fp;
    int c,  linecount;
    char filename[40], reply;

    printf("Enter file name : ");
    gets(filename);

    fp = fopen(filename, "r");     /* open for reading */

    if (fp==NULL)          /* check does file exist etc */
    {
        printf("Cannot open %s for reading \n", filename );
        exit();              /* terminate program */
    }

    linecount = 1 ;

    reply = '\0' ;
    c = getc(fp);             /* Read 1st character if any */
    while (c != EOF &&  reply != 'Q' && reply != 'q')
    {
        putchar(c);         /* Display character */
        if (c=='\n')
            linecount = linecount+ 1 ;
```

```
            if (linecount==20)
            {
                linecount = 1 ;
                printf("[Press Return to continue, Q to quit]");
                scanf("%c", reply );
            }
            c = getc (fp);
        }
        fclose(fp);
}
```

The char reply will contain the users' response. We check if this is 'q' or 'Q'.

Example 3 : Write a program to compare two files specified by the user, displaying a message indicating whether the files are identical or different. This is the basis of a **compare** command provided by most operating systems. Here our file processing loop is as follows :

```
read character ca from file A;
read character cb from file B;


while ca == cb and not EOF file A and not EOF file B
begin
    read character ca from file A;
    read character cb from file B;
end;


if ca == cb then
        printout("Files identical");
else
        printout("Files differ");
```

This program illustrates the use of I/O with two files. In general, you can manipulate up to 20 files, but for most purposes not more than 4 files would be used. All of these examples illustrate the usefulness of processing files character by character. As you can see a number of Operating System programs such as compare, type, more, copy can be easily written using character I/O. These programs are normally called **system programs** as they come with the operating system. The important point to note is that these programs are in no way special. They are not different in nature than any of the programs we have constructed so far.

/* Compare.c : Compare Two Files */

```c
#include <stdio.h>
void main()
{
    FILE *fp1, *fp2, *fopen();
    char ca, cb;
    char fname1[40], fname2[40];

    printf("Enter first filename :");
    gets(fname1);

    printf("Enter second filename :");
    gets(fname2);

    fp1 = fopen(fname1, "r");         /* open for reading */
    fp2 = fopen(fname2, "r");         /* open for writing */

    if (fp1==NULL)               /* check does file exist etc */
    {
        printf("Cannot open %s for reading \n", fname1 );
        exit(1);              /* terminate program */
    }
    else
    if (fp2==NULL)
    {
        printf("Cannot open %s for reading \n", fname2 );
        exit(1);              /* terminate program */
    }
```

```
    else                    /* both files opened successfully  */
    {
        ca = getc(fp1);
        cb = getc(fp2);


        while (ca!=EOF&&cb!=EOF&&ca==cb)
        {
            ca = getc(fp1);
            cb = getc(fp2);
        }
        if (ca==cb)
            printf("Files are identical \n");
        else if (ca != cb)
            printf("Files differ \n" );
        fclose (fp1);
        fclose (fp2);

    }
}
```

Writing to Files :

The previous programs have opened files for reading and read characters from them.

To write a file, the file must be opened (in write mode).

```
    fp = fopen( fname, "w" );
```

If the file does not exist already, it will be created. If the file does exist, it will be overwritten!

So, be careful when opening files for writing, in case you may destroy a file unintentionally. Opening files for writing can also fail. If you try to create a file in another users directory where you do not have access you will not be allowed and fopen will fail.

Character Output to Files :

The function putc(c, fp) writes a character to the file associated with the file pointer fp.

/* filecopy.c : Copy prog.c to prog.old */

```
#include <stdio.h>
void main()
```

```c
{
    FILE *fp1, *fp2, *fopen();
    int c ;

    fp1 = fopen("prog.c", "r");         /* open for reading */
    fp2 = fopen("prog.old", "w");       /* open for writing */


    if (fp1==NULL)                      /* check does file exist etc */
    {
        printf("Cannot open prog.c for reading \n" );
        exit(1);                        /* terminate program */
    }
    else if (fp2==NULL)
    {
        printf("Cannot open prog.old for writing \n");
        exit(1);                        /* terminate program */
    }
    else                                /* both files O.K. */
    {
        c = getc(fp1);
        while (c != EOF)
        {
            putc( c, fp2);              /* copy to prog.old */
            c = getc(fp1);
        }

    fclose (fp1);                       /* Now close files */
    fclose (fp2);
    printf("Files successfully copied \n");
    }
}
```

The above program only copies the specific file prog.c to the file prog.old. We can make it a general purpose program by prompting the user for the files to be copied and opening them appropriately.

/* copy.c : Copy any user file*/

```c
#include <stdio.h>
void main()
{
    FILE *fp1, *fp2, *fopen();
    int c ;
    char fname1[40], fname2[40];

    printf("Enter source file :");
    gets(fname1);

    printf("Enter destination file :");
    gets(fname2);

    fp1 = fopen(fname1,  "r");      /* open for reading */
    fp2 = fopen(fname2, "w");     /* open for writing */

    if (fp1==NULL)              /* check does file exist etc */
    {
        printf("Cannot open %s for reading \n", fname1 );
        exit(1);              /* terminate program */
    }
    else if (fp2==NULL)
    {
        printf("Cannot open %s for writing \n", fname2 );
        exit(1);             /* terminate program */
    }
    else                  /* both files O.K. */
```

```
    {
        c = getc(fp1);              /* read from source */
        while (c != EOF)
        {
            putc(c, fp2);           /* copy to destination */
            c = getc(fp1);
        }

        fclose (fp1);               /* Now close files */
        fclose (fp2);
        printf("Files successfully copied \n");
    }
}
```

Command Line Parameters : Arguments to main( )

Accessing the command line arguments is a very useful facility. It enables you to provide commands with arguments that the command can use For Example, in unix the command.

```
    % cat prog.c
```

takes the argument "prog.c" and opens a file with that name, which it then displays. The command line argument includes the command name itself so that in the above example, "cat" and "prog.c" are the command line arguments. The first argument i.e. "cat" is argument number zero, the next argument, "prog.c", is argument number one and so on.

To access these arguments from within a C program, you pass parameters to the function main(). The use of arguments to main is a key feature of many C programs.

The declaration of main looks like this :

```
    int main (int argc, char *argv[ ])
```

This declaration states that

- Main returns an integer value (used to determine if the program terminates successfully).
- argc is the number of command line arguments including the command itself i.e argc must be at least 1.
- argv is an array of the command line arguments.

The declaration of argv means that it is an array of pointers to strings (the command line arguments). By the normal rules about arguments whose type is array, what actually gets passed to main is the address of the first element of the array. As a result, an equivalent (and widely used) declaration is :

```
    int main (int argc, char **argv)
```

When the program starts, the following conditions hold true :

- argc is greater than 0.
- argv[argc] is a null pointer.
- argv[0], argv[1], ..., argv[argc-1] are pointers to strings with implementation defined meanings.
- argv[0] is a string which contains the program's name, or is an empty string if the name isn't available. Remaining members of argv are the program's arguments.

Example 4 : print_args echoes its arguments to the standard output – is a form of the Unix echo command.

/* Print_args.c : Echo Command Line Arguments */

```c
#include <stdio.h>
#include <stdlib.h>

int main(int argc,  char *argv[])
{
    int i = 0;
    int num_args;

    num_args = argc;

    while( num_args > 0)
    {
        printf("%s\n", argv[i]);
        i++;
        num_args--;
    }
}
```

If the name of this program is print_args, an example of its execution is as follows :

```
% print_args hello goodbye Pune
print_args
hello
```

```
goodbye
Pune
%
```

Example 5 : Rewrite print_args so that it operates like the Unix echo command.

Hint : You only need to change the printf statement.

The following is a version of the Unix cat command :

/* cat1.c : Display files specified as command line parameters */

```c
#include <stdio.h>
#include <stdlib.h>
int main(int argc, char *argv[])
{
    int i = 1;
    int c;
    int num_args = 0;
    FILE *fp;

    if (argc==1)
    {
     fprintf(stderr, "No input files\nUsage : % cat file...\n");
     exit(1);
    }

    if (argc>1)
        printf("%d files to be displayed\n", argc-1);

    num_args = argc - 1;

    while( num_args > 0)
    {
        printf("[Displaying file %s]\n", argv[i]);
```

```
        num_args--;
        fp = fopen( argv[i], "r");
        if (fp == NULL)
        {
            fprintf(stderr,"Cannot display %s \n", argv[i]);
            continue;    /* Goto next file in list */
        }


        c = getc(fp);
        while (c != EOF)
        {
            putchar(c);
            c = getc(fp);
        }
        fclose(fp);
        printf("\n[End of %s]\n--------------\n\n", argv[i]);
        i++;

    }
}
```

Note : The continue statement causes the current iteration of the loop to stop and control to return to the loop.

7.3.1 File Opening Modes

7.3.1.1 Text File

r	open existing file for reading
w	open (create if necessary), discard previous contents.
a	open (create if necessary), do not discard previous contents, write at the end of the file.
r+	open existing file for reading and writing. It behaves like 'r' with the option of writing.
w+	create and open file for reading and writing, discard previous contents. It behaves like 'w' with the option of reading.
a+	open (create if necessary) file for reading and appending. It behaves like 'a' with the option for reading.

7.3.1.2 Binary File

rb   open existing binary file for reading

wb   open (create if necessary), a binary file, discard previous contents.

ab   open (create if necessary), a binary file, do not discard previous contents, write at the end of the file.

r+b   open an existing binary file for reading and writing. It behaves like 'rb' with the option of writing.

w+b   create and open a binary file for reading and writing, discard previous contents. It behaves like 'w' with the option of reading.

a+b   open (create if necessary) a binary file for reading and appending. It behaves like 'a' with the option for reading.

7.3.2 Storing File on External Storage Device

Suppose x is a short integer variable and x = 125. So storage of x in text and binary files is given below.

Storing x in Text File :

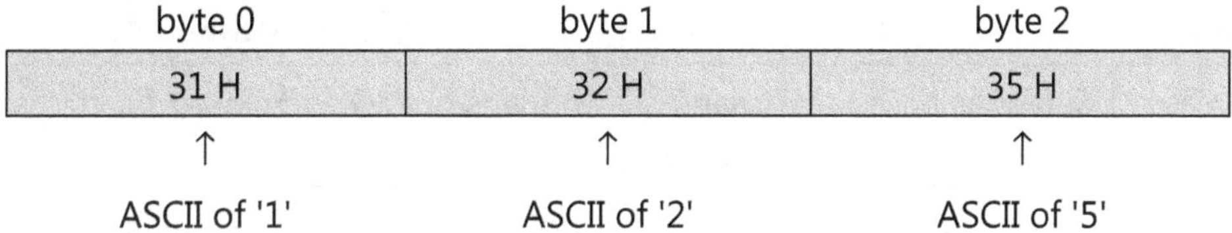

Fig. 7.4 : Storing 125 in text file needs 3 bytes

Storing x in Binary File :

Binary representation of 125 is 01111101

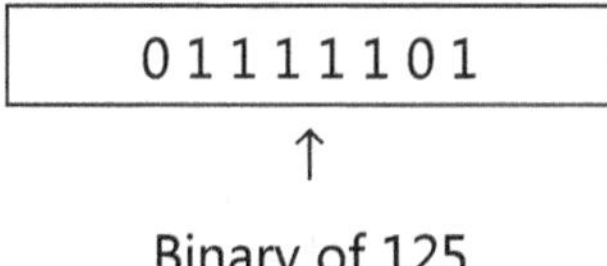

Fig. 7.5 : Storing 125 in binary file needs only 1 byte

7.4   PRIMITIVE FILE STREAM OPERATIONS AND IMPLEMENTATIONS IN C++

The I/O system of C++ contains a set of classes (such as fstream, ifstream and ofstream) that define the file handling methods. These classes are derived from fstreambase and from corresponding iostream class. These classes are designed to manage the disk files and are declared in fstream and therefore we must include this file in any program that uses file.

Input and output is initiated using the functions of the base classes istream and ostream.

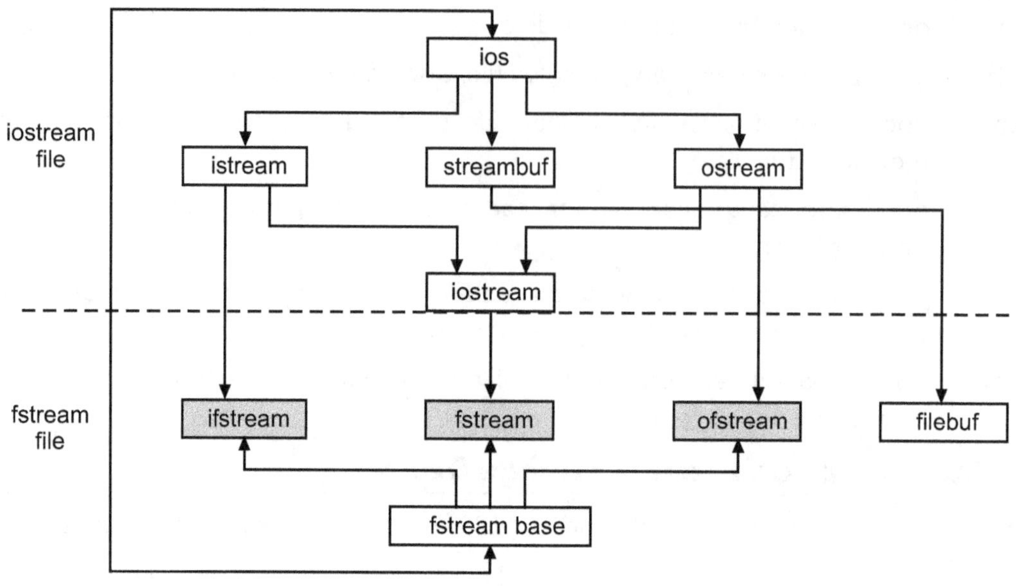

Fig. 7.6 : Stream classes for file operations

Class	Use	Contains functions
fstreambase	Serves as base for fstream, ifstream and ofstream class.	Contains open() and close() functions.
ifstream	Provides input (read) operations.	Contains open() with default input mode. Inherits get(), getline(), read(), seekg() and tellg() functions from istream.
ofstream	Provides output (write) operations.	Contains open() with default output mode. Inherits put(), seekp(), tellp() and write() functions from ostream.
fstream	Provides support for simultaneous input and output operations.	Contains open() with default input mode. Inherits all functions from istream and ostream classes through iostream.

7.5 PRIMITIVE FUNCTIONS IN C++ FOR FILES

1. File Creation

   - Basically, three classes are used for file creation.

     ➢ fstream class (used for reading as well as writing the data into the file).

     ➢ ifstream class (used for reading the data from the file).

     ➢ ofstream class (used for writing the data into the file).

- Observe the following code snippets
  - ➢ Open the file for reading

```
ifstream f_in;
f_in.open("myfile.txt");
```

  - ➢ Open the file for writing

```
ofstream f_out;
f_out.open("myfile.txt");
```

The most important thing while creating the file is the mode in which we are opening the file.

File mode parameters are

Mode	Meaning
ios : :app	Append data at the end of file
ios : :ate	Go to end of file after opening
ios : :binary	Open file in Binary mode
ios : :in	Open file for reading
ios : :nocreate	Open fails if file does not exist
ios : :out	Open file for writing
ios : :trunk	Truncates file to zero length.

Opening Files Using open()

The function open() can be used to open the file. In such cases, we may need to create a stream object and use it to open the file. This is done as follows :

file-stream-class stream-object;

```
stream-object.open("filename", mode);
```

The second argument which is called as mode, specifies the purpose for which the file opened. Above table gives information about various modes in which we can open the file.

Example :

```
ofstream outfile;
outfile.open("data.txt",ios : :out);
. . . . . . .
. . . . . . .
ifstream infile;
```

```
infile.open("data1.txt",ios : :in);
// for closing the opened files use following syntaxes
outfile.close();
infile.close();
```

Detecting end-of-file

Detection of end-of-file condition is necessary for preventing any further attempt to read data from the file. This is illustrated using the following statement.

```
while(f_in)
```

an ifstream object, such as f_in, returns a value of 0 if any error occurs in the file operation including end-of-file condition. Thus, while loop terminates when file returns a value zero on reaching the end-of-file condition.

There is one more approach to detect end-of-file condition, this approach we have used in the following program.

```
while(!f_in.eof())
{
//Read the file content
}
```

eof() is a function of ios class. It returns non-zero value if end-of-file condition is encountered and a zero otherwise.

Reading from a File :

```
#include<iostream.h>
#include<fstream.h>
#include<conio.h>

void main()
{
    ifstream f_in;
    char str[10];

    f_in.open("myfile.txt",ios : :in);
    while(!f_in.eof())
```

```
    {
        f_in>>str;
        cout<<"\n"<<str;
    }
    f_in.close();
    getch();
}
```

Writing into a File

```
#include<iostream.h>
#include<fstream.h>
#include<conio.h>
void main()
{
    ofstream f_out;
    char str[10]="awaneesh";

    f_out.open("myfile.txt",ios : :out);
    f_out<<str;
    f_out.close();
    getch();
}
```

Reading and Writing into a File

```
#include<iostream.h>
#include<fstream.h>
#include<conio.h>

void main()
{
    fstream f;
    char str[10]="awaneesh",str1[20];
```

```
    f.open("myfile.txt",ios : :in|ios : :out);

    f<<str;


    f.seekg(0,ios : :beg);


    f>>str1;

    cout<<str1;


    f.close();

    getch();
}
```

Sample File Program in C++

```cpp
#include<iostream.h>

#include<stdio.h>

#include<stdlib.h>

#include<fstream.h>

#include<string.h>


// class for storing passenger record
class passenger
{
    char f_name[15],l_name[15];
  int age;
 public :
  void get_data();
  void put_data();
};


class PassengerFile
```

```cpp
{
  private :
    char fname[12];
  public :
    void getfile();
  void create();
  void displayall();
};


// Function for getting passenger data

void passenger : :get_data()
{
    cout<<endl<<"Enter First name   : ";
    cin>>f_name;
    cout<<endl<<"Enter Last name    : ";
    cin>>l_name;
    cout<<endl<<"age : ";
    cin>>age;
}
// Function for displaying passenger data

void passenger : :put_data()
{
    cout<<endl << " \t" << f_name << "\t" << l_name  << "\t" << age;
}


void PassengerFile : :getfile()
{
    cout << "\n Enter filename : ";
    cin >> fname;
}
```

```cpp
void PassengerFile : :create()
{
    fstream file;
    passenger p;

    int n,i;
    file.open(fname,ios : :out|ios : :binary );
    cout<<"\nHow many records do you want to enter ?";
    cin>>n;
    for(i=0;i<n;i++)
    {
        p.get_data();
        file.write((char *) & p,sizeof(p));
        flushall();
    }
    file.close();
}

void PassengerFile : :displayall()
{
    passenger p;                 // object for passenger
    fstream file;
    file.open(fname, ios : :in );
    if(file.bad())
        cout<<"\nOpening error .....";
    else
    {
        cout << "\n id   Fname  Lname  Age \n";
        while(!file.eof())
```

```
        {
            file.read((char *) &p,sizeof (p));
            if (!file.eof())
            {
                        p.put_data();
            }
        }
    file.close();
    }


}

void main()
{
    class PassengerFile pfile;
    pfile.getfile();
    pfile.create();
    pfile.displayall();
}
```

Error Handling Functions :

- eof() : returns true if end-of-file is encountered while reading the file, otherwise it returns false.
- fail() : returns true when the input or output operation has failed.

Functions for Manipulation of File Pointers :

There are various functions that can be used to move the file pointer to the desired position. The file stream classes use the following functions :

Function Name	Used for
seekg()	Moves get pointer (input) to the specific location.
seekp()	Moves put pointer (output) to the specific location.
tellg()	Gives the current position of the get pointer.
tellp()	Gives the current position of the put pointer.

For Example :

```
        infile.seekg(20);
```

moves the file pointer to byte number 20. Remember the bytes in the file are numbered from zero. Therefore, file pointer will actually point to byte number 21.

Consider the following statements :

```
ofstream fileout;

fileout.open("awaneesh",ios : :app);

int p=fileout.tellp();
```

On execution of these statements, the output pointer is moved to the end of file "awaneesh" and the value of p will represent the number of bytes present in the file.

Specifying the Offsets :

seekg() and seekp() functions can be used with two arguments as follows :

```
seekg(offset, refposition);

seekp(offset, refposition);
```

The parameter *offset* represents the number of bytes the file pointer is to be moved from the location specified by parameter *refposition*. The *refposition* takes one of the following three constants defined in **ios** class :

- ios : :beg   start of the file
- ios : :cur   current position of the pointer
- ios : :end   end of the file

seekg() function moves the associated file's 'get' pointer while the seekp() function moves the associated files 'put' pointer.

7.6 COMPARISON BETWEEN TEXT FILE AND BINARY FILE [May 10]

Text File	Binary File
• The text file contains the data in the form of ASCII characters.	• The binary file consists of the data in binary form.
• The text file cannot store the graphical data. It can store only text.	• The binary file can store the data such as text, graphics, image, and sound.
• Text files can directly read and interpreted easily through editors.	• The binary files cannot be read directly. With the help of some tools the binary file can be read.
• Integer or real number requires more storage area when stored in text format.	• Binary file is more compact and takes less storage area.

7.7 SEQUENTIAL FILE ORGANIZATION   [Dec. 12]

The sequential file is organized by appending record to the file in the order, as they were entered.

Thus, the record found in the first position is the 'oldest' record and the last record in the file is the one most recently added.

- Records in the files are read or written sequentially.
- Records are of fixed length.
- Searching time is more because records are accessed sequentially from beginning.
- If we want to add a record, it can be always added at end of the file.
- Position of each field in the record and length of the field is fixed.

Drawbacks of Sequential File Organization :

- Insertion and deletion of records in between requires moving a large amount of data to create space for the new record.
- Accessing any record requires going through all the preceding records sequentially, which is time consuming operation. Therefore, searching a record takes more time.
- Needs to reorganize the file time to time whenever record is added or deleted.

Advantages of Sequential File over Unordered Files :

- Reading of records in order of ordering key is extremely efficient.
- Finding the next record in order of the ordering key usually does not require additional block access. Next record may be found in the same block.

Sequential File Operations :   **[Dec. 06, May 10]**

- Creation
- Insert record
- Display record
- Delete record
- Update record
- Searching of a record
- Packing.

The Structure used to Store Data in the File is given below :

```
struct student
{
    int roll;
    char name[20];
};
```

The Class Used to Hold Various Functions of Sequential File.

```
class database
{
    struct student st;
    public :
        void insert_data();
        void read_data();
        void search_data();
        void update_data();
        void delete_data();
        void sort_data();
};
```

1. **File Creation and Inserting a Record in it**   **[Dec. 12]**
   - Open the binary file in app mode (if file does not exist, it is created). Append mode will preserve the old content of the file and will help to write new content at the end of the file.

```
ofstream file;
file.open("database.txt",ios : :binary| ios : :out| ios : :app);
```

   - Accept the new record from the user.

```
cout<<"Enter the roll and name of the student";
cin>>st.roll>>st.name;
```

   - Write the record in the file.

```
file.write((char*)&st,sizeof(struct student));
```

   - Close the file after writing the record.

```
file.close();
```

Function for Writing Data into the File :

```
void database : :insert_data()
{
    ofstream file;
    file.open("database.txt",ios : :binary|ios : :out|ios : :app);

    cout<<"Enter the roll and name of the student";
```

```
    cin>>st.roll>>st.name;

    file.write((char*)&st,sizeof(struct student));

    file.close();
}
```

2. Displaying File Content   [Dec. 12]

- Open the binary file in read mode.

```
ifstream file;
file.open("database.txt",ios : :binary|ios : :in);
```

- Start reading the content of the file till file end encounters.

```
file.read((char*)&st,sizeof(st));

    while(!file.eof())
    {
        cout<<"\n"<<st.roll<<"\t"<<st.name;
        file.read((char*)&st,sizeof(st));
    }
    file.close();
```

Function for Displaying File

```
 void database : :read_data()
{
    struct student st;

    ifstream file;
    file.open("database.txt",ios : :binary|ios : :in);

    file.read((char*)&st,sizeof(st));
    while(!file.eof())
    {
        cout<<"\n"<<st.roll<<"\t"<<st.name;
        file.read((char*)&st,sizeof(st));
    }
    file.close();

}
```

3. Deleting Record from the File   **[Dec. 12]**

- Accept the roll number of the student whose record you want to delete.

```
cout<<"\nEnter the roll no. of the record that you want to delete :";
cin>>roll_number;
```

- Open "database.txt" file in read mode and "db1.txt" file in write mode.

```
file.open("database.txt",ios : :binary| ios : :in);
```

```
file.open("db1.txt",ios : :binary| ios : :out| ios : :trunc);
```

- Read the content from database.txt, if the roll number of the record is not matching with the roll number of that record which we want to delete, then copy the record into db1.txt, otherwise do not copy the record into db1.txt.
- So at the end db1.txt will hold all the record except the record that we want to delete.
- Now delete database.txt file.

```
remove("database.txt");
```

- Rename db1.txt into database.txt.

```
rename("db1.txt","database.txt");
```

- Now the new databse.txt file will not contain the record that we want to delete.

Function for Deleting Record from the File

```
void database : :delete_data()
{
    struct student st;
    int roll_number,flag=0,flag1=0;
    ifstream file;
    ofstream ofile;

    cout<<"\nEnter the roll no. of the record that you want to delete :";
    cin>>roll_number;

    file.open("database.txt",ios : :binary|ios : :in);
    file.open("db1.txt",ios : :binary|ios : :out|ios : :trunc);

    file.read((char*)&st,sizeof(st));

    while(!file.eof())
```

```
{
    if(roll_number==st.roll)
    {
        cout<<"\nRECORD FOUND!!!";
        flag=1;flag1=1;
    }
    if(flag==0)
    {
        ofile.write((char*)&st,sizeof(st));
    }
    flag=0;
    file.read((char*)&st,sizeof(st));
}
if(flag1==0)
{
    cout<<"\nRECORD NOT FOUND!!!\n";
}
cout<<"\n";
remove("database.txt");
rename("db1.txt","database.txt");

file.close();
}
```

4. Searching Record from the File   [Dec. 12]

- Accept the roll number of the student whose record you want to delete.

```
cout<<"\nEnter the roll no. of the record that you want to delete :";
cin>>roll_number;
```

- Open database.txt file. Read the content from the file sequentially. Compare the accepted roll number with the roll number of the record read from the file. If match found, record exists, then stop. If file end is encountered, then print "record not found".

Function for Searching Record

```cpp
void database : :search_data()
{

    struct student st;
    int roll_number,flag=0;
    ifstream file;


    cout<<"\nEnter the roll no. of the record that you want to search :";
    cin>>roll_number;


    file.open("database.txt",ios : :binary|ios : :in);
    file.read((char*)&st,sizeof(st));


    while(!file.eof())
    {
        if(roll_number==st.roll)
        {
            cout<<"\nRECORD FOUND!!!";
            cout<<"\n"<<st.roll<<"\t"<<st.name;
            flag=1;
            break;
        }
        file.read((char*)&st,sizeof(st));
    }
    if(flag==0)
    {

        cout<<"\nRECORD NOT FOUND!!!\n";
    }
    file.close();
}
```

5. Updating Record from the File   **[Dec. 12]**

- Record updation process is nearly same as that of the process of record deletion except one thing, whenever the record is found in the file, the new values for that record are taken from the user and then the record is written into db1.txt file.
- Accept the roll number of the student whose record you want to modify/update.

```
cout<<"\nEnter the roll no. of the record that you want to delete :";
cin>>roll_number;
```

- Open "database.txt" file in read mode and "db1.txt" file in write mode.

```
file.open("database.txt",ios : :binary|ios : :in);

file.open("db1.txt",ios : :binary|ios : :out|ios : :trunc);
```

- Read the content from database.txt, if the roll number of the record is not matching with the roll number of that record which we want to modify, then copy the record into db1.txt, otherwise accept the new values for that record and then copy the new record into db1.txt.
- At the end db1.txt will hold all the record as it is with the record which we want to modify with the modified values.
- Now delete database.txt file.

```
remove("database.txt");
```

- Rename db1.txt into database.txt.

```
rename("db1.txt","database.txt");
```

- Now the new database.txt file will not contain the record that we want to delete.

```
void database : :update_data()
{

    struct student st;
    int roll_number,flag=0,flag1=0;
    ifstream file;
    ofstream ofile;


    cout<<"\nEnter the roll no. of the record that you want to search :";
    cin>>roll_number;
    file.open("database.txt",ios : :binary|ios : :in);
    file.open("db1.txt",ios : :binary|ios : :out|ios : :trunc);


    file.read((char*)&st,sizeof(st));
    while(!file.eof())
```

```cpp
    {
        if(roll_number==st.roll)
        {
            cout<<"\nRECORD FOUND!!!";
            cout<<"\nEnter new name of the student";
            cin>>st.name;
            ofile.write((char*)&st,sizeof(st));
            flag=1;flag1=1;
        }
        if(flag==0)
        {
            file.write((char*)&st,sizeof(st));
        }
        flag=0;
        file.read((char*)&st,sizeof(st));
    }
    if(flag1==0)
    {
        cout<<"\nRECORD NOT FOUND!!!\n";
    }
    remove("database.txt");
    rename("db1.txt","database.txt");
    file.close();
}
```

/* Program of Sequential File in C++ */

```cpp
#include<iostream.h>
#include<stdio.h>
#include<conio.h>
#include<fstream.h>
#include<process.h>
```

```cpp
struct student
{
    int roll;
    char name[20];
};

class database
{
    struct student st;
    public :
        void insert_data();
        void read_data();
        void search_data();
        void update_data();
        void delete_data();
        void sort_data();
};
void database : :sort_data()
{
    ifstream file;
    ofstream out;
    struct student st[50],temp;
    int i=0,n,j;

    file.open("database.txt",ios : :binary|ios : :in);
    file.read((char*)&st[i],sizeof(st[i]));            //Important

    while(!file.eof())
    {
        i++;
```

```cpp
            file.read((char*)&st[i],sizeof(st[i]));
    }
    file.close();


    n=i;


    for(i=0;i<=n;i++)
    {
        for(j=i+1;j<=n;j++)
        {
            if(st[i].roll>st[j].roll)
            {
                temp=st[i];
                st[i]=st[j];
                st[j]=temp;
            }
        }
    }
    out.open("database.txt",ios : :binary|ios : :trunc|ios : :out);
    for(i=0;i<n;i++)
    {
        out.write((char*)&st[i],sizeof(struct student));
    }
    out.close();


}


void database : :read_data()
{
    struct student st;
```

```cpp
    ifstream file;

    file.open("database.txt",ios : :binary|ios : :in);

    file.read((char*)&st,sizeof(st));           //Important

    while(!file.eof())
    {
        cout<<"\n"<<st.roll<<"\t"<<st.name;
        file.read((char*)&st,sizeof(st));
    }

    cout<<"\n";

    file.close();
}

void database : :update_data()
{
    struct student st;
    int roll_number,flag=0,flag1=0;
    ifstream file;
    ofstream ofile;

    cout<<"\nEnter the roll no. of the record that you want to search :";
    cin>>roll_number;

    file.open("database.txt",ios : :binary|ios : :in);
    ofile.open("db1.txt",ios : :binary|ios : :out|ios : :trunc);
    file.read((char*)&st,sizeof(st));             //Important
```

```cpp
    while(!file.eof())
    {
        if(roll_number==st.roll)
        {
            cout<<"\nRECORD FOUND!!!";
            cout<<"\nEnter new name of the student";
            cin>>st.name;
            ofile.write((char*)&st,sizeof(st));
            flag=1;flag1=1;
        }
        if(flag==0)
        {
            file.write((char*)&st,sizeof(st));
        }
        flag=0;
        file.read((char*)&st,sizeof(st));
    }
    if(flag1==0)
    {
        cout<<"\nRECORD NOT FOUND!!!\n";
    }
    cout<<"\n";
    remove("database.txt");
    rename("db1.txt","database.txt");


    file.close();
}

void database : :delete_data()
```

```cpp
{
    struct student st;
    int roll_number,flag=0,flag1=0;
    ifstream file;
    ofstream ofile;

    cout<<"\nEnter the roll no. of the record that you want to search :";
    cin>>roll_number;

    file.open("database.txt",ios : :binary|ios : :in);
    ofile.open("db1.txt",ios : :binary|ios : :out|ios : :trunc);

    file.read((char*)&st,sizeof(st));            //Important

    while(!file.eof())
    {
        if(roll_number==st.roll)
        {
            cout<<"\nRECORD FOUND!!!";
            flag=1;flag1=1;
        }
        if(flag==0)
        {
            ofile.write((char*)&st,sizeof(st));
        }
        flag=0;
        file.read((char*)&st,sizeof(st));
    }
    if(flag1==0)
```

```cpp
    {
        cout<<"\nRECORD NOT FOUND!!!\n";
    }
    cout<<"\n";
    remove("database.txt");
    rename("db1.txt","database.txt");


    file.close();
}

void database : :search_data()
{
    struct student st;
    int roll_number,flag=0;
    ifstream file;

    cout<<"\nEnter the roll no. of the record that you want to search :";
    cin>>roll_number;

    file.open("database.txt",ios : :binary|ios : :in);

    file.read((char*)&st,sizeof(st));             //Important

    while(!file.eof())
    {
        if(roll_number==st.roll)
        {
            cout<<"\nRECORD FOUND!!!";
            cout<<"\n"<<st.roll<<"\t"<<st.name;
            flag=1;
```

```cpp
            break;
        }
        file.read((char*)&st,sizeof(st));
    }
    if(flag==0)
    {
        cout<<"\nRECORD NOT FOUND!!!\n";
    }

    cout<<"\n";

    file.close();
}

void database : :insert_data()
{
    ofstream file;

    file.open("database.txt",ios : :binary|ios : :out|ios : :app);

    cout<<"Enter the roll and name of the student";
    cin>>st.roll>>st.name;


    file.write((char*)&st,sizeof(struct student));
    file.close();
}

void main()
{
    database obj;
    int choice;
```

```cpp
clrscr();

while(1)
{
    cout<<"\n1.Insert Record";
    cout<<"\n2.Search Record";
    cout<<"\n3.Update Record";
    cout<<"\n4.Delete Record";
    cout<<"\n5.Sort Records";
    cout<<"\n6.Display Records";
    cout<<"\n7.Quit";
    cout<<"\nEnter your choice ";
    cin>>choice;
    switch(choice)
    {
        case 1 :
            obj.insert_data();
            break;
        case 2 :
            obj.search_data();
            break;
        case 3 :
            obj.update_data();
            break;
        case 4 :
            obj.delete_data();
            break;
        case 5 :
            obj.sort_data();
            break;
```

```
        case 6 :
            obj.read_data();
            break;
        case 7 :
            exit(0);
      }
  }


  getch();
}
```

7.8 DIRECT ACCESS FILE ORGANIZATION   [Dec. 11, May 12]

A direct access file allows arbitrary blocks to be read or written. Thus, we may read block 14, then block 53, and then we can write block 7. There is no restriction on the order of reading or writing for a direct access file.

Direct access files are of great use for immediate access to large amounts of information. They are often used in accessing large databases. When a query concerning a particular subject arrives, we compute which block contains the answer and then read that block directly to provide the desired information.

Random access file is a file in which records are accessed directly by referring to address where it is placed in a file.

Hash function is used in direct access file for accessing the record directly.

Hash function generates a natural address (whose range lies between 1 to file size) from the primary key of the record.

> Example, MOD (Primary key MOD N)

A good hashing function must minimize creation of synonyms. Synonym is defined as key which generates same address as address generated by another different key.

Primitive Operations   [Dec. 07, 08, May 09]

The primitive operations for the direct access file are.

- **Open :** It opens the file and set currency pointer to immediately before the first record.

- **Read-Next :** Returns the next record to user. If no records present, then EOF (end of file) condition will be set.

- **Read-Direct :** Set currency pointer to specific position and gets the record for the user. If the slot is empty or out of range, then it gives error.

- **Write-Direct :** Currency pointer is set to specific position and write the record to file at that position. If the slot is out of range, then it gives error.
- **Update :** Current record is written at the same position with updated values.
- **Close :** This will terminate the access of the file.
- **EOF :** If end of file condition occurs it returns true otherwise it returns false.

Program of Direct Access File Using C++

```cpp
#include<iostream.h>
#include<string.h>
#include<conio.h>
#include<fstream.h>
#include<process.h>
#include<math.h>
#define MAX 15
class employee
{
    public :
        char name[MAX];
        int empid;
        int chain;
        int delflag ;
};

class hashfile
{
    fstream hfile;
    public :
        hashfile();
        int hash(int x) { return x %  10};
        void insert();
        void search();
        void display();
};
```

```cpp
// function to initialize empty file
hashfile : :hashfile()
{
    int i;
        employee rec2;
        fstream iofile;
        iofile.open("hfile.dat",ios : :out|ios : :binary);
        strcpy(rec2.name,"\0");
        rec2.chain=-1;
        rec2.delflag=0;

        for(i=0;i<10;i++)
        {
            rec2.empid=0;
            iofile.write((char*)&rec2,sizeof(rec2));
        }

        iofile.close();
}

// function to insert a record in hash file
void hashfile : :insert()
{
        int i,flag=0,pos,cnt=0;
        long temp,start,size;
        fstream iofile;
        employee insertrec,rec3,trec;

        cout<<"Enter name";
        cin>>insertrec.name;
```

```cpp
cout<<"Enter no of empid";
cin>>insertrec.empid;

insertrec.chain=-1;
insertrec.delflag=0;

size=sizeof(insertrec);
pos=hash(insertrec.empid);

iofile.open("hfile.dat",ios : : in | ios : : out | ios : : binary);
iofile.seekg(0);

temp=pos*sizeof(insertrec);
iofile.seekg(temp);                         // move to position given by hash function

flag=0;
iofile.read((char*) &rec3,sizeof(rec3));

if(rec3.empid==0)                           // slot is empty
{
    flag=1;
    temp=pos*sizeof(rec3);
    iofile.seekp(temp);                     // move to position given by hash function
    iofile.write ((char*) &insertrec,sizeof(insertrec));
    return;
}
else              // slot is not empty
{
    if (hash(rec3.empid)==hash(insertrec.empid))
```

```cpp
    {
        while (rec3.chain!=-1)
        {
            iofile.seekg(rec3.chain * sizeof (rec3));
            pos=rec3.chain;
            iofile.read((char*) &rec3,sizeof(rec3));
        }
        flag = 2;
    }


    int nextpos=pos;
    trec=rec3;


    while(iofile.read((char*) &rec3,sizeof(rec3)))
                                    // find next empty position
    {
        if(rec3.empid==0)              // empty slot
        {
            iofile.seekp((nextpos+1) * sizeof(rec3));
            // move to postion given by hash function
            iofile.write ((char*) &insertrec,sizeof(insertrec));
            if (flag==2)
            {
                iofile.seekp(pos * sizeof (rec3));
                trec.chain=nextpos+1;
                iofile.write ((char*) &trec,sizeof(trec));
            }
            flag = 1;
        break;
        }
```

```cpp
                nextpos++;
            }
    }

    if(flag!=1)
    {
        cout<<"Error this rec was not inserted";
        cout<<"The file is full after this index";

        getch();
        return;
    }

    getch();
    iofile.close();
}                                       // end if insert


                                        // function to search a record of hash file

void hashfile : :search()
{
    int pos=0,t_empid;
    fstream iofile;
    employee rec1;

    cout<< "Enter the empid of the book to be searched.";
    cin>>t_empid;

    pos=hash(t_empid);                          // get the position of search record
```

```cpp
    iofile.open("hfile.dat",ios : :in|ios : :binary);
    iofile.seekg(0);
    iofile.seekg(pos*sizeof(rec1));

    while(iofile.read((char *)&rec1,sizeof(rec1)))                // read record at position
    {
        if(rec1.empid==t_empid)
        {
            cout<< " NAME "<<rec1.name<<" EMP. ID."<<rec1.empid;
            getch();
            iofile.close();
            return;
        }
        else
            if(hash(rec1.empid)==pos)                // if record is stored at position
            {
                iofile.seekg(0);
                if (rec1.chain!=-1)
                iofile.seekg(rec1.chain*sizeof(rec1));       // jump at position of chain
            }
    }

    cout<<" Error no such rec exist ";
    getch();
    iofile.close();
}

void hashfile : :display()
{
    int i=0;
```

```cpp
    employee rec2;
    fstream iofile;


    cout<<"\n\nSERIAL\tEMPID\tNAME\tchain";
    iofile.open("hfile.dat",ios : : in | ios : : binary);


    while(iofile.read((char *)&rec2,sizeof(rec2)))
    {
        cout<<"\n\n"<<i++;
        cout<<"\t"<<rec2.empid;
        cout<<"\t"<<rec2.name;
        cout<<"\t"<<rec2.chain;
    }


    getch();
    iofile.close();
}

void main()
{
    int ch,pos;
    float flag=1.1;
    hashfile file1;

    do
    {
        cout<<" \n 1. Insert a rec ";
        cout<<" \n 2. Disp all rec ";
        cout<<" \n 3. Search a rec ";
        cout<<" \n 4. Exit ";
```

```
        cout<< "\n Enter choice : ";
        cin>>ch;

        switch(ch)
        {
            case 1 :
                    file1.insert();
                    break;
            case 2 :
                    file1.display();
                    break;
            case 3 :
                    file1.search();
                    break;
            case 4 :
            exit(0);
            }
    }while(ch!=4);
}
```

Output :

1. Insert a rec

2. Disp all rec

3. Search a rec

4. Exit

Enter choice : 1

Enter name : Mita

Enter no of empid : 11

1. Insert a rec

2. Disp all rec

3. Search a rec

4. Exit

Enter choice : 1

Enter name : Ritesh

Enter no of empid : 22

1. Insert a rec

2. Disp all rec

3. Search a rec

4. Exit

Enter choice : 1

Enter name : Nilima

Enter no of empid : 33

1. Insert a rec

2. Disp all rec

3. Search a rec

4. Exit

Enter choice : 2

Serial	Id	Name	chain
0	0		-1
1	11	Mita	-1
2	22	Ritesh	-1
3	33	Nilima	-1
4	0		-1
5	0		-1
6	0		-1
7	0		-1
8	0		-1
9	0		-1

1. Insert a rec

2. Disp all rec

3. Search a rec

4. Exit

Enter choice : 1

Enter name : Adi

Enter no of empid : 41

1. Insert a rec

2. Disp all rec

3. Search a rec

4. Exit

Enter choice : 2

Serial	Id	Name	chain
0	0		-1
1	11	Mita	-1
2	22	Ritesh	-1
3	33	Nilima	-1
4	41	Adi	-1
5	0		-1
6	0		-1
7	0		-1
8	0		-1
9	0		-1

1. Insert a rec

2. Disp all rec

3. Search a rec

4. Exit

Enter choice : 1

Enter name : Ekta

Enter no of empid : 44

1. Insert a rec

2. Disp all rec

3. Search a rec

4. Exit

Enter choice : 2

Serial	Id	Name	chain
0	0		-1
1	11	Mita	-1
2	22	Ritesh	-1
3	33	Nilima	-1
4	41	Adi	-1
5	44	Ekta	-1
6	0		-1
7	0		-1
8	0		-1
9	0		-1

1. Insert a rec

2. Disp all rec

3. Search a rec

4. Exit

Enter choice : 3

Enter the empid of the book to be searched : 44

NAME Ekta EMP. ID.44

1. Insert a rec

2. Disp all rec

3. Search a rec

4. Exit

Enter choice : 3

Enter the empid of the book to be searched : 41

NAME Adi EMP. ID.41

1. Insert a rec

2. Disp all rec

3. Search a rec

4. Exit

Enter choice : 4

7.9 INDEX SEQUENTIAL FILE ORGANIZATION   [May 09, 10, Dec. 10]

What is Index?

Index is a data structure that allows locating a particular record in a file more quickly. For Example, Index in a book.

Indexing is used to speed up retrieval of records. Each record in the index file consists of two file. For Example, a key file and a pointer to the main file. To find a specific record for a given key value, index is searching for the given key value. Binary search can be used to search in index file. After getting the address of record from index file, the record in main file can be retrieved easily.

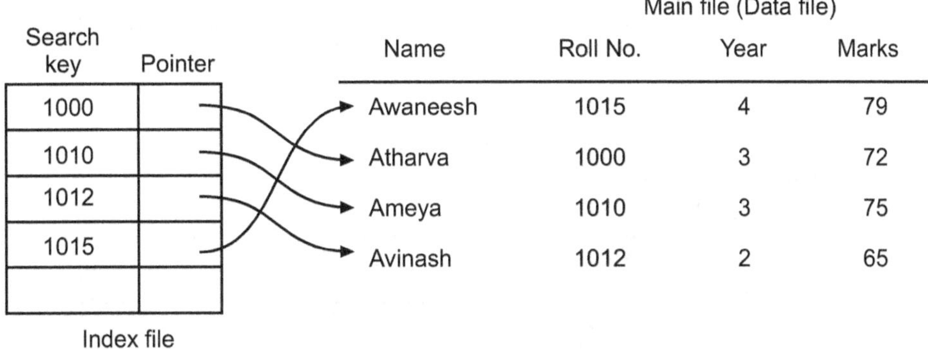

Types of Indexes :

- Primary indexes
- Secondary indexes
- Clustering Indexes

7.9.1 Primary Indexes (Indexed Sequential File)   [May 06, 07, 10, Dec. 06]

Indexed sequential file is ordered as well as indexed.

Records are organized by using primary key.

For supporting random access to the records, an index is used.

Index sequential file always maintain two major files : 1.Data file and 2.Index file.

Number of records in the index file is always equal to number of blocks in the data file. (Note that one block may contain multiple records).

See the following for example, carefully to understand the concept of data file and index file.

For creating primary index on the ordered file, we can use emp_no as primary key.

Every entry in the index file has two fields : emp_no and block pointer. Block pointer holds the address of the block.

The total number of entries in the index is same as that of the blocks in the data file.

Index file requires very few blocks as compared to the blocks of data file.

Binary search on the index file require very few block accesses.

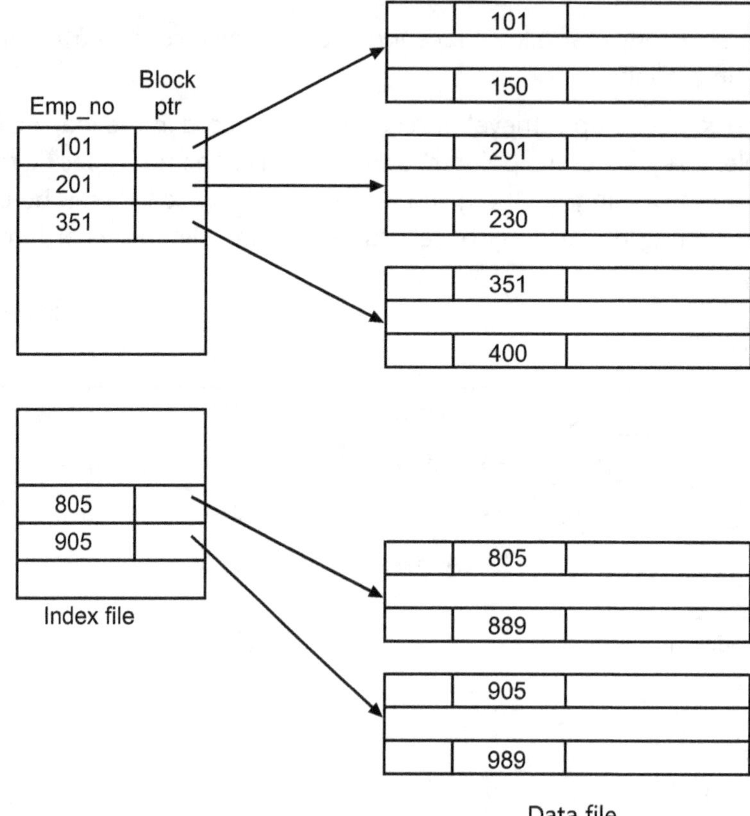

Data file

Fig. 7.7 : Primary index on ordering key field emp_no

7.9.2 Secondary Indexes (Simple Index File)   [May 10]

Sequential and indexed sequential files are not suitable for operations involving a search on a field other than ordering or hashed key.

If searching is required on various keys, secondary indexes on these files must be maintained.

A secondary index is an ordered file which contains following two fields :

- A block pointer
- Some non-ordering field of the data file.

The drawback of secondary index is, it requires more storage space and longer search time than that of primary index.

There could be several secondary indexes for the same file.

In secondary index file, there is a entry for every record in the data file.

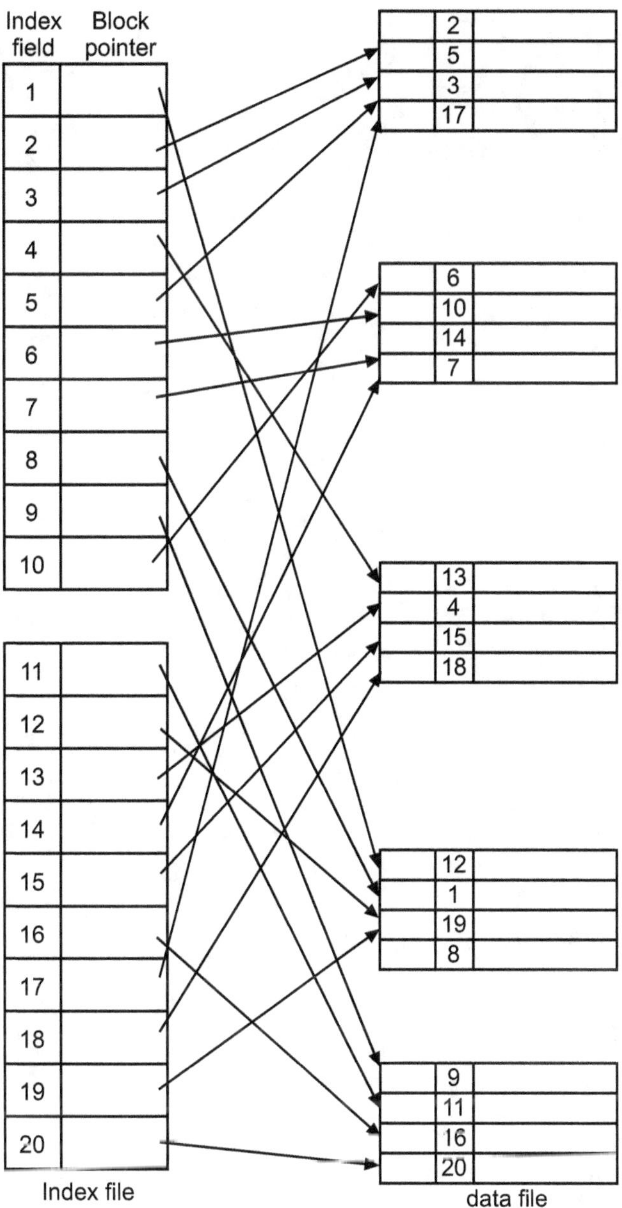

Fig. 7.8

Operations on Simple Index File :

```c
#include<stdio.h>
#include<conio.h>

struct itemrec
```

```c
{
    int itemcode;
    char itemname[20];
    float cost;
};

struct indexrec
{
    int itemcode;
    int position;
    int flag;
};

void displayindexfile()
{
    FILE *indexfile;
    struct indexrec index;

    indexfile=fopen("index.dat","r");

    printf("\n Index file is ");
    printf("\n Itemcode \t Position \t Del Flag");

    while (!feof(indexfile))
    {
        fread(&index,sizeof(index),1,indexfile);
        if (feof(indexfile))
                break;
        if (index.flag==1)
```

```c
            printf("\n\t%d\t\t%d\t\t%d ",index.itemcode,index.position,index.flag);
        else

    printf("\n\t%d\t\t%d\t\t%d?Deleted,index.itemcode,index.position,index.flag");
    }
}


insertrecord()
{
    struct itemrec item;
    struct indexrec index;
    FILE *indexfile, *itemfile;
    long position;

    printf("\n Enter itemcode : ");
    scanf("%d",&item.itemcode);
    printf("\n Enter itemname : ");
    scanf("%s",item.itemname);
    printf("\n Enter cost : ");
    scanf("%f",&item.cost);

    itemfile=fopen("item.dat","r");
    fseek(itemfile,0,SEEK_END);
    position=ftell(itemfile)/sizeof(item);
    fclose(itemfile);

    itemfile =fopen("item.dat","a");
    fwrite(&item,sizeof(item),1,itemfile);
    fclose(itemfile);

    indexfile=fopen("index.dat","a");
```

```c
        index.itemcode = item.itemcode;
        index.position= position;
        index.flag = 1;
        fwrite(&index,sizeof(index),1,indexfile);
        fclose(indexfile);
}

void search()
{
    int searchitcode;
    struct itemrec item;
    struct indexrec index;
    FILE *indexfile, *itemfile;
    long position,found=0;

    printf("\n Enter itemcode to be searched ");
    scanf ("%d",&searchitcode);

    indexfile=fopen("index.dat","r");
    while (!feof(indexfile))
    {
        fread(&index,sizeof(index),1,indexfile);

        if (index.itemcode==searchitcode&&index.flag==1)
        {
            found = 1;
            break;
        }
    }
```

```c
    if (found==1)
    {
        itemfile=fopen("item.dat","r");
        fseek(itemfile,(index.position)*sizeof(item),0);
        fread(&item,sizeof(item),1,itemfile);

        printf("\n Item Record is ");
        printf("\nItemcode \t  Item name \t  Cost");
        printf("\n\t%d\t\t%s\t\t%f",item.itemcode,item.itemname,item.cost);
        fclose(itemfile);
    }
    else
        printf("\n Record not found ");

        fclose(indexfile);
}

void deleterecord()
{
    int searchitcode;
    struct indexrec index;
    FILE *indexfile;
    long position,found=0,c;

    printf("\n Enter itemcode to be deleted : ");
    scanf ("%d",&searchitcode);

    indexfile=fopen("index.dat","r+");
    c=0;
    while (!feof(indexfile))
```

```c
    {
        fread(&index,sizeof(index),1,indexfile);
        if (index.itemcode==searchitcode&&index.flag==1)
        {
            found = 1;
            break;
        }
        c++;
    }


    if (found==1)
    {
        fseek(indexfile,c*sizeof(index),0);
        index.flag=0;            // Make a delete flag 0
        fwrite(&index,sizeof(index),1,indexfile);
    }
    else
        printf("\n Record not found");

    fclose(indexfile);
}

void main()
{
    int choice;

    do
    {
        printf("\n 1. Insert \n 2. Search \n 3. Delete a record");
        printf("\n 4. Display Index file \n 5. Exit");
```

```
    printf("\n Enter choice : ");
    scanf("%d",&choice);
    switch(choice)
    {
      case 1 :
              insertrecord();
              break;
      case 2 :
              search();
              break;
      case 3 :
              deleterecord();
              break;
      case 4 :
              displayindexfile();
      }
    }
    while (choice<5);
}
```

7.9.3 Clustering Indexes   [May 10]

A data file can associate with at most one primary index plus several secondary indexes.

In this organization key searches are improved. The single-level indexing structure is the simplest one where a file, whose records are pairs, contains a key and pointer. This *pointer* is the position in the data file of the record with the given key.

This is how a key search is performed : The search key is compared with the index keys to find the highest index key coming in front of the search key, while a linear search is performed from the record that the index key points to, until the search key is matched or until the record pointed to by the next index entry is reached.

Hardware for Index-Sequential Organization is usually Disk-based, rather than tape. Records are physically ordered by primary key and the index gives the physical location of each record. Records can be accessed sequentially or directly, via the index. The index is stored in a file and read into memory at the point when the file is opened. Also, indexes must be maintained.

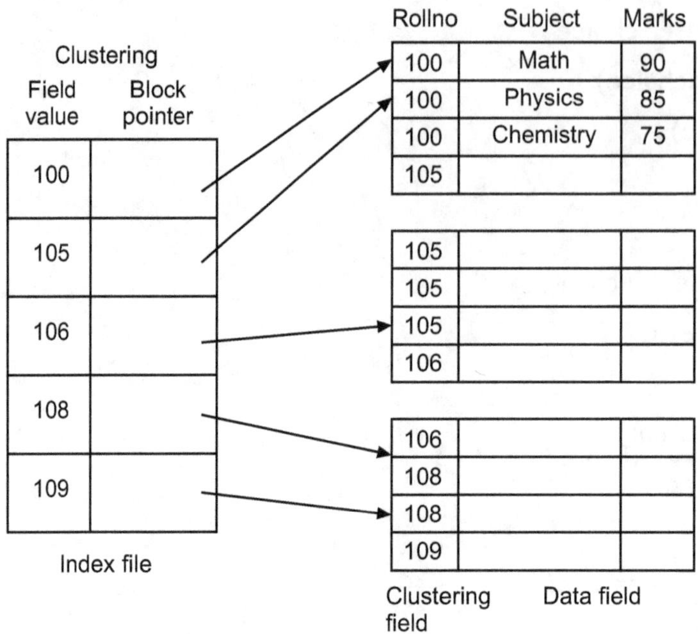

Fig. 7.9

7.9.4 Indexed Sequential Characteristics   [Dec. 07, May 09]

Records are stored sequentially but the index file is prepared for accessing the record directly.

Records can be accessed randomly. File has records and also the index. Magnetic tape is not suitable for index sequential storage. Index is address of physical storage of a record. When randomly very few records are required to be accessed then index sequential is better.

Faster access method. Additional overhead is to maintain index. Index sequential files are popularly used in many applications like digital library.

Advantages :   **[May 12]**

- Accessing any record is more efficient than sequential file organization.

- Large amount of data can be stored using this type of file organization.

- It can handle variable length records.

- A key can be quickly searched in the index file using binary search.

Disadvantages :   **[May 12]**

- Often more than one indices are needed for the records which occupies large storage area.

- Insert and delete operations are difficult and time consuming as data records needs to be shifted.

Operations on an Indexed Sequential File :   **[Dec 06, May 07]**

Following operations can be performed on the indexed sequential file.

- Create File
- Delete Record
- Search Record
- Display Record/Records
- Modify Record
- Insert Record
- Packing

A block is assumed to contain five records.

Index file is named as "index.dat".

Data file is named as "data.dat".

Program of Indexed Sequential File

```cpp
#include<iostream.h>
#include<conio.h>
#include<string.h>
#include<stdio.h>
#include<process.h>
#include<fstream.h>

struct student
{
    int rollno;
    char name[20];
    int status;
};
struct index
{
    int rollno,record_no;
}
class index_sequential
```

```cpp
{
    char data1[30];
    char index1[30];

    fstream data, index;

    public :
    index_sequential(char*str1,char*str2)
    {
        strcpy(data1,str1);
        strcpy(index1,str2);
        data.open(data1,ios : :binary|ios : :in);
        index.open(index1,ios : :binary|ios : :in);
        if(data.fail())
            data.open(data1,ios : :binary|ios : :out);
        if(index.fail())
            index.open(index1,ios : :binary|ios : :out);
        data.close();
        index.close();
    }

    void display(int record_no)
    {
        student rec1;
        data.open(data1,ios : :binary|ios : :in|ios : :nocreate);
        data.seekg(record_no*sizeof(student),ios : :beg);
        data.read((char*)&rec1,sizeof(student));
        cout<<"\n"<<rec1.rollno<<" "<<rec1.name;
        data.close();
    }
```

```cpp
    void create();
    void read();
    void readi();
    void insert(student rec1);
    void pack();
    void reindex();
    void update();
    int Delete(int rollno);
    int search(int rollno);
};
void main()
{

    class index_sequential object("master.dat","index.dat");
    int ch,rollno,recno;
    student rec1;
    clrscr();

    while(1)
    {
        cout<<"\n1.Print Record";
        cout<<"\n2.Insert Record";
        cout<<"\n3.Delete Record";
        cout<<"\n4.Update Record";
        cout<<"\n5.Search Record";
        cout<<"\n6.Pack";
        cout<<"\n7.Exit";
        cout<<"\nEnter ur choice : ";
        flushall();
        cin>>ch;
```

```cpp
switch(ch)
{
    case 1 :
        object.read();
        object.readi();
        break;
    case 2 :
        cout<<"\nEnter the record to be inserted (roll and name)";
        cin>>rec1.rollno>>rec1.name;
        object.insert(rec1);
        break;
    case 3 :
        cout<<"\nEnter roll no ";
        cin>>rollno;
        object.Delete(rollno);
        break;
    case 4 :
        object.update();
        break;
    case 5 :
        cout<<"\nEnter a roll no ";
        cin>>rollno;
        recno=object.search(rollno);
        if(recno>=0)
        {
            cout<<"\nRecord No : "<<recno;
            object.display(recno);
        }
        else
        {
```

```cpp
                    cout<<"\nRecord not found ";

                }
                break;
            case 6 :
                object.pack();
                break;
            case 7 :
                exit(0);
        }


    }
}

void index_sequential : :read()
{
    student rec;
    int i=1,n;

    cout<<"\n-----------Content of DATA.DAT-----------------";
    data.open(data1,ios : :binary|ios : :in|ios : :nocreate);
    data.seekg(0,ios : :end);
    n=data.tellg()/sizeof(student);
    data.seekg(0,ios : :beg);

    for(i=1;i<=n;i++)
    {
        data.read((char*)&rec,sizeof(student));

        if(rec.status==0)
```

```cpp
        cout<<"\n"<<i<<rec.rollno<<" "<<rec.name;
        else
        cout<<"-----Deleted..-----";
    }


    data.close();
}


void index_sequential : :readi()
{
    class index rec;
    int i=1,n;

    cout<<"\n-----------Content of INDEX.DAT----------------";
    index.open(index1,ios : :binary|ios : :in|ios : :nocreate);
    index.seekg(0,ios : :end);
    n=index.tellg()/sizeof(index);
    index.seekg(0,ios : :beg);

    for(i=1;i<=n;i++)
    {
        index.read((char*)&rec,sizeof(index));
        cout<<"\n"<<i<<rec.rollno<<" "<<rec.record_no;
    }
    getch();
}


void index_sequential : :insert(student rec1)
{
    student crec;
```

```cpp
int n,i,k;

data.open(data1,ios : :binary|ios : :in|ios : :nocreate|ios : :out);
rec1.status=0;
data.seekg(0,ios : :end);
n=data.tellg()/sizeof(student);

if(n==0)
{
    data.write((char*)&rec1,sizeof(student));
    data.close();
    return;
}

/*shift records till the point of insertion*/
i=n-1;
while(i>=0)
{
    data.seekg(i*sizeof(student),ios : :beg);
    data.read((char*)&crec,sizeof(student));

    if(crec.rollno>rec1.rollno)
    {
        data.seekp((i+1)*sizeof(student),ios : :beg);
        data.write((char*)&crec,sizeof(student));
    }
    else
    break;

    i--;
}
```

```cpp
    /*insert record at (i+1)th position*/
    i++;

    data.seekp(i*sizeof(student),ios : :beg);
    data.write((char*)&rec1,sizeof(student));
    data.close();
    reindex();
}

int index_sequential : :Delete(int rollno)
{
    student crec;
    int i,recno,n;

    recno=search(rollno);

    if(recno>=0)
    {
        cout<<"\nRecord is found ="<<recno;
        data.open(data1,ios : :binary|ios : :in|ios : :nocreate|ios : :out);
        data.seekg(recno*sizeof(student),ios : :beg);
        data.read((char*)&crec,sizeof(student));
        crec.status=1;
        data.seekp(recno*sizeof(student),ios : :beg);
        data.write((char*)&crec,sizeof(student));
        data.close();
    }
    else
    {
        cout<<"\nRecord not found...";
```

```cpp
        return 0;
    }
    reindex();
    return 1;

}

int index_sequential : :search(int rollno)
{
    class index indexes[50];
    student rec1;
    class index crec;
    int i,n,recno;

    index.open(index1,ios : :binary|ios : :in|ios : :nocreate);
    index.seekg(0,ios : :end);
    n=index.tellg()/sizeof(index);
    index.seekg(0,ios : :beg);
    index.read((char*)indexes,n*sizeof(index));
    index.close();

    if(n==0||rollno<indexes[0].rollno)
    return -1;

    for(i=1;i<n&&rollno>=indexes[i].rollno;i++)
    recno=indexes[i-1].record_no;

    data.open(data1,ios : :binary|ios : :in);
    data.seekg(recno*sizeof(student),ios : :beg);
```

```cpp
    for(i=1;i<=5&&!data.eof();i++; recno++)
    {
        data.read((char*)&rec1,sizeof(student));
        if(rec1.rollno==rollno&&rec1.status==0)
        {
            data.close();
            return(recno);
        }
    }
    data.close();
    return(-1);

}


void index_sequential : :pack()
{
    fstream temp;
    student crec;
    int i,n;

    data.open(data1,ios : :binary|ios : :in);
    temp.open("temp.txt",ios : :out|ios : :trunc|ios : :binary);
    data.seekg(0,ios : :end);
    n=data.tellg()/sizeof(student);
    data.seekg(0,ios : :beg);

    for(i=0;i<n;i++)
    {
        data.read((char*)&crec,sizeof(student));
        if(crec.status==0)
```

```cpp
        temp.write((char*)&crec,sizeof(student));
    }
    data.close();
    temp.close();


    temp.open("temp.txt",ios : :binary|ios : :in);
    data.open(data1,ios : :binary|ios : :out|ios : :trunc);
    temp.seekg(0,ios : :end);
    n=temp.tellg()/sizeof(student);
    temp.seekg(0,ios : :beg);


    for(i=0;i<n;i++)
    {
        temp.read((char*)&crec,sizeof(student));
        data.write((char*)&crec,sizeof(student));
    }
    data.close();
    temp.close();
    reindex();


}


void index_sequential : :update()
{
    int rollno,n,i;
    student crec;

    cout<<"\nEnter the rollno of the record to be updated ";
```

```cpp
    cin>>rollno;
    cout<<"\nEnter a new record (roll no and name) ";
    cin>>crec.rollno>>crec.name;

    if(Delete(rollno))
    insert(crec);

    else
    {
        cout<<"\nRecord not found ";
        return;
    }

    reindex();
}

void index_sequential : :reindex()
{
    int rollno,n,i;
    student crec;

    class index rec1;

    index.open(index1,ios : :binary|ios : :out|ios : :trunc);
    data.open(data1,ios : :binary|ios : :in);
    data.seekg(0,ios : :end);

    n=data.tellg()/sizeof(student);
```

```
    data.seekg(0,ios : :beg);

    for(i=0;i<n;i=i+5)
    {
        data.seekg(i*sizeof(student),ios : :beg);
        data.read((char*)&crec,sizeof(student));
        rec1.rollno=crec.rollno;
        rec1.record_no=i;
        index.write((char*)&rec1,sizeof(index));
    }
    data.close();
    index.close();
}
```

7.10 DIFFERENCE BETWEEN SEQUENTIAL FILE ORGANIZATION AND DIRECT ACCESS FILE

Sr. No.	Sequential File Organization	Direct Access File
1.	A sequential file access one record at a time, from first to last, in order.	A direct file access the records in any order, by record number.
2.	Each record can be of varying length.	Each record must be of identical length.
3.	A sequential file might look like this, with records separated by commas bear, skunk, moose, fish, alligator.	A direct file with same data would look like this bear_skunk_moose_fish_alligator.
4.	Sequential file access is similar to the tape drives where the files are accessed in a sequential manner.	Random access is similar to the one in hard disk and optical drives.
5.	No overhead of hash function.	Hash function needs to be calculated for direct access.

7.11 DIFFERENCE BETWEEN SEQUENTIAL FILE AND INDEX SEQUENTIAL FILE   [MAY 10]

Sr. No.	Sequential File	Index Sequential File
1.	It can be searched effectively on ordering key.	Search for a record on the basis of some other attribute.
2.	It usually takes more storage space.	An index file usually requires less storage space.
3.	Require movement of records, while inserting.	Records can be added at the end of the main file.
4.	Updation of sequential file requires more block access.	Upadation of index file requires fewer block accesses.
5.	When all records are to be processed, sequential files are suitable.	When random records are to be accessed, index sequential files are used.
6.	Slower access.	Faster access.

7.12 INDEXING AND HASHING COMPARISON [May 05, 06, 07, Dec. 06]

Hashing is often considered as a fastest method for accessing records. The speed of operation depends on number of block access.

In hashed files collision is a major problem.

If the number of records exceeds in number, the length of the linked list constituting the bucket will also increase. This will slow down the operation speed in hashed files.

Same thing can also be happen in case of indexed files as the number of records gets exceed.

Initial storage requirement for hashed file is very high. Indexing has no such initial requirement, as file grows blocks are acquired.

Batch processing of queries in database application is extremely difficult in hashed files.

Compared to hashed files, indexed files or sequential files perform better in batch processing of queries.

7.13 LINKED ORGANIZATION OF A FILE   [Dec. 07, 08, 11, May 08, 10]

Logical sequence of records is different from physical sequence.

Next logical record is obtained by following a link from the present record. (Like a linked list)

Linking of records with ascending value of primary key makes insertion and deletion easier.

When there is no index available it becomes difficult to search a record of the given primary key. As index is unavailable the only method one can use for searching is a linear search.

To facilitate searching on the primary key as well as secondary key it is necessary to maintain several indexes, one for each key.

We can set up indexes for each key. Each index entry contains key values pointer to list and the length of the associated list.

7.14 INVERTED FILE ORGANIZATION   [Dec. 05, May 07, 09, 10]

These files are similar to multilists.

In this file, only index structure is important record can be stored in any way.

Maintenance of index is complex than that of multilist.

Inverted files may also result in space saving compared with other file structures when record retrieval does not require retrieval of key fields. In this case, key fields may be deleted from the records. In the case of multilist structures, this deletion of key fields is possible only with significant loss in system retrieval performance.

Insertion and deletion of records requires only the ability to insert and delete within indexes.

E # index

510	
620	
750	
800	
950	

Index file

Occupation index

Analyst	B, C
Programmer	A, D, E

Sex index

Female	B, C, D
Male	A, E

9,000	E
10,000	A
12,000	C, D
15,000	B

Fig. 7.10 : Indexes for fully inverted file

7.15 CELLULAR PARTITIONS   [Dec. 05, 08, May 07, 08]

It is used in order to reduce file search times, where storage media may be divided into cells.

A cell may be an entire disk pack or it may simply be a cylinder.

Lists are localized to lie within a cell.

All records in the same cell may be accessed without moving the read/write heads.

In case if cell is a disk pack then using cellular partitions, it is possible to search different cells in parallel.

EXERCISE

1. Give any three points of comparison between Text files and Binary files. **(May 10, 6m)**

2. What are indices ? What are different characteristics of the index file organization ?

    (May 10, 4m)

3. (i) What is a sequential file ?

    (ii) Give any two advantages of sequential files over unordered files.

    (iii) Explain any-three operations on sequential files in brief ?   **(May 10, 6m)**

4. What are the differences between sequential and index sequential files ? **(May 10, 4m)**

5. Explain the concepts of :

    (i) Primary indexes

    (ii) Clustering indexes

    (iii) Secondary indexes   **(May 10, 6m)**

6. Write brief notes on :

    (i) Linked organization of a file.

    (ii) Inverted file organization.   **(May 10, 6m)**

7. What is file? Explain types of files.   **(Dec. 10, 4m)**

8. Explain different modes of opening files.   **(Dec. 10, 4m)**

9. Write a C/C++ program to create a file. Insert records in the file by opening file in append mode. Display all records and search for a specific record entered by user.   **(Dec. 10,8m)**

10. Explain in detail different file organizations.   **(Dec. 10, 6m)**

11. Write a C/C++ program to implement direct access file for employee database and perform insert a record and display database.   **(Dec. 10, 10m)**

12. What is a file ? What is a need of a file ? How are the files stored on external storage ? What are the basic operations to be performed on files ?   **(May 11, 8m)**

13. Write 'C' implementation of the primitives for sequential file organization.

    (May 11, 8m)

14. Compare sequential file organization with direct access file organization. Write 'C' implementation of the primitives for direct access file organization. **(May 11, 10m)**

15. Explain the various factors involved in selecting in a particular file organization for user. **(May 11, 6m)**

16. Write a C/C++ program to create a file. Insert records in the file by opening file in append mode. Display all records and search for specific record entered by user.

(Dec. 11, 8m)

17. What is file? List different file opening modes. Explain Index sequential file organization in brief. **(Dec. 11, 8m)**

18. List different file organizations. State features of sequential file organization. What is need of A file organizations? List different primitive operations on files and explain any two operations in brief. **(Dec. 11, 10m)**

19. Explain in brief :

    (i) Linked file organization

    (ii) Direct file organization. **(Dec. 11, 6m)**

20. Write a C/C++ program to perform create, insert, display and search operations for sequential file organization. **(May 12, 8m)**

21. What is index sequential file organization? State its advantages and disadvantages.

(May 12, 8m)

22. List different file organizations. State the need of file organizations. List different primitive operations on files. Compare sequential file with index sequential file organization. **(May 12, 10m)**

23. Explain in brief direct access file organization with example. **(May 12, 6m)**

24. Write an algorithm to perform create, insert, display and search operations for sequential file organization. **(Dec. 12, 8m)**

25. What is index sequential file organization? State its advantages and disadvantages.

(Dec. 12, 8m)

26. What is file? List different file opening modes. Explain Index sequential file organization it brief. **(Dec. 12, 8m)**

27. Explain in brief   **(Dec. 12, 8m)**

   (i) Linked file organization

   (ii) Direct file organization

28. What is file organization? Explain any three types of file organization.   **(May 13, 8m)**

29. Write a C/C++ program to create a sequential file and to implement primitive operations for the same.   **(May 13, 8m)**

30. Compare sequential file organization, indexed file organization and direct file organization.   **(May 13, 8m)**

31. Explain different modes of opening file.   **(May 13, 8m)**

32. Compare text and binary files.   **(May 13, 8m)**

SAMPLE QUESTION PAPER

End-Sem. Theory Examination

Time : 2 Hours   **Max. Marks : 50**

1. (a) Define binary search tree. Construct binary search tree from following set of strings. Show all steps. Also write height of final tree. **[4]**

JAN FEB MAR APR MAY JUN JUL AUG SEP OCT NOV DEC

(b) Explain the necessity of representing expression in prefix and postfix notation. For the given postfix expressions, evaluate it for the values given. Show stepwise stack contents. **[8]**

A B C * D E F ^ / G * –1 * +

A = 61 B = 1, C = 4, D = 16, E = 2, F = 3, G = 2, H = 5

where ^ = exponential operator

(c) Implement the following functions in 'C' to implement circular queue using array. **[8]**

    (i)   Insert an element,

    (ii)   Delete an element,

    (iii) Queue full,

    (iv) Queue empty.

Assume data elements to be integer.

OR

2. (a) Write an algorithm to convert infix expression to postfix. Convert the following infix expression to postfix using stack.

A / B $ C + D * E – A * C where $ is an exponentiation. Show stepwise conversion. **[8]**

(b) What is Priority Queue? Write Pseudo 'C' function to insert and delete item from Priority Queue. **[8]**

(c) From gives traversal, construct the binary tree. **[4]**

Inorder   :   DBFEAGCLJHK

Preorder   :   DFEBGLJKHCA

3. (a) Explain the following traversals for threaded binary tree with suitable example **[6]**

    a. Preorder

    b. Inorder

(b) Explain the concept of red and black trees with suitable example. **[3]**

(c) Create an AVL tree for the following data.   **[6]**

40 20 10 30 70 60 55

OR

4. (a) Create an AVL tree for the following elements. Show all steps with rotation.

CAR BAG MAN SAD TAN FAN ADD   **[6]**

(b) Comment on "Threaded binary tree can be traversed without using stack".   **[3]**

(c) Explain the concept of B tree and B+ tree with suitable examples   **[6]**

5. (a) Explain in detail different file organizations.   **[6]**

(b) Write a C/C++ program to implement direct access file for employee database and perform insert a record and display database.   **[6]**

(c) Write 'C' implementation of the primitives for sequential file organization.   **[3]**

OR

6. (a) Compare sequential file organization with direct access file organization. Write 'C' implementation of the primitives for direct access file organization.   **[6]**

(b) Explain in brief :   **[3]**

(i)   Linked file organization

(ii)   Direct file organization.

(c) What is index sequential file organization? State its advantages and disadvantages.**[6]**

Time : 2 Hours   **Max. Marks : 50**

Instructions to the candidates :

   (i) Answer four questions.

   (ii) Neat diagrams must be drawn wherever necessary.

   (iii) Figures to the right indicate full marks.

   (iv) Assume suitable data if necessary.

---

1. **(a)** Clearly indicate the contents of stack for evaluating the following postfix expression:**[6]**

    Assume $A = 10$, $B = 2$, $C = 13$

    (i) A B + C – B A – C + –

    (ii) A B C + * C B A – + *

  (b) Consider the following circular queue of character and size 5.   **[6]**

0	1	2	3	4
		A	C	

Fig. 1

Front point to index 1 and Rear point to index 3 For addition operation, first increment the corresponding index by 1 and then add the new element at the index location. For deletion operation, fist increment the corresponding index by 1 and then delete the element at the index location Show the queue contents as per the following operations at every step :

   (i)   F is added to the queue

   (ii) Two letters are deleted

   (iii) K, L, M are added to the queue

   (iv) Two letters are deleted

   (v)   R is added to the queue

   (vi) Two letters are deleted

OR

2. **(a)** Clearly indicate the contents of stack during conversion of given infix expression to prefix: **[6]**

    Infix expression : A + (B * ((D – E % F) / H))

  (b) The dq is an input restricted doubly ended queue, implemented as a linear queue. The delete functions return the element that is deleted and also stores 0 (Zero) at the location of deleted element. Clearly indicate the contents of queue after each add and delete operation given below: **[6]**

```
{
        int front;
        int arr[10];
        int rear;
        };
        struct dqueue dq = {-1, {0}, - 1};
        int i = 0;
        addqatend (&dq, 11);
        addqatend (&dq, 12);
        addqatend (&dq, 13);
        i = delqatbeg (& dq);
        i = delqatbeg (& dq);
        i = delqatend (& dq 22);
        addqatend (&dq, 22);
        addqatend (&dq, 23);
        i = delqatbeg (& dq);
        i = delqatbeg (& dq);
        addqatend (&dq, 24);
```

3. **(a)** Convert the following generalized tree into a binary tree: **[4]**

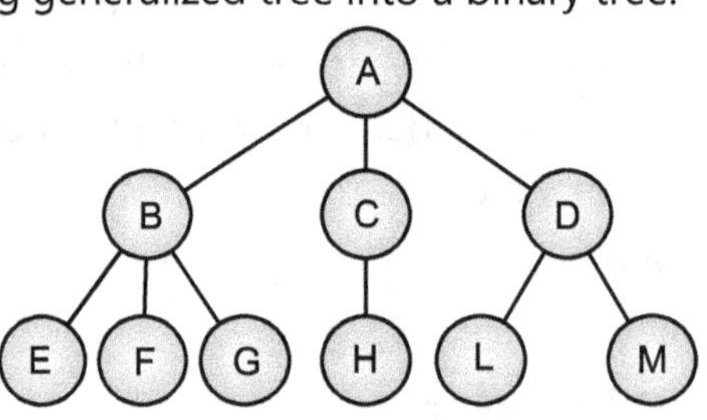

Fig. 2

(b) Construct binary tree using tree traversals given below: **[4]**

Preorder traversal : P A Q B R S D E F

Inorder traversal : A P B Q D S E R F

(c) For the graph given below, find BFS and DFS.   **[4]**

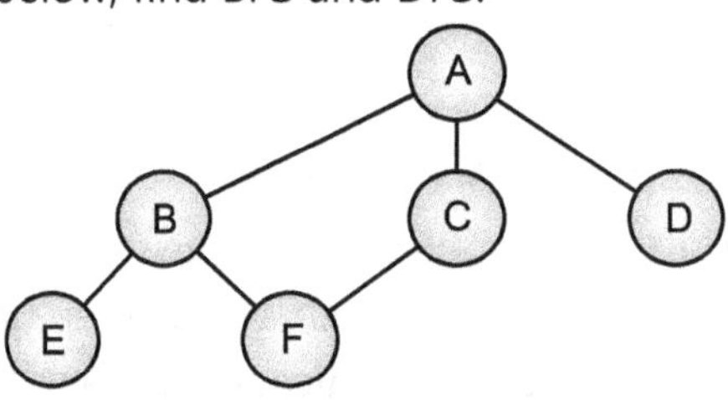

Fig. 3

OR

4. (a) Draw the threaded binary tree equivalent for the tree represented by the following array assuming root node of tree is stored at index 0 in the array.　　　**[4]**

Index	Data
0	10
1	-
2	20
3	-
4	-
5	30
6	-
7-	-
8	-
9	-
10	-
11	-
12	40
13	-
14	-
15	-
16	-
17	-
18	-
19	-
20	-
21	-
22	-
23	-
24	-
25	50
26	-
27	-
28	-
29	-
30	-
31-	

(b) For the graph given below, show stepwise representation of MST using Kruskal's algorithm. **[4]**

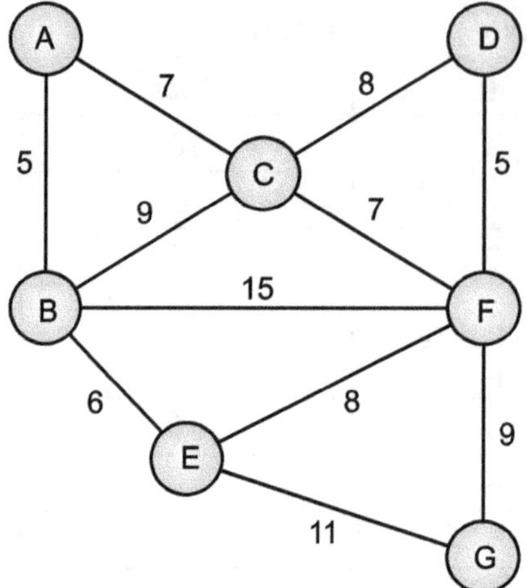

Fig. 4

(c) Consider the following graph, each node contains subject course number: **[4]**

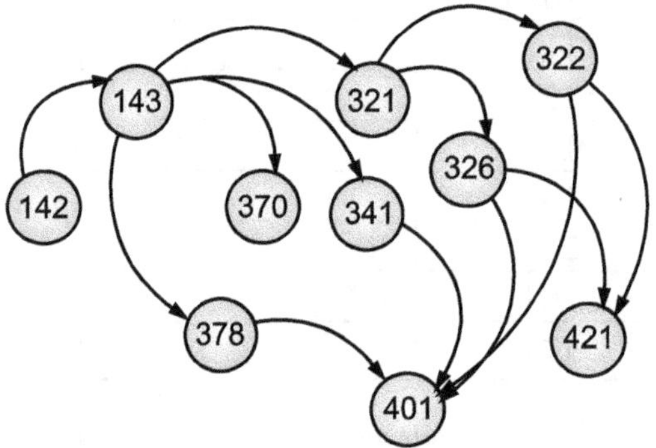

Fig. 5

To complete a course, students need to take all the course subjects. Students need to take into consideration which courses are prerequisites for other courses when making a schedule for the upcoming semester so that 370 can not be taken before 143, nut the former can be taken along with 341 and 370. Help the students by giving the order of subjects they need to take to complete the course. [Hint : Topological sort]

5. (a) Show stepwise construction of maxheap for the data :

40, 50 10, 60, 20, 30, 70 **[5]**

(b) What is symbol table ? What are the operations on symbol table. Give symbol table ADT. **[5]**

(c) Convert the following binary tree into AVL tree. **[4]**

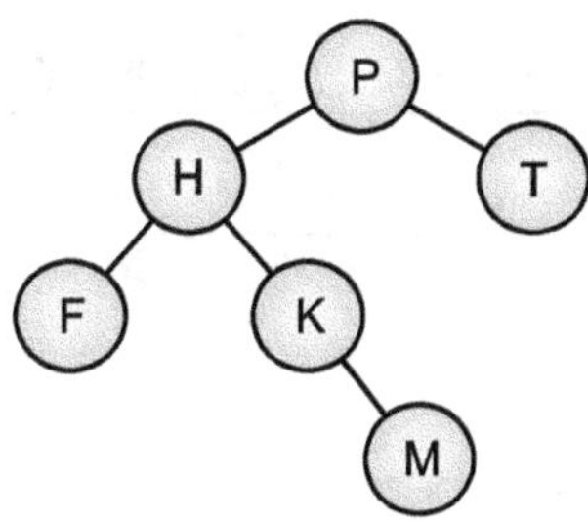

Fig. 6

OR

6. (a) Assume a hash table of size 10 and hash function:

H(X) = X mod 10

Perform linear probing with and without replacement for the given set of values :   **[6]**

71, 63, 59, 20, 75, 105, 216, 89, 8, 29

(b) Construct optimal binary search tree, for the following data :   **[8]**

N = 4, Key set = {do, if, read, while}

{p1, p2, p3, p4} = (3, 3, 1, 1)

{q0, q1, q2, q4} = { 2, 3, 1, 1, 1}

The p's and q's are multiplied by 16 for convenience.

7. (a) Explain how records are logically deleted from a file.   **[6]**

(b) Explain 'C++' file open function with syntax, example. Explain the difference between 'C++' ios :: app and ios :: ate flags associated with file open function.   **[6]**

OR

8. (a) Explain the following 'C' file functions with syntax and example.   **[6]**

(i) Create file

(ii) Read (data and record from a file)

(iii) Delete file.

(b) Some N employee records are stored in a sequentially organized file (emprec.dat) Write C++ code to find the value of N, without reading the records from the file one after another.   **[6]**

```
{
    Unsigned int empid;
    Char fname [10];
    Char Iname [10];
    Char gender;
    Float salary;
};
```

END SEM. EXAM. NOVEMBER 2016

Time : 2 Hours   **Max. Marks : 50**

Instructions to the candidates :

   (i)   Answer four questions.

   (ii) Neat diagrams must be drawn wherever necessary.

   (iii) Figures to the right indicate full marks.

   (iv) Assume suitable data if necessary.

1. **(a)** Clearly indicate the contents of stack during conversion of given infix expression to postfix expression. Consider $\wedge$ as exponent operator: **[6]**

   $A* (B - C)E^{\wedge}F + G$

   (b) Explain the concept of multiqueue, Double Ended Queue and Priority queue.   **[6]**

OR

2. **(a)** Implement stack as an ADT using sequential organization.   **[6]**

   (b) Consider the following circular multiqueue of integers and size 6.   **[6]**

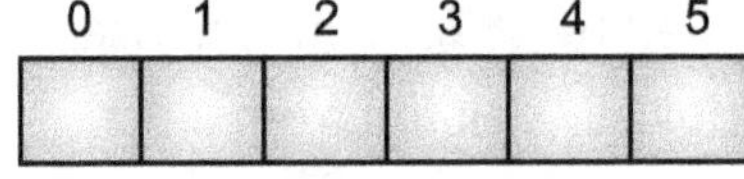

Fig. 1

Front of Q1 = -1 Rear of Q1 = -1 Q1 starts at 0

Front of Q2 = -1 Rear of Q2 = -1 Q2 starts at 3

Show the circular queue contents as per the following operations at every step :

   (i)   Insert 21 in Q1

   (ii)   Insert 23 in Q1

   (iii) Insert 9 in Q2

   (iv)   Insert 8 in Q1

   (v)   Insert 10 in Q2

   (vi)   Insert 11 in Q2

   (vii) Delete Q1

   (viii) Insert 81 in Q2

   (ix)   Delete Q1

   (x)   Insert 25 in Q 2

   (xi)   Insert 100 in Q1

   (xii) Delete Q2

3. (a) Write an algorithm for the inorder traversal of a Threaded Binary Tree.   **[6]**

(b) Write the pseudo code for Kruskal's algorithm and find minimum spanning tree for the following graph :   **[6]**

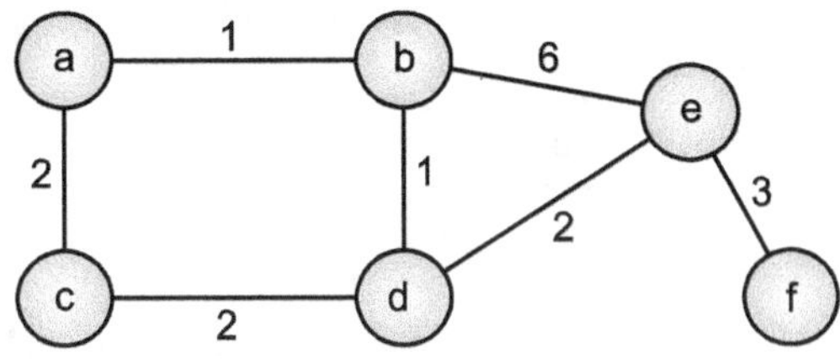

Fig. 2

OR

4. (a) Construct binary tree using tree traversals :   **[4]**

Inorder   : H, D, I, B, E, A, J, F, K, C, G

Postorder   : H, I, D, E, B, J, K, F, G, C, A.

(b) Explain with topological sorting using example.   **[4]**

(c) Give a graph, perform DFS and BFS. Assume starting vertex 1.   **[4]**

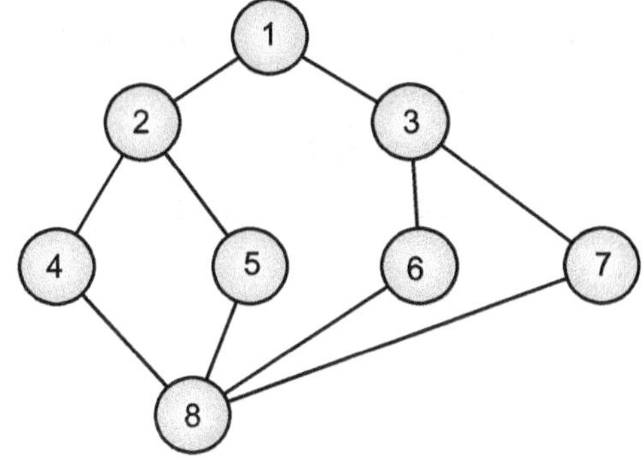

Fig. 3

5. (a) How many Binary Search Trees (BSTs) can be constructed for the given 'n' identifiers? Construct all possible BSTs for the following identifier set. Compute the cost of each BST. Which BST is an optimal binary search tree ? The identifier set a [ ] = (a1, a2, a3) = do, if while) with the successful and unsuccessful probabilities.   **[10]**

P [ ] = (0.5, 0.1, 0.05)

Q [ ] = (0.15, 0.1, 0.05, 0.05)

(b) Write a note on rehashing.   **[4]**

OR

6. (a) Construct an AVL for the following data set :   **[10]**

30, 5, 3, 18, 19, 4, 6, 35, 33, 15

(b) Huffman encoding and decoding.   **[4]**

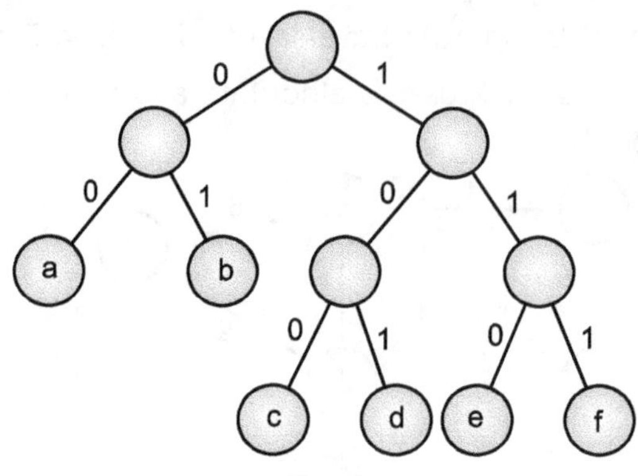

Fig. 4

Encode :

(i) addef

(ii) deaf

Decode :

(i) 0010000111

(ii) 11100101110

7. (a) Write the pseudo code for search and insert operations in indexed sequential file.   **[6]**

    (b) Compare binary file with test file.   **[6]**

OR

8. (a) What is file? Explain different types of file organizations.   **[6]**

    (b) Explain :   **[6]**

       (i)   Primary index

       (ii) Secondary index

       (iii) Cluster index.